Regency RAKES

2 Glittering
Regency Romances

THE UNEXPECTED BRIDE
by Elizabeth Rolls

THE MARRIAGE TRUCE
by Ann Elizabeth Cree

THE Regency RAKES

A further collection from some of Mills & Boon Historical Romance's most popular authors

THE
Regency
RAKES

by
Elizabeth Rolls &
Ann Elizabeth Cree

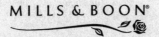
MILLS & BOON®

*All the characters in this book have no existence outside the imagination
of the author, and have no relation whatsoever to anyone bearing the
same name or names. They are not even distantly inspired by any
individual known or unknown to the author, and all the incidents are
pure invention.*

*All Rights Reserved including the right of reproduction in whole or in part in
any form. This edition is published by arrangement with Harlequin
Enterprises II B.V. The text of this publication or any part thereof may not
be reproduced or transmitted in any form or by any means, electronic or
mechanical, including photocopying, recording, storage in an information
retrieval system, or otherwise, without the written permission of the publisher.*

*This book is sold subject to the condition that it shall not, by way of trade
or otherwise, be lent, resold, hired out or otherwise circulated without the
prior consent of the publisher in any form of binding or cover other than
that in which it is published and without a similar condition including
this condition being imposed on the subsequent purchaser.*

*MILLS & BOON and MILLS & BOON with the Rose Device
are registered trademarks of the publisher.*

*First published in Great Britain 2004 by
Harlequin Mills & Boon Limited,
Eton House, 18-24 Paradise Road,
Richmond, Surrey TW9 1SR*

THE REGENCY RAKES © Harlequin Books S.A. 2004

The publisher acknowledges the copyright holders of the
individual works as follows:

The Unexpected Bride © Elizabeth Rolls 2000
The Marriage Truce © Annemarie Hasnain 2000

ISBN 0 263 83672 X

138-0104

*Printed and bound in Spain
by Litografía Rosés S.A., Barcelona*

THE UNEXPECTED BRIDE
by
Elizabeth Rolls

Elizabeth Rolls was born in Kent but moved to Melbourne, Australia, at the age of fifteen months. She spent several years in Papua New Guinea as a child, where her father was in charge of the Defence Forces. After teaching music for several years she moved to Sydney to do a Masters in Musicology at the University of New South Wales. Upon completing her thesis, Elizabeth realised that writing was so much fun she wanted to do more. She currently lives in a chaotic household in Melbourne with her husband, two small sons, two dogs and two cats. Readers are invited to contact Elizabeth at elizabethrolls@alphalink.com.au

Chapter One

An impartial observer might have been excused for stating that the crowd at Almack's Assembly Rooms on that fine spring night was entirely made up of members of the Ton who were intent upon enjoying themselves to the hilt. Young ladies dressed demurely in silken gowns of various pastel shades swirled past escorted by nattily attired beaux. Anxious mothers chatted together in groups, each certain that her daughter outshone every other girl in beauty and elegance. All in all it was a scene of great interest to the student of human nature.

One fair-haired young gentleman stood apart, however, looking the picture of gloom. Although dressed with great elegance and propriety he did not appear to be entirely at ease in his surroundings. He returned an occasional polite rejoinder to greetings from various acquaintances, all of whom registered surprise at finding him in such a place. Otherwise the Honourable George Carstares seemed to be very much in a brown study, with a frown of worry in his blue eyes.

He looked with ever-decreasing expectation and hope at the entrance doors of Almack's Assembly Rooms. It wanted but ten minutes to eleven. If Peter doesn't arrive soon, he thought, they won't let him in at all. Lord! If those high-nosed ladies wouldn't relax their rules for England's hero, his Grace the Duke of Wellington, they'd certainly refuse admittance to Peter Augustus Frobisher, Seventh Earl of Darleston! Not for all his handsome looks and undeniable charm would they unbend!

It occurred to him on a wave of optimism that if Peter didn't arrive in time there was nothing to stop him leaving and seeking more convivial entertainment elsewhere. The Patronesses might insist arbitrarily that no one should enter after eleven, but there was nothing in the rules to stop a fellow leaving whenever he pleased. Mr Carstares devoutly hoped that such a thought would not occur to any one of the six great ladies who presided over Almack's. He had little doubt that they would be able to persuade the Ton to abide by such a decree, and then one would be in the basket!

A faintly surprised drawl brought an end to these depressing reflections. 'You here too, George! Whatever for? Don't tell me Darleston is sacrificing both of us this evening!'

Carstares swung around, the gloomy expression giving way to something more like his usual merry smile. 'Good God! Carrington! Did Peter ask you as well? What the devil is he up to?'

'Standing us up, by the look of things!' answered Viscount Carrington. 'Never mind, in less than ten minutes we can go and wait for him in the street! Give him another few minutes out there and then toddle off to more entertaining pastures!'

'Just what I was thinking!' said Carstares with a grin. He ran a hand through his fair locks. 'D'you know *why* he asked us to meet him here?'

'Not the least notion. Do you?' asked Carrington curiously.

Carstares rubbed his nose thoughtfully. 'Got a slight suspicion. Was with him, you know, when he heard about the death of young Nicholas Frobisher in that hunting accident last winter.'

Carrington looked more than a little puzzled. 'Well, yes. I know Peter was cut up about it. He was fond of the lad, and he *was* Peter's heir after all, but there's nothing in that to make the fellow run mad!' Then, in very polite tones, 'Good evening, Lady Sefton. How delightful to see you!'

The kindly-looking peeress smiled gently at him and said, with not a trace of sarcasm, 'And so unusual to see you here, Lord Carrington and Mr Carstares! But you must come further in. The young ladies do not linger at the front doors in hope of dance partners, you know. I shall make it my especial concern to introduce you to the very prettiest!' Not a muscle in her face betrayed what George Carstares knew must be her considerable inward mirth at the expression of startled horror on the Viscount's face.

The Patroness delivered her final thrust with a dead straight face, 'And, of course, my lord and I shall look forward to your company at supper!' She departed to mingle with the crowd, not waiting to hear their response to what amounted to a royal command.

Carstares groaned. 'I knew one of them would think of it!'

'Think of what?' asked Carrington. 'Oh, never mind! We're done to a cow's thumb now! Get on with your theory, and later on we can toss for the honour of calling Peter out!'

After a moment to gather his wits Carstares continued,

'So Nicholas is dead. Don't suppose you know who the heir is now?'

'Can't say I do,' replied Carrington. 'I don't keep track of all my friends' distant relations!' Then, in tones of shock as a possibility struck him, 'My God! It couldn't be! Not Jack Frobisher?'

George nodded.

Carrington thought about it. 'Peter won't stand for that. He'll have to remarry. Unpleasant for him after his experience with Melissa, but he might choose better this time!'

'Hope so,' said George. 'Because I think that's what we're doing here. Helping Peter choose a wife! Or at least providing moral support while he chooses! And thank God—if he's here, he ain't contemplating marriage to Caroline Daventry!'

Whatever Lord Carrington might have said in response to his friend's suspicions was destined to remain unspoken. At that moment a startled hush came over the crowd and they realised that most people were staring in disbelief at the entrance. An even more startled murmur replaced the hush as the tall gentleman in the doorway moved into the room.

He seemed quite unconcerned by the collective gaze and whisper of the assembled throng, but stood and surveyed the scene carefully. His was a tall, athletic figure, dressed with unobtrusive elegance in the satin knee-breeches and swallow-tailed coat which were *de rigueur* for a ball. His cravat was tied with an artistry calculated to turn any aspirant to fashion pea-green with envy. The curly black hair was brushed into the fashionable Brutus and the dark brown eyes seemed to search the room.

After a moment this direct gaze fell upon Lord Carrington and Mr Carstares. A smile lightened the rather sombre countenance as the gentleman came towards them. This was Peter Augustus Frobisher, Earl of Darleston, veteran of the Peninsular War and hero of Waterloo.

He reached his friends and said with a faint twinkle, 'How kind of you not to depart! Had you quite despaired of me?'

'You'd have had two friends the less if you hadn't shown your front, my boy!' said Carrington trenchantly.

The Earl looked amused. 'How very extreme! You could have left, you know! In fact the thought occurred to me, while I was screwing up my courage in the carriage, that all I had to do was wait and the pair of you would shortly emerge. There's nothing in the rules to stop you leaving!'

His friends stared at him in speechless dudgeon. George was the first to recover the use of his tongue. 'Oh, yes, there is, when Lady Sefton has personally commanded your presence at supper!'

Darleston said soothingly, 'Never mind, there are worse fates!'

Before either of his indignant friends could draw breath to ask exactly what he had in mind, an attractive woman of about fifty came up behind them and tapped Darleston on the arm.

'Peter! You dreadful boy! What on earth are you doing here at the Marriage Mart?' Her voice held deep affection and Earl turned around with a smile of delight on his face.

'Aunt Louisa!' He bent to kiss her on the cheek. 'Simply for the joy of seeing you dressed like the Christmas beef! Can you doubt it?'

'Easily, you trifler! Oh, it is good to see you! And you too, George and Michael! How long it seems since you were all schoolboys racing around Darleston Court. Making the place hideous with your noise and muddy boots!' She smiled at the recollection.

The three gentlemen grinned, and Carstares said, laughing, 'Seems like yesterday for you, Lady Edenhope. You appear to remember our sins only too well!'

'I've cause enough!' she replied with a chuckle. 'I never did find out who put the frog in my bed!'

'All of us!' admitted Darleston. 'Carrington caught it with George's boot and I climbed up the ivy with it. A joint effort, in fact! And didn't we feel like sweeps when you simply gave it to Meadows the next morning and asked him to return it to the owner with thanks? He was furious with us!'

Lady Edenhope laughed up at them. She was not, in point of fact, related to Darleston, but had been his mother's dearest friend, and she cherished a deep affection for him. Knowing him as well as she did, she too had a very fair notion of the interpretation to put on his presence at Almack's after so many years. No doubt so did many of the Ton, she thought ruefully. The matchmaking mamas would be in full cry after the quarry in no time! Enough to make any man turn tail and bolt for cover!

At thirty-two, the widowed Earl was a matrimonial prize of the first stare. Extremely wealthy and possessed of an ancient and honourable name, he had charm and good looks that were the final seal upon his fate. Perfectly aware of this, for the past few years he had avoided the more respectable entertainments afforded by the Metropolis, preferring to spend his time in pursuits unlikely to bring him within the range of marriageable young girls and their mamas.

'Well, it is lovely to see you all here,' said Lady

Edenhope. 'Now I must run along. I'm supposed to be chaperoning a friend's daughter and I mustn't neglect my duty. Not that it's very onerous. The dearest girl, and already snapped up!'

She departed into the throng and the three gentlemen looked at each other reminiscently. Darleston broke the silence, saying lightly, 'Well, ''Once more unto the breach, dear friends,'' as the Bard would have it! No doubt enough people know us that we shan't find ourselves utterly ignored.' This last was said in distinctly sarcastic tones.

They suited the action to the word and began to mingle with the crowd. One by one they found themselves being presented to various young ladies, all of whom seemed flatteringly anxious to please and entertain them. George Carstares and Lord Carrington took this in good part, and even found that they were quite enjoying themselves.

For Lord Darleston, however, it was quite another matter. Despite the fact that he had been introduced to the very attractive Miss Ffolliot, his mind persisted in wandering. Here at Almack's twelve years earlier he had met his first wife and fallen madly in love with her lovely face and charming ways. What a fool I must have been! he thought bitterly. Calf love! He had been *aux anges* at the thought that such a divine creature should favour him over so many suitors who had appeared to him far more eligible. A modest young man, he had been quite innocent of the lure of his prospective title and fortune. He had seen himself as a callow youth, miraculously favoured by the loveliest debutante of the season.

With an effort he jerked his mind out of the past and back to his companion. 'I beg your pardon, Miss Ffolliot, I was wool-gathering. What were you saying?'

Miss Ffolliot smiled up at him and said in a soft voice,

'It was of no consequence, my lord. Just a polite com-
monplace. Should we take our places now?'

'Most certainly we should,' he answered, and led her
into a set. Really she was a very pretty girl, he thought
to himself. Many spiteful matrons would have described
her hair as red, but in fact it was a deep rich auburn and
she had the delicately fair complexion which goes with
such hair. Wide-set grey eyes gazed up at him in innocent
enjoyment and her smile was quite delightful. Her figure
was just what he liked too, slender but with a suggestion
of womanly curves. All in all, thought Darleston, she was
quite lovely!

As they danced he attempted to engage her in conversation, but she had very little to say for herself besides
polite rejoinders to his comments. The only question to
which she replied with any enthusiasm was his query as
to whether she was enjoying her visit to Almack's.

'Oh, yes, my lord! Very much! It is nice to see so
many new people and to dance all night!'

From all of which Lord Darleston came to the swift
conclusion that this young lady would not do at all. While
he did not wish to marry a chatterbox he preferred to
seek a lady who had a little more to add to a conversation. Without wishing to be unkind, he found Miss
Ffolliot a little dull for his taste. Very charming and
sweet, but just not his sort!

At the end of the dance he returned Miss Ffolliot to
her mother to find that she had been joined by her husband, a kindly-looking man of medium height, as well as
Miss Ffolliot's next partner. He was introduced to
Darleston as Mr Richard Winton, a gentleman of roughly
the same age as the Earl, who recognised him as a fellow
member of White's. The two of them chatted politely

before Mr Winton excused himself and Miss Ffolliot to join a set.

Darleston noted without the least rancour that Miss Ffolliot was chatting merrily to her new partner without the slightest hint of shyness.

Mr Ffolliot watched the pair and said, 'Mr Winton is a neighbour of ours in the country. Phoebe always finds it easier to chat to old acquaintances!'

Darleston smiled and said, 'I tend to agree with her! And the dreadful thing is when someone who has been presented to you once should chance to recognise you and you simply cannot remember the right name!'

'Dear me, yes!' said Mrs Ffolliot with a chuckle. 'And they always seem so hurt if one admits one can't remember them! Mr Ffolliot has a truly terrible memory for names.'

'Nonsense, my dear! You do exaggerate!' protested the maligned gentleman.

'Not by very much!' she asserted with a twinkle. 'Still, no doubt Lord Darleston is not afflicted too badly. I'm sure people are only too glad to recall themselves to his mind!'

'Only too true, ma'am. You can have no notion of the number of people who claim long acquaintance on the basis of one meeting years before!'

'I can imagine!' laughed Mrs Ffolliot. 'Never mind, my lord! My husband and I shall remember to cut you the next time we meet, and Phoebe shall be given strict instructions to do the same.'

Laughing at this, Darleston made his farewells and departed to seek Carstares and Carrington. George was easy enough to spot. He was taking part in the same set as Miss Ffolliot and Mr Winton. And after a few moments' searching Darleston found Carrington listening very politely to Lady Jersey, another of the Patronesses, wickedly, if aptly, known as 'Silence'.

'Darleston, my goodness! I didn't believe Maria Sefton when she told me you were here! It must be years! Lord Carrington too! What a catch for us! Why, I declare there has not been so much excitement all season! Did I see you stand up with Miss Ffolliot? Such a sweet child, but a little shy. Parents charming, but the brother! Oh, my goodness! Oh, well! He's only her half-brother. The first Mrs Ffolliot died very young, I believe, and John Ffolliot remarried a few years later. It does happen, you see, Darleston! Now I must be off! Do come again! I'm sure it does us good to have such a shock!'

She fluttered away to inform all and sundry that it was just as she had suspected. Darleston was going to remarry. And about time too! After all, he owed it to his name! Oh, goodness me! Just think if one had to acknowledge that odious Jack Frobisher as Earl of Darleston! Besides, it was time and more that Darleston got over smarting about the way that baggage Melissa had treated him. Running off with Barton in that vulgar way! Just as well she did break her neck in that carriage accident! At least it spared Darleston the scandal of divorcing her!

Carrington and Darleston watched her go with a fairly accurate idea of what she must be saying. Half-annoyed and half-amused Darleston enquired, 'Did she stop to draw breath while she spoke to you?'

Carrington grinned. 'Not so that you'd notice! But she's as shrewd as she can hold together for all she rattles on so fast.'

'No need to tell me that!' answered Darleston with a grimace. 'I got the distinct impression that dear Silence knew everything about me! Right down to what brought me here this evening!'

In some amusement, Carrington said, 'Doing it far too brown, dear boy! I should imagine everyone who knows you worked that out the moment they laid eyes on you! Especially when they saw you stand up with that pretty little redhead!'

Darleston sighed, 'I suppose it must be glaringly obvious. But what choice do I have?'

'None, regarding your duty,' answered his friend seriously. 'But plenty as to the shape it must take. Let's face it, Peter, you are the most eligible of men. Wealthy, titled, and the ladies seem to find you tolerably pleasing to the eye. You could probably have your choice of brides.'

'How very dull!' complained Darleston. 'You make it all sound so respectable!'

'Well, that's what you want, isn't it?' asked Carrington bluntly.

Darleston sighed again. 'God knows why I bear with you, Michael! You have such an appalling habit of being disgustingly right! Ah! Here comes George. Did you enjoy yourself?'

'As a matter of fact I did,' answered Carstares. 'My partner, Miss Blackburn, was quite charming, and at least I won't have a head tomorrow morning from dancing with her! Or pockets to let, for that matter!'

'You'll find yourself with pockets to let all right and tight if you let your susceptibilities lead you astray and find yourself in Parson's Mousetrap!' observed Darleston caustically.

Carstares looked shocked. 'Me? Parson's Mousetrap! Not likely. Younger son, you know! That's your fate,

Peter, at least so I believe! We'll see you falling in love and waiting at the altar in no time!'

'Love!' ejaculated Darleston. 'You can't be serious! I tell you, I'm done with that rubbish! This is to be a marriage of convenience. As long as the girl is well brought up to know her duty and is not a positive antidote…' He left the sentence unfinished.

Carstares and Lord Carrington looked at each other in concern. This was even worse than they had thought! What hope had the poor chap of happiness in marriage if he was this bitter? Not to mention the poor girl who accepted his offer.

After a moment's silence Carstares said thoughtfully, 'Then you'd better make damn sure the girl don't care a rush for you! After all, you don't want to treat some poor child to the same dirty trick you were served! Oh, Lord! Here comes Lady Sefton. Lay you handsome odds she's going to snabble Peter as well.'

The arrival of the amiable Lady Sefton effectively ended the conversation, but Carstares' observation had gone home deeply. The thought that he might hurt some unsuspecting innocent in the same way he had been hurt gave Peter furiously to think.

Although he bore his part at the ensuing supper party with charm and wit, his mind was frequently elsewhere. Until now his future bride had been a very hypothetical and unreal figure. Suddenly, even though her face and figure remained in the shadows, she became a person, with thoughts and feelings, perhaps a heart to be wounded. George was right, he thought. Better make sure she doesn't care too much, whoever she turns out to be!

Two days later the lovely Lady Caroline Daventry sat in her cushioned pink drawing room, glaring at the door as it closed after her fifth morning caller. Her normally languishing blue eyes were glittering with fury and every line of her lushly curved body was stiff with rage. Even the blonde curls piled so becomingly on top of her head seemed to quiver with emotion. She had been hard put to it to bite back a savage rejoinder as yet another sweetly smiling lady had told her in strictest confidence that it seemed 'Dear Peter' was considering a second marriage.

His appearance at Almack's and dance with Miss Ffolliot had lost nothing in the telling. The fact that he had remained chatting to her parents for several minutes gave weight to the wildest flights of fancy. It was even rumoured that Mr Richard Winton, hitherto the most likely candidate for her hand, was in a way to being cut out!

Caroline Daventry was no fool. She knew enough to discount the more fanciful accounts, but even so what was left alarmed her. It was a fairly open secret that she had been Darleston's mistress for the past year. Never had it occurred to her that he might consider remarrying. He had appeared to be perfectly satisfied with her favours, and she had been content to maintain her position as his mistress. But if he was to remarry then clearly the situation was altered.

Restlessly she rose to her feet and began to pace up and down. She must think! Obviously Darleston must dislike Jack even more than she had thought. That had to be the reason for this change of direction. So far so good! At least he wasn't fancying himself in love with some simpering little debutante! That made her task a little easier. Far less difficult to detach his thoughts from an abstract goal than from a specific person, but she must work fast. If Darleston *was* going to marry again then she fully intended to be the new Countess!

* * *

That same morning Lord Darleston had decided to try the paces of a new mare. He had bought her at Tattersall's the previous week, and every time he'd thought of taking her out something had cropped up to distract him. This morning he was determined that nothing should be allowed to deflect him from his purpose.

Therefore the unfashionable hour of eight o'clock had seen him swinging into the saddle of a mettlesome bay mare who appeared to be under the erroneous impression that her new master would be disconcerted by her habit of plunging a little as he mounted. Amused by these fidgets, Darleston had settled himself in the saddle and spoken to her soothingly.

The groom who had brought her around from the mews said apologetically, 'Very lively she is, my lord! She needs a good gallop!'

'Not to mention a firm hand!' said his master as he brought the mare's head up. 'Steady there you silly creature! It's early enough that we can probably get away with a bit of a gallop in the park. Thank you, Fred. I'll bring her around when I get back.'

The groom touched his cap respectfully and stepped back as his master gave the mare the office to move. Having revised her opinion of the man on her back, the mare moved off at a decorous pace and tried to convey the impression that this was the way she always behaved. Fred watched the pair of them depart and then went back to the mews to tell his cohorts that the master could handle anything that ever looked through a bridle, even that flighty piece of blood and bone Griselda!

Upon reaching the park, Darleston was relieved to discover that it was practically deserted. Several horses were being exercised by grooms and a very few people were strolling along the paths. No carriages and no sign of anyone who might recognise him. Hardly a surprise at this ungodly hour, he thought. Most members of society would still be abed after the entertainments of the previous evening.

The mare, Griselda, was dancing impatiently, itching to go. For the good of her education Darleston held her to a steady trot for a hundred yards before pressing her to a canter. After another hundred yards and a quick glance around he gave Griselda her head and touched his heels lightly to her flanks. No further encouragement was necessary. The mare took off down the path with a delighted snort. For over a week she had been cooped up in a stable or led out in a string and she had had quite enough of such boredom. This was much more to her taste.

Darleston sat firm in the saddle and kept a light hand on the mare's mouth. Her paces, he concluded, were excellent. Smooth and effortless, with an impressive turn of speed. Her mouth, too, was good; she was extremely responsive to his hand on the rein. Her only fault, if fault it could be called, was her flightiness. Ah, well, we're all young once! he thought tolerantly.

On the thought he sat back and steadied the mare. A phaeton was being driven towards him at a smart trot and an incredibly large grey hound was running alongside. Good heavens, he thought. Who on earth would be out at this hour? He reined Griselda in to a trot so as not to startle the pair harnessed to the phaeton.

As the carriage drew nearer he realised that he knew the occupants. The gentleman driving nodded politely, but obviously would have continued had not Darleston reined in and said in tones of mock indignation, 'I didn't think you were serious when you threatened to cut me, sir! How do you do, Mr Ffolliot? And Miss Ffolliot! No need to ask how you are! You are looking charmingly!'

'Lord Darleston! This is very pleasant,' replied Mr Ffolliot. 'I don't believe you have met my—' He stopped suddenly.

Darleston, a trifle puzzled, said, 'But of course I have met Miss Ffolliot! She granted me the honour of a dance at Almack's the other night!'

'Oh, of course…er…quite so!' said Mr Ffolliot in some confusion. 'I beg your pardon, Lord Darleston!'

'Think nothing of it, sir. Mrs Ffolliot warned me of your lamentable memory!' said Darleston with a chuckle. He liked this unpretentious man with the kind eyes.

He turned to Miss Ffolliot and said, 'I do hope our dance holds a stronger place in *your* memory, Miss Ffolliot! Or do you have so many dancing partners that neither you nor your parents can disentangle us all?'

Miss Ffolliot gave vent to a delightful choke of laughter and said, 'Oh, no, Lord Darleston. That dance is firmly fixed in my mind! It was most enjoyable!'

Darleston blinked a little. This merry creature was a far cry from the shy girl he had danced with at Almack's! And there was something different about her this morning. Something about her eyes. Although she smiled at him delightfully, he had the odd feeling that those wide grey eyes were looking right through him. Trying to gather his thoughts, he asked, 'And may one enquire what brings you out at this unfashionable hour, Miss Ffolliot? Surely you should be recruiting your strength after whatever party you graced last night.'

She laughed and said, 'Oh, but the park is so much more pleasant when there is nobody about! And much better than a stuffy ballroom! Besides—' she indicated the dog who sat panting next to the phaeton '—poor

Gelert needs a great deal more exercise than he'd get if we came out at a fashionable hour and had to stop continually to be polite!'

'I do sympathise, Miss Ffolliot!' answered Darleston. 'I brought this lunatic mare out early for much the same reason.'

'She's a pretty thing,' said Mr Ffolliot. 'Quite a youngster too. How is she called?'

'Yes, she is young. Just over three. I bought her last week. Her name is Griselda. Steady you idiot!' This last to the mare as she fidgeted nervously. 'She is a little impatient as yet!'

'Surely she is ill-named then, my lord!' said Miss Ffolliot with a smile. 'Wasn't Griselda supposed to be very patient?'

'Do you mean that mawkish creature in Chaucer?' asked Darleston in some surprise. Most young ladies were well read in Byron, but he had yet to meet one with a knowledge of medieval literature!

'That's the female. She comes in *The Decameron* too you know,' answered Miss Ffolliot. 'How nice to find someone else who thinks she was a fool for putting up with that odious husband. She should have simply told him he was being an idiot!'

'Quite so, Miss Ffolliot,' he agreed with a twinkle. 'I can easily believe that you'd do just that!'

'I'd probably let Gelert bite him!' was the answer.

'That would certainly bring him to his senses in a hurry!' said Darleston, grinning.

He looked at the dog curiously. Never before had he seen quite such an enormous hound. Tremendously long legs and a deep barrelled chest gave the impression of immense power. He must stand at least three feet at the shoulder, thought Darleston in awe. The breed was nevertheless familiar to him from a horse-buying trip to Ireland years before. 'An Irish wolfhound, isn't he? I've never seen such a magnificent specimen of the breed.'

Miss Ffolliot smiled at him and said, 'That's right! Most people enquire about his breeding in the most patronising tones and it makes me simply wild!'

Darleston chuckled. 'I can just imagine!' But all the while an odd voice in his mind was nagging at him. Surely Miss Ffolliot had been an entirely different girl in the ballroom! If asked, he would have sworn she wouldn't say boo to a goose! And hadn't she said the other night that she enjoyed dancing and meeting new people? And now she preferred the park at an early hour because it was empty and better than 'a stuffy ballroom'!

He quizzed her gently. 'I think you were not telling the truth the other night, Miss Ffolliot. I distinctly recall you saying how much you enjoyed meeting new people and dancing!'

Again he heard that appealing choke of laughter. 'Good heavens! Surely you don't expect a girl to inform a gentleman to whom she has just been introduced that she hates meeting new people! Let alone that she dislikes balls when the poor man is dancing with her! How very rude that would have been in me! Besides, that dance was, as I said, very enjoyable.'

'Mere flattery, Miss Ffolliot!'

'Not at all, my lord. You dance very well!' she added in tones of great kindness.

He roared with laughter and said, 'That amounts to toad-eating, Miss Ffolliot! You are a baggage, I take leave to tell you!'

Then, as Griselda sidled restlessly in the cool breeze, 'I must not keep my "Impatient Griselda" standing any longer. Sir! Your most obedient servant! Miss Ffolliot, your most humble!' They bade him farewell and, raising his hat to Miss Ffolliot, he pushed the mare into a trot and continued on his way. It occurred to him that he would enjoy meeting Miss Ffolliot again. She was a most refreshing, if contradictory young lady!

Chapter Two

Lord Darleston had been a trifle over optimistic in thinking that the park would be bereft of all the Ton that morning. At least two other people had seen him exercising the mare, and had also observed his conversation with the Ffolliots. The murmurs of interest which followed this episode came inevitably to the ears of Lady Caroline, who began to be seriously worried. Worried enough to be betrayed into making some rather snide remarks to Miss Ffolliot at a ball. Miss Ffolliot did not attempt to reply but simply looked extremely puzzled.

Quite apart from all the gossip, Lady Caroline had noticed an even greater degree of detachment in her lover than was normal. Never one to indulge in displays of demonstrative emotion, Darleston seemed to her to be more aloof and untouchable than ever. It was as though his mind was far away, even when he made love to her with all his usual skill and expertise. Lady Caroline turned various schemes over in her mind and finally decided on a course of definite action, for which she prepared by ensuring that Darleston did not see her privately for over a week.

The first direct step in her campaign was a discreetly

worded invitation bidding his lordship to supper one evening. She knew that she would have to step warily.
Darleston was neither to lead or drive. If he once suspected what she was up to then she might as well give
up. Hence the supper invitation. A delightfully romantic
evening *à deux* with his favourite wines and food would
serve her turn. Afterwards, when he was in a relaxed
mood, she could begin her task of distracting him from
immediate thoughts of matrimony. Convincing him that
she would be a suitable wife was much further on in her
plans!

Accordingly Lord Darleston presented himself for a
late supper on the designated evening, in a mood of
agreeable anticipation. Lady Caroline kept a talented
chef, and knew his taste in wine to a nicety, besides
which her personal attractions were definitely alluring.
He had seen little of Caroline recently, except at parties
where perforce discretion was necessary. It did not occur
to him that the lady had deliberately made quite sure he
had had no opportunity to see her alone for some time.
Better for her plans if he was eager to see her and enjoy
her favours, she reasoned.

Darleston entered the drawing room to find Lady
Caroline attended by her companion, Miss Jameson, a
depressed-looking creature of about sixty. She was a
cousin of the late Sir Neville Daventry and was supposed
to lend an air of respectability to her relation's ménage.
In reality Lady Caroline did very much as she pleased,
dispensing with Miss Jameson's chaperonage whenever
it suited her convenience.

Darleston greeted both ladies politely, and was especially kind to the older lady. 'Miss Jameson! What a pleasure to see you. I hope you are keeping well?' It was
part of his charm that he was always kind to those less

well off than himself. Kind, but never patronising, and Miss Jameson, as always, responded to his friendly greeting with a smile that very few ever saw.

'I am very well, Lord Darleston. And you? We have not seen you for an age!' she said.

Lady Caroline cut in at this point, 'Yes, I am sure Lord Darleston is well, Cousin Lucy, or he would not be here! Now, we wouldn't want to keep you from your bed at this late hour, so we will bid you goodnight!'

This abrupt dismissal brought a slight frown to Darleston's brow, not because he was eager for Miss Jameson's company, but because he found the ruthless manner of it faintly distasteful. Lady Caroline did not notice the frown. Like many self-centred people, she was unable to comprehend that anyone would put up with an inconvenient companion from a combination of good manners and kindness.

Miss Jameson appeared unsurprised by the curtailing of her evening. She had known perfectly well from the outset that Caroline would get rid of her as quickly as possible. The two years since Sir Neville's death had left her few illusions about her charge's character, and she had no doubts at all about the nature of Lady Caroline's relationship with Lord Darleston. It was certainly not her place to remonstrate with Lady Caroline, she reflected, but it seemed a dreadful thing to see such a fine man as Lord Darleston in her coils.

'I shall bid you goodnight, then, dear Caroline, and you, my lord,' she responded in a dignified manner, which afforded no hint of the sense of hurt she felt. It would give her great pleasure, she thought, to put a spoke in Lady Caroline's wheel. She was not quite sure what Caroline was up to, but she knew her charge well enough to know that something was afoot.

Darleston went immediately to the door and opened it for her, saying, 'Goodnight, Miss Jameson. It is most unkind of you to deprive us of your company. Perhaps I shall be luckier on another occasion!'

She looked up at him in wry amusement as she exited the room and her soft reply reached only him. 'Most unlikely, my lord! Goodnight, and God bless you!'

After shutting the door behind her, Darleston turned back to his hostess, who looked a little miffed. 'Really, Peter dear, I cannot imagine why you bother with Cousin Lucy! I only keep her here to silence all the tabbies!'

Darleston was silent for a moment, and then said with an assumption of lightness, 'Kindness costs nothing, Caroline, and I think her situation as a dependant cannot be a happy one.'

Although she could not understand his attitude, Lady Caroline was quick enough to realise that she had erred in some way. She glided across to him and twined her arms around his neck, 'Oh, Peter! 'Tis not that I meant to be unkind to poor Lucy! But I have seen so little of you recently that I longed to have you all to myself!' The blue eyes gazed up at him meltingly from under long curling lashes. A provocative smile was on her lips, deepening as she felt his arms slide about her waist.

Darleston looked down at her with a faint smile. Perhaps it was as well to let Miss Jameson have an early night, he thought as he kissed Lady Caroline. Her response was immediate and demanding. Nothing loath, Darleston tightened his arms about her and set about the enjoyable task of satisfying her obvious desire. His own physical desire was easily a match for hers, but as always some small part of him remained detached and indifferent.

After a few moments he released himself carefully and

said, 'Perhaps we should have supper first, Caroline! Otherwise I fear your chef's talents will be quite unappreciated in comparison with your own charms!'

Satisfied that she had well and truly aroused him, Lady Caroline agreed. 'Whatever you wish, my lord. Just as long as the supper does not spoil your appetite!' She cast a meaning glance over her shoulder as she led the way to the small table set for two. A side-table nearby held a small but choice supper and several decanters.

As they sat down Lady Caroline said languidly, 'Do you know, Peter—except, of course, for your presence—London is so dreadfully dull at the moment? One gets so tired of seeing the same faces and hearing the same gossip! I declare it is beyond anything!'

Darleston was amused. 'My dear, are you contemplating a repairing lease in the country? I fear you will find that even more dull!'

A shudder of horror greeted this suggestion. 'The country! At this season! What an insupportable idea! Of course not! I am thinking of going to Paris. I have friends there, you know. And it seems such a long time since I visited France! And Paris is always so gay! Will you have a little duckling, Peter?' She judged that she had said enough for the time being.

Having accepted the duckling, and some asparagus, Darleston returned to the subject of Lady Caroline's projected sojourn in Paris. 'And what will be so different about Paris, my sweet? New clothes, admirers? New gossip?'

She gave a tinkling laugh. 'But of course, my dear! All those things! Now, enough of me! Tell me what you have been doing to keep you away from me all these days!'

Darleston hesitated for a moment. The last thing he

wanted to do was confide in Caroline! 'Oh, just catching up with old friends and seeing to some business,' he said easily. 'Carstares and Carrington are in town at the moment. I've seen a lot of them.'

'Do you know, I even heard that the three of you had been seen at Almack's?' she said daringly. 'Surely a most unlikely place to find any of you! Let alone all three together! You must have raised such hopes in the hearts of all the young ladies and their fond mamas!' This last was followed with another tinkling laugh.

Sipping her wine, she watched his reaction carefully. She was perfectly aware that practically every woman in town with a marriageable daughter would be in full cry after such a prize as Darleston. She was also tolerably certain that this would be irking her lover almost unbearably.

His quick scowl confirmed her suspicions, and again she changed the subject. 'Do tell me. How does Mr Carstares, and Lord Carrington, of course?'

'Oh, they are well enough. Carrington has gone down to Bath to visit his young sister for a few days. She is at school there and has been unwell.'

'Poor child,' said Lady Caroline, thinking it was as well that one of Darleston's close friends was out of town. Carstares and Carrington together might manage to spike her guns!

She kept the conversation to neutral topics until the end of the meal.

When Darleston reached for the brandy decanter she rose to her feet and said with a smile, 'Perhaps you would excuse me briefly, Peter.'

He stood up and said, 'Only very briefly, Caroline! I'm sure you would not wish to keep me waiting!' After escorting Lady Caroline to the door and closing it behind her Darleston returned to the table and poured himself a glass of the late Sir Neville's very fine old brandy. Sipping it reverently, he sat down to give some thought to Caroline's scheme to visit Paris. He suspected that her main reason for finding London dull was simply that she had been subtly but effectively ostracised by quite a number of influential society hostesses.

Caroline had not been quite discreet enough with one or two of her lovers. It was even said that she had entertained a number of gentlemen at her Scottish home during her period of strict mourning. The Patronesses of Almack's had let it be quietly understood that for her to apply for vouchers would be useless. Nothing was said openly, of course, but Lady Caroline did not make the attempt. To be publicly denied would be insupportable.

Although she vowed that such entertainments were insipid and not at all to her taste, Darleston was perfectly aware that she wanted that entrée, even if only for the pleasure of spurning it. Obviously if she were in Paris there was no question of Almack's, and her reputation would not be such a barrier where she was not so well known.

The excellence of the brandy gave rise to more thought, and to a great degree mitigated against his lordship's rising impatience at the inordinate length of time Lady Caroline was taking. It did not occur to him that she wanted him to be extremely eager or that she wanted to give him time to think over her plans.

It suddenly struck Darleston that if Caroline decamped for Paris it would be deucedly inconvenient for him. He enjoyed her favours very much and was loath to go to all the effort of finding and setting up a new mistress. His own married experience led him to eschew all married women. Something in his nature revolted at the

thought of offending another man as he had been offended. Unfortunately his preference was for women of
his own order, which therefore meant a widow, and he
was damned if he could think of another likely candidate
to fill the position which would be left vacant by Lady
Caroline's departure.

He had no illusions about the quality of Caroline's
affection for him. She might go to Paris alone but she
would certainly not return so. Not that she needed a pro-
tector in financial terms for she was quite well off! In
fact that was one of the things that Darleston found agreeable about the relationship. It was conducted on equal
terms with none of the necessity to buy expensive presents to keep his mistress happy.

He was just beginning to toy with the notion of following Lady Caroline to Paris when she returned. Her
elegant gown of deep blue satin had been replaced by a
dressing gown which consisted of floating layers of pink
gauze. It was quite evident to Darleston that her ladyship
was not wearing a stitch beneath it. He said nothing, but
tossed back the last of his brandy with scant respect for
so noble a vintage and stood up.

Lady Caroline glided to the sofa and seated herself
with an inviting smile. The dressing gown fell open, exposing one elegant white leg which Caroline did not
bother to cover. Darleston shrugged himself out of his
coat and removed his cravat without taking his eyes from
her face. He walked over to the sofa unhurriedly, but
Lady Caroline could see the tension in every line of his
athletic body. He stood before her, looking down at her
voluptuous curves with increasing lust.

'Do you like my dressing gown?' she asked provocatively. 'It's a new one.'

He answered lightly enough, 'Very elegant my sweet, but I'll appreciate it more when I've torn it off you!'

The following morning Darleston slept late, not having returned home until four in the morning. His lordship's valet, Mr Fordham, was finally summoned from the servants' hall by his master's bell at midday.

Fordham found his lordship fully dressed except for the finishing touches to his cravat. He waited quietly, not wishing to disturb so delicate and important an operation.

Darleston caught his eye in the mirror, 'Ah, there you are Fordham. Good morning, or rather, since I perceive the day to be advanced, good afternoon!'

'Good afternoon, my lord. I trust your lordship enjoyed an agreeable evening?' replied Fordham very politely.

The long, powerful fingers on the cravat stilled in the act of setting a crease and the brown eyes glanced into the mirror again. 'Very agreeable, Fordham,' answered the Earl gravely.

'I am glad to hear it my lord. May I remind your lordship that you had promised to wait on Lady Edenhope this morning?' asked Fordham.

'You may remind me, and you may also tell me why the devil you didn't awaken me over an hour ago to this purpose!' said Darleston, carefully examining the results of his labours.

'Your lordship may remember that upon the last occasion I ventured to do such a thing you hurled a boot at my head with great accuracy and consigned me to a place of extreme heat!' was the unperturbed reply.

Darleston, satisfied that his cravat would pass muster, swung around with a distinct twinkle in his eye and asked curiously, 'Why do you bear with me Fordham?'

The valet answered simply, 'I like you, my lord, and

even if you did hit me with the boot you apologised later and informed me that you would prefer I remained in your employ rather than seeking the post you had recommended in the heat of the moment.'

Darleston chuckled and said, 'Very well, Fordham! Did you by any chance send a note round to Lady Edenhope?'

'Certainly, my lord. She sent this note back for you.' He handed Darleston a sealed billet.

'Thank you, Fordham.' He broke the seal and read the enclosed missive.

> My Dear Darleston
>
> I shall forbear to ask exactly how you amused yourself last night if only you will have the goodness to be my escort tonight! My little protégée is unwell and my lord has gone into the country so I am bereft of a companion for the concert at the Hanover Square Rooms this evening. I know you love music and the programme this evening is rather lovely: all Mozart. So if you feel you can bear my company I shall look forward to seeing you this evening.
>
> All my love, Louisa Edenhope.

Darleston grinned. He wouldn't put it past Lady Edenhope to know perfectly well where he had been last night. He glanced at Fordham and said, 'You may send a footman round to tell Lady Edenhope that I shall be delighted to be her escort this evening.'

'Very good, my lord. I will go myself, if your lordship has no further need for me this afternoon.'

'Yourself, Fordham?' said Darleston in surprise. 'You are welcome to do so if you wish, but why?'

'Some exercise will do me good, my lord. Mr Meadows has informed me that I am getting fat!' There was a slight hint of indignation in Fordham's tone of voice.

'I see,' said Darleston, somehow preserving a straight face. 'You have my permission to take a walk every day if you deem it necessary. You know my routine. No doubt you can pick a time which will be mutually acceptable to us both. That will be all for now. You will lay out my clothes later, of course.'

'Naturally, my lord.' Fordham left on his message and Darleston gave himself up to laughter. No doubt Meadows, the old butler, was enjoying himself at Fordham's expense, but there was no denying that Fordham was starting to look a little tubby!

Darleston did enjoy the concert that evening. He found Lady Edenhope's company restful, and it was pleasant to sit back and listen to the music. One of the things he missed most about his mother was her music. She had been a fine singer and had played the pianoforte with great talent. There had always been music in his home and he missed it greatly. He thought idly to himself that he must try and choose a musical wife.

During the interval he remained with Lady Edenhope, chatting about the performance. Two of Mozart's string quartets had been played, and Lady Edenhope felt that a better balance of the parts had been needed.

They returned to their seats for the second half. 'That cellist was by far too loud in places, Peter. Particularly in the slow movements!' she asserted, and then realised that Darleston was not listening. He was staring at a lady she had already noted as being most oddly dressed.

All in severe black and heavily veiled, the lady sat two rows ahead of them and slightly to the right. She was escorted by a young person who was obviously a maid-servant and had made no effort to speak to anyone during the interval. Looking at her more closely, Lady Edenhope came to the conclusion that she was quite young. The severe black was extremely flattering to an already slender figure.

Darleston continued to stare until his companion gave him a gentle nudge and asked, 'Do you know that girl, Peter?'

'What...? Oh, I'm sorry, Aunt Louisa! I wasn't really attending,' he apologised.

'I noticed,' she said dryly. 'Is the young lady an acquaintance of yours?'

'I'm not quite sure,' said Darleston slowly. 'I *think* I know who it is, but I can't for the life of me imagine what she is doing dressed like that!'

'Most odd!' agreed Lady Edenhope. 'Oh, here is the orchestra. We had better stop chattering.'

They sat back to enjoy the two symphonies which followed. The last one was Mozart's final essay in this genre. Darleston had never heard the work before and was taken aback by the power of the music, particularly in the final movement. Here the closely knit interweaving of the melodies was utterly exhilarating, and when the end came Darleston felt that he wanted to leap up and yell like a boy. He contented himself with clapping vigorously.

The slender lady in black appeared to be similarly affected. She was leaning forward, applauding enthusiastically, and Darleston became more and more certain that he knew her.

Turning to Lady Edenhope as the audience began to make its way to the doors, Darleston said, 'Would you excuse me for a moment, Aunt Louisa? I should like to speak to that lady.'

'Of course, Peter,' she replied. 'I shall wait here.'

Darleston made his way forward against the crowd, nodding to acquaintances as he went. The girl in black had not moved from her seat, but seemed to be waiting for the crush to disperse. No one spoke to her, although many curious glances were cast in her direction.

She did not notice Darleston until he sat down beside her and said, 'Good evening, Miss Ffolliot! Did you enjoy the concert?' Several heads turned at once as he identified the mysterious lady.

There came a startled gasp and she swung around towards him. What he could see of the lovely face behind the veil suggested shock and consternation. Rather surprised, he said, 'I'm sorry. I did not mean to startle you.'

For a split second she hesitated, and then said, 'It is Lord Darleston, is it not?'

He smiled and said, 'Quite correct! Although I am surprised you can see a thing through that veil!'

'But I…' She stopped, appeared to recollect herself, and said with an assumption of lightness, 'Well, my lord, you have lost me my wager!'

'Miss Ffolliot, I most humbly beg your pardon! What wager was that?' he asked in amusement.

'Why, that no one would recognise me like this! I did not think it possible. And indeed I do not think anyone else did know me!' she said, laughing.

Darleston chuckled and said, 'I'm sure they didn't. Certainly my companion Lady Edenhope did not. But I'm afraid that I gave the game away by speaking your name so loudly.'

She shrugged her shoulders and said surprisingly, 'Oh,

well, I dare say it does not matter too much now. Did you enjoy the concert?'

'Yes, very much indeed. Especially the last symphony. I had not heard it before.'

'Had you not?' she asked. 'I have once. I think it is my favourite of his works. The last movement—I wish it could go on for ever!'

'That movement is particularly splendid,' he agreed. 'What is it that *you* like about it?'

She thought carefully for a moment and then said, 'It's all the melodies, I think. You know, how he fits them all together, especially at the end in the coda, where they seem to be tumbling over one another. It makes me want to run and jump. It makes me forget...' Again she stopped herself in mid sentence.

'Forget?' he asked curiously. 'What can a child your age wish to forget?'

'Oh, nothing really, my lord,' she answered awkwardly. 'I really should be going now.' She turned to the maid. 'Anna?'

'The crowd is gone, miss. Just his lordship, and a lady seems to be waiting for him,' was the reply.

Darleston was very puzzled by now. Wishing to prolong the encounter, he asked, 'May Lady Edenhope and I escort you home, Miss Ffolliot? I assure you it would be no trouble.'

She shook her head firmly. 'Thank you, my lord, but the carriage will be waiting for me.'

Sensing that she would really prefer to be alone, Darleston did not press her, but said, 'Then I had better return to Lady Edenhope! Goodnight, Miss Ffolliot, it was delightful to run across you again so unexpectedly. Please convey my regards to your parents, and of course to your dog!'

'Oh, Gelert!' She choked on a giggle. 'Not even I would dare try to bring him to a concert! Goodnight, my lord! If I had to lose my wager, I'm glad it was to you!'

'You are very gallant, Miss Ffolliot! Goodnight!' Darleston returned to Lady Edenhope, who was looking distinctly amused.

'Well, you have stirred up the gossips! Was it really Miss Ffolliot?' she asked as they went out into Hanover Square.

Before Darleston could answer, a bluff, hearty voice was heard from a carriage. 'Hello Darleston. Was that Miss Ffolliot? Charming lass! Good for you, boy!'

Darleston blinked into the amiable countenance of old Lord Warboys, who tipped him a knowing wink and continued to his coachman, 'Well, drive on, man! Drive on! Catch me death of cold!' The carriage clattered off, leaving Lord Darleston staring.

Several more encounters of a similar nature served to finish the job begun by Lord Warboys' example of well-meant but tactless jocularity. By the time Darleston had escorted Lady Edenhope back to Half Moon Street he had quite made up his mind to end all the gossip and speculation at least temporarily.

Five days later Lady Caroline Daventry left London for Paris. Three days after that Lord Darleston was reliably reported to be on his way to Dover to catch the next packet. Society shrugged its collective shoulders and forgot all about the momentary excitement raised by Darleston's supposed pursuit of the lovely Miss Ffolliot and invented other gossip for its amusement.

Lord Carrington, returning to town, shook his head at George Carstares and said, 'It will be the same next season! If only the silly fool doesn't take it into his head to marry Caroline Daventry!'

George looked up, shocked, from his copy of the *Gazette*. 'Don't think he's that taken with her, do you?'

Carrington looked cynical and said, 'I'd be prepared to lay odds that's what *she's* after! As for Peter, he seems to think that all women are much the same as each other. In that mood, there's no saying what he might do!'

'Good God!' said George, staring in disbelief at the *Gazette*.

'What's that?' asked Carrington, momentarily diverted.

'Says here that Mr John Ffolliot has been killed in a driving accident!' answered George.

'Lord, that's bad. Young Geoffrey isn't up to much. Doubt he'll make the grade. He'll be running through his inheritance in no time! Hard on Mrs Ffolliot. I believe they were devoted to each other.'

George nodded, 'Sad. Oh, well. Just have to wait and see what happens when Peter comes back. No good us taking a trip to Paris. He'd be furious if he thought we were checking up on him!'

'Can't say I'd blame him,' said Carrington. 'He's two and thirty and ought to be capable of looking after himself, even if he is an ass at times!'

Chapter Three

To the intense concern of Carstares and Carrington, Darleston spent the entire summer and most of the autumn in France. After a lengthy sojourn in Paris, during which he was reported to have danced scandalous attendance on Lady Caroline, he proceeded to attend a series of house parties in various *châteaux*, all of which were notable for the presence of *la belle veuve anglaise*, Lady Caroline Daventry.

At last, towards the end of October, George received a brief note from Darleston Court informing him that its noble owner had returned and would be perfectly happy to entertain the recipient as soon as might be convenient for him. The note ended: 'I have invited Carrington as well and hope you will both make a long stay. Christmas if you like! Sorry to have been such a rotten correspondent. Darleston.'

George breathed a sigh of relief. It seemed his lordship had no immediate plans involving Lady Caroline. He resolved to inform his married sister, with whom he had promised to spend Christmas and New Year, that he would be bringing Darleston. Not for anything would he willingly leave his friend alone at that season. He had as a boy spent a couple of Christmases with Darleston's family and knew that Peter would be more lonely than ever at that time.

Accordingly, he and Carrington drove down to Darleston Court hatching plans to keep Peter out of trouble. All went well, and when Carrington departed six weeks later, to join his mother and sister in Bath, Carstares bore Peter off to spend the holiday with Lord and Lady Fairford and their young family.

It seemed to George that when Peter returned to Darleston Court in late January he had lost much of his bitterness and was far closer to being his old self than would have seemed possible the previous spring.

In early April Darleston House in Grosvenor Square became a hive of activity as it was readied for the arrival of his lordship. Every room was turned out and cleaned as though it were not always kept in readiness for any unexpected visit my lord might choose to make.

Lord Darleston flung himself into the festivities of the season with no hint at all that he was an unwilling participant. The Marriage Mart was honoured with his frequent presence, and he danced assiduously with all the prettiest debutantes, but no one could detect the slightest sign that he was more attracted by one than another. To be honest, he appeared no closer to fixing his interest than last year!

It takes very little, however, to nudge a man into precipitate action. The hand of fate, once dealt, takes no account of rank or wealth but plays its cards with ruthless efficiency. Thus Darleston was sitting idly reading an estate report in his study one afternoon in late May when he was interrupted by his butler.

He looked up. 'Yes, Meadows? What is it?'

The butler coughed apologetically, 'I'm sure I'm sorry to disturb your lordship, but there is An Individual to see your lordship. Quite determined, he is. Says he'll wait in the hall as long as it takes to see you. I hope I know my duty, and I would have had him removed, but he seems terribly worried about something that concerns your lordship and wouldn't trust any of us to give a message! Wouldn't even give his name!'

Darleston looked startled. 'Good heavens! This sounds most melodramatic! Is he a Respectable Individual, Meadows?'

'I should say he was in one of the Trades, my lord. He was, I *will* say, very respectful,' replied Meadows.

'Very well, Meadows. Send this mysterious person in,' instructed Darleston.

He sat back to await his visitor, agog with curiosity.

He had not long to wait before a respectably dressed man of about forty stood before him. 'Good afternoon, Mr...er?'

The man said slowly, 'If your lordship will not be offended I'd be better pleased to leave names out of it for now. I will only say that I am employed by the *Gazette* as an editor. A couple of hours ago one of my boys brought this to me.' He held up a note with a broken seal.

'Go on, then,' said Darleston encouragingly. 'I assure you I am listening.'

'Well, my lord, the lad is very sharp, and he said the lady who delivered it seemed very upset and kept on asking odd questions about how we verified the accuracy of notices and suchlike. Almost as if she wanted to warn the boy! He took the money and gave her a receipt, but then he got worried and brought it in and told me the whole story. So when I read the notice I thought I'd just come along and check with you. Read it for yourself my lord.' He held out the note across the desk.

Darleston opened it and was at once aware of a very familiar scent which clung to it. He read the note and his brows contracted sharply. His visitor blenched as he looked up and asked in freezing accents, 'Did the lad describe the lady?'

'He did, my lord. He said she was quite old, maybe fifty or even sixty. Dressed very plain. Gave him a shilling, which he didn't want to take on account of he didn't think she looked as if she'd have too many shillings, despite being a lady, which he reckoned she was.'

Darleston was silent for a moment, then he said, 'I am much obliged to you and the lad. This notice has not my authority, and I will be further obliged if you will keep it to yourselves that it ever crossed your desk.'

'Begging your pardon, my lord, but there's no question of the lad or myself saying a word to anyone about this!' said the man.

'Good! I am more grateful than ever, and while I realise that you are a man of integrity and did not come with the idea of a reward, I beg that you will accept something. If not for yourself then for the lad.' So saying, Darleston reached into a drawer in his desk and drew out a roll of soft. He peeled off several notes and held them out. 'As I said, you are a fellow of honour. You will divide this fairly between yourself and the lad.'

His visitor flushed as he accepted the money and said, 'I'll take it for the boy, my lord. Not for myself, thanking you kindly. Well, I'll be going, then. I take it you'll know how best to deal with the matter. I…I wish you luck! No, don't ring that bell. Your butler makes me nervous!'

He departed quickly, leaving the angriest man in London behind him.

Darleston strode over to the fire which was burning in the grate and cast the note into its flames. He watched it burn for a moment and then went back to his desk. 'Thank God for Lucy Jameson!' he said to himself.

He penned a brief note and then rang the bell. When Meadows came in response he handed him the note and spoke abruptly. 'Be so good as to have that delivered to Lady Caroline Daventry immediately. That will be all.'

Meadows took the note and left the room without a word.

Darleston left his mansion in Grosvenor Square shortly after ten o'clock that evening, clad in the satin knee-breeches and swallow-tailed coat which proclaimed his destination was a ball.

A footman, springing to open the door of the waiting town carriage, and being rewarded with a curt nod, wondered what had happened to put the master in such a temper. Generally he was pleasant enough, if rather aloof. This evening, however, the expression on his face was positively forbidding. Roger shut the door carefully. Whatever had put that look on the master's face, he preferred not to be involved.

'Brook Street. We are picking up Mr Carstares at his lodgings,' was the terse order. The carriage rolled away, clattering over the cobbles. Its occupant leaned back against the squabs, prey to bitter thoughts, all of which were directed at the fairer sex. To Lord Darleston, at that moment, the goddess Aphrodite held no charms whatsoever.

He shuddered at the thought of the ball he had promised to attend. Hordes of gauche young girls, all in hopes of catching a husband, all with ambitious mamas eager to make sure they danced with the most eligible bachelors or, as in his case, widowers. Blast them all, he thought furiously. He would stay in the card room drinking brandy!

The carriage drew to a halt in Brook Street unnoticed by him. Then George's cheerful voice said, 'Anyone home? Wake up, Peter, you're away with the clouds!'

He looked up in surprise into the open countenance. 'Oh. Here, am I? Sorry, George. I was thinking.'

'Bad habit that,' said George, getting into the carriage. 'People might notice and then where would you be?' Observing the frown as he looked closely at his friend, George asked, 'What's happened, Peter? Your face is enough to turn the milk!'

Peter was silent for a moment before replying savagely, 'Caroline!'

Momentarily puzzled, George enquired, 'Is she ill?'

'Not in the least! She sent a notice of our engagement to the *Gazette*!' was the sufficiently startling reply.

Speechless with amazed horror, George could only stare at his friend with a dropped jaw. His brain whirled as he contemplated the uproar which would greet the Seventh Earl of Darleston's betrothal to his mistress.

Finally he managed to say, 'Er...do I congratulate you?'

'You do! Fortunately the editor had the good sense to check with me before printing! I was able to stop it being published, thank God.'

'Anyone else know about this?' asked George.

'I hope not! Except for old Miss Jameson, who delivered the notice. From what the editor said she deliberately went out of her way to put them on their guard.'

After some thought, George said, 'Seems to me that if Lady Caroline has told people the notice is going to appear, and it doesn't, she'll look like a fool.'

'Good!'

'Won't like that, Peter.'

'She's not supposed to like it! I sent a discreet note to her house informing her that after a most interesting conversation with an editor of the *Gazette* I would be returning to Darleston Court tomorrow and did not expect to see her again!'

'Oh!' George digested the news that Peter had broken irrevocably with his mistress, then said cautiously, 'Probably a good thing.'

'I'm damned sure it is! Tonight I'm celebrating. Cards, dice and brandy are the order of the evening. Curse all women! The problem is that I have to marry! Caroline knows that, but if she thinks I want a child of hers to succeed me any more than my revolting cousin Jack…!'

George was fully in agreement with this sentiment. So Carrington had been right after all! No doubt she had subtly manoeuvred Peter into spending all those months in France. His retreat to Darleston Court and the Fairfords' for the entire winter, though, must have made her desperate. No doubt she had decided to risk all on this last throw when Darleston had returned to town and begun attending the sort of parties where one met eligible young ladies.

The problem, to George's way of thinking, was Peter's ridiculously low opinion of women generally. Much of this could, of course, be attributed to Melissa's behaviour. Lovely, faithless Melissa, who had run off with another man just as her husband returned, wounded, from Waterloo. Her defection had been no surprise to anyone, least of all Darleston, who had rejoined Wellington's forces as a volunteer in full knowledge of his wife's character. It struck George that Peter had an absolute genius for choosing the wrong woman. First Melissa and now

Caroline. Expecting women to be like that, he could pick them unerringly!

Hoping to change the subject, he said casually, 'Had a letter from my sister this morning. In the family way again. Hoping for a girl this time. Says three boys in row is quite enough. She and Fairford want me to visit. Probably wouldn't mind if you came along again. Do you good to get out of London for a while.' He knew that Peter liked and respected Lady Fairford very much. In fact, on reflection, there were plenty of women whom Peter liked and respected but all of them were happily married!

Peter hesitated before answering, 'Thanks, George, I'll hold you to that later. But first I think I'll go to Darleston alone. I need to do some thinking. A terrible habit, as you say, but necessary. I must marry, but I don't want to find myself saddled with a second Melissa!'

'Certainly not,' said George. Then, 'Don't any of the debutantes interest you? You certainly interest them!'

Peter laughed cynically. 'Not really. They all admire my wealth and my title and most of 'em are absolutely tongue-tied when I dance with them. That or disgustingly arch!'

George thought about that for a moment. 'Well, if you take my advice you'll marry the first eligible girl you meet with whom you can hold a rational conversation!'

Peter chuckled. 'I did meet one, now I come to think of it. Last year it was. Young Ffolliot's sister. Can't think of the girl's name now. Something beginning with a P anyway. But I haven't seen her this year.'

'Believe their father died suddenly last year. Driving accident. Carrington and I saw it in the paper,' said George thoughtfully. 'They'd still be in mourning.'

'But young Ffolliot has been on the town just as

usual!' said Peter, very much surprised. 'He's not in mourning, surely!'

'Ffolliot wouldn't!' said George in disgust. 'Young waster! Carrington said something about it at the time. He'll be running through his fortune before long if he doesn't settle down.'

Their arrival at Lady Bellingham's ball put an end to the conversation as they stepped out of the carriage to join the crush of people flocking up the steps.

Lord Darleston's behaviour that evening was described by some as disgraceful and by others as exemplary. The first camp was almost entirely composed of young ladies and their ambitious mamas, all of whom were disappointed that such an eligible *parti* should elect to spend the entire evening in the card room, dicing while consuming untold quantities of brandy. The gentlemen in the card room, however, were of the opinion that under the circumstances Darleston's forbearance was remarkable. Admittedly he was badly foxed, not vulgarly drunk, as young Ffolliot was, for example, but on the whole he carried his drink very well.

The evening was a successful one for Darleston. He had begun with piquet, playing with George Carstares for chicken stakes. His lordship made it a rule never to play for high stakes with relatives, and had extended this taboo to include his best friend. After a couple of rubbers, in which the run of cards was fairly evenly divided, Darleston suggested they should give up trying to fleece each other.

'Had enough, George? Maybe we should try our luck with the rest of the world?'

'Not on my account, Peter. I can afford losing to you!'

answered George cheerfully, hoping he would be able to check his friend.

'My dear George, may I recommend that you go to the devil?' asked Peter in amusement. 'Do you imagine I am so drunk I can't see through your appallingly clumsy efforts to keep me out of mischief. Believe me, I have no intention of adding to my problems by dissipating my fortune! Only myself!' He had been drinking steadily, but his speech was in no way impaired. Only the odd glitter in his eye betrayed the state of his temper. To any not intimately acquainted with him he appeared amiability itself.

George, having tried to hold him in as tactfully as possible, bowed to the inevitable and grinned at his friend's recommendation, merely saying, 'You'll have the devil of a head in the morning! I'm going back to the ballroom. You never know. I might meet the girl of my dreams on the dance floor!'

'More likely meet a sticky end!' said his lordship sardonically, raising his glass in salute.

He watched George depart and then turned back to the room in search of amusement. Someone tapped his shoulder. 'Hello, Manders,' he said, recognising a comrade from Peninsular days. 'Rubber of piquet?'

His friend demurred without hesitation. 'Not with you, Darleston! Even when you're foxed, you play out of my league. Wouldn't even be entertaining for you! But I don't mind taking you on at dice.'

'Whatever you please, old boy, but first I think I'll find some more brandy!' said his lordship agreeably. He caught at a passing footman. 'Do you think you could find me a bottle of brandy? You could? Splendid!'

He turned back to his companion. 'There we are! What more could we ask for?'

Manders grinned. 'Well, a couple more people to liven up our game, do you think? Here's your cousin Frobisher with a friend. Shall we ask them?'

In point of fact the last person in the world that Darleston would have chosen to dice with was his cousin Jack Frobisher, but he responded politely.

'Dear boy, whatever you wish.' He beckoned to Frobisher, saying, 'Good evening, Cousin. Manders and I are going to have a little game of dice. Do you and your friend care to join us?' He looked closely at the young man accompanying Frobisher. The youth was vaguely familiar, lank sandy hair, a chin which the charitable might have described as weak but was in reality non-existent. Darleston searched his memory. Young Ffolliot, that was it.

Unable to detect any hint that the young man was in mourning, he asked curiously, 'Heard you'd lost your father a while back, Ffolliot, but I suppose it's only a rumour?'

'Oh, Lord, no. It's true enough. Couldn't see much point in going into all that business of mourning when the whole world knows we didn't get on!' was the unconcerned answer.

Darleston was taken aback. Such casual disregard for a parent's death was nothing less than shocking. He cast his mind back. He had been only slightly acquainted with John Ffolliot, but his memory was of a kindly man with a well-developed sense of humour. Hardly the man to engender dislike in his offspring! In fact he recalled that the last time he'd seen the elder Mr Ffolliot he had been driving his daughter in Hyde Park.

That was right! It all came back now! He'd danced with the chit at Almack's and then spoken to her in the park. Met her at a concert too. Red hair, well, auburn anyway, and dreamy grey eyes. That was the girl! It occurred to him that there had appeared to be no lack of affection between father and daughter.

In a tone that was little less than a rebuke he said, 'Then perhaps you would be so good as to convey my condolences to your sister, Mr Ffolliot? I am sure from what I have seen of her that she held her father in considerable affection *and* respect. Now, shall we play dice? I have my own set here.'

Ffolliot turned red with anger, but a nudge from Frobisher recalled him to his senses, so he sat down at the table with the other three. Darleston raised his eyebrows slightly, but held his tongue. He produced his dice and the game began.

At first the luck all went Frobisher's way. A pile of guineas grew steadily in front of him, to the annoyance of his friend Ffolliot, who grumbled continuously. Eventually, tired of the incessant whining, Darleston said lazily, 'Mr Ffolliot would appear to resent your luck, Cousin. Surely not the part of a good friend!'

'Perhaps not,' was the unconcerned reply. 'However, the game does begin to lose savour. Might I be excused, gentlemen?' Frobisher rose to his feet, bowed gracefully and departed with his winnings.

As the game continued between the three remaining players Lady Luck chose to turn her face to Mr Ffolliot. Emboldened by this, and the amount of champagne he had consumed, he recklessly raised the stakes.

'Double each throw, gentlemen?' he challenged.

Darleston nodded imperturbably, but Manders said bluntly, 'Too high, Ffolliot. Don't be a fool! Luck won't stay with you all night. Especially if you can't afford it! I'm out!' He rose to his feet. 'Excuse me, Darleston, I'll see you later.'

Darleston smiled up at him, saying amiably, 'Thanks for the game, Manders. You must dine with me soon. I feel sure our tastes have much in common!'

He tossed back his glass of brandy, refilled it, and said to Mr Ffolliot, 'Fifty a throw, wasn't it?' The game proceeded, but Lady Luck, possibly affronted by Mr Ffolliot's behaviour, began to favour Darleston. That pile of guineas slowly made its way across the table. Finally they were all in front of Darleston.

'Do you wish to continue, Mr Ffolliot?' he asked politely.

'Yes! Damn you! Double the stakes!' slurred Ffolliot. The luck had to change! He glared at his opponent defiantly.

Darleston looked at him carefully. It was not in his nature to refuse a challenge, but it went against the grain to win money from a drunken youth who most certainly could not afford it. Wryly he admitted to himself that he had certainly provoked Ffolliot earlier. His code of honour dictated that it was time to call a halt.

The words were on the tip of his tongue when Ffolliot said loudly, 'I don't like your dice, Darleston!' A dead silence came over the room. People turned to stare in disbelief. To accuse Darleston of cheating was unthinkable! His courage, honour and pride were a matter of public record. George Carstares, who had just come back into the room with Lord Carrington, stopped dead in his tracks, fully expecting Darleston to call Ffolliot out.

Darleston, however, managed to hold his temper in check. His eyes blazed, but he leaned back in his chair and asked softly, 'Do you not, indeed, Mr Ffolliot? And what would you like to do about it? We can of course break the dice. But then of course you will owe me a new set.' Almost as an afterthought he added, 'And…

er…satisfaction as well. Your choice, Mr Ffolliot! Or perhaps you have a set of dice we can use, and break at the end of the game, of course!'

Ffolliot's eyes fell. 'I…don't have a set with me…I…I must have been mistaken!' he stammered.

'Then shall we continue?' asked Darleston sweetly. The other occupants of the room lost interest, but George Carstares, watching closely with Lord Carrington, breathed a huge sigh of relief. He had no fears for Darleston's safety in a duel with Ffolliot, however, the law was strict about these little affairs.

'Damn it, George,' muttered Carrington. 'Can't this be stopped somehow? Ffolliot can't afford to lose. He's a blasted little squirt, I agree, but his sisters and stepmother have enough problems without Peter ruining him and calling him out!'

George shook his head. 'He'd tell us to go to the devil! Already done that once this evening! At least he accepted the boy's apology. No one can do anything with Peter in this mood!'

The game continued and Ffolliot's losses mounted steadily. His face became sickly as his vowels grew in number. From time to time he made a little headway, but this was always short-lived. Darleston threw a ten, those mocking eyes daring his opponent to call a halt to the game. Ffolliot's hand trembled so that his throw was clumsy and the dice fell to the floor. He bent to retrieve them, fumbling a little. Slightly flushed, he straightened up. 'I beg your pardon, Lord Darleston!'

Darleston nodded for him to throw again. He threw a twelve and shot a triumphant glare at the Earl.

Carstares and Carrington exchanged startled glances. 'Did you see what…?' began George.

'Let's wait and be sure,' murmured Carrington, placing

a restraining hand on his companion's arm. They continued to watch the game carefully.

Now the game began to run in Ffolliot's direction. Lady Luck, it would seem, had relented towards Mr Ffolliot. Carstares and Lord Carrington drifted over to the table. Laying his hand on Ffolliot's arm, the latter said coldly, 'Mr Ffolliot, did I not hear you inform Lord Darleston that you had no dice with you when he offered to let you change the dice?'

'That's right,' said Ffolliot, shrugging off the hand. 'What of it Carrington? I'm happy enough with the dice now! All a misunderstanding, eh, Darleston?'

Darleston looked in annoyance at George and Carrington, but what he saw in their faces made him hold his tongue. Again the whole room was focused on that small table.

Carrington was speaking again, 'I have little doubt that you are only too happy with these dice, since they came out of your pocket! Strange how the luck turned so quickly after you retrieved the dice from the floor, wouldn't you say? Carstares and I saw you make the exchange! Shall we break them for you?'

Ffolliot grabbed the dice. He was shaking, but tried to bluster. 'How…how dare you? I…I don't care for your tone, Carrington. Darleston has made no complaint!'

An expectant silence had pervaded the whole room. The assembled company looked with scorn at Ffolliot and with great interest at Darleston for his reaction.

His blazing eyes seemed to burn holes in Ffolliot's face, but his voice was as urbane as ever. 'I think this concludes our little game, Mr Ffolliot. You will hear from me in the next day or so to arrange the terms of payment for your debt.'

The host, Lord Bellingham, came forward to say icily,

'I am afraid I must ask you to leave, Mr Ffolliot, unless you are prepared to have those dice broken!' He waited a moment, but Ffolliot did not respond. Still clutching his dice, he stood up unsteadily and walked to the door. Men turned aside from him, disgusted. Bellingham gestured to a footman. 'See that he leaves!'

Darleston rose to his feet, saying calmly, 'How very unpleasant. Ah, Bellingham! I do beg your pardon for this little contretemps! I shall also take my leave. Please accept my apologies.'

'Nonsense, Darleston, no need for you to leave!' said Bellingham. 'I'm sure Carstares or Carrington will join us for a game of cards! Why leave just because of that infernal little mountebank?'

Darleston resumed his seat, saying obligingly, 'Of course, Bellingham.'

When Darleston reached Grosvenor Square again it was four in the morning. He let himself into the house and found a candle burning on a small table. He picked it up and went upstairs to his bed-chamber where he proceeded to undress himself. Despite the acid comments of Fordham on the subject, Darleston insisted that he was perfectly capable of putting himself to bed at night.

The evening's events had done little to alleviate his temper, and the comment dropped by Carrington on the way home, that he very much doubted Ffolliot's ability to meet the debt he had contracted, had infuriated him. If it hadn't been for the loaded dice Darleston would have quietly cancelled the debt. Unfortunately the public exposure of Ffolliot's dishonesty made that impossible.

Ffolliot's suggestion that he himself had been using loaded dice also continued to rankle. Well, if Ffolliot couldn't pay the debt in one way, he should pay it in another! At this point the problem of Lady Caroline drifted back into his brandy-fogged mind. 'Blast Caroline!' he said aloud. 'The only way to be safe from her is to marry someone else. But who?'

He pulled the nightshirt laid out for him over his head. What had George said? Marry the first eligible girl who can hold a rational conversation! Well, that was Ffolliot's sister! Damn! what was her name? Might have been Phoebe, but he couldn't really remember. It occurred to him that she would be made devilishly uncomfortable over the night's doings. That bothered him, he had been oddly attracted to her. Usually young girls bored him, but she had a spark of humour that appealed to him. Not on the occasion he'd danced with her at Almack's, to be sure, but in the park and at the concert she'd seemed a different creature entirely. And she had that unusual dog.

He was about to get into bed when the idea struck him. To his somewhat tipsy logic it seemed perfectly reasonable, although an irritatingly sober voice warned him not to do anything rash. Impatiently he thrust the warning voice aside to consider his idea. Then he pulled on a dressing gown, sat down at the writing desk in the corner and penned a brief letter. He read it through owlishly, nodded, and sealed it. That would take the trick! he thought triumphantly. Must get it off immediately!

A little unsteady on his feet now, he went back downstairs to leave the letter on the hall table for the post.

A glow of satisfaction pervaded his being as he returned to bed, convinced he had solved all his problems in the most sensible way imaginable. The idea seemed so neat and logical that he could not for the life of him think of a single objection to it: a circumstance which must be ascribed in great part to the quantity of brandy he had consumed.

Never, even when sober, prone to worry about a decision once it was made, Lord Darleston drifted off to sleep. His only concern was the devilish head with which he was bound to be afflicted when he awoke.

Chapter Four

Clad in sober grey muslin, Miss Ffolliot and Miss
Phoebe Ffolliot stepped off the terrace and moved
through the shrubbery towards the rose garden accompanied by a large Irish wolfhound. A basket hanging from
Miss Ffolliot's arm suggested that the pair were engaged
upon an expedition to gather flowers. The scent of roses
hung heavily in the early-morning air and the cloudless
sky gave promise of a lovely day.

Miss Phoebe took a deep breath, remarking, 'This is
the best part of the day. No one else about, just us and
the sun.'

Miss Ffolliot looked amused as she answered, 'Surely
Mr Winton would improve the morning? You'd scarcely
notice if the sun disappeared, let alone Gelert and I!'

Phoebe blushed, but said with spirit, 'You know perfectly well what I mean, Penny. Gathering the flowers for
Mama with you gives us a chance to be private, and talk.'

'About Mr Winton?' asked Penelope, with a faint
smile.

'Oh, Penny, he's so wonderful!' said Phoebe, giving
up all attempt at dignity. 'I wonder why he is coming to

see Mama…do you think he might possibly make an offer?'

'Not being in Richard's confidence, I can't say,' answered Penelope. 'But it does seem likely. Even Mama seems to think so, and certainly the fact that he went to town for the season last year, danced with you everywhere, took you driving, sent you flowers and came home when we did because of…of…Papa, and has danced attendance on you ever since, suggests that he takes an interest in you!' She gave her twin an affectionate hug.

This reference to the death of Mr Ffolliot put an end to conversation for several moments, and the twins gathered roses in silence. Phoebe selected the best blooms, cutting them carefully to place in her sister's basket. Penelope broke the silence, saying, 'I'm sure he would have spoken sooner but thought it would be in bad taste. As it is you will have to wait until we are out of mourning to be married. But that's only a month now.'

'Geoffrey doesn't let that stop him from enjoying life!' said Phoebe in disgust.

'Just because Geoffrey chooses to behave badly and gamble in every hell in town is all the more reason to act with some propriety,' said Penelope. 'Mama is very worried. She has no control over Geoffrey, even Papa didn't have much, and now he is without any restraint.'

'I wish he would come home,' said Phoebe. 'I mean, I don't, because he is always perfectly horrid, but we should at least know what he was up to.'

Penelope didn't answer immediately, but presently, after several more roses had been placed in the basket, she said reluctantly, 'Geoffrey is home. He arrived about four o'clock this morning.'

Phoebe stared at her sister. 'Are you sure? Does Mama know?'

'I'm quite sure,' said Penelope dryly. 'He made such a devilish noise coming up to bed that I woke up and heard the hall clock chime. He was not entirely sober and his language was most edifying. I'm surprised that you didn't wake up. As for Mama, Tinson knows that Geoffrey is home, and by now I am sure he will have informed Mama of the delightful treat in store for her.'

'Oh, dear,' said Phoebe. 'Poor Mama! Is it very dreadful, do you think, that we should be so uncaring about our half-brother?'

'No,' replied Penelope decisively. 'Geoffrey is an odious little beast, and considering the way he treats our mother it would be wonderful if we *did* like him!'

Phoebe was obliged to acknowledge the justice of this comment. Not only was Geoffrey appallingly rude to his stepmother, but he made it abundantly clear that he resented the existence of his three half-sisters, particularly Penelope, who frequently told him exactly what she thought of him with scant regard for her mother's remonstrances or Geoffrey's blustering threats. Phoebe glanced sadly at Penelope. It was hard to believe that the girl who moved so confidently beside her, one hand resting lightly on the dog's collar, was practically blind.

A serious accident four years earlier had left Penelope unable to do more than distinguish light and dark very faintly and perceive movement. Though perfectly confident in familiar surroundings, she had refused utterly to enter into last Season's festivities, declaring that she preferred to hear about them from Phoebe rather than have the strain of dealing with strangers and strange places. She had accompanied her parents and Phoebe to London but had remained mostly at home, so that few people even realised that Phoebe had a twin. From time to time she had attended concerts with a maid, but always veiled to avoid recognition.

By the time the roses were gathered it was nearly breakfast-time, so the young ladies turned their steps towards the house. They were met at the side-door by Tinson, the elderly butler. 'Shall I take the basket, Miss Penny?' he asked.

'Yes, please, Tinson, we'll arrange them after breakfast. Is Mama down?' asked Penelope.

'Mrs Ffolliot is in the breakfast parlour with Miss Sarah. She was wondering where you were, but I informed her that I thought you were in the rose garden and would be in shortly.'

'Thank you, Tinson. We will join them at once. I assume Mr Geoffrey is still abed?' said Penelope.

The butler's voice was impassive as he answered, 'Mr Geoffrey has not stirred since he went to bed and he did not express a desire to be wakened for breakfast.'

'Good!' said the twins in unison. They burst out laughing at their impropriety and Phoebe pulled Penelope's hand through her arm as they moved towards the breakfast parlour.

Mrs Ffolliot looked up, smiling, as her elder daughters entered the room. She deeply regretted that Penelope had refused point-blank to make her debut or even meet many people. Phoebe had been very successful, and Mrs Ffolliot knew that Penelope's lively personality would have been more than sufficient to overcome any disadvantage caused by her blindness. There was nothing to choose between the girls in terms of looks. Indeed, until Penelope's accident she herself had often not been able to tell them apart. They had the same curling dark red hair and grey eyes, were of identical height and figure and possessed the same charming countenance. But now, despite her usual gaiety, there was occasionally a withdrawn, shut-in look to Penelope's face, and if that had not been enough to distinguish the pair she was accompanied everywhere by the huge hound, Gelert, who acted as a self-appointed guide for his young mistress.

'Good morning, Mama; good morning, Sarah,' said the twins.

'Good morning, dears. Were there plenty of roses? We must have a good display in the drawing room for our guest, don't you think, Phoebe?' asked Mrs Ffolliot with a faint smile.

Phoebe blushed and Penelope chuckled. 'That's too bad of you, Mama. I've already made her blush and now you're doing it.'

Phoebe laughed at her twin as she sat down. 'Penny, how do you always know?'

'I told you, I can feel it. The room temperature just rose several degrees!' answered Penelope as Gelert guided her to an empty chair beside thirteen-year-old Sarah. 'Is there anything left, or did Sarah eat the lot?'

Sarah giggled at this reference to her notorious appetite and said, 'There's plenty. Shall I butter a scone for you?'

'Yes, please, love. I'm nearly as hungry as you!'

'Two scones for now, then, Sarah,' teased Phoebe. 'And I'll ring for Tinson to fetch another dozen!'

Breakfast passed merrily, without mention of Geoffrey or any other unpleasantness. The twins were perfectly aware that Mrs Ffolliot did not wish to discuss the situation in front of Sarah. They lingered over the teacups until it was time for Sarah to depart to the drawing room to practise the pianoforte.

When she had left Mrs Ffolliot sighed and said, 'Your brother is home again, Tinson informs me. I believe he arrived late last night, or rather early this morning. There is bound to be some unpleasantness, but he may not stay long and at least he does not have anyone with him this time.'

On his previous visit Geoffrey's friend Mr Frobisher had accompanied him. Mrs Ffolliot had considered that the young man's conversation was most unsuitable for the chaste ears of her daughters. She was also aware that he led her stepson into every low gambling hell in London.

Penelope had never revealed to anyone that he had attempted to take unwelcome liberties with her person, and had received a slap in the face in addition to being well bitten by Gelert. The incident was one she preferred to forget.

'It is a pity that he should come just now, but I dare say he will sleep until past noon, and anyway, Richard Winton is so well-acquainted with us that he will not be overly concerned. Phoebe, dear, a note came over this morning to tell me why he is visiting us today. He has made an offer for you, and begs my permission to pay his addresses to you. He is most generous and offers to house Sarah, Penny and myself if, as he puts it, our present situation should become untenable. You have only to consider your answer, my dearest.'

Phoebe stared at her as if unable to believe what she heard. Her grey eyes filled with tears and she hugged her mother in joy.

Penelope contemplated her sister's future with real delight. Richard Winton was a close friend of the family, well-born and possessed of an easy fortune coupled with a good estate ten miles distant. He was passably good-looking, kindly, and he had been, in Penelope's opinion at least, in love with Phoebe for the last two years. He was one of the few people who had never had the

slightest difficulty in telling the twins apart. For this reason alone Penelope had been disposed to favour his suit.
As she had said once in a moment of candour to her
mother, 'The idea of marrying a man who thinks you are
your sister is not to be borne!' Absently she stroked
Gelert's rough head, then rose to hug her sister. 'Oh,
Phoebe, you'll be so happy together, and it's quite close
so we shall see lots of both of you!'

'They might like to be alone!' laughed Mrs Ffolliot.

Phoebe protested indignantly, 'Of course we'll want
you, Mama. Why, his letter says so!'

'Nevertheless, my love, I think we will give you time
to become used to being Mrs Winton before we descend
upon you for good. Now go and dry your face. You must
arrange the flowers before he arrives,' answered Mrs
Ffolliot.

Phoebe departed singing, but Penelope remained behind. 'Mama, do you have any idea why Geoffrey is
home?' she asked.

'No, my dear. Why do you ask? I take it that you heard
the noise? Tinson merely informed me that he was home.
I gathered, from what Tinson *didn't* say, that Geoffrey
was not at all sober when he arrived, but that is not unusual,' answered her mother.

Penelope was silent for a moment, and then said, 'I
did wake up. Phoebe and Sarah didn't, so I...I...I went
out into the corridor when I heard his door shut. Mama,
something is really wrong. He was raving about Lord
Darleston and...and some debt. He said, ''He'll take the
lot, damn his eyes!'' Mama, do you suppose he has lost
a terrible amount of money?'

Mrs Ffolliot went white, but managed to say calmly,
'We must suppose he has lost some money. Perhaps a
great deal. You have not said anything to Phoebe?'

Penelope shook her head. 'Good. Let us not spoil this day for her. Richard will be here in an hour or two, so we must put this out of our minds for now.'

'Yes, Mama, but what do you know of Lord Darleston? I met him once with Papa when we were driving, you know. He seemed…well, not the man to be found in the sort of hells we know Geoffrey frequents. Not at all like his odious cousin,' said Penelope, repressing a shudder with difficulty.

'When did you meet Lord Darleston?' asked her mother. 'Your father never mentioned it,'

'Oh, Lord Darleston thought I was Phoebe, and Papa didn't correct him because I kicked him under the driving rug. I think he had stood up with Phoebe at Almack's. Yes that's right, because I asked Phoebe about him and she said he was the most handsome man she had ever seen. That was before she fell in love with Richard, of course.' This observation was delivered with an absolutely straight face.

'Penny!' exclaimed Mrs Ffolliot, trying unsuccessfully not to laugh.

'Anyway, I thought his lordship was charming, and he admired Gelert! I suppose Papa didn't tell you because he knew you'd be cross with us for deceiving an Earl, so I warned Phoebe and that was that! Except that I met him again at a concert,' finished Penelope.

Despite herself, Mrs Ffolliot smiled. Genuine admiration of Gelert was a sure road to Penelope's liking. 'His lordship is very charming, and I would have been extremely cross with the pair of you for imposing on him like that!' said Mrs Ffolliot. 'I know very little of him except what the world knows, which is that he is a hero of Waterloo, that his first wife ran off with another man and that he has avoided marriageable women ever since.

I remember his standing up with Phoebe; it was most unlike him. Someone told me later that he is considering remarriage because of the succession. And considering that his heir is that odious Jack Frobisher, one cannot wonder at his decision!'

Penelope laughed. 'Why, Mama, you are a positive fund of information. I must go and confer with Sarah on a suitable gift for the bride. Come along, Gelert.'

The pair left the room together, leaving Mrs Ffolliot alone to worry about the shortcomings and possible—or probable, as she admitted to herself—gambling debts of her stepson. She thought on reflection that it was entirely likely that Geoffrey had lost a great deal of money, and she wondered how, if that were the case, it was to be paid.

They were not wealthy. Phoebe's season had been paid for with money left by the twins' godmother specifically for that purpose. Penelope had insisted that her share be put aside for Sarah. Mrs Ffolliot and her husband had acquiesced because, despite her raillery and outward laughter, it was evident that the thought of braving a critical world she could not see frightened Penelope.

Mrs Ffolliot sighed, wondering if they had been right in allowing Penelope to shut herself away. It would appear from what the child had said that she had met and liked at least one total stranger. This was encouraging, even if the pleasure had in part stemmed from a deplorable sense of mischief on the part of her daughter and, she had to admit, on the part of her husband. John Ffolliot would have enjoyed the joke as much as his eldest daughter. He would have been most unlikely to tell his wife of the meeting. Not from any fear of censure, but to spare her embarrassment when next she met Lord Darleston.

Casting her eye around the cosy breakfast parlour, Mrs

Ffolliot wondered how much Geoffrey had lost this time. Last month it had been ten thousand pounds. She knew the estate would not be able to weather many such blows. Already their circumstances were uncomfortably straitened, and she thanked God that at least Phoebe was now provided for. Sarah was bidding fair to rival her elder sisters' beauty, and Phoebe could be counted upon to find a husband for her when the time came. It was only Penelope whose future exercised her mind. Perhaps if she stayed with Phoebe and Richard for a while, to meet people, it would rid her of this absurd notion that she was unfit to marry. After all, the blindness was the result of an accident, not something that she could pass on to a child!

A discreet knock at the door disturbed her thoughts. 'Come in,' she called.

Tinson entered. 'Excuse me, madam, but Mr Winton has called to see you. He is in the morning room.'

'To see *me*, Tinson, are you sure?' she responded.

'Mr Winton thought he should see you *before* he sees Miss Phoebe,' said Tinson, with the ghost of a twinkle in his eye.

Mary Ffolliot burst out laughing. 'Oh, Tinson, where should we be without you? I shall come at once. Please tell Miss Phoebe that if she waits in the rose garden I shall send Mr Winton to her there. And you might tell Miss Penny to keep Miss Sarah occupied!'

'Certainly, madam, but as to Miss Sarah, she is still in the drawing room, helping Miss Penny to learn a new piece of music,' answered Tinson.

Richard Winton rose to his feet as Mrs Ffolliot entered the morning room and held out her hand to him. He bowed over it. 'Dear Richard, I received your letter. Need I tell you how happy this makes me?'

'Mrs Ffolliot, I can only say that I hope I shall be worthy of your good opinion and that Phoebe's father would have approved,' he answered. 'Perhaps even more importantly, does Penelope approve?'

'Of course she does!' answered Mrs Ffolliot. 'Apart from Tinson and their father, you are the only man who never had the slightest trouble telling them apart.'

Richard roared with delighted laughter. 'God help the man who takes her to wife. He'll never know a minute's peace!'

Noting the sudden sadness in his hostess's face, he said, 'I beg your pardon, that was clumsy. Does Penelope still favour the life of a recluse? Phoebe told me about it once. Perhaps once she and I are married Penelope can come to stay and meet new people. That might help her to gain confidence in herself.'

Despite the fact that her mind had been running along these lines, Mrs Ffolliot was taken aback. 'Richard, you are probably one of the kindest men alive. If anyone can help Penny it will be you and Phoebe. I am not quite close enough to Penny, dearly though I love her. The bond between those two is very strong and I think that Phoebe's marriage to you will give her the insight to help Penny. Now, Phoebe is in the rose garden and must be wearing away the turf, so you had better go to her, and we shall expect both of you for a nuncheon!'

The rest of the day passed very happily. Richard stayed until the late afternoon, finally taking his leave most reluctantly to receive his sister who was coming to stay. He and Phoebe were to marry as soon as she was out of mourning for her father. 'I wish it could be sooner, sweetheart,' he whispered as he kissed her goodbye in the hall.

'But society is terribly fussy about these things, even though your father is probably very annoyed at our sense of propriety!'

Phoebe floated back to the drawing room, to be brought down to earth by the presence of her half-brother. Never a prepossessing sight, Geoffrey, suffering the after-effects of the previous night, looked particularly repellent, in addition to which he reeked of brandy. Unshaven, with lank sandy hair and bloodshot eyes, he did not compare well with the just departed Mr Winton who, in addition to being impeccably turned out, had the advantage of a good pair of shoulders as well as a chin. Penelope had once said disgustedly that her brother reminded her of a mangy weasel, scrawny and slippery.

It appeared that Penelope had been voicing her opinion of his person in no uncertain terms, to judge from what he was saying. 'A fellow can have a drink in his own house, I hope, without being nagged by his sister! Damn it all, I need a drink with you about and after all I've been through! Anyway, don't preach to me about your mother's drawing room, it won't be hers for very much longer. It'll all belong to Darleston, blast his eyes!'

A stunned silence followed this announcement. 'Sarah, please go upstairs at once,' requested Mrs Ffolliot.

'Don't be silly Mama, she'll have to know soon enough,' said Penelope. 'Would you care to explain yourself, Brother?'

'Mind your own business, girl!'

'It is my business! How much did you lose this time?' she asked fiercely. Gelert growled menacingly in response to her mood, but Penelope gripped his collar firmly.

'Keep him off!' shrieked Geoffrey in panic. 'I saw what he did to Frobisher's arm!'

'How much Geoffrey? Or shall I let him go?'

'Penny!' gasped her mother.

'Thirty thousand pounds, and he wants it immediately!' answered Geoffrey as he rushed from the room.

Mrs Ffolliot and her daughters were too horrified even to gasp. The silence was eventually broken by Sarah.

'It sounds like an awful lot of money for an evening's fun, doesn't it?'

There was not really much more to be said.

Penelope awoke early the next morning after a restless night. Phoebe had cried herself to sleep but Sarah was too young to be alive to the full consequences of the affair. Penelope knew that her father would have been mortified at Geoffrey contracting a debt he could not meet and she herself writhed with shame. Darleston of all people!

She thought back to those brief meetings. He had certainly mistaken her for Phoebe the first time, for he had thanked her for the dance and asked how she was enjoying the season. At their second meeting they had merely spoken of the Mozart symphony they had just heard. The hint of humour in his deep, husky voice had appealed to her at once. Phoebe's description of him as tall, dark and excessively handsome had not told her nearly as much as that attractive voice.

The fact that he had been the only person to recognise her behind the veil had also made a deep impression on her. A man who could spot a near stranger like that was obviously very perceptive and observant.

Resolutely Penelope thrust that train of thought from her mind, forcing herself to concentrate on the current situation. How was Darleston to be paid? The estate could not bear a debt like that. Everything would have to be sold to pay it! Even then she doubted that the whole sum could be raised. Her musings continued fruitlessly until Phoebe awoke, but for the life of her she could think of no honourable way out of the tangle.

The three girls went down to breakfast in a subdued frame of mind. Even Sarah had realised from her elder sisters' attitude that the situation was disastrous.

They found their mother looking pale and worn. 'Good morning, dears,' she said, trying unsuccessfully to be normal. Her voice sounded tired.

Penelope frowned and said, 'The devil take Geoffrey! Mama, did you sleep at all last night?'

'Hush, Penny, you mustn't speak like that,' remonstrated Mrs Ffolliot gently.

'Did you?' pressed Penelope, ignoring the rebuke.

'Not very much!' admitted her mother.

'Well, Geoffrey won't be at breakfast anyway!' said Sarah, seating herself. 'At least, it would be unusual if he did come down this early!'

'What are we to do, Mama?' asked Phoebe in fearful tones.

Her mother smiled slightly, and answered, 'You at least needn't worry too much! Richard is to look after you!'

Phoebe's indignation spurred her into unaccustomed vehemence. 'Mama, how could you possibly think I would not be concerned about the three of you? Besides, if you are to be thrown out to starve I shall refuse Richard's offer and go with you.'

A burst of laughter from her twin greeted this announcement. 'Oh, for heaven's sake, Phoebe! I don't often hanker after my eyesight, but what wouldn't I give to see Richard's face when you told him! You pea-goose!

He'd drag you to the altar before you could draw breath!
And what's more, we'd help him!'

Phoebe had the grace to look a little sheepish. 'Was I
being silly?'

'Very silly, love!' said her twin emphatically. 'What
good would it be for you to starve with us when we are
depending on you for the occasional charitable hand-
out?'

'I trust it won't be quite as bad as that!' intervened
Mrs Ffolliot. 'May I suggest that we leave this unpleasant
discussion for now and eat our breakfast?'

The girls dropped the subject immediately, not wishing
to upset their mother any further. Their chatter about the
weather, music and whether or not Sarah should be permitted to read *The Mysteries of Udolpho* might not have
been exactly cheerful, but at least it avoided the topic of
Geoffrey and his disgrace.

After breakfast Sarah was sent off to the drawing room
for her usual hour's practice and the twins and Mrs
Ffolliot repaired to the Morning Room. They went over
the situation carefully and decided that it would be possible for Mrs Ffolliot, Penelope and Sarah to manage in
a small house, or cottage even. Mrs Ffolliot's jointure
was not large but it would be enough.

These plans were thrown into complete disarray by the
arrival of Richard Winton in a towering fury. He announced himself and told them without any roundabou-
tation that he knew the whole story, his sister having just
come from London where it was the talk of the town.

'Elizabeth had heard something of the affair in town.
She mentioned it to me when she arrived last night,' he
said. 'Carrington and George Carstares caught Geoffrey
switching the dice on Darleston and denounced him publicly. Unfortunately it was at Lady Bellingham's ball.

Created the devil of a row, apparently. I'm afraid Geoffrey had already had to apologise for accusing Darleston of using loaded dice.'

'Dear God,' said Mrs Ffolliot faintly. 'I am afraid the debt will have to be met if Darleston insists.'

'I could see Darleston,' offered Richard. 'He might drop his claim if he knew that the position for you and the girls would be so disastrous. I don't know him well, but he is a decent enough fellow.'

'On no account! The debt will have to be paid, at least in part,' snapped Mrs Ffolliot. Phoebe and Penelope nodded in agreement.

'Besides,' said Penelope, 'if we get him out of it this time, how long do you think it would be before it happened again? And most likely to someone who wouldn't care in the slightest. In fact I wouldn't put it past Geoffrey to trade on it!'

'True,' agreed Richard reluctantly. 'But how many gentleman would play with him, do you think?'

'None, I should hope!' answered Penelope, 'What about money-lenders, though? The estate will not bear what Geoffrey wants to spend. It is only a matter of time before he goes down that path.'

Her auditors looked shocked but did not bother to contradict her. They knew that what she said was all too true.

A knock at the door heralded the arrival of Tinson. 'The post, madam. And Mr Geoffrey is up.' This last rather apologetically.

Silence greeted the announcement, to be broken by Penelope. 'Never mind, Tinson, we know you couldn't help it!'

Despite the seriousness of the situation Phoebe could not repress a giggle, and even Tinson's well-trained mouth twitched. His voice gave no hint of this, however. 'Certainly not, Miss Penny.' He left the room with a dignified gait.

'Really Penny—' began Mrs Ffolliot, only to be interrupted by Richard.

'Anyway, there's only one thing to be done, Mrs Ffolliot. You and the girls are coming to live with Phoebe and myself. I'm damned if I'll have my wife's sisters and mother thrown into penury!'

'Oh, yes!' agreed Phoebe enthusiastically. 'How good of you, Richard!' She looked up at him with melting gratitude and adoration.

'Richard, you can't possibly want all of us foisted onto you!' said Mrs Ffolliot. 'My jointure will be enough to support the three of us in a small establishment. We shall have to be careful, but no doubt we will manage.'

Richard's scathing reply was barely launched when the author of their misfortunes strolled in, saying airily, 'Everything's settled. Don't know what you were all in such a taking over!' Then he saw Richard Winton and looked scared.

Mr Winton eyed him forebodingly and asked in deceptively polite tones, 'And just what do you mean by that, Ffolliot?'

Geoffrey tried to bluster. 'None of your damned business, Winton. Private family matter, and I'll thank you to get out so we can discuss what has been decided!'

'Decided by whom, Geoffrey?' Penelope cut in.

'By me, miss! I'm head of the family!' was the reply.

'Then I'll certainly stay,' said Richard. 'Since I am to be a member of your family!'

Geoffrey shot him a scared and startled glance.

Mrs Ffolliot said quietly, 'We did not get a chance to tell you last night, Geoffrey, but Phoebe has accepted an offer of marriage from Richard. He has every right to be present.'

A crack of laughter from Geoffrey greeted this news, 'Marriage, eh? Well, they can forget that—unless Winton likes to put up thirty thousand pounds for her! She's going to marry Darleston! Got a letter from him. Cancels the whole debt in return for her hand in marriage! Told you it was all settled.' He brandished the letter in front of them.

The horrified silence was broken by Phoebe's incoherent wail of protest, and would have been further broken by Richard assaulting Geoffrey had not Phoebe cast herself into his arms, sobbing. As it was Richard had too much on his hands to do more than glare at Geoffrey and snap, 'Over my dead body, Ffolliot!'

'Geoffrey, you must see it is out of the question!' said Mrs Ffolliot. 'I will not give my consent to such a marriage!'

'Give me that letter!' Richard put Phoebe into Penelope's comforting arms and marched over to Geoffrey, who tried to protest.

'Nothing to do with you—!' He broke off and handed the letter over mutely, afraid of the expression on Richard's face.

Richard read aloud.

Dear Sir

I understand from mutual acquaintances that your estates will not bear the debt which you owe me. On the occasions when I chanced to meet your sister, Miss Ffolliot, I formed an agreeable impression of her person and character. I am prepared to forgo the entire debt in return for her hand in marriage.

If you are agreeable to this, please arrange the wedding for the fourteenth of July, by which time I understand she will be out of mourning, and let me know so that I may procure a special licence. Naturally I will let it be known that I have cancelled the debt due to my engagement to your sister.

I remain your obedient servant, etc. Darleston.

Richard crumpled the letter into a ball and hurled it from him. 'This is outrageous, but it changes nothing for you, Ffolliot!' he said evenly. 'Let me inform you that it becomes you neither as a man nor a brother to attempt to force your sister into marriage to clear your debts. And that would be my opinion whatever my own feelings towards her!'

'This is terrible,' said Mrs Ffolliot quietly. 'If this gets out we are ruined more than just financially.'

'Didn't he write ''Miss Ffolliot''?' enquired Penelope suddenly.

'What does that matter? Yes, he did!' answered Richard irritably.

'It matters a great deal. I am Phoebe's elder by twenty minutes, therefore *I* am Miss Ffolliot. Moreover, Lord Darleston has met me twice, whether he knows it or not!' said Penelope triumphantly. 'I'll marry him, and that will settle Geoffrey's debt for once and for all!'

'Penny, you can't!' gasped Phoebe in shock. 'I won't let you do this for me!'

'Fiddle,' said Penelope. 'I liked the man, when I met him. After all, what can he do? He said ''Miss Ffolliot''. If he'd said ''Miss Phoebe'' it would be different; we'd have to tell him. As it is he won't know until it's too late. Which will serve him right for being so arrogant about it! He'd take more care over buying a filly!'

Geoffrey, stunned at first, finally found his tongue.

'You! What the devil do you think Darleston or any man would want with a blind wench?'

That broke the remnants of Richard's self-control. He took two swift strides and floored Geoffrey with a savage blow, just as Sarah came in to discover what all the noise was about.

She took in the scene and said delightedly, 'Oh, well done, Richard! That was a nice flush hit! You drew his cork beautifully!'

'Sarah! You mustn't use language like that!' protested her mother.

'Oh, but it was! Wasn't it Penny?' Sarah defended herself.

'Well, it did *sound* like a nice flush hit,' agreed Penelope. 'But I'll have to take your word that Geoffrey's cork has been drawn! Thank you, Richard!'

Geoffrey struggled to his feet, clutching a handkerchief to his streaming nose, and Richard, taking him by the shoulders, thrust him into a chair, saying, 'If you have any more comments like that, I suggest you keep them under your tongue or I'll take a horse whip to you!'

'Penny, no! You can't marry a near stranger!' said Mrs Ffolliot·weakly.

'Mama, it's the only way. If all this gets out we are ruined. Think of Sarah, for heaven's sake!' pleaded Penelope.

'Darling, I can't let you do it!'

'Mama, don't be foolish. I'll be all right. Darleston is a gentleman, isn't he, Richard?' asked Penelope.

'I've always thought so, but I'm beginning to wonder!' said Richard. 'Mrs Ffolliot, you mustn't let her do this. I'll see Darleston, explain the situation. He won't force the issue.'

'No!' exclaimed Mrs Ffolliot. 'That would be intolerable.'

'Besides, I'll only do it on one condition!' said Penelope suddenly.

They all turned to her in surprise. She continued quietly to her brother, who listened in something akin to terror at the note of implacable determination in her voice. 'You will have the lawyers draw up a trust which gives you access only to the income from the estate and whatever is left in the funds. You will be not be able to touch the capital or sell anything without the consent of Mama and Richard or Phoebe, Sarah and myself as we come of age. Furthermore, if you die without issue then the estate must revert to Sarah!'

'Me? Why me?' gasped Sarah.

'Phoebe and Richard don't need it and neither will I. Darleston is so wealthy he could buy the whole county, let alone one estate!' said Penelope bluntly. 'Well, Geoffrey, those are my terms. If you don't like them find another way out! And don't think for a moment that you can bully Phoebe into it!'

Geoffrey stared at her in disbelief. He was caught and he knew it. Penelope's ultimatum was the only avenue of escape open to him.

'Damn you! What choice do I have?' he raged.

'None that I can think of,' she answered quietly. 'Well, do you agree?'

'Very well!' He rushed from the room in fury, slamming the door behind him.

'Mrs Ffolliot, you can't let her do this!' protested Richard. 'The whole idea is repugnant! She barely knows him!'

'What does that matter? Lots of marriages are arranged,' argued Penelope. 'And he doesn't know me! I should have thought you'd be much sorrier for him!'

'There is that, of course!' admitted Richard dryly. 'Nevertheless, this cannot be the only solution!'

'Probably not, but it does seem the neatest,' said Penelope. She turned to her mother, 'Well, Mama?'

'Penny, are you quite sure? The fourteenth of July is only a matter of weeks away.'

'Yes, Mama, quite sure.'

Chapter Five

Geoffrey Ffolliot tipped the brandy bottle up over his empty glass. A mere trickle came out. He stared at it blearily, then hurled the bottle from him with a curse as his brandy-fogged mind absorbed the fact that he had finished the bottle. He sniffed self-pityingly. No one cared that he sat drinking alone in his bed-chamber! No one seemed to think that he deserved the slightest sympathy for getting so deeply into debt! And as for that little bitch Penelope! She had used the whole situation to make him sign that blasted deed consigning all control of his property over to the trustees! Damn her!

He groaned, remembering that it was her wedding day tomorrow. Had to give her away, didn't he? God, he felt sick! Get her out of the house at least! Good thing! Hah! Perhaps Darleston would teach her a thing or two about the respect due to a fellow! Geoffrey gloated over the thought for a moment. Better if it were Jack Frobisher, of course. He'd have known how to deal with the wench! Break her in the same way he'd break a rebellious filly! But it wasn't Jack; it was Darleston himself!

The memory of those scornful brown eyes boring into him at the Bellingham House ball made him shudder.

Needed more brandy if he had to face both of them. Penny and Darleston together! Oh, God, where was the bottle. Finished it, hadn't he? Better ring for another! No! Old Tinson wouldn't bring one, most likely. Get it himself! Get two. Lots in the cellar! Go down now!

Geoffrey got to his feet very carefully and stood swaying for a moment. Then with unsteady steps he left the room. Fortunately he was so far gone that he completely forgot to take a candle. Otherwise he would have probably burned the entire house to the ground. As it was he made his stumbling way down to the kitchens, knocking over a number of chairs on the way.

He made it safely down the back stairs and into the kitchen. Now, where was the door to the cellar? Swaying giddily, he tried to get used to the darkness. Finally he thought he could find the door and walked very slowly and unsteadily towards it. His outstretched groping hand met the latch.

Ah! That was it! He pulled the door open. The blackness before him was absolute. Vaguely he thought about a light, but an odd thought of Penelope drifted into his mind. Didn't need a light! If that stupid wench could manage, then so could he!

He took one step down into the yawning blackness. No! He would need a light. Have to find the brandy, down there! Penelope wouldn't need to find the brandy but he did. Therefore, need a light!

It all seemed terribly logical. He swung around sharply, too sharply, and lost his footing. For a split second he teetered on the first step. His arms flailed wildly, trying to find something to grab and save himself. His fingertips caught the door frame and for a moment he hung there. Then his tenuous hold slipped and with a despairing scream he fell backwards into the waiting dark.

Penelope awoke to birdsong outside her bed-chamber window. She sat up in bed to stretch. For the past weeks she had been waking very early. The days had been so busy that this was the only time she got to think without interruption. Change had come into their lives with a vengeance after so many tranquil years. Tonight only Sarah would sleep in the room the three of them had shared for so long. Phoebe had been married a week ago. This morning she herself would marry the Earl of Darleston.

The ceremony promised to be very different from Phoebe's wedding, which, although rushed, had been a joyful occasion. Lord Darleston had waved aside the suggestion that he should meet his prospective bride again before the ceremony, though Mrs Ffolliot had insisted that he be given the opportunity to visit. If he had agreed Mrs Ffolliot would have told him everything, depending upon his generosity to accept Penelope openly instead of in the hole-and-corner fashion to which they were reduced. Phoebe therefore, was to remain very much in the background today, to avoid arousing suspicion. This would be helped by the fact that the Earl had requested his bride be prepared to leave almost immediately after the ceremony because of the distance to Darleston Court. This exclusion of her twin was, to Penelope, one of the worst aspects of the whole affair.

She was a country girl and had seen enough farm animals to understand the mechanics of what marriage involved physically. According to Phoebe's panegyric it was simply wonderful. Also, from the sound of it, a great deal of kissing was involved. That seemed odd to Penelope. The only occasion on which a man had at-

tempted to kiss her she had not enjoyed at all, except for
the dubious pleasure of slapping Mr Frobisher's face and
hearing his yells when Gelert bit him. Mama had told her
only that in the marriage bed it was her duty to acquiesce
to her husband and that in all probability she would enjoy
it. Mrs Ffolliot had based this prophecy upon her own
experience of marriage as well as her sneaking suspicion
that Darleston was sufficiently experienced to know precisely what he was doing.

Geoffrey, of course, as her nearest male relative was
to give the bride away. This, to Penelope, was not a
pleasant thought. She felt far more like a sister to Richard
Winton than to her own brother, who would have forced
Phoebe into the marriage had he been able to get away
with it.

Richard was such a contrast to Geoffrey. He was still
shocked that Mrs Ffolliot was permitting the marriage to
go ahead. Perhaps Penelope's likeness to his own bride
had increased his sensitivity to the situation, but he had
bowed to Phoebe's knowledge of her sister.

Phoebe had said thoughtfully, 'Penny has hated being
blind, or nearly so, because she feels a burden to us rather
than because it inconveniences her. Now she feels that
she is doing something to help us. Also it has voluntarily
brought her out of her seclusion, which is probably better
than us trying to winkle her out by stealth.'

Mrs Ffolliot had concurred with this opinion, when
Richard had protested on the grounds of Darleston's approach to the whole business, saying, 'Darleston has been
betrayed by one woman and treated very badly by one
member of the Ffolliot family, yet he said in his letter
that he had formed an agreeable impression of "Miss
Ffolliot". Phoebe tells me that she barely spoke to him
when he stood up with her, so I suspect any impression

was made by his meetings with Penny. From that point of view we are not cheating him, and I have every confidence in Penny's ability to handle him. Losing her sight has made her very sensitive to people's moods and natures. She can tell more from a person's voice in one brief encounter than I can in several.'

'She will have her work cut out with Darleston, ma'am. He seems made of ice these days!' Richard had answered. 'I wish you will reconsider! He may be furious!'

'Penny described him as charming,' was all Mrs Ffolliot had said.

Penelope, of course, knew nothing of these discussions, but she had an idea that at least initially his lordship was going to be very angry when he was told about the switch. Richard had wanted to do it, but Penelope had said firmly that since it would be her husband and her marriage she would prefer to break the news herself. As she lay in bed she wondered how she was going to raise the subject. Obviously the change of name had not meant anything to Darleston. Perhaps he had never known what 'Miss Ffolliot's' Christian name was. Well, she would simply have to tell him the whole sordid story.

What really worried her was having to tell him that she was very nearly blind. Penelope hated being pitied. The mere thought that he might pity her was galling. She would have to make it very clear that, with Gelert, she could be perfectly independent of his assistance once she knew her way about Darleston Court, which she understood to be huge.

She had got thus far in her ruminations when Sarah, who had been awake for a while but reluctant to disturb her, asked, 'Penny, are you scared?'

The question forced Penelope to think carefully.

Honesty forced her to admit that she was. 'A little, Sarah. But don't you dare tell the others!'

'Why are you doing it, then?'

'Being scared is not a reason not to do something,' said Penelope.

'Don't be an idiot, Penny!' said Sarah. 'You don't even know him. It's hardly necessary to get married just to prove you aren't scared!'

Penelope hesitated. 'Sarah, we have tried not to talk about all this in front of you, but what Geoffrey did was very dreadful. He wrongly and publicly accused Lord Darleston of cheating and then cheated himself. The debt must be paid somehow. The scandal is already appalling. It could hurt Mama, Phoebe and you. I can stop all that by marrying Darleston.'

'Will he be very cross with you when you tell him?'

'I hope not, but if he is I dare say it will not be for long,' said Penelope, with a convincing display of confidence that she was far from feeling. 'Now, that's enough questions for the bride! Isn't it time to get up?'

'Yes, my lady!' answered Sarah, and was obliged to dodge a well-aimed pillow.

Tinson came downstairs especially early that morning, just as he had for Miss Phoebe's wedding a week earlier. All the Ffolliot girls were close to his heart, but Miss Penelope was perhaps the dearest. He was quite determined that nothing and no one should be allowed to spoil her wedding day.

He was fully aware that Master Geoffrey had been drinking late the night before, and it had occurred to him that the boy would need sobering up before church. When Tinson reached the kitchen, prepared to make some very strong coffee, he found the housekeeper, Mrs

Jenkins, and Mrs Ffolliot's abigail, Susan, there before him.

As he entered Susan said, 'Here's Mr Tinson! He'll remember!'

'Remember what?' asked Tinson.

'The cellar door,' replied Mrs Jenkins. 'I'm sure it was shut before we went upstairs last night. But it's open now, or have you been down already this morning?'

Tinson shook his head and looked at the open door. 'No, Mrs Jenkins, I have not. And, yes, the cellar door was shut. I shut it myself.'

Susan nodded. 'There now! That's just what I said to Mrs Jenkins! "Depend upon it," I said. "Mr Tinson shut it. I saw him with my own eyes!" I said.'

Tinson shrugged and said, 'No doubt the master came and helped himself to another bottle of brandy later on. I'd better see what sort of a mess he's made down there. Fetch me a light, please, Mrs Jenkins!'

She went into the scullery and returned with an oil lamp already lit. Tinson took it with a word of thanks and ventured through the door. He had only descended a few steps when the yellow glow of the lamp revealed Ffolliot's body lying sprawled at the foot of the steps.

His gasp of horror brought Mrs Jenkins and Susan through the door behind him.

'Oh, my goodness!'

'Is he dead?'

Tinson didn't bother to reply, except for a terse, 'Stay here!' but got down the steps as quickly as he could. He bent over his master and felt for the pulse in his throat. Slowly he straightened and looked up at the two women, shaking his head.

They stared at him as he came back up. The three of

them went back into the kitchen, which was otherwise still empty.

'What will the mistress say?' asked Susan in shocked tones. 'And it's Miss Penny's wedding day and all! Why, she mightn't be able to get married today at all with this nasty business!'

Mrs Jenkins and Tinson exchanged a long glance. The rest of the staff would have informed any outsider that these two frequently disagreed. Despite this they were good friends and old allies, and there was one subject upon which they had but a single mind. Miss Penny was the finest, bravest lass you could wish for and they would have given their lives to spare her distress.

'Shut the door, Mr Tinson,' said Mrs Jenkins quietly. He nodded and did so.

Turning to Susan, he confirmed her sudden suspicion. 'Nothing is going to spoil Miss Penny's day! Say nothing to the mistress or to anyone! We'll lock the cellar door and I'll tell the mistress and Mr Winton *after* Miss Penny and her lord have left. I'll let them think only I knew.'

Susan glared at him and replied, 'Well, and it's a good idea, barring the bit about you getting all the credit for it! Shame on you, Mr Tinson! Mrs Jenkins and I aren't scared to own up! Are we, ma'am?'

'Not likely!' came the staunch reply. 'Silly old fool!'

As Lord Darleston was driven in his well-sprung chaise towards the church from the inn at which he had put up the night before, he wondered if he had taken leave of his senses. Certainly George Carstares, his groomsman, seemed to think so. He had protested vehemently when Darleston had first told him what he meant to do, the day Mrs Ffolliot's polite letter accepting his offer had arrived.

'For God's sake Peter, this is sheer persecution. Why,

the girl may be in love with someone else but feel obliged to marry you! What if you take one another in dislike? She may be a dead bore, or find you a dead bore.'

'She's not a dead bore,' had said his lordship indignantly. 'I admit I thought her a little dull the first time I met her, but I dare say she was minding her dance steps. On the other two occasions that I met her she was very lively and showed a good understanding. You were the one who advised me to marry the first eligible girl I could talk to rationally! Besides, I like her dog!'

George had spluttered in his indignation at being cited as an influence in Peter's decision. 'What a wonderful basis for proposing to a girl! If you can call it a proposal! I made a joke and you like her *dog*? It's to be hoped the dog likes you, if it's the size you say it is. It's probably the one that mauled your cousin when he stayed with Ffolliot.'

Peter had remained silent. Not even to George could he admit that he had still been as drunk as a wheelbarrow when he wrote to Geoffrey Ffolliot and that he had been completely and utterly dumbfounded when he received an acceptance of his offer.

Carstares had been rather silent this morning since they'd got up at the inn. He had done his best to dissuade his friend from what he thought must be a disastrous step but he could do no more on that head. Now he shrugged mentally and said, 'Well, Peter, I suppose I should stop being such a prophet of doom. I hope it will all work out for you and I hope you know I've only spoken out because I care about you. All the same, I wish you would tell me why you are getting married like this.'

Darleston was silent for a moment, and then said evenly, 'You already know why. I married once for love and look what happened. Even as we rompéd Boney

Melissa was betraying me with Barton. If it weren't for the succession I wouldn't marry again, but I'm damned if I want my cousin Jack to step into my shoes. And I'm damned if I want to be dodging women like Caroline for the rest of my life! This seemed a good way of securing a sensible wife who wouldn't expect me to dance attendance on her. I don't mean to be in love with my wife and if she cuckolds me I can divorce her without any qualms!'

George had enough sense to make no comment on this explanation. They drove the rest of the way in silence.

Just as they were about to alight at the church, Peter turned to his friend and said, 'Thank you for bearing with me, George. I don't mean to bully the girl or make her the scapegoat for Melissa's sins, believe me. I just don't want any emotional tie. But if you think it best I'll speak to Miss Ffolliot before the ceremony to make sure she is not being coerced and that she perfectly understands the situation.'

George wrung his hand, 'Better late than never!' he agreed fervently.

They were greeted by the rector of the parish, Dr Pearson, who was a little surprised when the groom requested that he might be permitted to speak to the bride for a moment before the ceremony.

'My lord, with all respect, this is *most* irregular. However, if you will wait in the vestry I will tell Miss Ffolliot when she arrives that you wish to see her.'

'Thank you, sir,' answered Peter, and followed the sexton to the vestry, where he awaited the bride on a very uncomfortable chair.

He was not kept waiting long. The bride, veiled and all in ivory satin, was escorted into the vestry by Dr Pearson, who then stepped outside to wait. Darleston cleared his throat, glaring at George who promptly followed the rector.

Nervously he cleared his throat and looked at his bride. He had forgotten how slender she was, almost fragile, he thought, and a faint scent of flowers accompanied her. Silently she waited for him to speak.

'Miss Ffolliot, I realise this is a little late, but my groomsman has represented to me that you may have been coerced into taking part in this ceremony. I wished to ascertain that you had no prior claim to your affections and that you are indeed willing to marry me,' said the Earl stiffly.

Penelope listened very carefully and decided that candour was the best approach. 'My Lord, if I had taken you in dislike on the occasions upon which we met, or if my affections had been engaged, I should have sent you a note recommending you to go to the devil. As it is I am aware that my brother's behaviour has the potential to damage my family, so I am only too happy to marry you if it will save them pain. Like you I ''formed an agreeable impression''. On that basis I am willing to become your wife.' She felt a few qualms about her blindness and Phoebe, but told herself that his lordship would have expended more interest in selecting a new filly than he had on his marriage!

Peter blinked at his bride's blunt assessment of the situation, but told himself firmly that she was definitely sensible, which was all to the good. 'Thank you, Miss Ffolliot. George will be relieved that he is not assisting at a tragedy!' he said, and could have kicked himself, but the bride said nothing as she moved to the door, although he could have sworn the odd noise she made was suppressed laughter.

Five minutes later Peter Augustus Frobisher, Earl of

Darleston, was awaiting Miss Penelope Ffolliot at the altar steps, feeling that he was in for some surprises where his bride was concerned. His groomsman, on the other hand, upon noticing the bride's twin sister in the church, had suddenly remembered an interesting piece of information about the daughters of the late Mr John Ffolliot. He wondered whether it was the part of a friend to warn the groom, but decided against it. That's what you get for buying a pig in a poke! he thought with a certain wry amusement.

Penelope proceeded up the aisle on her brother-in-law's arm, feeling extremely nervous about getting through the ceremony without making a fool of herself. She could see practically nothing in the dimly lit church. All her reliance was on the fact that she knew the place very well and had been walked through the ceremony a dozen times. And thank God it was Richard at her side, rather than Geoffrey, although just where Geoffrey had disappeared to was a complete mystery to her. The knowledge that Sarah was just behind her was an added comfort.

Penelope's confession of why she was doing this had touched Sarah's childish heart to the core. She had known her sisters loved her but, that one of them would do this to save her from scandal made the knowledge very real to her. Sarah was no fool; she knew Phoebe was protected by Richard and that the brunt of society's anger would have made it difficult for Mama to launch her into society. Sarah vowed to herself that there must never be anything she was not prepared to do for Penny.

So serious did she look that the groom was quite disconcerted by the frown on her face. He wondered if his bride was that solemn, but the memory of that stifled chuckle in the vestry reassured him.

The marriage service was brief and the bride and groom took their vows clearly. Penelope listened closely to the Earl's voice. It was just as attractive as she remembered. Their brief conversation in the vestry had confirmed that. He sounds a little nervous, thought Penelope, but she was aware few others would realise this. Her own nerves must be much more obvious!

The Earl thought initially that his bride was suffering no nervous jitters at all. Until, that was, her hand was placed in his by Richard Winton. Then he became aware that she was trembling slightly. George's comments on his behaviour rose mercilessly in his mind; he felt a cad. He could sense the girl staring at him and gave her hand a comforting squeeze. At least, he hoped it was comforting.

As for Penelope, she had become suddenly aware of the Earl's physical presence as he took her hand. The sun shone brightly through one of the windows and she was dimly aware of his height beside her, though his voice came from way over her head. She tried to stop shaking, but could not. Then, as she tried in vain to pierce her darkness and see him, she felt him press her hand gently. The trembling stopped and Penelope resolved to thank the Earl as soon as they were away from the church.

Darleston felt less guilty when his bride stopped shaking. He followed the rector through the service carefully, placed the ring on Penelope's now steady hand and heard them declared man and wife. My God I've done it now. There's no going back! he thought wildly, and then became aware that something was expected of him.

'You're supposed to kiss her, Peter!' came George's agonised whisper. The rector looked as though he were trying not to laugh.

Very carefully Darleston lifted the veil back from his

wife's face to gaze into her dark grey eyes. Strange eyes, he thought. They seemed to look straight through you, as though you weren't quite there. He put a gentle hand under Penelope's chin and bent to kiss her lightly on the mouth. Her lips were warm and soft. The Earl decided that he would definitely enjoy kissing her again later on.

Penelope was unprepared for this. Although she had known it would happen it was the one thing that had not been rehearsed, and the strange feeling of yearning which swept over her at the touch of his lips was a complete surprise. She wondered if he had wanted to kiss her. George's whisper had been quite audible to her, and she was unsure whether to be amused or miffed. She felt the Earl draw her hand through his arm to lead her from the church and realised that the hardest part was still to come. She still had to tell him that he had been duped to a certain extent, and that was beginning to weigh heavily on her conscience.

The bridal party moved to the Rectory, where Phoebe, Sarah and Mrs Ffolliot whirled Penelope upstairs to change out of the wedding dress, which had been worn by Phoebe a week earlier. 'Darling Phoebe, thank you for letting me wear it. It was like being held by you all the time,' said Penelope, hugging her twin. 'Oh, Sarah! I couldn't have managed without you. You were wonderful!' Sarah blushed and blew her nose noisily.

'Penny, are you sure you don't want Richard to tell Lord Darleston?' asked her mother.

'Quite sure, Mama,' said Penelope. 'You see, if I don't tell him it will be because I am scared. Even if it is all a bit irregular I don't want to start by not trusting him enough to tell him myself.'

In no time at all it seemed she was being handed into the chaise. Some surprise had been expressed by the groom when he realised that Gelert was going to accompany them, and George had proved no help at all, saying enthusiastically to the new Countess of Darleston, 'Just the thing, Lady Darleston. Peter was telling me how much he admired your dog!'

Peter had glared at him and given in gracefully, thinking that as the dog was bound to join the household anyway it might as well be now as later. He followed his wife and her dog into the chaise, and the door was shut behind him by Richard Winton, who said in affectionate accents, 'Behave yourself, Penny,' then, in a more challenging tone of voice, 'Look after her, Lord Darleston.'

His lordship accepted this blunt command with commendable meekness, merely saying, 'I shall hope to receive both you and Mrs Winton at Darleston Court in the very near future so that you may assure yourself that I am doing so. Goodbye, Winton, and thank you.'

He noticed that as Winton stepped back from the chaise his arm was tapped by a nervous-looking old man who had sat at the back of the church with the Ffolliot's upper servants. Peter rather thought that he must be the butler. He dismissed the matter from his mind as his bride spoke.

'I am afraid Richard has become very older-brotherish since he became engaged to my sister,' said Penelope apologetically as the chaise rolled away.

'So it would appear,' said Peter. 'Are you tired, Lady Darleston? I dare say you were up early and have been very busy. Perhaps you would care to rest? We have some sixty miles to travel to Darleston Court.'

Concealing her surprise at the formality of his address, Penelope admitted that she had been awake early and that a nap would be welcome. Sleep was far away, however, so she settled herself back in the corner of the chaise to count to five thousand while she worked out how to start explaining herself to her husband. My husband, she thought. If only I could *see* him! I don't even know what he looks like, only Phoebe's description. She reached five thousand and sat up, ready to begin her confession, when a gentle snore informed her that his lordship was asleep.

It appeared to Penelope that a couple of hours passed before her husband awoke as they pulled into an inn-yard to change the horses. Lord Darleston procured a basket of food and they were on their way again. This was it, decided Penelope. She had to get it over with! Before she could start, however, Lord Darleston spoke.

'My lady, I think it is important that I make my position quite clear to you at the start. As you are possibly aware, this is my second marriage. My first wife disgraced my name and I would not have chosen to marry again except for the recent death of my cousin and heir. His death means that the title must go, after me, to a man I consider totally unworthy of it. To be perfectly honest with you I have married to beget an heir. I am sorry if you are shocked at my plain speaking, but I deplore deceit and you had better know that I have every intention of... of consummating our union as soon as possible.'

Penelope was speechless. She laid one trembling hand on Gelert's head and drew a deep breath. 'It is my turn to be honest now, my lord. I...I am not the person you think I am!'

Darleston was puzzled. 'What on earth are you talking about? You are, or rather were, Miss Penelope Ffolliot, aren't you?'

'Yes, but when you met me the first time, at Almack's, it wasn't me you met but my twin, Phoebe!' said Penny desperately, and a trifle incoherently.

Absolutely staggered, the Earl stared at her in disbelief.

Then, as he recalled odd differences between the girl he had danced with at Almack's and the girl driving in the park and at the concert, he realised the mistake he had made.

'Phoebe…I *thought* that was the name! What in heaven's name were you two playing at, then? It was you, though, with your father that day and at the concert. I would swear it!' said the Earl angrily.

'Yes, that was me both times.' Privately she was amazed he was so sure.

'Why? Did you share your come-out to economise?' This in a menacingly quiet tone.

'No! I didn't want a come-out. I simply went to London to be with Phoebe. Hardly anyone knew about me; when you met me you thought I was Phoebe, so I let you continue to think it!' cried Penelope. 'Then Geoffrey lost all that money, and it wasn't the first time and we couldn't pay, so he tried to force Phoebe to marry you, even though she was betrothed…'

'He did *what*?' The shock and horror in the Earl's voice were unmistakable. She gasped in fright as he took her roughly by the shoulders. This was too much for Gelert, who rose, growling fiercely in warning.

'No, Gelert!' cried Penelope.

Darleston released her and said in a milder tone of voice, 'I beg your pardon. Please forgive me, I did not mean to startle you. You say your brother tried to force your sister to marry me?'

'Yes. We knew you meant Phoebe, but she had just become engaged to Richard so I said I would marry you. It was true what I said in the vestry, my lord. I would not have married you if I had not liked you. Anyway, you didn't seem terribly interested in whom you married or Mama would have told you. You shouldn't have bought a pig in a poke!' she finished, unconsciously echoing George Carstares's unspoken thought.

'Why the devil didn't you tell me all this in the vestry?' demanded the Earl furiously. 'Good God! I shall be the laughing stock of town if this gets out! Well, it needn't alter my plans. You and your sister are so alike I dare say it doesn't make any odds which of you lies in my bed tonight! Is there anything else I need to know? God help you if there is, my girl!'

Penelope was shaking. This was far worse than she had imagined and she bit her lip to keep from crying. She still had to tell him she was blind, but she remained silent, terrified of bursting into tears if she spoke. Too late she realised that she had underestimated the insult to his pride in being so duped. It occurred to her that he had probably decided the whole family were cheats. Finally she asked in a very wobbly voice, 'Would you have married me if you had known that there were two of us?'

Darleston, already feeling guilty over his loss of temper, but by no means prepared to admit it, answered very angrily, 'Very well, *no*! it *wouldn't* have changed my mind!' He refrained from adding that it would have made a difference if he had been confronted with Phoebe. Mrs Ffolliot had been perfectly right in guessing that it was Penelope's stronger personality which had caught his attention. Goaded beyond endurance he added, 'And my intention to consummate this marriage stands, so I suggest you get used to the idea!' He then dragged the frightened girl into his arms and brought his mouth down savagely on hers.

Taken totally by surprise, Penny tried to struggle in vain. The Earl, however, had forgotten the presence of Gelert, who had become increasingly anxious about this

stranger shouting at his mistress. He took instant exception to the situation and leapt at Darleston barking fero-
ciously, forcing him to release Penelope. Half fainting,
Penelope was unable for a moment to call Gelert to order,
and she groped helplessly for his collar, finally dragging
him back. Shaken with sobs, she slid off the seat onto
the floor, her arms about the dog's neck, crying into his
rough coat. Gelert whined and licked her face frantically,
pausing only to direct a few warning snarls at Darleston.

Stunned by the dog's attack, Darleston sat back in his
seat wondering just what he should do. His bride sat dishevelled and weeping on the floor of the carriage, her
dog displaying every sign of flying at him again if he
dared move towards her. He tried to apologise. 'My
lady…I mean, Penelope, I'm sorry for losing my temper
and frightening you…I hope you will forgive me.' Then,
on a more practical note as she continued to cry, 'Would
you care for a handkerchief?'

A choked voice answered, 'Thank you,' and a small
hand was held out. He placed his handkerchief in it and
then put his head in his hands in disbelief at the mess he
had made of the whole affair. His temper had ebbed. He
felt very guilty, but somehow still annoyed with Penelope
for having witnessed it. He groaned inwardly. Tonight
was definitely not the night to bed his bride. It would be
tantamount to rape.

The rest of the journey was passed without conversation. The Earl had no idea what to say to ease the tension
and Penelope was completely numbed by the thought of
the night to come. She had been terrified when Darleston
seized her. There had been no hint of gentleness in his
embrace. His mouth had completely and brutally possessed hers and his arms had admitted of no escape. She

began to feel sick with fear at the thought of being alone with him.

By the time they reached Darleston Court in the falling dusk Penelope was in such a state of fright that she could not stop shaking. When the chaise drew up at the front of the house a footman opened the carriage door and let down the steps. His Lordship leapt down, holding out his hand to assist Penelope to alight. Not realising, she attempted to get down unaided but completely missed the steps. She fell with a cry of fright and found herself once more in her husband's arms. 'Careful!' he said 'You will hurt yourself if you don't look out.'

There was real concern in his voice, and this undid her totally. Perceiving that she was about to burst into tears, he swept her up and carried her into the house, past the row of waiting servants, saying only, 'Dinner in fifteen minutes, if you please. I have something to show her ladyship in the study!' Closely followed by Gelert, he strode to the study door with Penelope in his arms. A footman rushed to open the door and close it behind them and Darleston deposited his wife gently on the sofa.

She turned towards him, saying shakily, 'Would you please ask one of your people to take Gelert to the stables for the night and feed him?'

Darleston blinked. 'Are you sure you would not feel safer if he remained?' he asked quietly.

'I would prefer to be able speak to you without worrying about his behaviour,' answered Penelope proudly. She suspected that her husband was going to be even angrier than before at what she was about to tell him. If Gelert attacked him a third time he might insist the dog be sent away. Besides, she was ashamed of her own fear. All her life her father had taught her to look her fears in the face and conquer them. She would not permit herself to hide behind Gelert's protection.

'As you please,' said Darleston. He tugged the bell-pull by the desk. The butler appeared and Darleston gave him his instructions, 'Meadows, please have her Ladyship's dog conveyed to the stables and fed.'

'Yes, my lord,' said Meadows.

Penelope heard the apprehension in his voice and said with tolerable composure, 'He will be good, I promise. Come, take his collar from me.' Meadows crossed the room to her side to grasp Gelert's collar. 'Go with him, Gelert,' she commanded. He obeyed reluctantly, giving a last growl as he passed Darleston.

'Thank you, Meadows. Her ladyship will ring for him when she wants him,' said the Earl.

Penelope turned towards her husband's voice and said nervously, 'There is one last thing I must tell you, my lord.'

'Yes? I doubt you can shock me any further, but go ahead.'

Bracing herself for the explosion, she said simply, 'I am blind.'

The silence lengthened, only to be broken by the Earl saying bitterly, 'I appear to have married into a family of cheats. Do you imagine I wish my heir to be blind? Dinner will be served in ten minutes. Ring for Meadows when you are ready to join me.'

Penelope heard his footsteps cross the room then the door slammed behind him. She realised too late what he was doing and sank back onto the couch in the knowledge that she would have to wait there until it occurred to him that she had no idea where the bell-pull was.

Darleston waited an extra twenty minutes for his bride, before giving up and starting his own dinner. He was furious. Doubtless the staff was agog at the situation, and the wretched girl's last admission was the outside of enough. He ate several courses without even tasting them and downed a bottle of burgundy with no noticeable effect. Could he repudiate the marriage? Not without a shocking scandal which would leave him looking a total fool. Also, he suspected that the law was on the Ffolliots' side.

Blast the girl. Couldn't she even have joined him for dinner to make a show of wedded bliss for the servants? His conscience pointed out firmly that he had given her little cause to care what he wanted and that in all likelihood the girl was terrified of him.

Finally, after the footman had placed the brandy on the table, he began to consider the whole situation from Penelope's perspective. He tried to understand why she had done it. Obviously she must care for her sisters and mother very much. It occurred to him, on a wave of shame, that his behaviour would have terrified even a girl who could see. What Penelope must have felt appalled him. He thought it must have resembled a nightmare for her and found himself unexpectedly thankful that the dog had been there. The courage she had shown in sending Gelert out before making her final admission became plain to him. At least I didn't do anything, he thought, but that was small comfort as he recalled his final bitter comment.

He dismissed the footman and asked him to find Meadows. The butler arrived and said, 'The dog has been fed and suitably housed for the night, my lord.'

'Thank you, Meadows. Tell me, when you conducted her ladyship upstairs…'

'I beg your pardon my lord, but her ladyship is still in

the study, I believe. She certainly did not ring to be conducted upstairs.'

At this point the true reason for Penelope's non-
appearance struck Darleston with all the force of a thun-
derbolt. He leapt to his feet in horror at his stupidity. 'My
God! Meadows, please bring some hot soup and rolls to
her ladyship's room in twenty minutes, do you mind?
There's a good chap. I'll explain later and you can comb
my hair for being such a fool!'

He raced out of the dining room across the hall to the
study door. He recollected himself enough to knock
lightly. There was no answer, so he opened the door and
stepped in quietly. The inadequate words of apology died
on his lips as he saw his bride, sound asleep on the sofa
with traces of tears on her cheeks. He cursed himself
silently for what he had done. All his anger had been
unjust. The situation was his own fault for being arrogant.
He would simply have to make the best of it and try to
make the girl happy.

Softly he stepped over to the sofa and knelt beside it
to take her hand. 'Penelope! Wake up,' he said gently.
She did not stir immediately but when he spoke again,
sat up in terror, trying to pull away from him. 'Penelope,
it's all right. I have come to apologise and take you up
to your room. Meadows is bringing you some food and
then I shall leave you to sleep, I give you my word.'

He was horrified at the fear on her face but, to his
relief, she relaxed slightly at his words. 'That's better. I
cannot tell you how ashamed I am of the way I have
behaved towards you. It was inexcusable, all of it. In
truth it was my meetings with you, not your sister, which
prompted me to believe ''Miss Ffolliot'' would be a suitable bride, so I can scarcely complain about which twin
I received. As for your blindness, I can only say that my

reaction was contemptible and I beg your pardon most humbly.'

Penelope was scarcely able to believe her ears at the change in his voice. She found her own voice with difficulty. 'It is I who should apologise, Lord Darleston. We played a shabby trick on you, especially with regard to my blindness. If you wish to repudiate our marriage I would not blame you.' She blew her nose and wiped her eyes, wishing that she could see him as she awaited his reply.

It surprised her. Peter put his hands on her shoulders and very gently pulled her into his arms. He held her lightly, resting his cheek against the auburn curls. 'That seems a little drastic, since I got the right bride through no fault of my own. Unless you prefer to have nothing more to do with me I suggest we get to know each other and try to wipe out this bad start to our marriage.'

Penelope listened with tears trickling down her cheeks and whispered, 'Thank you, my lord.'

Chapter Six

Penelope awoke the next morning to a gentle knock on her door. 'Come in!' she called. The door opened and she heard Gelert's bark as he bounded into the room. Delighted to find his mistress, he leapt onto the bed to nuzzle her face. The rosy-cheeked maid who had brought him said shyly, 'His lordship sent me to wait on you milady. I've brought some tea for you and his lordship's compliments. He will be at your disposal this morning to show you over the house.'

'Thank you,' said Penelope, finding it odd to be called 'milady'. She gave Gelert a last hug. 'Off now.' He jumped down beside the bed his tail beating a rhythmic tattoo on the floor. Penelope heard her maid approach the bed, and held out her hands for the tea. It was placed in her grasp very carefully.

'Have you got it safely, milady?' came an anxious enquiry. 'We were told that you're blind, and his lordship's orders are for all of us to be sure to help you find your way about.'

'That will be wonderful, thank you,' said Penelope, sipping her tea. She smiled in the direction of the pleasant, eager voice. 'What is your name?'

'Ellen, milady.'

'Will you be able to show me around until I know where everything is?' asked Penelope hopefully. 'Once I know the way to rooms and know the layout of the grounds I shall be all right with Gelert here. But if you are free to help at first, Ellen, I should be very grateful.'

'Oh, milady, it would be a pleasure. Shall I pull back the curtains now?'

Penelope nodded and heard the girl cross to the window. Light flooded in. She was instantly aware of the difference, probably the room faced east, she thought. Thoughtfully she finished her tea while Ellen busied herself around the room. It seemed that the Earl was taking some thought for her well-being. When he had carried her upstairs the previous night he had seen to it that she finished the soup and rolls, had all that she needed and knew she could reach the bell-pull from her bed, but after that her memory was vague, for she had been very sleepy. Suddenly she realised that she was wearing a nightdress and wondered how she had got into it. Frowning, she tried to remember, but all she could recall was someone with very gentle hands and a tender voice. It dawned on her that her husband must have put her to bed. She blushed hotly at the thought of him undressing her.

'Would you like to get up now milady?' Ellen's voice broke in on these embarrassing reflections.

'Yes, I should get up. What is the time?'

'Just after ten, milady. His lordship wouldn't let us wake you any earlier. He said to take the dog up at ten and not before, unless you rang.'

'Thank you, Ellen,' said Penelope as she got up. 'Did Gelert behave himself?'

'Oh, yes, milady, except for frightening one of the grooms half to death, being as he didn't know a dog was in that stall and he is such a size! Johnson, the head groom, told Mr Meadows that he'd had to persuade Fred not to give notice!'

Penelope laughed. 'You don't seem to mind him. I think someone made a lucky choice of maid for me!'

'Oh, no, milady! The master told Mr Meadows to line up all the maids and ask which ones liked dogs, without telling them why, and then to bring in your dog and see if they still liked dogs! I was the only one who did!' This last was said with great pride, and Penelope, after a startled moment, had to sit back on the bed, so hard did she laugh at this unorthodox method of selecting an abigail.

Half an hour later Ellen conducted her downstairs to the study, where Lord Darleston was awaiting her. She was a little nervous, both of her reception and of Gelert's possible reaction to her husband. Ellen was a good guide, explaining the passages and doors very clearly so that by the time they reached the study Penelope knew she would be able to find her own way back. 'Thank you, Ellen,' said Penelope as they reached the study door. She knocked, and upon hearing her husband call, 'Come in,' she entered.

Peter was sitting at his desk, looking over some estate business, 'Good morning, Penelope.'

Good morning, my lord.'

'Peter.'

'I beg your pardon?'

'Peter. My name is Peter. Peter Augustus, actually, but that's almost as formal as my lord. Unless you prefer not to, please call me Peter in private.'

Penelope listened very carefully. All she could hear in her husband's voice was a friendly warmth. All yesterday's anger seemed to have disappeared. She relaxed visibly. Peter, watching her intently, could see the tension ebb from her slender frame and was immeasurably relieved. He had slept badly the previous night. Every time he had nearly dropped off, his conscience had pricked him back to wakefulness. His behaviour continued to appal him; he could scarcely believe what he had done and he had resolved to make every effort to help Penelope settle in.

Furthermore he had received a very disquieting letter from Richard Winton that morning, which had been delivered by a messenger who had ridden all night to reach Darleston Court. He did not quite know how to reveal the contents of the letter to his wife. With any other girl he would have simply given it to her to read, but that was obviously impossible.

He decided to approach the matter obliquely. 'Tell me, Penelope, were you very much disappointed that your brother did not appear to give you away?'

Penelope flushed and hesitated. She could not lie and say she *had* been upset when in reality she had been relieved! On the other hand it seemed so improper to tell Darleston—oh, dear, Peter!—just how much she disliked her half-brother.

Eventually she said quietly and without rancour, 'I am afraid, Peter, that I was not in the least upset. My half-brother and I share a mutual dislike. I was far happier for my brother-in-law to give me away. Indeed, given the circumstances of our marriage, I should not be surprised to learn that Geoffrey was too embarrassed to face the pair of us!'

Peter was not really surprised. He could not imagine that there could have been much affection between young Ffolliot and his proud sister. For she was proud, not arrogant or above herself, it was just that she had a certain dignity and gallantry in her bearing. The contrast with

Geoffrey's whining and somewhat shady character could not have been more marked. It occurred to him that she must have been bitterly galled by the knowledge that her brother was a cheat.

In his turn Peter hesitated, then he said simply, 'Then I hope you will not be too upset to hear, that one of your grooms followed us here bearing a letter from Richard Winton. In it he asks me to break the news that your brother must have fallen down the cellar steps the night before last. Your mother's butler found him early yesterday morning with a broken neck. He decided that it was better to wait until after our wedding to inform your mother. He did not wish to spoil your wedding day. I am sorry, Penelope.' Peter could think of nothing further to say to his bride.

Her mouth dropped open in amazement. She looked to be completely stunned, and then shook her head, saying in disbelief, 'Geoffrey is dead? Oh, dear God! And on our wedding day! I married you to avoid scandal! Not to inflame it! Whatever will people say?'

Peter had already thought about this and he had a ready answer. 'We will just tell the truth. Accidents do happen, you know, and we can emphasise the story of the faithful old retainer not wishing to ruin his young mistress's happy day!' No need to tell the world that the bridegroom had seen to that without any outside assistance, he thought ruefully.

Penelope looked unconvinced. 'Sell them a Banbury story, do you mean? Does Richard happen to mention just what Geoffrey was doing down in the cellar? Not that I need ask. No doubt he was in his cups as usual!'

Her husband nodded in embarrassment, and then realised how useless that was. 'Er, yes, Winton does say that it appears Geoffrey was a trifle bosky.'

'Bosky? A *trifle* bosky?' was the scornful rejoinder. 'I'm only surprised that he could get as far as the cellar!' Then she recollected herself and said shamefacedly, 'I beg your pardon, my lord—I mean Peter. But Geoffrey could be simply horrible. When your letter came he tried to bully Phoebe into marrying you even though she was already betrothed to Richard! And he wouldn't even wear mourning for Papa! The kindest, most loving father!' Tears stood in her eyes as she said this.

'He didn't bully you, I hope?' asked Peter in real horror.

'Certainly not!' she retorted. 'I would have told him to go to the devil if it had been just the debt. It was more the stigma for my mother and sisters. Besides, I used the situation to force Geoffrey into putting the whole estate under the control of a trust so that he could not continue to waste it. Under that trust it now goes to my little sister Sarah, since Phoebe and I don't need it!'

'I see,' he replied slowly. 'Then we need only consider the practicalities of the situation.' Thoughtfully he eyed the gown of grey muslin in which his bride was arrayed and said, 'I shall send to London for some new gowns for you. You are out of mourning—for your father, of course. And for a half-brother I believe a month's half-mourning will suffice. So, since we are spending our time here quietly at Darleston Court, it should not be necessary to be terribly strict. Just as long as you don't dash about the countryside in bright colours! Yes, some new gowns definitely!' He hoped this would change the subject, since Penelope was obviously chafed by it.

It certainly did effect a change of subject, but not quite in the way he had intended. Penelope flushed even more vividly than before. What must he think of her, not having suitable clothes for her new status? Well did she know that the simple gowns Phoebe and Mama had fashioned for her were out of place here. She lifted her head and said proudly, 'There is not the slightest need, my lord. I have quite enough clothes for my needs.' It occurred to her that she had been a trifle ungracious, and she stammered, 'I...I mean it is very kind of your lordship, but I do not require new clothes or wish you to be spending a great deal of money upon me!'

Peter was taken aback. It was the first time in his career that an offer to supply new finery to a woman had been refused. Most of 'em, he thought cynically, would have presented him with a detailed list! Belatedly he remembered that the Ffolliots were not well off and that there had been very little time for Penelope to acquire any new gowns. He realised that his offer had sounded like a condemnation of her attire. Careful now! he thought.

'Of course not!' he said cheerfully. ''Twas just that I thought since you'd had no time to buy new clothes since you came out of mourning for your father it would give me great pleasure to do it for you! You can trust me to know what colours will suit you. I shall avoid pink. Something tells me that it will not be one of your favourites! And since you are to be in half-mourning initially, perhaps deep blues, even pale colours such as a lemon-yellow will be acceptable!'

Self-consciously Penelope raised a hand to her auburn curls and admitted, 'Indeed, pink is not a favourite! Neither Phoebe nor I ever wear it! We both prefer blues and greens.' With an effort she smiled at her husband, saying, 'I beg your pardon, my lord. If you wish to buy me some new gowns, I should like it very much.'

He smiled in relief. 'Excellent. Ask Ellen to take your measurements and leave the rest to me.' She could hear the smile in his voice.

'Oh, one other little thing, Penelope…'

'Yes, my lord?'

'I think you are cheating.'

'Cheating!' The outrage in her voice was unmistakable.

Peter grinned at the reaction and continued, 'Yes, cheating! I distinctly recall asking you to call me by my Christian name. You are being extremely disobedient, and if I do anything about it your dog will probably try to bite me again!'

'Oh!' She stopped in confusion. 'I'm sorry he was so badly behaved, my…I mean, P-Peter. He is generally very good, but…'

Peter interrupted her, saying seriously, 'You must not apologise for his behaviour, Penelope. I deserved it. I shouted at you and then tried to force my attentions on you. I'm glad he was there. Which brings me to something else.'

'Yes, Peter?' It was much easier as you went along, she discovered.

She heard him clear his throat. He sounds nervous, she thought in amazement.

'Our relationship,' he said carefully. Oh God! How to put it? He rustled some papers. 'At the present I have no intention of insisting upon my…my rights as a husband.'

And just what, wondered Penelope, does the well-bred bride reply to that? To her absolute horror she heard herself asking, 'Why not?'

Peter was also rather taken aback. That was the last response he had expected! 'Well, we don't know each other very well yet. I…I don't wish to force myself upon you.'

'Because I am blind.' It was not a question, but a statement. She flushed in embarrassment. It was the same old problem. Someone unable to accept her affliction without pitying her. Perhaps he even found it distasteful.

Peter heard the pain in her voice, saw the crimson stain her cheeks and was puzzled. What had he said to hurt her? 'Yes,' he said gently. 'I think it would be unfair for me to insist you share my bed before you have learnt to know me and trust me, especially after yesterday.'

All she could hear in his voice was sincere concern. Yes, he was kind, this husband of hers, despite his loss of temper the previous day. He was not extending patronage or pity, but simply behaving in accordance with the dictates of his honour. 'Thank you, Peter.' She did not know what else to say, how to apologise for her suspicions.

He looked at her carefully, not really understanding what had upset her. It occurred to him that it would be just as important for him to understand her, to avoid future mistakes.

Diffidently he said, 'I thought that today I should perhaps show you over the house and part of the gardens. Ellen, your maid, will also help you. Unfortunately she has not had much experience as a lady's maid, but…'

'She likes Gelert!' Penelope finished his sentence with a chuckle. 'Thank you, Peter. Ellen told me about how you chose her. If you have time to show me around today that would be lovely. Once I know where everything is Gelert will be able to guide me.'

'Gelert? What on earth do you mean?'

A demonstration was always most effective in Penelope's experience. 'You are sitting down, aren't you?'

'Well, yes.' How the devil did she know?

'At a desk. Is the desk between us?'

'Yes.'

She walked straight towards him in absolute confidence with her hand on Gelert's collar and stopped about eighteen inches from the desk. 'The desk is about a foot and a half away, isn't it?'

'Good God! How did you do that? You even knew I was sitting!'

'Your voice, of course. The height is wrong for you to be standing. And I heard you move some papers so I thought you must be at a desk. As for knowing where the desk was, Gelert stopped me.'

Peter stared at them in disbelief. 'And he does that all the time?'

'Yes. It makes it much easier if I don't have to wait about for people or take them away from whatever they are doing. I prefer to be as independent as possible.'

Good heavens! Here he'd been thinking that he was tied to a girl who would need constant help and attention. He began to revise his ideas very quickly. This was no helpless child to be nursed over every obstacle. She would probably give him a sharp set-down if he tried!

He wondered what to say, and then thought, When in doubt, be direct!

'I find myself in an awkward situation, then, my dear. My instinct is to shepherd you around every chair, make sure you never take a step without an attendant, but something tells me you would not appreciate this!'

Penelope smiled. 'Not at all, Peter. It would drive me quite demented! I like my privacy and I prefer to know that someone has sought my company for pleasure rather than a sense of duty or charity.'

'I take your point, Penelope, but there may be times when you will need my assistance which may not occur to me. I would like to think that you will have no hesitation in asking for help.'

'Thank you, Peter. I will remember that.' There was still a certain reserve in her voice and Peter realised at once that she would probably find it difficult to ask him for help. He wondered how much of this was due to his own behaviour and how much to pride and—well, to put it bluntly, sheer cussedness!

Wisely he dropped the subject, resolving to leave it to time. 'Shall we start our tour in the breakfast parlour, then, Penelope? Are you hungry?'

'Yes, please, Peter.'

He moved to her side, wondering how the dog would react, but Gelert, sensing no alarm on the part of his mistress, merely looked at him indifferently. 'Will you take my arm, Penelope?' Wordlessly she held out her hand. He kissed it and tucked it through his arm to lead her out. Penelope wondered at the odd thrill that ran through her at the touch of his lips.

After breakfast Peter began their tour of the house. After careful thought he had decided to concentrate on making sure she could find her way about. The servants had been warned that nothing must be left lying about and nothing moved without warning their mistress.

He told her this as they entered the study. 'Thank you, my lord—I mean, Peter. But they needn't worry too much. Gelert would never let me fall over anything. He has been my eyes for the last four years. It would have been much harder without him. As it is I have been able to retain some independence of movement.'

Peter stopped in surprise. 'You were not always blind, then?'

'Oh, no. It was an accident. Geoffrey let off a gun near my horse one day. When I was thrown off my head hit a tree root. I was unconscious for days. When I did come to I had the most dreadful headache and couldn't see. I can distinguish light from dark a bit, and I notice movement, but that's about it.'

Peter said nothing but his mind was relieved of one worry. Repudiating the marriage was out of the question, but he had been concerned about the possibility of his wife passing on her affliction to a child. At least now he had only to consider the best way of wooing the girl so that he could start a family.

Despite his discretion on this subject, Penelope sensed his slight change of mood and was quick to realise the reason. 'Peter, it was bad enough that we didn't tell you about Phoebe, or that I was blind, but I would never have married anyone if there had been the slightest possibility of passing my blindness on to a child. Please, you must believe that.'

Peter stopped dead, staring at his wife, utterly amazed. 'How the devil did you know what I was thinking?' he demanded at last.

'I...I don't know, your voice or something. I can do it with Phoebe all the time, because we are so close. I always know when something is wrong and she always knows about me.'

Peter looked at his bride in consternation. 'I shall have to behave myself if you are going to read my mind like that. Even my thoughts will have to mend their manners!' Certainly some of his thoughts would have to be put firmly to the back of his mind for a while. Looking at Penelope, he realised just how hard it was going to be stopping himself from making love to her. The memory of the softness of her lips in church and putting her to bed the previous night was vivid. He had restrained himself nobly on that occasion, but hoped to God that the situation would not arise again.

Honesty compelled him to admit that the chances of

him showing a similar level of self-discipline another time were about zero! The delicate curves of his wife's body would have been a constant temptation under any circumstances, but to know that he had the right to take her and make love to her made his decision to wait doubly hard. Hoping devoutly that she couldn't sense what he was thinking now, he concentrated on his description of the study. It was a very masculine room, furnished with comfortable leather chairs, a large desk and walls lined with books. All the Frobishers had enjoyed collecting books, and this library was justly famous for its collection of seventeenth century manuscripts of poetry.

Penelope, listening to her husband, was perfectly aware that something was bothering him, but this was one subject on which she could not possibly understand his thoughts. With no experience of love it did not occur to her that she could be the object of his desire. She supposed that he would tell her when he wanted to consummate the marriage, which made her a little nervous. Would he just come to her room one night and get into bed with her? Of course, Phoebe had thought it was wonderful. But then Phoebe and Richard were in love; surely that made a difference. Still, even Mama had said she would probably enjoy that part of married life. Suddenly she realised that she had not heard a word Peter had said for several minutes and dragged her mind back to the study.

After the study came the State Dining Room followed by the Small Dining Room, which were both on the ground floor, after which they descended to the kitchens where Penelope was introduced to the French cook, François, and his minions. François excelled himself in his Gallic address, assuring his new mistress that he would be inspired by her presence to create new dishes for her delectation. Penelope responded delightfully, thought Peter, quite unaware that his feelings for his wife were not at all along the lines he had intended.

Finally they repaired to the Morning Room, where a light meal had been laid out. Over this Darleston told his wife a great deal about the history of the house and his family. The Earldom went back to the Restoration of King Charles II. The then Viscount Darleston had fought bravely for his King and had been duly rewarded upon his return from exile. The house itself had been built in the following century, after the Elizabethan manor house burned down. Penelope could hear the passion in Peter's voice as he told her all this. She could understand his pride in the title and his reluctance to permit it to go to one who would soil its lustre. Jack Frobisher, she thought, was the last man Darleston would wish to have to acknowledge as his heir!

In the afternoon Peter took her back over the part of the house he had shown her in the morning and was amazed to realise that she could find her way about without much difficulty. She laughed at his surprise, saying only that she had become very quick to remember things like that. 'You are quite incredible, my dear,' he insisted. 'Why, George got lost between his bedroom and the dining room the first time he stayed here!'

'You and George are very close, are you not?'

'Yes, we fought together under Wellington in the Peninsula, and at Waterloo. Both of us came back here to recover after we were wounded at Waterloo. George's parents are dead, his sister was close to her confinement and I had no desire to be alone at that point—' He broke off, not wanting to mention his first wife's disastrous flight with her lover when she'd heard of his return from war.

Penelope heard the bitterness in his voice so she changed the subject adroitly. 'Did you admire Wellington very much? Papa used to read all the newspaper reports aloud to us for my sake. I always felt that Wellington sounded very aloof and unapproachable. Did that make it hard to serve under him?'

'Not at all,' answered Peter. 'We knew he was out to get the job done and that he would do it. Also I assure you, my dear, that you will not find him in the least unapproachable when you meet him, as you are bound to do!' Peter knew quite well that his erstwhile commander would be fully appreciative of the charms of the new Lady Darleston.

They moved out into the garden together with Gelert. Peter was fascinated to see how the great dog guided his mistress, protecting her from any mishaps. He always stopped before steps, pushed her to the centre of any doorway and guided her safely around obstacles. 'Did you train Gelert on purpose, Penelope?'

'Not really. We hoped for a while that my sight would return, or at least improve, but it didn't. Gelert was about a year old then. Papa gave him to Phoebe and me when he was a puppy and we shared him, but after the accident he spent more time with me and gradually began guiding me about. I couldn't do without him now.'

Peter took her to the herb garden, where an almost tangible cloud of fragrance greeted them. He said, laughing, 'I've no idea what they are all called, but I know which ones smell the loveliest.' To his surprise Penelope could identify most of them by their scent or texture, and it was obvious that she took a great deal of pleasure in the garden.

Peter began to realise that his wife's other senses appeared to be highly developed. If he stepped away she had no trouble locating him from the sound of his voice. He also began to have an inkling of the extent of her independence and pride. She did not cling to him nervously in the new environment she faced, but rather stepped out boldly into the unknown with a courage that left him wondering how he would acquit himself under a similar affliction.

'Do you ever long for your sight?' he asked abruptly as they left the herb garden to wander through the shrubbery.

She hesitated before answering, 'Yes. Very often, when I meet new people, but I try to avoid that because they annoy me by being pitying and patronising.'

'Was that why you didn't come out with Phoebe?'

'Yes, meeting lots of people all at once is terribly confusing. I can't see them and the headaches come back because I get scared of the crowd. My parents took me to a local Hunt Ball but it was awful. You see, I can't dance any of the figured dances, only the waltz. None of the men wanted to dance with me, so Phoebe pretended to be me for half an hour and I had some of her waltzes!'

Peter roared with laughter. 'So I wasn't the first victim after all! Was that your idea, to dance for your sister?'

'Goodness, no! Phoebe dared me to do it, but Mama was very cross with us and I didn't really enjoy the ball, so I refused to go to any more. I suppose it was cowardly but it seemed much easier to stay at home.'

Peter thought he detected a note of sadness in her voice, but her face told him nothing. 'Do you find it frustrating not knowing what I look like?' he asked unexpectedly.

'But I do know! Phoebe described you in great detail after our first meeting. Tall, about six foot two, with black hair, brown eyes and an olive complexion. You have a fine figure and are very handsome, according to her.'

Peter chuckled at the unmistakable mischief in Penelope's voice. The chit was teasing him! Thank God his behaviour hadn't frightened her off.

When they stopped to sit on a garden bench Penelope said shyly, 'Perhaps when we are…are a little better acquainted, you would permit me to…to touch your face. You s…see that way I can *feel* what you look like.'

The request startled Peter. He had seen how she had touched a rose and explored its petals. The idea that those gentle, soft hands might touch him in the same way was very pleasant.

She was facing him with that odd listening look on her face, but his silence disconcerted her and she flushed, saying, 'I'm sorry, I didn't mean to offend you.'

'You have not offended me at all,' he assured her, adding, 'Would you like to do it now, while we are alone?' His voice told her that he was perfectly sincere, so she lifted her hands to his face, gently tracing the strong line of his jaw and chin. The nose was finely modelled, his cheekbones high, his mouth warm and firm. His hair curled crisply and she liked its texture. In fact she liked what she found very much.

Peter sat utterly still as her hands moved over his face. It was very like a caress, and he found himself deeply aroused, although he was aware she had not intended it thus. Her face was turned up to his as she concentrated, her dark red hair curling around her brow, her lips slightly parted. Finally Peter could deny himself no longer. Very gently, so as not to scare her, he slipped one arm about her waist to draw her nearer. Those soft fingers quivered, were still, and her listening look intensified.

Not taking his eyes from her face he said huskily, 'May I join in, Penny?' The diminutive disarmed her and she nodded mutely, not trusting her voice.

He raised his free hand to her face and stroked her cheek lightly, enjoying its soft smoothness. The column of her white throat was equally soft. He could feel her trembling in his arms yet she did not try to draw away from his embrace. His fingers passed gently over her tender mouth and with a groan of pleasure he bent his head to cover her lips with his own. This time Penelope made no attempt to struggle, rather she melted against him, returning his kisses as best she could. From the moment he had put his arm about her waist she had known he would kiss her and had schooled herself not to draw back, but the sensations his mouth aroused took her completely by surprise. Her heart was pounding erratically, something seemed to have happened to her breath, and she was conscious of a spreading weakness in her body.

As for Peter, he found his wife's innocent response to his advances a revealing experience. The relationship he had enjoyed with Lady Caroline and other even less respectable partners since his first wife's defection; had not prepared him for the protective instinct aroused by Penelope's timid return of his embrace. Her mouth was unbelievably sweet. He was ashamed when he recalled how brutally he had taken it the previous day. Now his mouth moved gently yet passionately over hers as his arm tightened around her waist. The other hand slid over the curve of her breast under the muslin gown and he felt her gasp in surprise. Reluctantly he released her. He wanted to bed her, most certainly, but for her sake he did not want to rush his fences.

'Thank you, Penelope. I...I...think we should return to the house,' he said. His voice betrayed his confusion.

Dear God, he wanted her so much. It would be torture to know she was asleep in the bedroom next to his, that all he had to do was walk through the connecting door and get into her bed. He remembered how lovely he had thought her when he'd put her to bed last night, still with the tears on her cheeks. It had been impossible to resist the temptation to caress one of those delicate white breasts, and she had smiled so tenderly in her sleep!

Penelope rose slowly to her feet, rather surprised to discover that her legs would still obey her commands. She did not know what to say. His kiss had left her shaken physically and with her emotions in a whirl. The feelings he had aroused in her were beyond her comprehension. Her gasp when he touched her breast had been one of pleasure, and she wondered if her response had disgusted him. On the whole she thought not, he had released her very gently, not at all as though he were angry.

Peter's thoughts were also in turmoil, but of a different kind. A nasty suspicious voice in his mind was warning him to watch his step, that he was becoming interested in his wife as a person, perhaps even as a lover. Better not to care, just be civilised, keep a distance. Remember Melissa. You don't want to make the same mistake twice. But she's not like Melissa, he argued. Melissa had been a virgin, certainly, but she had not been the total innocent this girl was. The nagging doubts persisted. Perhaps it would be better to keep some emotional distance between them.

By the time they reached the house Penelope was aware of Peter's change of attitude. His manner towards her was still friendly but he made no attempt to win her confidences, merely speaking of the route they were taking back to the house. She was a little saddened by this, assuming that somehow she had caused his withdrawal, and decided firmly that she had better not become too attached to her incalculable husband!

Chapter Seven

A month later Darleston sat in his sunny breakfast parlour consuming a plate of ham and eggs, wondering if he would see his wife at breakfast or indeed at all that day! In the time since their wedding the couple had made very little progress in their relationship. Peter acknowledged to himself that this was his fault.

For perhaps a week Penelope had tried very hard to get to know him and he had politely rebuffed her every time. Then she had given up and had appeared to avoid his company. After a week of being effectually ignored, Peter had begun to feel piqued and had made tentative advances, hoping to mend the breach.

Penelope it seemed, had other ideas. She had made it quite clear that she had plenty to do and was not pining for his company! She spent a great deal of time with his housekeeper, learning the ways of the house, and even more time in the drawing room, playing the piano. He had frequently paused outside the door to enjoy the music, knowing from experience that if he went in she would not continue past the end of the movement.

'Good morning, Penelope,' said Peter now, looking up

from his letters as his wife entered the breakfast parlour with Gelert. 'Did you sleep well?'

'Very well, thank you, Peter.' answered Penelope.

Peter rose to his feet to help her to a chair and bestowed a pat upon Gelert, who had completely accepted him as a friend. 'Would you like a cup of tea?'

'Yes, please.'

He poured one for her, saying as he passed it to her, 'There you are, my dear. Are you very busy today? I thought we might go for a drive together.'

'That is very kind of you, Peter, but I will be in the stillroom for much of the day. Perhaps another time.'

'As you please.'

Having seen that Penelope had everything she needed, Peter continued reading his correspondence, feeling that he had perhaps been too thorough in avoiding any emotional involvement with his wife! Despite the fact that she generally used his Christian name in private, the polite formality of her manner always made it *sound* as though she were calling him my lord.

To make matters worse for Peter, he was having a great deal of difficulty remaining on his side of the door which connected their rooms. He was not sleeping particularly well, and when he did sleep he was disturbed by dreams which made it even harder not to be able to go through that door. He had not attempted to kiss her since that first day in the garden and the memory of her response haunted him.

It was difficult to believe that the remote girl on the other side of the table had responded so sweetly to his embrace. She seemed as distant and cool as the moon. Peter gazed at her in frustration as she sat in the sunlight from the window, munching a scone and sipping her tea. Her dark red hair showed gleams of copper in the light and there was a slight tinge of pink in her usually pale cheeks.

Penelope was perfectly aware of Peter's scrutiny, as she always was. It was not distaste for his company that made her avoid him, but a profound distrust of her own feelings. She was uncomfortably aware it would be only too easy to fall in love with her husband. Obviously that was the last thing he wanted. He had made no further attempt to kiss her, or to do anything else a marriage should involve, so she must assume that either he was not attracted to her or that she had disgusted him. Therefore it would be most unwise to indulge in any affection for him. She continued to sip her tea, conscious of her husband's regard but utterly unconscious of the fact that he was jealous of the teacup.

'I have received a letter from George Carstares. Would you object if he came to stay, Penelope?'

'Not at all, Peter. I should like to know your friends. When will he arrive?'

'I shall write telling him to come when he likes, which means he will come as soon as he receives my reply, in all probability.'

'Then I shall inform Mrs Bates and ask her to have a room made ready for him at once. I am glad you will have some company.' Having finished her breakfast, Penelope arose. 'If you will excuse me, Peter, I will go about my day now.'

'A moment please, Penelope, if you would not mind.' Peter had made up his mind swiftly; he must try to breach the gap between them.

She turned towards him with a questioning look on her face, said, 'Very well, my lord,' and sat down again.

He winced at the chilling formality of her response, which made it quite clear she waited from duty, not inclination. For a moment he hesitated, before saying, 'I would very much like you to come for that drive with me, my dear. We seem to see very little of each other and I grudge your company to the stillroom and Mrs Bates. Besides, Gelert will enjoy the run!' Gelert, hearing his name coupled with the word 'run', uttered an enthusiastic bark and wagged his tail.

'You really want me to come out with you?' Penelope was surprised. Always before he had accepted her refusals with equanimity, which had reinforced her belief that he preferred it that way and merely requested her company out of duty.

'Yes, I do want your company, Penelope. I think it is time you met some of my tenants. As my wife that is one your duties,' he said, wondering just how he should go about convincing her that it was time she fulfilled all her wifely duties.

'If that is your wish, Peter, of course I will accompany you. When do you wish to set off?'

'I should finish reading my letters and reply to some of them… an hour from now shall we say?' answered Peter, glancing idly at the rest of his letters.

One of them caught his attention. 'Oh, here is a letter for you, Penelope, from your mother!'

'From Mama? Please read it to me, Peter!' said Penelope in unabashed delight.

'Read it to you?' It had not occurred to Peter that he would have to read his wife's correspondence.

Misunderstanding his exclamation, Penelope blushed. 'I beg your pardon, my lord. I will ask Ellen to read it for me if you are too busy.' She went to Peter's side and held out her hand for the letter.

Realising that he had unintentionally hurt her, Peter ignored her outstretched hand and slipped his arm about her waist. 'Silly child, of course I'm not too busy! It was just that I had not really thought about how you were to read your letter. Come, sit down again and I'll read it for you at once.' Before she could protest he had pulled her onto his lap. 'There! Comfortable? I do hope your mama hasn't written anything too personal! What should I do if she has, my dear?'

Stunned to find herself sitting in her husband's lap, with his arm around her waist, Penelope was taken off her guard and answered without thinking, 'Don't listen, of course!' Peter burst out laughing.

'I suppose I could try that, or shutting my eyes might help!' He opened the letter and began to read aloud.

'"Dear Penny, Thank you for your note letting us know you are well—" Did you write, Penelope?' Peter was very surprised.

'Yes, just a short note to say I was well. I can write if I am very careful and don't rush. Ellen addressed it for me. I asked her to post it when she went to the village. Should I not have done so?'

'You most certainly should not!' said Peter. 'Why didn't you get a frank from me, and leave it on the table in the hall, you silly girl? Your mother will think I won't let you write to her!'

Penelope blinked. 'A frank! Oh, dear, I forgot you could give me one. I hope she didn't think that you are a sort of Bluebeard! Perhaps I'd better write again.'

'I think you should, or I'll have that ferocious brother-in-law of yours down upon me!' teased Peter. 'Now, where was I? Ah, yes. "Could his lordship not give you a frank?"—see! "Or did you merely forget that he could do so? Sarah gives it as her opinion that Darleston has you locked in a dungeon and that you were forced to write the letter. I think it was a mistake permitting her to read *The Mysteries of Udolpho* and Richard has apologised for giving it to her. I suggested that if Darleston had wished to behave in such a dastardly fashion he probably would have franked the letter and made you write more, but she informed us that criminals always make one fatal error and that this is his. She was more convinced by Richard's comment that Darleston would have chosen a really wealthy victim like Emily if he'd wanted to behave like Montoni!'''

Peter had to stop reading at this point, to regain some control over his voice. 'Good God, what an imagination! Penelope, you are to write immediately! I intended to offer my services as your amanuensis, but no doubt that will afford your sister fresh grounds for suspicion. Stop laughing, girl, this is my reputation at stake!'

Penelope tried to contain her mirth, but failed totally. Peter was delighted to see her quiet reserve shattered and continued with the letter.

Phoebe and Richard are very well. They have spent a great deal of time with us and are very happy but I believe Phoebe is writing to you, so I won't spoil any of her news.

Ariadne has had her foal and it is a filly. Richard thinks she is very promising!

Sarah sends her love and she is also writing, although I believe she is uncertain whether to address a letter of encouragement to you, Penny, or threats to Darleston. She is consoling herself with the thought that Gelert will probably take the first opportunity of dealing with the situation!

I am glad Darleston was not out of reason cross about the affair. You must now show yourself to be equally generous. Be a good girl, Penny darling, and a kind and loving wife.

Your Devoted Mama.

Peter was silent for a moment after finishing the letter. Penelope was leaning confidingly against him, smiling tenderly at her own thoughts. He studied her delicate profile, delighting in her proximity. Gently he reached up to stroke her cheek, marvelling at its softness. Startled out of her thoughts, she turned to him enquiringly. He gave her a hug and said, 'Perhaps we should write to your family this evening to allay the fears your little sister entertains.'

Unable to resist the temptation to tease him, Penelope said, 'Goodness no! She'll enjoy it far more if we fuel her suspicions. It will be a very good idea for you to write the letter and me merely to sign it! Think what a thrill for her to be the heroine and to dream of rescuing me from your clutches!'

'Thanks very much. My clutches don't seem to be that unbearable to you!' said Peter in amusement. 'If we do that she will probably disguise herself as a boy and run away to rescue you. I shall give her a copy of *Northanger Abbey* at the first opportunity!'

'What's that about?' asked Penelope curiously.

'A young lady who reads too many sensational novels, *The Mysteries of Udolpho* in particular, and allows too free a rein to her fancies! It was written by the same woman who wrote *Pride and Prejudice* and *Mansfield Park*. Do you know them?'

'Mama read *Pride and Prejudice* aloud to us. We all liked it.'

'Good! I shall recommend *Northanger Abbey* with a clear conscience.' He stood up and set Penelope gently on her feet. 'Come along, Penelope. If we are to go for our drive I had better finish the rest of these letters and write to George at least. That is, if you really don't mind him visiting us. Shall we invite Sarah later on as well— just to lull her suspicions of course!'

Penelope's face plainly mirrored her delight. 'Could we. Peter? I mean, I'm sure she doesn't really believe you are a villain, but I should like to see her.'

'Of course you may invite her,' said Peter, happy to have hit on such a simple way of pleasing her. Surely now they would go on better than they had been doing. He held the door open for her and watched her departure with Gelert, an odd smile on his face. Slowly he walked to the study, still chuckling at the letter Penelope had received.

Penelope came to seek him out an hour later, ready to go for their drive. She had spent a great deal of time discussing her bonnet with Ellen and was feeling particularly frustrated that she could not judge the effect for herself. She knocked at the study door shyly, amazed at the slight feeling of breathlessness that took hold of her as she heard his deep voice. 'Come in, Penelope.'

Peter looked up from his desk as she entered and smiled. 'Ready, my dear? My letters are finished, so we shall go?' He added, 'You look charming in that bonnet.' She did. The bonnet framed her face and the dark green ribbons that were tied under her chin emphasised the fairness of her complexion.

Penelope did not really know how to respond to the compliment. She wondered why he was being friendly again and how long it would last. 'Thank you,' she said at last, feeling that she must say something.

Peter led her out to the waiting phaeton and lifted her up into it effortlessly. Penelope trembled as she felt his hands encircle her waist. She told herself fiercely to stop being silly. After all he was only lifting her into a carriage!

Peter told himself exactly the same thing, and reminded himself that an open carriage, especially with a groom up behind, was not a good place to make love to a girl, even if she was your wife.

He leapt up into the vehicle, trying very hard not to think about the delicious curve of Penelope's waist, or how she had sat in his lap while he read her letter. It would be positively dangerous to dwell on such thoughts while driving a high-couraged pair like his matched greys!

The drive was very pleasant. They called at several farms on the estate, and while Peter discussed the crops and harvest with the farmers Penelope was entertained by their wives. She discovered that Peter was looked up to as a good landlord and that he was genuinely concerned with the welfare of his tenants. The last farm they visited was particularly interesting.

'We may not be able to stay long here, Penelope,' said Peter. 'Jewkes got married last year and his wife is expecting their first baby very soon. As a matter of fact she is Ellen's sister!'

'Peter, if only you'd told me I could have brought a note from Ellen,' said Penelope.

'I'm sorry, dear, I didn't think. But at least you may take a message back,' he apologised.

Jewkes was in the farmyard when they arrived and was extremely proud that the Earl had brought his new Countess to be introduced. 'Proud to meet ye, milady. My Martha's in the 'ouse. Come y' in to meet 'er. She'd be that sorry to miss ye! Take my arm, milady. Ellen tells us ye're blind but once ye know the way ye never forget!'

'I'll wait with the horses, Tom, and not intrude on Martha,' said Peter.

'Why, she'd not think it a trouble, milord!' expostulated Jewkes, but Peter insisted, thinking that the two women would talk more easily without him.

Tom Jewkes rejoined him a moment later. 'Goin' along like winkin', they are! Cheers Martha up to have a visitor, not that she's gloomy, but we'll both be glad when it's all over.'

'Hoping for a fine lusty son, are you, Tom?' asked Peter.

The farmer thought about it and said, 'Well, in a manner of speaking, yes. But bein' a farmer ye get so used to wantin' a heifer, it's hard to break the habit! And I'll tell ye summat, milord, I'll be glad whichever it is just so long as Martha's all right! And so will you be when it's your turn, if ye'll forgive my speakin' so bold!'

Peter gripped his shoulder and the conversation turned into agricultural topics.

Presently Penelope appeared at the kitchen door and Gelert, who had waited with Peter, bounded across the yard to her side. She placed her hand on his collar for him to guide her to Peter and Jewkes.

The latter was highly impressed. 'Ellen said as how ye had a dog to be guide ye, which I couldn't believe, but Martha says if a dog can herd sheep and cattle, why not guide a human?'

'He is very good at it,' said Peter. 'And now I think we should be getting back for our nuncheon and letting you get on with your work, Tom. We'll call again to see how Martha is going on. Mind you let us know if you need anything.'

'Oh, Mr Jewkes,' said Penelope. 'I told Martha that I would send Ellen over for a few days when she is…confined. Just send a message when you need her.'

The farmer flushed. 'Why, milady, I know Martha will be easier in her mind if she knows that. Thank ye.'

Penelope smiled and said, 'It's nothing, Mr Jewkes. I know I should like to have my sister with me, and so I thought Ellen had better come. Goodbye.'

Peter lifted her into the carriage and leapt up beside her. They drove off at a spanking trot, Peter negotiating the turn out of the yard with ease. 'That was kind of you, Penelope. I know how much you depend on Ellen.'

Penelope was silent for a moment, and then said, 'Martha is so glad to be having a child, but I thought she sounded a little scared. She didn't say much but I know she was glad when I said Ellen would be coming over.'

They drove on in silence for a mile, but it was not an awkward silence. Peter was thinking of his wife's generosity in volunteering to do without her maid. He realised guiltily that he had spent so little time with Penelope recently that she must be doubly dependent upon Ellen for company. Yet she never complained, although she had admitted that she found her blindness to be frustrating in company. But, no! It was not the actual blindness which had bothered her but people's reaction to it. What had she said? *They annoy me by being pitying and patronising…*

Almost without thinking, he asked her, 'Penelope, what frustrates you most about being blind?' She did not return an answer immediately and he said gently, 'I'm sorry. I didn't mean to pry. Forget it.'

'I'm not offended, Peter,' she said, laughing. 'It's just that there are so many things which frustrate me that I didn't really know where to start!'

'But you never say anything!' he said in surprise.

'Well, what good would it do?' she answered. 'I suppose the thing I miss the most is reading. But even then my family were always happy to read aloud. Reading music too. My sisters used to help me to learn new pieces. Sometimes we would learn them together. One of them would practice and I would learn the piece by ear! They helped me to learn lots of poetry by heart too, so it's always there when I want it.'

Peter suddenly understood fully just what a leap of faith she had taken to marry a total stranger for the sake of her family. He felt a surge of tenderness for her, an urge to look after her. Transferring the reins to one hand, he slipped his arm around her shoulders and said, 'Well, I can't help you with new music, but I can certainly read aloud to you!'

'But I don't wish to make demands on you!' protested Penelope, trying to ignore the odd fluttering of her heart as she felt his hand caress her shoulder.

'My sweet, it is merely a fair return for all the pleasure your music gives me! I often listen outside the door,' he admitted with a smile. 'I love music, you know, Penelope.'

'I...I thought it would disturb you!' she said in surprise.

'The only thing that disturbs me is that you won't let me sit down in comfort to listen!' he said. 'I have to skulk around the door because you always stop if I come in, you silly child.' He gave her a light hug and returned his full attention to his horses. The last thing he wanted was to tip his wife into a ditch because he couldn't keep his hands off her!

Penelope did not know what to say. She could not understand his change of mood. Not that he was ever

unkind or rude. Simply distant, so that she hesitated to
approach him. Did he really wish to be friends now? Or
would he revert to his formal coolness? It was lovely
when he was being kind and approachable. Then she felt
that there was nothing she could not ask him. But be
careful, she warned herself. Just respond to as much as
he offers, when he offers it. It occurred to her that it
would be easier said than done to switch her feelings on
and off.

Falling in with her abstracted mood, Peter drove home
swiftly. He did not resent her silence, rather it was refreshing to drive out with a woman who did not feel
obliged to fill up every moment with chatter. He hoped
that he had managed to at least partially bridge the chasm
he had created.

'Gelert seems to have enjoyed his run,' said Peter, as
they walked into the Great Hall. 'We must take him out
more often, I think. Did you enjoy yourself my dear?'

'Yes, I did, thank you, Peter. Gelert is used to more
exercise. P…Papa and I used to drive out together.' The
slight hesitation told him how much the loss of her father
had hurt.

'You miss him very much, don't you?' asked Peter,
touched.

'Always. We were very close, you see. But I am glad
now that he died when he did. He would have been so
ashamed of what Geoffrey did.' She turned and faced
him. 'I have been meaning to apologise to you for his
behaviour, but I just didn't know how to bring the subject
up…'

'There is no need, Penelope. I was also at fault for not
calling a halt to that damned game of dice when I had
the chance. Don't give it another thought, I beg of you.'

Penelope went into her nuncheon feeling much easier

in her mind over the whole matter. Perhaps things were finally sorting themselves out, she thought hopefully.

The rest of the day passed peacefully. Penelope spent the afternoon in the stillroom, helping her housekeeper to sort out and dry herbs. Her mind drifted over the morning's drive and she wondered again why Peter had suddenly become friendly. Perhaps he was just moody, she thought. Then, as she relived the visit with Martha Jewkes, another possibility occurred to her. He wanted an heir, didn't he? Was all this kindness a ploy to get her into his bed willingly? She blushed at the idea, but the more she thought about it, the more likely it seemed.

Having reached that conclusion, she examined her own feelings. She had to admit to herself that she was fond of her husband, despite his recent coolness towards her. In fact, if she were honest with herself, she liked him very much. He was unfailingly polite to her, and the respect and liking she had observed in his tenants were indicative of a fine man. Finally she came to her physical reaction to him. When he touched her in any way she enjoyed it. The time he had kissed her in the garden she had not wanted him to stop. Why had he stopped? Should she not have kissed him back? Had she disgusted him? Perhaps he didn't find her attractive but felt he must do his duty and beget an heir!

She took extra care over her toilet that evening, asking Ellen to dress her in a gown of dark green silk which had arrived from London. Ellen had taken great pleasure in describing all the lovely new gowns which had been ordered. They all suited Penelope's colouring perfectly, setting off the glowing curls and the fairness of her complexion.

By the time she joined Peter for dinner Penelope was so nervous that she had withdrawn behind her barriers again. Peter noticed the change immediately and set himself to drawing her out once more. He teased her about the suspicions her brief letter had aroused, suggesting ways they could reply to Sarah's letter when it arrived. Gradually Penelope relaxed, forgetting her worries and simply enjoying her husband's company.

For his part Peter was more than content with his companion. His eyes dwelt appreciatively on her slim figure, not missing a single curve. The silk of her gown clung to every contour and he thought with pleasure of the softness of her body when he had lifted her into the carriage. Mellow candlelight caught highlights in the dark red hair, which seemed to glow with an inner fire. The memory of the sweetness of her mouth was a constant temptation, but he controlled himself nobly. Surely it could not have been quite so yielding, so responsive!

After dinner they sat in the drawing room and Penelope played the piano for him. She played with a sensitive touch and Peter listened with real pleasure. His bride never ceased to amaze him with the things she could do for herself, despite her blindness.

By the time she had played through a Haydn sonata he had come to a decision. He could wait no longer; he wanted her so much it hurt. Surely after a month, he told himself, she would not mind! After all, he had warned her that he wanted an heir.

Penelope finished the sonata and stood to close the piano. Peter went to help her. Standing so close to her was too much for his self-control. His hand caught her wrist and he pulled her gently but inexorably into his arms. Startled, Penelope froze, instinctively turning her face up to his.

Peter felt her stiffen. His conscience told him to release her, but the sensation caused by holding her against him made short work of this gentlemanly impulse and he pressed his lips firmly upon hers. One hand slid up her back while the other caressed her throat and cheek. For a moment Penelope fought the urge to respond, but when that wandering hand moved to stroke her breast she gave an involuntary moan of pleasure and yielded to his embrace, slipping her arms around his neck to cling to him.

Peter felt her response and tightened his arm to support her. Her lips, so incredibly tender and soft under his, parted slightly and, unable to resist the temptation, Peter slid his tongue into her mouth. He groaned as he fully tasted her sweetness. Dear God, he thought wildly, I could take her right here on the floor!

His hand slipped into the bodice of her gown and Penelope thought for a moment that the world had turned upside down. Her whole body trembled and she wondered if she were about to faint. The straying fingers in her bodice teased and caressed the tender flesh, his mouth possessed hers completely.

He released her mouth, only to murmur against her cheek, 'Penny, I cannot wait much longer. I want you in my bed. Do you understand?' He took her mouth again, gently at first, then more insistently as his desire for her took control. Scarcely knowing what he was doing, he lifted her in his arms and carried her effortlessly back to the sofa. He sat down with his wife nestled in his lap to continue his assault on her already weakened defences. Again his hand slid into her bodice and he stroked the velvety flesh as his mouth moved over her throat, making her shiver in delight.

Penelope was lost on a sea of sensation; his hands and mouth were igniting a blaze which threatened to consume her utterly. She stroked his face and returned his kisses shyly, unsure of herself. Peter felt a surge of tender affection. She was so sweet and lovable in her innocence, he thought. Then, realising that he was about to lose control of his emotions completely, he suddenly released her, saying harshly, 'Penelope, I think you should go up to bed now. If you do not I cannot be responsible.' His hands were shaking as he put her from him and stood up. He told himself that he didn't want to rush her, but in truth his own feelings were frightening.

Penelope couldn't believe her ears. What had she done wrong? Confused by Peter's rejection, she stood up slowly and moved to the bell pull. She heard Peter cross swiftly to the door, heard it open and slam as he left. Her body still trembled from his caresses. She yearned for more. Why had he left? He had said he wanted her. Surely he hadn't thought that she was unwilling! Unable to answer her own questions, she pulled the bell and waited for Meadows.

He came almost immediately. 'Meadows, please send Ellen to me in my room. I am ready to retire for the night.'

'Yes, milady.'

Slowly, sadly she went out of the room with Gelert and made her way through the house to her bed-chamber. She wondered where Peter had gone. Probably the study, she thought. It was his refuge and she never sought him out there.

When Ellen came she found her mistress abstracted, even depressed. This was surprising; Lady Darleston was generally very cheerful. Tonight she was not at all inclined to talk, indeed she seemed close to tears. Ellen had been told already that she would be going to stay with her sister and was very grateful to her mistress for thinking of this. She chattered gaily as she brushed Penelope's hair and readied her for bed. Perhaps the mistress had disagreed with the master over some matter, she thought as she put away clothes.

'Goodnight, milady. Come along, Gelert,' said Ellen as she prepared to leave. She noticed that the connecting door was open and wondered if she should shut it. No, if the mistress and master had argued it would be better to leave it open. You couldn't make up through a shut door!

Penelope lay in her great bed, feeling frustrated and depressed. She was quite sure she had annoyed Peter by responding to his advances so willingly. Well, then, next time he kissed her, she wouldn't respond. At least, not if she could help it! She was obliged to admit to herself that it might be very difficult not to respond to her husband's sensuous embrace. His mouth and hands were so very persuasive, she thought as she drifted off to sleep. Perhaps she could simply pretend not to enjoy his advances!

Coming up to bed an hour later, Peter stood at the open connecting door to gaze at his sleeping wife. He too was feeling frustrated, and the confused look of pain on Penelope's face when he thrust her away refused to be banished from his mind. Why, he asked himself, couldn't he initiate a physical relationship with his wife without all these unwelcome emotions creeping in? Perhaps it would be safer not to take her to bed if it was going to stir up feelings best forgotten? But he had to take her to bed if he wanted an heir! Blast it all, why did she have to be so sweet, so damned responsive and yielding? He didn't want to care for the girl. He liked her very much; she was a charming companion. That was all he wanted to feel!

Chapter Eight

Penelope entered the breakfast parlour the next morning determined to try and recapture the friendliness of the previous day. She had taken particular care with her choice of gown, selecting a dark blue morning dress which Ellen and the housekeeper assured her was most becoming. Her efforts were not entirely wasted.

Peter looked up as she entered and caught his breath. The deep blue emphasised the fairness of her complexion. Her hair was caught at the nape of her neck with a wide blue bow and lay carelessly over one shoulder, the burnished curls blazing against the dark fabric. An affectionate smile hovered around the delicately cut lips. He remembered how they had yielded to his demands the evening before…soft, trembling… Hell and damnation! He wouldn't think of it! He would not be undone by a pretty face again!

'Good morning, Peter.'

'My lady.' He rose and pulled out a chair for her. 'I trust you slept well?'

'Er…yes,' she lied gallantly. In truth she had not slept well at all. Nervously she seated herself. The formality of her husband's greeting chilled her. His tone was simply arctic.

'Would you like a cup of tea?'

'Thank you, my lord.'

He poured it and passed it to her, trying to ignore his conscience, which told him that he was behaving badly. He retired into his newspaper.

Penelope tried again. 'I did enjoy the drive yesterday, Peter. If you are going again, may I come?'

'I will be going on horseback today. It will waste less time.'

He looked into her face. For one fleeting instant he thought he saw her mouth tremble, but then an expression of cold indifference settled over her face. 'I beg your pardon, my lord.' She would not try again; his rejection hurt too much and it was too much like begging. Next time he invited her out he could go to the devil!

The following hour found Penelope in a restless mood, longing to go out. She tried to concentrate on her music but found the charms of Handel were nothing compared to the prospect of exercise. A ride would have been enjoyable, even on the inevitable leading rein. She told herself firmly that it was merely for Gelert's sake that she wanted to escape from the house. Innate honesty forced her to admit to herself that she had wanted to spend time with her husband.

The memory of his passionate kisses the previous night had disturbed her sleep. He had been so gentle, yet demanding. He had even said that he wanted her! Her fingers slowed on the keys as she dwelt on the memory. What had she done wrong? She longed for the courage to ask him, but his greeting at breakfast had been so distant and icy. A waste of time! What on earth was wrong with the man? One moment he behaved as though he liked her, the next as though she were a nuisance.

A rebellious thought crept into her mind. Why should she not go out? After all, she did not have to wait on Peter's pleasure for her entertainment! One of the grooms could just as easily escort her! Her decision made, she closed the piano, and went to change.

Ellen was predictably horrified. 'Riding? But, milady, what will the master say?'

'The master,' said Penelope between her teeth, 'may go to the devil! Please just find my riding habit.'

Ellen did as she was bid, reflecting that her mistress surely couldn't come to much harm on a leading rein. The head groom, Johnson, was very reliable. But what the master was going to say she hardly dared to think!

The master, having spent a busy morning visiting tenants and discussing improvements to his estate and crops for the coming winter, was startled to say the least at the sight which met his eyes as he rode homewards across the park. His wife, atop his favourite retired hunter, with his head groom and her dog in attendance, was cantering off goodness knew where!

Good God, what the hell did Johnson think he was up to? Swearing under his breath, Peter galloped his mare over to intercept them.

Hearing the hoofbeats, Johnson turned around and immediately said, 'We'd best stop a moment, your ladyship. The master is back and he's coming this way.'

Penelope bit back the very unladylike rejoinder which rose to her lips and merely said, 'Very well. Perhaps his lordship wishes to join us.'

Observing the grim look upon the Earl's face, Johnson could think of nothing less likely. Gloomily he wondered just why he had let his mistress cajole him into this foolishness and whether the master would give him a reference or not.

Penelope on the other hand was quite calm. She was determined to give as good as she got. After all, he had not told her that she might not ride any of his horses! It occurred to her that Johnson might be in a certain amount of trouble, however.

'Don't worry, Johnson. It will be me he'll be annoyed with. I'll tell him you didn't like the idea,' she said encouragingly.

'I'd appreciate that, milady!'

Peter pulled the mare in beside his errant bride and her escort and glared at them.

'What the devil do you think you're doing?'

His head groom wilted at the outrage in his voice, but Penelope faced him squarely with her chin up and answered in dulcet tones, 'Riding, my lord. Do you care to join me? I understood you to be otherwise engaged this morning, but if you have finished your business early and would not be wasting your time of course you are most welcome.'

He stared at her and said angrily, 'I do not consider it safe for you to be on horseback, my lady. You will please oblige me by returning to the stables at once. And as for you, Johnson, you must be out of your mind!'

Penelope sniffed disdainfully. 'My lord, I have been riding since I was a little girl. If my parents saw no need for me to stop when I lost my eyesight, I can see no reason for you to concern yourself with my safety. Johnson merely obeyed my orders in saddling a suitable horse and accompanying me. You had given no contrary orders, so you can scarcely blame him.'

Unable to think of a single answer which would not shock his servant, Peter was at a loss for a moment. Then he said curtly, 'Change horses with me, Johnson. Griselda is too lively to lead another horse from. I will take your mistress for a ride.' He suited the action to the word and dismounted.

Johnson obeyed, and gave the reins of his quiet hack to the Earl, who vaulted effortlessly into the saddle. He took the leading rein and said, 'You may return to the stables, Johnson.' Then, seeing the woebegone look on the man's face, 'Oh, for heaven's sake man! You can't imagine that I'd sack you for obeying orders!'

'Yes, sir! I mean, no, sir. Thank you, sir!' Johnson mounted and set off, leaving the Earl and his unrepentant Countess confronting one another.

Peter drew a deep breath and said, 'Shall we go, my lady?'

'Certainly, my lord.'

Peter pressed his mount into a trot, observing that his bride sat the old hunter with easy confidence.

'In future, Lady Darleston, I would appreciate it if you checked with me before setting my household by the ears!' The fury in his quiet voice was unmistakable. Inwardly she quaked but lifted her chin even higher, facing him defiantly.

'Indeed, my lord? I cannot conceive what concern it is of yours how I choose to spend my time, always provided I do not waste yours, of course!' she replied.

'You are my wife! Of course I am concerned with your safety!' he said furiously.

'Oh. I'm afraid that didn't occur to me, my lord. I was not aware that you had any interest whatsoever.'

Her air of calm detachment galled him. Damn it, the impertinent chit had as good as told him to mind his own business! Despite his anger he had to acknowledge that her seat on a horse was magnificent. She rode so well that he could understand her reluctance to give up after her accident. He decided that there was nothing to be gained in arguing the point. Obviously she was quite capable of controlling a horse and he was making a fool of himself.

'Well, you are obviously able to handle a horse. As long as you ride with either myself or Johnson you should be safe enough. Believe it or not, I do take an interest in your well-being!'

'How kind of you, my lord. However, I beg that you will not concern yourself with me. I shall be more than happy to ride out with Johnson. You must have a great deal of estate business to occupy your time.' Her voice spoke volumes of indifference she was far from feeling. The thought that he would offer to spend time with her as an unwelcome duty stung her pride unbearably.

Peter immediately realised that he had offended her deeply. He changed the subject at once. 'How do you find Nero's paces, Penelope?'

'Very comfortable, my lord.'

He winced at the formality of her reply but forbore to comment upon it. After all, he had started it!

She continued, 'Johnson informed me that Nero is practically retired but is the most reliable mount in the stables.'

'He certainly is,' said Peter with a fond glance at his old friend. 'I rode him at Waterloo. But for him and George Carstares I should have been killed.' He was silent for a moment, reliving the battle, lost in a haze of smoke, the roar of guns and the screams of dying men and horses. He shook his head to dispel the hellish vision.

'What happened, Peter?' Her voice was gentler, drew him back. Something in his voice had told her that the

horror of the things he had seen that day would live with
him for ever.

After a moment he went on. 'I was rallying my men.
They were in a square, holding their ground, but the
French columns kept coming. There were shots flying
everywhere but Nero was as steady as though he'd been
in his stable. Finally a musket ball hit me. All I remember
is a pain in my side and lying in the mud, staring up at
Nero's belly. The men said it was the strangest thing they
ever saw. Any other horse would have taken to his heels,
but he stood right over me until our men managed to beat
back the French. Otherwise I would have been trampled.'

'And Mr Carstares?' prompted Penelope softly.

'George saw it happen. When he could, he fought his
way to me and got me back on Nero, had one of the men
lead me to the rear.'

Penelope was silent for a moment. Perhaps his anger
had simply been at seeing her on a horse he must regard
as very special. Eventually she said, 'I'm sorry I rode
Nero without your permission, Peter. I can understand
that you would prefer no one else to ride him.'

'It's no matter Penelope,' said Peter in embarrassment.
'He needs to be ridden, and since he is getting on a bit
now I don't ride him as much as I used to. If you will
exercise him I shall be glad of it. I still ride him occasionally, for old time's sake, but otherwise please consider him as your own.'

'Thank you, Peter.'

They rode on in silence. When Peter spoke again he
had reverted to formal indifference. With a sigh Penelope
gave up trying to regain lost ground. If his lordship
wished for a relationship distinguished by cool propriety
he should have it!

* * *

The following morning Penelope arose and sent a message to the stables to find out when it would be convenient for Johnson to ride out with her. The answer came back before she was out of her bath that Johnson would be at her disposal whenever she wished.

Penelope thought about this carefully as she dried herself. 'Very well, Ellen. Please lay out my riding habit, and then when I am dressed you may send someone to tell Johnson that I shall be down directly after breakfast.'

'Yes, my lady.'

'And, Ellen.'

'My lady?'

'I think I will go for a good long walk after my ride and take something with me to eat. Just fruit, bread and cheese will do, and whatever you would like to eat if you will come with me.'

Ellen blinked in surprise. 'Don't you think you'll get tired, my lady?' Then, remembering her place, 'I mean, of course I'll come, but…'

Penelope set her jaw and said firmly, 'No buts. Just lay out my habit and think about what you'd like to eat for lunch!'

Ellen did as she was told and shortly, arrayed for riding, Penelope made her way down to the breakfast parlour. As she passed along the corridors and galleries she told herself firmly that she would *not*, absolutely would *not* give her husband the slightest reason to think she cared about his attitude towards her. If he felt like being friendly, or even amorous, she would simply be polite. Constant rejections when she overstepped some invisible boundary were too hurtful.

It did not occur to her that Peter was the one who kept on stepping over the emotional boundaries which he had set for their relationship.

Peter rose to his feet at her entrance and laid down his morning paper. 'Good morning, Penelope. Would you care for a cup of tea?'

'Thank you, my lord, that would be lovely.' She congratulated herself silently on the cool, but polite tone of her voice.

It was on the tip of Peter's tongue to remonstrate with her for being so formal but he decided to let it pass. Something in her face warned him to tread warily. She was wearing what her mother and sisters would have described as 'Penny's keep-out look'.

He poured her tea and set it down before her. Observing the snugly fitted habit, he enquired, 'Were you planning to ride this morning Penelope?'

'Thank you, my lord. Yes, I have sent a message down to the stables and Johnson is expecting me after breakfast.'

Peter sat down and thought about this. He knew perfectly well that he had behaved badly the previous day and that he should offer to escort his wife, but her very next words showed how little that would be appreciated.

'I think I shall enjoy riding out with Johnson,' she said sweetly. 'He seems very easy to talk to. And afterwards Ellen and I are going to take Gelert for a long walk with a picnic lunch.'

'Good heavens, girl! You'll be exhausted!' he exclaimed before he could stop himself.

Penelope looked amused and replied, 'You must not concern yourself about me. I am perfectly capable of judging how far I can ride or walk.' And, changing the subject, 'How are you spending the day, my lord?'

'Estate matters. I have to see a tenant. If you would care to join me…'

He got no further. 'How kind, my lord, but I am sure

that Johnson will prove an acceptable escort. And of course I would not wish to be in your way.'

The cold indifference in her voice stung, but Peter merely shrugged and said, 'As you please, Penelope.' Having finished his breakfast, he excused himself politely and left to go about his business.

As the door shut behind him Penelope relaxed with a sigh of relief. It had been far more difficult than she'd expected to maintain a pose of icy formality. She was annoyed to realise that her hands were trembling slightly as she finished her cup of tea. Silly little fool! she told herself crossly as she made her way to the side table and helped herself carefully to a boiled egg. Somehow her appetite seemed to have deserted her.

Johnson met her as soon as she entered the stable yard. 'Good morning, my lady. Nero is saddled and ready. The master said as how you would be riding him in the future. For which we're all glad. He's a nice old chap and he does get a bit bored not going out as often.'

Penelope smiled and said, 'Well, I'm afraid that I won't be providing him with too many thrills, just a quiet ride every day or so!'

'Just the thing for the old fellow,' said Johnson cheerfully. 'Fred! Bring Nero out for her ladyship, and Misty for me.'

'Yessir!' Penelope heard the clatter of hooves on the cobbled yard and then a voice saying respectfully, 'Here they are, Mester Johnson, sir. Will that be all, sir?'

The voice sounded just a little nervous, and something stirred in Penelope's memory. 'Ah, would this be Fred who got such a terrible shock to find Gelert here in a supposedly empty stall?'

'Aye, that's him, my lady. Silly clunch! Well, say something, lad!'

'Good morning, my lady. I'm sure 'e's a nice dog, but I'd never seed sech a big un afore!'

Penelope smiled and said, 'I don't suppose Mr Johnson had either! Never mind, Gelert really is quite harmless, I promise! Now, shall we be going?'

'If your ladyship is ready,' said Johnson. He brought Nero around to her and, taking her foot, threw her into the saddle. She settled herself quickly, sorting out her skirts and finding the stirrup. Carefully she gathered up the reins so that she could just feel Nero's mouth and waited quietly while Johnson mounted.

He did so and asked, 'Are you ready my lady?'

'Yes, Johnson.'

They trotted out of the yard together, with Gelert bounding around them, and Johnson said, 'There's a pretty ride through the park towards the village, my lady. Plenty of room for a canter if so be your wish, and we can circle back around the Home Farm and through the woods. About an hour and a half it would take.'

'That sounds excellent, Johnson,' said Penelope cheerfully. 'You pick a ride that you would enjoy, it doesn't really make much difference to me.'

Johnson glanced at her and said slowly, 'Well, I suppose not, my lady, but when spring comes around again and the violets are out in the Home Wood, or even now when all the birds are about and the smells are nice anyway…well, that's why I thought we'd go this way. Ellen was saying how you like the herbs and we thought you'd like this.'

Penelope turned towards him and said, 'Thank you, Johnson, for giving it so much thought. I do appreciate that.'

Penelope enjoyed the ride very much. Johnson was an excellent guide, telling her all about the route they were taking and describing the scenery. It was a glorious day and she could feel the sun warming her as the horses trotted along. To her great delight there was even a lark swinging high above them in a rapture of song. They halted the horses and she listened entranced for several minutes, and Penelope then said, 'You know, Johnson, a neighbour of ours at home, Mrs Knighton, had one trapped. She put the poor little thing in a cage in her drawing room and it just drooped and fretted. Wouldn't eat, wouldn't sing. My sister and I got into the most awful scrape because we let it out into her garden and of course it was gone. When it took off and realised it was free again...oh the song! You'd have thought its heart had been breaking in that horrid cage!'

Johnson snorted and said, 'Them as puts any wild bird, leave alone a lark, in a cage needs to be caged theirselves. 'Tisn't right for a lark, of all birds! They need the sky and the wind, my lady. And anyway, do you think as how a lark singing caged inside would sound like this one?'

Penelope shook her head and said softly, 'No, he'd sound stunted, like his soul would be.'

'That's right,' said Johnson. 'And I'll warrant you and your sister didn't care much about the trouble you got into!'

His mistress grinned engagingly. 'Not very much!' she admitted. 'Mama promised all sorts of dire retribution in front of Mrs Knighton and revoked it all when we got into the carriage to go home!'

The groom gave a shout of laughter. 'That's the way. I dessay she was a-wishing she'd done it herself!'

The rest of the ride passed agreeably. Johnson, who had known the Earl since boyhood, like all the older servants, had had little time for the previous Countess. This one he reckoned to be a far better bargain! Old Meadows had it right when he said she was quality through and through. A real lady she was. Not too high in the instep and had a brain as well as a heart. As they turned to ride homeward Johnson silently congratulated his master on a good choice!

Penelope returned to the house to discover that Ellen and François between them had contrived an extremely hearty picnic lunch which included a large bone for Gelert. Despite Ellen's misgivings Penelope still felt fresh after her ride, and was determined to go for a walk. Quite apart from her genuine desire to get out of the house and give Gelert enough exercise she was unwilling to give his lordship the slightest reason for thinking she was moping about or pining for his company.

They set off together through the kitchen garden and orchards with the lunch split between two small satchels and Ellen further laden with a rug. Ellen said she knew a good spot for a picnic about a mile and half away, where the stream dropped several feet in a tinkling cascade to a deep pool. It was, she said a sheltered, sunny spot and would save them having to carry any water. They reached the place after about forty-five minutes of steady walking and spread out the rug in the filtered shade of a spreading oak close to the pool.

Myriad sounds came to Penelope's ears: the plash of the water falling into the pool, a constant ripple of bird-song and the occasional splash of a leaping trout. Contentedly she sat on the rug and helped Ellen set out the lunch. Cold pasties, a cold chicken, bread rolls, cheese, a very large slab of plum cake, and fresh fruit. Fortunately François was adept at simple meals of this sort, being as how, said Ellen, the master often liked to come out like this with a gun or fishing rod.

'He's not much of a one for ceremony,' said Ellen, completely forgetting that it was not her place to pass comment on her master to his wife. For her part Penelope didn't care. If she couldn't get to know her husband and his likes and dislikes one way then she would have to resort to more devious means!

The afternoon passed peacefully and Penelope found out a great deal about Ellen's family, especially her sister, Martha. Ellen was terribly excited about becoming an aunt for the first time. Occasionally she stopped and begged pardon for rattling on, but her mistress simply laughed and said she liked to hear it all. And indeed Penelope was finding, in Ellen's stories of her family life, some surcease from a homesickness she had hardly dared to admit to herself.

Separated from her mother and sisters for the first time in her life, without anyone to really talk to or confide in she had begun to feel almost unbearably lonely. If only Peter was consistent, they could be friends, she thought. There was a great deal about him that she liked, and it was obvious that his servants held him in considerable affection as well as respect. This to her mind was indicative of a fine man! With a smile she remembered the scene in *Pride and Prejudice* where Lizzy discovered how wrong she had been about Darcy by listening to his housekeeper praise him to the skies. Firmly Penelope put aside the reflection that Lizzy then proceeded to fall very much in love with her erstwhile enemy! Love, thought Penelope, was definitely out of the question!

Chapter Nine

Over the next few days Penelope continued to ride out in the mornings or go out with Ellen. She saw very little of Peter except at breakfast or dinner, when their conversation was limited to polite enquiries about each other's health and activities. Even breakfast she tried to avoid, only coming down when she was fairly sure that Peter would have left.

When it rained heavily one afternoon she found plenty to do helping Mrs Bates in the stillroom. That lady said that the mistress was a great deal more helpful than some fine ladies who couldn't tell one herb from another even with their eyesight! Together they brewed simples and arranged herbs for drying while through it all Mrs Bates gossiped comfortably about the house and its traditions. Penelope heard all about the wonderful parties the previous Earl and his lady had given, and how broken up the old Earl had been when his wife died of a wasting disease.

'He only lived a twelvemonth my lady, just didn't seem to care any more. Master Peter was in the Peninsula then, but the Earl, he wouldn't call him home. In the end Mr Meadows wrote to Master Peter and told him just how things was without his lordship knowing. He sold out and got home within a month but 'twas too late. His lordship died and Master Peter married eighteen months later. Ah, 'twas a bad business.' She sighed lugubriously, but went on more cheerfully, 'Well, it's all different now, dearie—my lady, I should say! Now, I'll just go to the sewing room and find some more muslin bags for this lavender. Such a lot we've got this year!'

She bustled out of the room and the door shut behind her. Penelope mused over what she had been told. She wished she had known Peter's parents. They sounded rather nice. Her thoughts were interrupted by the door opening and she swung around quickly. The footsteps were not those of Mrs Bates. Then a distinct odour of shaving soap reached her and she could hear Gelert's tail thumping the floor enthusiastically.

'Good afternoon, my lord,' she said politely.

Peter had long since stopped being openly amazed at her uncanny ability to know who had entered a room so he just answered, 'Good afternoon, Penelope,' and wondered how the devil she did it.

'Mrs Bates will be back very soon if you wish to speak to her,' said Penelope.

'Actually, Penelope, it was you I came to find,' said Peter steadily, as he tried to remember just how long it was since he had seen his wife alone. At least four days he thought, and then it had only been by chance that she had come to breakfast before he'd left. It was almost as if she were avoiding him!

Penelope looked a trifle surprised and said, 'You wish to speak to me, my lord?'

Peter took a deep breath and said, 'Er, yes. I thought that I had better inform you that my cousin Jack has arrived unexpectedly. He tells me that he is on his way to visit a friend and simply stopped to wish us happy, but I felt obliged to offer him lodging.'

He looked keenly at his wife. She suddenly looked very pale and her voice was not quite steady as she said, 'I...I...thought you did not like your cousin.'

'No, I don't, but he is my heir and I cannot in all honour refuse him the hospitality of this house without a better reason than that,' Peter replied. 'Has something disturbed you, Penelope? You are acquainted with Jack, I believe. Was he not a friend of your brother's?'

'Yes. Yes, he was. He stayed with us once,' answered Penelope, making a tremendous effort to calm herself. She felt that it was impossible to tell Peter the truth: that she feared and loathed his cousin. She would simply take good care never to be alone with him. 'Will he be staying for long—and when does Mr Carstares arrive?'

'Jack will only stay two or three nights, and I had a letter from George. He is staying a little longer with his sister to bear her company while Fairford is away. He'll be along in a week or so.'

'Very well, my lord. I will see you and Mr Frobisher at dinner, then,' said Penelope politely.

Peter was suddenly piqued at this cool dismissal. Damn it! She can't just dismiss me like that! He reached out and took her hand, firmly pulling her towards him. She stiffened and tried to pull away, but he ignored this and with his free hand pushed her chin up. She stopped resisting but the expression on her face was cold. Nevertheless he could feel that she was trembling and he bent his head to kiss her, expecting the same warm response that she always gave him. It was not there. She stood submissively in the circle of his arm and remained seemingly aloof.

In reality Penelope was finding it extremely difficult to

control her instinctive desire to respond to Peter's gentle kiss. As always her heart pounded, and she felt that her knees would give way at any moment, but somehow she clung to her resolution and remained outwardly unresponsive. Just when she thought she could bear it no longer and must return his kiss, he stopped and released her.

Unhurriedly she stepped away and asked steadily, 'Will that be all, my lord?'

Puzzled, Peter looked at her. Her whole body seemed to radiate relief and her expression suggested that she did not find his attentions in the least bit agreeable. After a moment he gathered his wits and answered slowly, 'That was all I had to tell you. I beg your pardon, Penelope. I will see you at dinner.'

He left the stillroom in some confusion and returned to the study where, instead of settling to the work he had intended to do, he sat wondering what on earth he had done wrong. It did not really take him very long to work it out. Penelope *was* avoiding him, and she had obviously taken his hints that he did not wish for a close relationship. That, he told himself firmly, was all to the good. The only problem was that he did not really enjoy making love to a statue, especially when the said statue had hitherto responded to his advances with a tantalising mixture of innocence and passion.

But that's just the problem, he thought irritably. You found her too appealing, too—he flinched at the word—lovable. Surely now you can simply get on with it and...? *No!* He couldn't do that! He couldn't force himself on the child if she found his attentions distasteful. But did she? he wondered. Then he understood fully. His wife was protecting herself from being hurt in the only way she could: by retreating behind a barrier of complete indifference.

He cursed as he realised what he had done. The only way he could break the impasse was to confide in her, apologise and explain his odd humours. And to do that he would have to step out from behind his own barriers, thus creating the very situation that he wished to avoid: a relationship of emotional intimacy with his wife!

As he had expected, Peter did not see Penelope again until dinner time. He heard her in her bed chamber, chatting away to Ellen as she changed for dinner. Briefly he considered knocking on the door and escorting her down to the drawing room, but then decided against the idea. After all, he'd got what he wanted, hadn't he? A wife who would make no demands on his time or feelings.

His thoughts turned to his cousin as he tied his cravat. What did Jack want this time? Money, no doubt. Peter already made his heir a generous allowance, but it never seemed to be quite enough to support Jack in the lifestyle he enjoyed. Idly Peter wondered what Jack would do when he was cut out of the succession by a child. I'll have to settle some money on him, thought Peter, and he certainly won't be happy about it! Oh, well, plenty of time before we need to consider that!

He went on down to the drawing room, where he found his cousin lounging in a wing chair. 'Good evening, Jack. I hope the staff have made you comfortable,' said Peter in a friendly manner.

'Oh, yes, Cousin, I always feel quite at home here,' replied Frobisher. 'But where is your bride? I am looking forward to renewing my acquaintance with her.'

'No doubt she will be down shortly,' answered Peter, wondering why the thought of his cousin meeting Penelope was so distasteful. He began to ask Frobisher about his journey, and for how long they were to have the pleasure of his company, when Penelope entered the room.

The first intimation that he had of her arrival was an utterly blood-curdling growl from the doorway. He swung around in consternation to see Penelope with her hand gripping Gelert's collar firmly. And just as well! The dog was snarling viciously. What on earth had got into him? Only once had he seen the beast react like that, in the chaise on his wedding day. Suddenly he realised that Gelert's attention was focused on Frobisher, and turned to look at his cousin, who had whitened and was backing away.

Penelope spoke quickly. 'I am sorry, my lord. Perhaps you might ring for Meadows and I will ask him to take Gelert down to François in the kitchens. We will wait in the hall.'

'That seems an excellent suggestion Penelope, if you think François won't mind,' said Peter in relief.

'Oh, no, he and Gelert are good friends. He says Gelert is the only dog he has ever known who doesn't try to steal in the kitchen,' said Penelope as she dragged the still snarling dog out of the room.

Peter turned back to Frobisher, unsure of what to say. He could only think of one reason why the dog should react so savagely. It also made sense of Penelope's evident upset at the news of Jack's arrival. Peter was stunned by the fury which arose in his breast at the mere suspicion that Frobisher might have taken advantage of Penelope's blindness. Somehow he managed to mask his anger and turn the dog's behaviour off with a casual apology. He couldn't accuse his cousin on the basis of a dog's testimony—however much he might wish to!

Penelope returned alone and Peter immediately went

to her and took her arm. Damn her independence! He was determined that she should not feel any fear of Frobisher just because she had sent Gelert out. He remembered the other occasion when she had refused to hide behind Gelert's protection and paid silent tribute to her courage.

'Penelope, I believe you are already acquainted with my cousin Jack Frobisher.'

He led her up to him reluctantly, but Penelope was in complete control of herself and responded cheerfully, holding out her hand. 'Indeed, yes. How do you do, Mr Frobisher? I do beg your pardon for keeping you waiting. Perhaps we should go straight into dinner, before François's creations are quite ruined.'

'What a marvellous idea, fair cousin. But first I must extend my condolences to you on your recent sad loss! I was very much distressed to hear of it!'

Penelope looked rather puzzled at first, but then answered, 'Oh! Yes, of course. Geoffrey's death. Thank you, Mr Frobisher.'

'And on the very morning of the wedding, I understand,' continued Frobisher. 'No doubt Peter has been at pains to console you in your…er…time of grief. On a happier note, do permit me to welcome you to the family, and to congratulate Darleston on acquiring such a charming bride!' Frobisher bowed low over her hand but did not kiss it. Not with his formidable cousin standing right there. He looked at Penelope appraisingly. Just as appetising as ever, he thought nastily. All that fresh loveliness, but not for him! Darleston got everything, damn his eyes!

They went into dinner and Frobisher exerted himself to try and charm his companions. He missed very little and was quick to notice the constraint between the couple. Good! he thought unpleasantly. It certainly suited him if they were ill at ease with each other! It was delightful to think that all his cousin's reputed skill with the ladies had not helped with this one! He asked his cousin about the estate, and even managed to conceal his boredom at Peter's answers.

Turning to Penelope, he said, 'It sounds as though my cousin is spending a vast deal of time on his estate! How do you contrive to occupy yourself?'

Penelope answered easily, 'Oh, I go for walks with my maid and Gelert, or I ride out with Johnson—the head groom, you know. That is if the weather is fine. Otherwise I find there is plenty to do in the house.'

'You ride out?' said Frobisher, surprised. 'I'm surprised Darleston permits such a thing! Most unsafe isn't it? And with only a groom!'

'Penelope is quite capable of deciding what is and isn't safe for her to attempt without my interference, Jack,' said Peter, annoyed that Frobisher's comment so closely tallied with his own initial reaction. He also suspected that Penelope was about to deliver a blistering set down!

'Of course,' said Frobisher hurriedly. 'And where do you ride, Lady Darleston?' Something told him that it would be as well not to assume terms of familiarity with his hostess.

Penelope answered politely, Peter's interjection having given her time to recall the impropriety of administering a severe snub to her husband's cousin and guest. 'Oh, I let Johnson decide. We usually go through the park and into the village and then swing around to come back around the Home Farm and the woods.' She left it at that. Not for anything would she have shared the joy of those rides and Johnson's descriptions of the countryside with someone like Jack Frobisher!

'Ah, yes,' said Frobisher smoothly. 'And back over

that picturesque old bridge into the park. How very pleasant.'

'That's right,' said Penelope. 'You must know it well, of course.'

'Indeed I do,' was the reply. 'Well, it seems with all this activity on your part, Lady Darleston, that Peter's company is entirely superfluous!'

Over the next couple of days Penelope had no difficulty in avoiding Frobisher's company. Gelert's behaviour on that first evening had seen to it that he was just as eager to avoid her when he knew the dog to be with her.

Nevertheless it was with real relief that she saw him off two days later. For one thing, good manners had dictated that she must put in an appearance at the breakfast table and not simply disappear for a walk in the middle of the day. Peter, of course, was being hospitable as well so that meant they'd had to be together a great deal more than she would have liked. His manner remained politely distant, and although this was what she expected and told herself she preferred a nagging ache persisted.

Frobisher left immediately after breakfast and Penelope, having sent a message down to the stables for Johnson, set off with a light heart for her morning ride, her first in three days. It was a pleasant day, with the sun going in and out, but there was a fresh wind blowing which added a nip of autumn to the air.

They took their usual route and came out of the woodland path just near the bridge over the stream. Johnson leaned forward to unclip the leading rein from Nero's bridle. The bridge was too narrow to ride abreast and he generally let Penelope ride over first, knowing that of all horses Nero was one he could trust to behave.

Penelope pushed Nero into a trot, knowing that the

wise old fellow would head straight for the bridge. She was taken completely by surprise when, at the first rumble of his hooves on the planks, the horse stopped dead in his tracks and tried to pivot around on his haunches, snorting nervously. Controlling him with hands and heel, she soothed him. 'There now, you old idiot! What's the matter? Come on then. You know this bridge!' Firmly she gave him the office to go ahead, and reluctantly, snorting at each step, the old horse obeyed.

Suddenly an ominous creak was heard. Nero, whinnying in fright, tried to back off the bridge but it was too late. Johnson, spurring forward with a terrified yell of warning, was helpless as he saw the horse pitch forward as the bridge collapsed under him, flinging his rider over his head into the rocky stream.

Horrified, Johnson threw himself from the saddle and leapt into the stream, slipping on boulders in the fast-running water in his efforts to reach his mistress, who was lying between two rocks with her face in the water. Gelert beat him to it. The great dog was there with a mouthful of his mistress's hair, dragging her clear of the water.

'Good lad,' gasped the groom as he got to the pair. 'Here now, let me lift her. That's it!' He made his way carefully to the opposite bank with his limp burden and laid her down on the grass. Quickly he loosened the buttons at her throat, turned her onto her front and began pressing on her ribcage rhythmically. Water poured out of Penelope's mouth and in a moment she began coughing weakly as she tried to drag air into her lungs.

'Thank God!' whispered Johnson, and helped her to sit up. She appeared dazed, but by some miracle seemed to have no major injuries. Far more worrying was the fact that in the brisk wind she was already beginning to shiver violently. Shock too, thought Johnson. He had to get her home, fast!

Thinking quickly, he stripped off his coat and put it on her. 'Just stay right there, lass—my lady. I'll be back in a brace of shakes!' Swiftly he waded back across the stream to get his own horse. Old Nero had scrambled to his feet and was making his way over, but both knees were badly cut up and he was limping on his near hind. Johnson's heart contracted at the old horse's plight, but he had to help his mistress. Cursing, he went on and caught his quiet mare, leading her back to Penelope.

Gently he helped the shaken girl to her feet, talking to her encouragingly, and somehow managed to get her into the saddle. She swayed dangerously and Johnson realised that she could not possibly remain there with the amount of support he could give from the ground. Praying that she would not fall off, he vaulted up behind her and eased her forward so that he could get into the saddle himself. Once he was sure he had her safely he set out slowly for home. Sparing a brief glance back, he saw that Nero was limping along behind. Gelert trotted just ahead.

They were halfway home on that torturously slow journey when a startled shout was heard to the right. Johnson looked around with a sigh of relief. It was the master, galloping towards them on the mare Griselda.

He pulled her in beside them and asked furiously, 'What the devil happened, Johnson? Is she all right? You're supposed to look after her!'

'There's no need to tell me that, my lord. I think she'll be well enough, when we can get her home and into a warm bed. Bridge collapsed, and, yes, 'tis my fault for not thinking fast enough that Nero would never have baulked at a bridge without a damn good reason!'

Peter was silent for a moment while he took this in,

then, 'I'm sorry, Johnson. Don't blame yourself. I'll ride on, and bring a carriage back for her. Can you manage for now, or shall I take her and you ride in on Griselda?'

'Better if you take her, my lord. My arm is going numb for all she's such a slip of a thing. Begging your pardon, my lord.'

Peter brushed this aside and leapt off his mare. He steadied Penelope while Johnson dismounted carefully and then vaulted onto the gentle Misty. Johnson was in Griselda's saddle and riding fast before Peter had Penelope fairly settled in his arms. He put Misty into a walk and continued the slow ride home. Penelope leaned against his shoulder and he could feel the shivering which shook her whole body. 'Home soon, sweetheart,' he said encouragingly, and wondered if she was even aware that he had taken Johnson's place. She seemed only half conscious.

Talking quietly to her, he came to the conclusion that she was aware of him, but simply lacked the strength to reply. She had turned her head slightly so that her cheek rested on his chest in an attitude of trust.

With a mile to go across the park, his travelling coach came to meet them down the ride, driven hard by Johnson himself with Fred beside him. Another groom leapt out as the coach pulled up. Fred jumped off the box and ran to the horses' heads.

'Well done, Johnson,' said Peter in relief.

'I sent for Dr Greeves, my lord. And a message up to the house. They'll be expecting us at the main entrance. 'Tis easiest for the carriage. Jim here can bring Misty and Nero back.'

'Nero!' said Peter. 'I forgot all about him!' He looked around. The old horse was still limping along behind, his head nodding at every painful step. Peter winced as he realised that his old friend was badly hurt.

No time to think of that now. Johnson was waiting to help him with Penelope. Together they got her off Misty and into the coach. Peter got in with her and settled her along the seat, wrapping her in the rugs he found, then knelt on the floor himself to steady her against any bumps. Gelert jumped in beside him and Johnson closed the door.

Johnson drove back to the Court as quickly as he could without too much jolting. He drew up at the front door and found Ellen, Meadows and Mrs Bates anxiously awaiting them. The Earl carried his semi-conscious wife up to her chamber where Mrs Bates and Ellen took over, shooing him from the room with scant respect which spoke whole volumes about their regard for the mistress.

Peter left obediently and went down to the entrance hall to receive the doctor who, to his relief, arrived very soon. He escorted Greeves upstairs and left him at Penelope's door, saying, 'Her ladyship's maid and Mrs Bates are in there. I shall wait out here for you.'

Greeves nodded. 'Very well, my lord,' he said, and went in.

Peter sat down on a chair in the corridor and waited impatiently. He was reasonably certain that Penelope had taken no serious injury, but, like Johnson, the wetting and cold wind frightened him. A lungful of water too!

It seemed a very long time before Greeves reappeared, although it was actually only half an hour. 'Sorry to keep you waiting, my lord,' said Greeves, who was experienced with distraught husbands.

'How is she?' asked Peter at once.

'She'll do well enough. Strong constitution although she looks so fragile.' Peter heaved a sigh of relief. The doctor continued, 'A wee bit of concussion and a fair few bruises. The main problem will be the wetting she got and the water she took in. You can be grateful to that groom of yours for thinking so fast or she'd not have had a chance. As it is you can expect her to be unwell for about a week, I'd say. And keep her quiet for another week after that. Just carriage exercise, no riding or walking, and keep her well rugged up and out of draughts. I've left some medicine. Mrs Bates and Ellen know what to do. Someone had better sit up with her for a couple of nights. She's a bit feverish and may become disorientated at times. Nothing to worry about, just reassure her.'

'Thank you, Greeves,' said Peter.

'Not at all, my lord, and congratulations on your marriage,' said Greeves. 'I'm just sorry to meet her ladyship in these circumstances. I'll come again tomorrow to check on her. Now, don't come down with me: I know my own way after all these years! You go in and see her ladyship. And for heaven's sake relieve her mind about the horse. She's badly worried over him. Lie if you have to, but make it convincing! Goodbye, my lord!' He held out his hand.

Peter gripped it warmly and said, 'Thank you again, sir. I'll see you tomorrow.'

Pausing only for a perfunctory knock, he went straight into Penelope's room, where he found her propped up in bed with several pillows and Ellen carefully spooning the last of some chicken broth into her.

Mrs Bates came to him and said, 'Oh, Master Peter, what a terrible thing!'

'Never mind, Bates,' said Peter kindly. 'The doctor says her ladyship will be quite well very soon. He wants us to sit with her for a couple of nights, so if you or Ellen can be with her until after dinner I'll take over then.'

'If that's what you want, my lord, that's what we'll do,' said Mrs Bates. 'Her ladyship seems inclined to sleep at the moment, but if she wants you earlier we'll send for you.'

'Of course,' said Peter. 'I'll be in the house all day, and I'll make sure Meadows knows where I am. Now I'd better speak to her.'

He went over to the bed and leaned over his sleepy wife. 'Warmer now, little one?'

She opened her eyes and smiled up at him, 'Much warmer,' she said weakly. 'Just very tired.'

'You sleep, then. I'll leave you with Ellen and Mrs Bates for now and come back to sit with you later,' said Peter gently.

'Nero, is he hurt badly?' she asked. 'He didn't want to go onto the bridge but I made him. He tried so hard to stop!' There were tears in her eyes.

'A few cuts and bruises,' lied Peter, who had no idea just how badly hurt the horse might be. 'He'll be fine by the time you're out and about again, so don't worry. Now, settle down and go to sleep.' He bent over, kissed her gently and left.

Returning after dinner, he found Ellen with Penelope. There was a fire burning brightly on the hearth which cast a dim glow over the room. Ellen put a finger to her lips and he nodded in acknowledgment.

The maid tiptoed over to him and spoke softly. 'Her ladyship has just gone back to sleep. I've given her some broth and her medicine. She needs it again in four hours, or when she wakes up. Doctor says she's not likely to sleep more than a few hours at a time. There's a full kettle by the fire to make her a hot drink if she coughs. Mrs Bates left some valerian and chamomile in the little blue jar on the mantel. She says 'twill help the mistress sleep better. Just put a little in the hot water.'

Peter nodded. 'Thank you, Ellen. I'll go through to my room to change for the night and come back. I won't be long.'

He went out quietly and returned ten minutes later in his nightshirt and dressing gown. He dismissed Ellen with a kindly word of thanks and went quietly over to the bed. Penelope was sleeping soundly enough, although her breathing sounded a little laboured. A small table had been pulled close to the bed. On it he found the medicine, a jug of lemonade with a tumbler and a bowl of lavender water.

Reassured that he had everything he might need, he walked around to the other side of the bed and carefully got onto it. Might as well be comfortable, he thought, sliding under the eiderdown. As he lay there listening to Penelope's breathing he wondered about the bridge. His bailiff, Stanwyck, had gone out with Johnson to look at it. He had come back to say that some of the supports had worked loose and was threatening all sorts of dire punishment for the man he had sent out to overhaul it at the start of the summer. Peter was a little puzzled. The bridge had apparently been in good repair; he could see no reason why a previously reliable man should suddenly skimp on a job, especially when it might cost lives, not to mention his own employment.

Eventually Peter dozed off. He awoke shortly before midnight to find Penelope stirring beside him. She was coughing badly and seemed a little confused.

He spoke immediately to reassure her. 'It's me, Penelope. Peter. How are you feeling?'

Unfortunately this only served to confuse her further. She could not for the life of her think what her husband was doing in her bed. 'Peter? Why? What do you want?' Her voice sounded scared and Peter resisted the impulse to inform her that it was not unusual for a husband to spend the night in his wife's bed.

'Er, I'm the night nurse, Penelope,' he explained.

Penelope thought about that carefully. Night nurse? Why should she need a night nurse? Gradually her mind cleared of all the odd dreams she had been having and she remembered what had happened. 'Oh, I...I fell off Nero, didn't I? And got wet.' She stopped to cough again and tried to sit up.

Peter helped her, saying, 'Just wait a minute and I'll get you a drink.' He climbed over her carefully and poured a tumbler of lemonade, putting it into her hand. She nodded her thanks, unable to speak for the coughing. Peter racked his brains and remembered the kettle. Quickly he went over to the fire to put the kettle on the hob. It was quite warm already, and in a moment he had a tisane of valerian and chamomile ready for her.

He took it across to her and said, 'Try this—Mrs Bates's recommendation, a tisane. Then I'll give you your medicine.'

'Thank you,' she said as she took the cup from him. She sniffed it. 'Valerian and chamomile. This will make me sleepy!'

'At midnight that's probably not a bad thing,' observed Peter with a tinge of amusement in his voice.

'M...midnight? But you were in my bed!' She sounded absolutely shocked.

This time Peter said dryly, 'There's nothing improper about *that*, my sweet. We *are* married, you may recall!'

'Yes, b...but,'

He interrupted her, half-amused and half-annoyed. 'Rid yourself of the notion that I am harbouring any villainous designs upon your person, Penelope. I am merely concerned with your health and trying to make sure that Mrs Bates and Ellen get enough rest!'

'I...I beg your pardon, my lord,' said Penelope stiffly, extremely embarrassed both at finding Peter in her bed and at having been so rude.

'Very well. Now finish that tisane and you can take your medicine.'

She did as he bade her and took the dose, screwing up her face in disgust as she tasted it. 'Ugh! How horrid!'

'No temptation to stay sick, then,' said Peter unsympathetically as he settled himself in an armchair by the fire.

Startled at the direction of his voice, Penelope asked, 'Why are you in the chair?'

'I thought you objected to me in your bed,' was the blunt reply.

'Yes, but... I mean, no! I mean... I didn't mean to ...' She stopped, tired and uncertain about just what she *did* mean!

Peter looked up sharply at the tone of exhaustion and confusion in her voice. Infamous of him to tease her when she was ill and needed his kindness! 'Never mind, Penny,' he said gently. 'If it will not disturb you I will come back to bed.'

'Yes, please,' she whispered, half asleep.

By the time Peter reached the bed she was sound asleep again. Very carefully he got into bed and made himself comfortable.

His slumbers were disturbed by some very detailed and delightful dreams in which Penelope had obviously quite overcome her shock at finding him in her bed. Eventually one of these dreams was so vivid as to jerk him out of sleep. He woke up completely to discover that Penelope had rolled over in her sleep and was snuggling up to him in a confiding manner which made his heart pound and his blood seem several degrees warmer. That spelt the end of sleep for Peter. He spent the remainder of the night with gritted teeth, reminding himself that his wife was sick and moreover that he had foolishly assured her that he had no villainous designs upon her person.

When Penelope awoke again it was to find Ellen with her. His lordship, Ellen informed her would come back to sit with her during the afternoon, while she and Mrs Bates would sit up in turns at night. Penelope tried not to feel hurt. After all he was a busy man and theirs was only a marriage of convenience.

Chapter Ten

Ten days later, shortly after tea, George Carstares's curricle bowled up the driveway drawn by a pair of chestnuts. Penelope, much recovered, was in the drawing room playing the piano when she heard the commotion in the Great Hall. A cheerful voice was saying, 'Hello, Meadows, you old rascal. Where's his lordship? Out? Shooting rabbits? Oh, well, I suppose we'll get a rabbit pie out of it.'

She walked out onto the gallery overlooking the Great Hall feeling very nervous about greeting her guest. Did he know she was blind? What had Peter told his friend about the marriage?

Just as she was wondering whether to call out Carstares looked up and saw her. 'Good evening, Lady Darleston. I hope my arrival won't inconvenience you.'

'It's Mr Carstares, milady,' explained Meadows. 'Now let me take your coat and hat, Master George, then you can join her ladyship. Master Peter—his lordship, I mean—won't be very long.'

'Do come up, Mr Carstares,' said Penelope with a friendly smile. 'Unless you would prefer to rest in your room.'

'Rest? Good God, no, ma'am!' said George. He came up the stairs to her and said, as he saw Gelert, 'That hound of yours is even bigger than I remembered! How are you, Lady Darleston? Recovered from your wetting and fall, I hope!'

'I'm much better, Mr Carstares. Shall we go into the drawing room?' She moved towards the door with Gelert, and George, who had received a long explanatory letter from Peter, leapt to open it for her. She smiled and thanked him.

'Please make yourself at home, Mr Carstares. There is a brandy decanter on a side table, I believe, or I can send for some tea if you would prefer that.' Penelope seated herself on the Queen Anne sofa and Gelert lay down, resting his head on her feet.

'Thank you, but I'll wait for Darleston. How is he?'

'Very well, but the estate has been keeping him rather busy.' In sober fact Penelope had been very little in her husband's company for the last few days. And since he had most uncharacteristically exerted his authority with her to confine her to the house she had been extremely bored.

George heard the constraint in her voice. He remembered what Peter had said about not wanting any emotional involvement and correctly deduced that his friend had achieved his aim. Rough on the girl, he thought sadly. She was a pretty little thing, and if Peter was doing his well-known impersonation of an icicle it must be rather uncomfortable for her.

He asked politely after her family, and when Peter came in ten minutes later he found them roaring with laughter over a letter Penelope had received that morning from Sarah. Neither one noticed him at first, and he stood watching them from the doorway. He had not seen his wife in so merry a mood for days. Penelope felt the draught and turned towards him with a questioning look on her face. It seemed to him that all the animation died out of her face to be replaced with a look of guarded enquiry.

George followed her gaze and said, 'Hello, Peter! Your sister-in-law seems to have the most unflattering notion of your character. Read this!'

Peter came forward and took the proffered letter. 'May I, Penelope?'

'Of course, Peter.'

He read aloud.

Darling Penny

I hope you are better. Why didn't Lord Darleston frank your first letter? It seems awfully mean to me. Mama says you probably forgot, but I think that is a hum. It's a pity that he's so mean, because he looked quite nice at the wedding. It just goes to show, you can never tell.

I have been reading *The Mysteries of Udolpho* and Mama says I have let it prey upon my imagination too much. I suppose Darleston hasn't really got you locked in a dungeon, has he? And where was he when you fell off your horse? It would be too good to be true, but even Richard doesn't think it's very likely. He and Phoebe are very well and absolutely sickeningly in love. I hope you aren't. It would be nice to have one sister in possession of her senses.

At this point Peter stopped to laugh a little awkwardly. Nothing seemed more unlikely than that Penelope should even like him, let alone love him! If anything he would have said that Penelope had settled into dislike of him.

He handed the letter back to her, saying lightly, 'Well, my dear, I suppose I had better live up to my reputation and find a nice damp dungeon for you! How are you, George?'

'Very well, thanks, Peter. Penny has been looking after me admirably. You know I don't think I congratulated you sufficiently at your wedding, you lucky dog!' said George, laughing even while he groaned inwardly at the obvious discomfort between his hosts. Peter, you idiot, he thought. You've made a mess of this all right and tight!

Penelope blushed as she rose to her feet. 'I must go and change for dinner, if you gentlemen will excuse me,' she said. Peter attended her to the door and opened it. 'Thank you, Peter. Did you shoot any rabbits?'

'Three,' he answered.

'Oh, good. George, you'll get your rabbit pie!' said Penelope with a chuckle as she went out.

Peter followed her into the hall and shut the door. 'Penelope?'

'My lord?'

'So formal, my dear?'

There was a wistful note in his voice which pierced her defences, but she replied steadily, 'I find it preferable to maintain consistency in our relationship, my lord.'

She was aware of his closeness, but jumped when she felt his hands grip hers gently. 'Penny, this is foolish…' he began.

Her fingers trembled in his. As always his touch drew a response from her. He drew her closer, gazing into her wide grey eyes with their incredibly long lashes. His gaze dropped to her mouth. The delicately shaped lips looked softer, more inviting than ever. Desire flared in him. He leaned towards her, but at the last moment she pulled away from him.

'I...I must change for dinner. Please excuse me, my lord.' He released her hands reluctantly and watched her go, longing to undo the damage he had done.

Dispiritedly Peter returned to George and said, 'You and Penelope seem to have taken to each other.'

'Delightful girl,' said George. 'A pity she's blind, but it doesn't seem to stop her doing much. How do you get along with the dog?'

'Fine, now,' said Peter.

'Oh, don't tell me he went for you!'

'Only when I richly deserved it,' said Peter, in the sort of voice which suggested that he would prefer not to discuss the subject. 'A brandy, George?'

They talked casually about mutual acquaintances for a while, and then Peter said, 'Well, what's bothering you, George? You said in your letter that you had something to tell me that you preferred not to commit to paper. Out with it.'

George looked worried. 'Yes. If it wasn't for that I wouldn't have dreamed of butting in at the moment.'

Peter was puzzled. 'Why on earth not?'

'Why not? For goodness' sake, Peter, as if it wasn't bad enough having to remind you to kiss the bride in the church! The best man doesn't usually come along on the honeymoon!'

'Oh, rubbish. We're not exactly lost in love, you know. Get on with your story or whatever it is.'

George took a deep breath, 'I'm concerned about your cousin Jack Frobisher. There are some very ugly rumours going around.'

'George, there are always nasty *on dits* circulating

about my cousin! You should ignore them. I do!' said Darleston in amusement.

'Seems he's getting desperate. The money lenders have got their claws into him, apparently. A couple of weeks ago Frobisher attempted to elope from Bath with Carrington's sister, Amelia.'

'Good God!' exclaimed Darleston in distaste. 'Don't tell me that this is common knowledge!'

'No, it was all hushed up,' said George reassuringly. 'In fact that's the main reason Carrington didn't call him out. These things always get about, and naturally it wouldn't do the girl's chances much good. Told me in confidence because he wanted you to be warned. Thinks Jack did it in response to your marriage. You know, being cut out and all!'

'But you said there were rumours about Jack!' Darleston pointed out

'The rumours are not about him but spread by him. At least, so I suspect.' George cleared his throat, uncomfortably aware that he was venturing onto dangerous ground. He continued. 'Peter, Frobisher was there the night you had your turn-up with Ffolliot. He probably knew quite well that Ffolliot's estate would never bear a debt of that size. He was furious about your marriage, you know. Been saying that you only did it to spite him and that he'll make you regret it. He's been stirring up all sorts of gossip about Penny too. Saying the marriage was a put-up job to clear Ffolliot's debt. Which is true. But you don't want everyone to know it!'

Darleston stared at him in shock. 'Good Lord! Are people taking him seriously?'

'Well, you'll admit the story makes good telling! People are listening, Peter. The most popular version is that the whole thing was a plot to entrap you into marriage. Which, if you ask me, is a little hard on your wife! I should say she has enough problems without that! If anyone was trapped into marriage she was!' said George bluntly.

'Is there anything more?' asked Darleston, ignoring this rider.

'Well, there is one thing.' said George reluctantly. 'Carrington thinks Frobisher is in enough of a mess to try and dispose of you. You must know he made no secret about the fact that he didn't expect you to remarry.'

'George, are you seriously suggesting that Jack is going to try and kill me so that he can inherit? You must be crazy!' burst out Darleston. 'This is nineteenth-century England, not medieval Italy!'

'I know! I know it sounds mad. But it's just possible he might be desperate enough to do it. Trying to elope with Miss Amelia was pretty desperate! Another thing,' George continued, 'if you'll forgive me for touching on a private matter. If Frobisher wants to inherit, it's possible he might also try to harm Penny.'

Darleston stared in amazement. 'Penelope? Why?'

'Well, she is your wife, you know. An heir and all that,' said George, extremely embarrassed. This was delicate ground for even the closest of friends.

'You needn't…' Darleston only just stopped himself informing George that the chances that Penelope might be carrying an heir were zero. 'Does anyone else know about this?' he asked

'No. Only Carrington. He said I should warn you at once. Knew something about the lender Frobisher went to. From what Carrington said, if your cousin is in his clutches it could be very serious.'

Darleston took a turn around the room. 'This sounds like pure nonsense, but I suppose I had better look into it. Don't say anything to Penelope just yet, will you? If Jack does try anything his only hope of getting away with it is to make it look accidental, and I have every confidence in Gelert's ability to protect her. Something will have to be done about the gossip, of course. I won't have anyone gossiping about my wife!'

'You said accidental,' said George slowly. 'What about that fall she had? Didn't you tell me that Jack was staying with you just before it happened? Could he have tampered with the bridge?'

'Good heavens! I doubt that he even knew she was riding at all, let alone where she… Wait a minute, maybe he did know! I recall something being said about her riding at dinner one night. That's right! He thought it was dangerous. Penelope would have bitten his head off if I hadn't interrupted.'

'Did he know where she would ride?' asked George.

Peter racked his brain but couldn't remember. 'Goodness knows. Anyway, this is too fanciful! It was sheer fluke that Penelope rode onto the bridge first.'

'Might have been worse if she hadn't,' George pointed out thoughtfully. 'Your letter said that Nero refused to go on. Now, if Johnson had gone ahead, and then Penelope got Nero to go, the bridge could have collapsed under the pair of them!'

'Maybe. Come on, we'd best change for dinner. François gets very angry if we are late!'

Dinner that night was a far more cheerful meal than it had been for the previous few nights. George and Penelope were in a way to becoming fast friends. It was obvious to Peter that his friend admired Penelope and that she treated him with much the same open friendliness she had once shown to her husband. She even unbent towards him a little, but he was uncomfortably aware of a demon of jealousy gnawing at him. That he had only himself to blame for her air of polite indifference did nothing to reconcile him to it.

George and Penelope were discussing the late war with France. It was evident that Penelope had followed it very closely and Peter was conscious of a twinge of pride at the intelligence displayed in her questions and comments. 'I wish more women had an understanding of the war!' said George. 'Some of them say such stupid things!'

'Oh, come, George! So do lots of men!' protested Peter.

Penelope smiled and said, 'Yes, like my brother's friend Mr Frobisher. He thought that it was a lot of fuss about nothing and bemoaned the fact that he couldn't go to Paris.' It suddenly occurred to her that Jack Frobisher was her husband's cousin and heir. Perhaps it was not quite the thing to be rude about him. She flushed and said, 'I...I do beg your pardon, my lord. I had forgotten that Mr Frobisher is your cousin.'

Darleston gave a short laugh, saying, 'You needn't worry about that, Penelope. My opinion of my cousin is well-known to George, who fully agrees with me. I would greatly prefer the entire world to forget that he is my cousin.'

There was an awkward silence which George tried to fill. 'By the way, Penny, do relieve my curiosity! What happened to Frobisher's arm when he stayed with your family? It was bandaged for weeks and all he'd say was that he'd been bitten by a dog.'

'Gelert didn't like him,' said Penelope, and refused to elaborate.

George didn't press the issue and Darleston had a shrewd idea as to what must have happened. 'Jack Frobisher is a toad. He probably deserved it!' he said, feeling again that unexpected rage at the thought of any other man touching Penelope. He looked at her closely. Her expression was often difficult to read, but he thought she had paled at the mention of Frobisher's arm.

Penelope left the gentlemen very correctly to enjoy their port, and retired to the drawing room. When they came in she was playing the piano. She stopped, but they begged her to continue and disposed themselves to listen. The instrument sang under her fingers, and it was obvious that she was completely absorbed in the music. Darleston thought to himself that she looked particularly lovely when she was concentrating hard on something.

He ran a distracted hand through his hair, trying desperately to concentrate on something other than the soft enticing curves of her figure. He raised his eyes to her face. The dark red curls were piled high on her head to fall in soft ringlets; they jostled for position, caressing her neck in careless abandon. One particularly vagrant lock tickled her cheek in a way that made Peter's fingers itch to stroke it back.

He nearly groaned aloud in frustration and dropped his gaze to her hands which drew rippling magic from the instrument. He tried to focus on the music, but found himself remembering the occasions when she had touched him. Good Lord, he was behaving like a lovesick schoolboy! With a massive effort of his will he turned away and wrenched his mind from contemplating Penelope.

He thought over what George had told him. Would Jack really try to murder him? Surely not! And yet the notion could not be dismissed. It occurred to him that it was even more a matter of urgency for him to consummate his marriage. The sound of George's voice roused him from his thoughts. Penelope had finished playing and

George was offering to read to her. He had the *Gazette* in his hand and Penelope was delighted.

Darleston began to feel annoyed. Dash it all, she didn't have to be that friendly! And why was George so damned assiduous in his attentions? To be calling her Penny as though he had known her for ever! The contrast between the polite, reserved manner Penelope kept for him and the way she treated George was marked, and although he had encouraged her reserve he was piqued. By the time Penelope excused herself for the evening he was determined to visit her room for the express purpose of telling her plainly to behave herself!

George and Darleston remained chatting for a while, the former cheerful and unrestrained, his host a little gloomy. Finally George decided to put the cat among the pigeons. He was quick to observe and understand the demons which drove his best friend. The tension between the pair was not lost on him and he thought he could make a shrewd guess as to the cause of it.

'Peter, you're a lucky dog. If I organised a marriage for myself, as you did, it would be a total wash-out. She'd turn out to be a half-wit, or bad-tempered, or worse. But you! You end up with the most charming, intelligent girl imaginable! Even has a nice dog! I take it all back. You couldn't have chosen better if you'd known the girl for years. Nothing like Melissa either, thank God!'

Peter looked a bit startled at this panegyric. He didn't answer for a moment, but finally said, 'Yes, I suppose you're right. It could have been a lot worse.'

George left it at that. Hopefully Peter would give it some thought. It was obvious to him that Peter was annoyed by the ease with which he had made friends with Penelope. With a bit of luck it might make him realise that the girl wasn't a dangerous charmer, like Melissa, and that he could treat her as a friend, rather than a distant and not overly liked acquaintance, without disaster.

George excused himself early, saying the drive had tired him and that he would see Peter in the morning. Peter said, 'I'm unfortunately obliged to see my bailiff in the morning. Do you mind entertaining yourself? We might take guns out in the afternoon.'

'Of course I can entertain myself. Might even take Penny riding. She tells me you let her ride old Nero and that she's back in action after the accident.'

For some reason the thought of Penelope riding with George enraged him. Why, when he had offered to take her out yesterday she had refused. No doubt she would accept George's invitation with alacrity! Angrily he pushed away the knowledge that his own offer had been less than inviting. He was more than ever determined to suggest to his wife that she should be more reserved with George. With this in mind he changed himself for bed and then knocked firmly on the connecting door.

A brief silence followed his knock, and Peter wondered if his wife were already asleep. Then a startled voice bade him enter. Penelope was sitting up in bed brushing her hair. He walked over to the bed to stand looking down at her. She faced him nervously, uncertain of what he wanted. A pulse hammered in her throat and she realised to her annoyance that she was trembling.

'Peter?' Her voice was commendably steady, but her husband caught the hint of uncertainty.

'May I speak with you, Penelope?'

'Of course.' Was that *all* he wanted, drat him?

Darleston didn't mince words. 'I'm pleased, of course, that you like George, Penelope, but it is scarcely necessary for you to be quite as friendly, or to be on Christian name terms with a man you have only just met! With any other man I would be very angry indeed. Please remember that I require discretion in my wife and would prefer her to maintain a ladylike reserve with other men.'

Penelope was stunned. 'Are you seriously telling me that you expect me to be boring with everyone just because *you* happen to have a preference for it? Don't be an idiot, Peter!'

It had not occurred to Peter that she would argue with him. Surprised, he snapped back, 'If that is how you see it, yes! I'm not prepared to be cuckolded twice!'

Penelope's jaw dropped in amazement. For a moment she was rendered utterly speechless at the implied insult, and then she lost her temper. Before she could stop herself she was out of bed, standing before him shaking with hurt and rage. The angry words spilled from her, 'How *dare* you? Just because I am pleased to see someone who treats me as a…a *friend*, rather than an unwelcome guest! You are suggesting that I would be unfaithful to you? If that's what you think of me, I'm not surprised you go to such pains to avoid me. I hate you, Peter. Get out!'

It had not dawned upon Peter that his gentle bride had a temper, and he was startled to say the least. He had rather expected a continuation of her polite reserve. What he might have said in response would never be known. He found to his horror that the extremely diaphanous nightgown in which Ellen had arrayed her mistress did little, if anything, to conceal her charms. On the contrary, it displayed her slender figure to admiration. He stood staring at her, with desire rising in his blood, unable to think of anything save that he longed to tear the flimsy silk from her with a minimum of ceremony.

Furious that he was still there, and totally unaware that she might as well have been naked, Penelope repeated her command. 'Get out, Peter, and leave me alone!' She accompanied this with a stamp of her foot and pointed to the door. Peter, observing the lift of one delectable breast under the almost non-existent nightgown, forgot he was meant to be having a fight with his wife. He grasped her by the shoulders, pulled her against his body and kissed her fiercely.

The ringing slap he received across the face, coupled with the fact that his wife stood on his foot very hard indeed, brought Peter to the realisation that he had chosen an inauspicious moment to kiss her. He released her at once and stepped back, saying angrily, 'I beg your pardon, ma'am. I will relieve you of my presence! Goodnight!'

He left the room immediately, slamming the door behind him. Penelope got back into bed slowly, buried her face in the pillow and cried herself to sleep. Darleston, standing silently cursing himself on the other side of the door, heard the muffled sobs but was too mortified to go back and apologise. The memory of the hurt on her face lashed at his conscience. Blast the girl!

Chapter Eleven

The following morning Peter was not surprised to be informed by Meadows that the mistress was breakfasting in bed, having passed an indifferent night. He merely nodded and returned to his perusal of the morning papers.

George looked up and said, 'Meadows, please ask her ladyship if she would care to go riding with me this morning. Or driving if she prefers.' Turning to Peter, he said, 'Driving might be better, do you think?'

'Probably,' was the unconcerned reply.

George took the hint and concentrated on his breakfast. As he ate he wondered how long it would take Peter to relax and at least trust his wife. He was quite aware that Peter was annoyed at the ease with which he and Penelope had struck up a friendship. 'Damned fool that he is!' muttered George under his breath.

'I beg your pardon?' said Peter.

'Oh! Er…just talking to myself!' George excused himself hurriedly, startled to realise that he had spoken aloud.

Peter nodded and left it at that, but he had very little doubt of the identity of the 'damned fool'! He was beginning to agree with George. What on earth was wrong with him? Surely he could manage to be consistently kind to the chit and not keep losing his temper? It wasn't as though she was annoying in any way. She was attractive, even beautiful, she was gentle, but with plenty of spirit. He grinned reluctantly as he recalled how she had turned on him last night.

He was physically attracted to her, no doubt of that! It would be very easy to be extremely fond of her. And that, he admitted to himself as he sipped his coffee, was just the problem. He didn't want to care at all. If he didn't care, then he couldn't be hurt by her. But she can be hurt, his conscience nagged. Why should Penny be hurt because of Melissa's sins?

His mood had lightened considerably by the time he had finished his breakfast. He was still confused, but his innate sense of justice was forcing him to the realisation that he would have to do something permanent about his behaviour. It wasn't in anyone's interest for him to continue blowing hot and cold on Penelope's feelings. He would only succeed in driving her into estrangement, if indeed he had not done so already.

Meadows came into the room just as they were finishing. 'Her ladyship is at your disposal whenever you would care to go, Master George. She would prefer to drive with you, if you have no objection,' he said.

'Thank you, Meadows. Please send a message to the stables for my chestnuts to be harnessed and tell her ladyship that I will be ready as soon as the horses are. Sure you can't come, Peter?'

'Quite sure,' said Peter with genuine regret. 'But why don't you try the paces of my new greys? They need exercise and your own team could probably do with a rest after your journey.'

George correctly deduced from this that Peter was trying to apologise for his earlier bad temper, and he suppressed a grin with some difficulty. 'With pleasure, dear boy. I'll try not to lame 'em for you. The greys, then, Meadows.'

'Very good, Master George, but don't tire her ladyship! She has been extremely unwell!' With that Meadows departed on his errands.

Peter stared after him in some bewilderment. 'Good Lord! Next thing you know Meadows will be calling her "Miss Penny", just as if he had known her from childhood! How amazing!'

'Not at all!' said George, amused by Peter's surprise. 'Very lovable girl, Penny. Reminds me of my sister!'

Half an hour later George and Penelope were bowling along behind Peter's prized Welsh greys with Gelert running beside them. Penelope was rather quiet at first, and George noted the faint circles under her eyes. She cheered up a bit when George told her that Peter had offered to lend them his greys. Surely if he would lend his beloved greys he wasn't too angry with her, she thought.

'Where shall we go, Penny? Your choice.'

'Oh, could we visit the Jewkes farm? Martha's baby will arrive soon and I should like to visit her. I have a note from Ellen for her, and some clothes for the baby. Do you know the farm?'

'We'll find it. I've been there once with Peter.'

A child gave them directions to the farm, and as they drove along George wondered if he should try to explain something of Peter's confusion to Penny. Peter would be furious if he knew, but the sight of Penelope's troubled face decided him. 'Penny?'

'Yes, George.'

'Hope you won't be offended, but could I talk to you about Peter?'

'About Peter?' echoed Penelope.

'Mmm. Odd fellow, Peter. Seems very moody at the moment. Thought it might be easier for you to handle him if you knew more about him. Generally he's the kindest chap alive, but after we got back from the War he changed.'

'Melissa?'

'That's it. You see, he married her for love, despite the fact that everyone else knew she married him for his money. When she ran off with Barton and got killed it was pretty hard on Peter. Of course he knew before he rejoined what she was like. She wasn't very discreet. Probably volunteered hoping he'd be killed. But the fact that she dragged his name in the mud, well, he just can't seem to forget about it. Don't know if you knew any of this.'

'Peter told me a little,' said Penelope. 'But he is so withdrawn most of the time, and then sometimes he is quite friendly. I find it very hard to understand his moods and…and I don't think he likes me very much.'

George's heart ached at the sadness in her voice as she said this. 'Thing is,' he continued, 'Peter finds it almost impossible to trust a woman now.' He refrained from mentioning Lady Caroline Daventry and her connection with Peter. 'But if you can just bear with him until he comes to his senses…don't let him upset you too much…' he left the sentence unfinished and they drove on in silence for a while.

Finally he said with difficulty, 'When Peter said he was getting married again I thought he'd gone mad, the way he went about it. Think now that he couldn't have chosen better. Told him so last night. Must be plain as a pike-staff, even to him, that you're not like Melissa. Probably he'll be a bit easier to live with soon. He's the very devil when he's moody!'

Penelope thought over his words of advice as the greys cantered along in the autumn sunshine. Would Peter become more predictable? George was his best friend, so presumably he understood him. She did not want to be estranged from Peter. Surely they could be friends, even if they weren't in love!

And that, she realised, was her problem. Despite all her efforts to remain aloof, Peter's charm and kindness, when he was not being disagreeable, had got past her guard. She had, almost without knowing it, fallen in love with her husband! A husband, she told herself, who only wanted her to provide an heir, who didn't really care twopence for her. More than anything in the world she wanted to prove to him that she was worthy of his trust and respect, even if he never loved her.

She groaned inwardly at the mess she was in. Well, she thought, it's too late to back out now!

Their arrival at the farm interrupted her thoughts. As George swung the curricle into the farmyard she realised that she had ignored him for at least a mile.

'I beg your pardon, George, I didn't mean to be so dreadfully rude. I was thinking over what you said about Peter. I'll keep trying. I know he can be kind…he was so good about finding out that I am blind and that it was really my sister he thought he was marrying—' She broke off in horror. 'Oh, dear, I shouldn't have said that!'

George laughed. 'Peter told me in his letter what had happened. Serves him right. But from what he said to me on the way to the church it was actually you that he meant to marry!'

Penelope was startled. 'He said that, but I thought he was just being polite!'

'No, one of the things he liked about you was Gelert!'

Penelope giggled. 'Did he tell you how he chose a maid for me? He had Meadows line up all the house-maids to ask them if they liked dogs. Then he showed them Gelert and they picked the only one who was left!'

George chuckled and said, 'One of the things that gives me hope about Peter is that he has never completely lost his sense of humour. He'll be all right! Also, Meadows likes you. He couldn't stand Melissa! Peter takes a lot of notice of Meadows because the old boy looked after him as a child. Meadows was quite insistent that I mustn't tire you out this morning. Made Peter think a bit!'

'Meadows has been very kind to me,' said Penelope. 'And I notice that he nearly always calls you "Master George" and quite often calls Peter "Master Peter." He's like our old butler. I'm sure Tinson will never call me Lady Darleston!'

'Probably not. In fact I wouldn't be surprised if Meadows forgets himself one day and calls you "Miss Penny"! He nearly did this morning,' said George with a grin, 'Gave Peter something to think about. Meadows was so correct with Melissa that it was embarrassing!'

A cheerful hail from the farmhouse put a stop to their conversation. Jewkes had heard them and come out to see who was there. He was brimming over with excite-ment, and as he rushed towards them his words became distinguishable '...on'y sent a lad ten minutes ago! Took ye at yer word, my lady. It's a boy, and he come so fast I barely 'ad the midwife 'ere in time. Ellen will be real disappointed, but we was all caught short as ye might say!'

'Jewkes, is the baby here already?' gasped Penelope. 'Oh, how dreadful! I promised to send Ellen! Poor Martha! George, we must go home at once to tell Ellen.

One of the grooms will bring her over immediately, Jewkes. I'm terribly sorry!'

Jewkes roared with laughter. 'Why, there's no call to feel bad, my lady. We didn't expect the little lad for another week. An' it's right kind of ye to send Ellen at all. I'll tell Martha. She's asleep now. Tired her out it 'as, for all it 'appened so quick. Ye'll forgive me if I get back to 'er?'

'Why of course you must, Jewkes!' said Penelope warmly. 'Here, I've a letter from Ellen and some clothes for Baby. We'll go back now and send Ellen over. Goodbye—and congratulations!'

George turned the curricle out of the yard and said, 'Home, then, Penny?'

'Yes, please, George. I must send Ellen to her sister as quickly as possible. She was so anxious about Martha, and excited about being an aunt!' said Penelope. 'You do not mind, George?'

'Of course not! We can go out again, if you like, once you have given the message,' said George obligingly. 'Pity to spend a day like this inside if you don't have to!'

'We could ask the lodgekeeper to send the message up to the house!' suggested Penelope. 'That way we won't waste any time or get caught up.'

'Good idea! There's a very nice drive around the edge of the park, which should exercise the greys nicely and get us back in time for a late nuncheon!'

The greys quickly covered the distance back to the lodge and the message was delivered. The ten-year-old son of the lodgekeeper was only to happy to earn a penny by going up to the Court.

That done, George set the greys in motion again. They were eager to be off, yet they responded willingly to his light touch on the reins. He steadied them as he said cheerfully, 'Peter stole a march on me over this team. He used to own the prettiest team of chestnuts, knew I admired them and offered to sell them to me. Next thing we know Camley sells up and Peter's got his greys! Don't know how he hears the news so fast. He offered to let me call him out, but he's too good with a pistol for me! And he's not bad with a sword either.'

Penelope laughed. 'I can just see you calling him out because he sold you a pair of horses that you coveted. He'd have simply said that he thought you wanted the chestnuts so he gave you first refusal, since he didn't need them any more!'

'You know him uncommonly well, Penny,' said George in amusement. 'That's exactly what he did say!' They lapsed into a companionable silence. George Carstares thought that for all her liveliness Penelope didn't seem to feel the need for constant conversation. He knew she needed time to think over what he had said earlier. It sounded as though Peter was very confused about his marriage. He suspected that Peter was fonder of the girl than he was willing to let on.

Penelope enjoyed the swift rhythm of the hooves on the road and the swing of the curricle. Before her accident she had been taught to drive by her father. The easy motion of the carriage and the steady pace of the team told her that George was a good driver. She found herself wishing bitterly that she did not have to sit passively, but could take the reins.

Generally she did not waste time sighing over what could never be, but several times just recently she had caught herself in the middle of what felt suspiciously like a wallow of self-pity. Stop it! she told herself with a mental shake. Then she realised that it would be far better to work out the reason for her mood and face it.

That was how she had reconciled herself to the loss of her sight. She had faced her fury with Geoffrey and conquered it with the help of her father. He had made her see that bitterness would harm only herself. He had forced her to be as independent as possible, refusing to pity her. Above all he had understood the pride which made pity a totally unacceptable reaction to her affliction.

So why, after all these years, should self-pity creep in? Frustration, yes. She often felt frustrated, but she had discovered long ago that it was better to consider a problem dispassionately to see if there was a solution. If not, then it was best to move on to something else.

Peter. She wanted to see Peter. She wanted to know what he looked like, this man she had married and so foolishly fallen in love with. That he was handsome, she knew. Phoebe's description had told her that. At first she hadn't minded, hadn't even thought about it. Now it was suddenly important. She felt at a complete emotional disadvantage not being able to see him. Well, bad luck, she thought, there is no solution.

Having made her way through the tangled skein of thought, Penelope set herself to thinking about how to win Peter's trust and liking. Slapping him in the face and stamping on his foot was probably not a good start! She considered apologising for her loss of temper but rejected the notion. It wouldn't harm him to realise just how angry and hurt she had been. Besides which she was *not* going to emulate 'Patient Griselda'!

The pounding of another set of hooves disturbed her thoughts. A rider, approaching at a gallop from the rear, by the sound. She felt George turn to glance over his shoulder as the newcomer drew close.

'Chap's in a big hurry.' He pulled over a little.

The next few seconds were filled with confusion.

There was a shattering explosion, swiftly followed by a startled yell from George. Something hurled her from the seat to the floor of the curricle.

'Stay down Penny!' Another explosion mingled with George's frantic command. She could hear the terrified neighing of the horses as George fought to control them. The curricle swung madly as they plunged in fright, attempting to bolt. Penelope clung to George's legs as she crouched on the floor. Gelert was barking furiously and she could hear the other horse galloping away at top speed. Gelert's barks receded into the distance.

Gradually George calmed the greys until they stood sweating and restless in the road. He looked around, but their assailant had made good his escape. Gelert had chased him, but his instinct to stay with Penelope had obviously prevailed and he was coming back. George looked down at Penelope.

'Are you all right? He's gone. You can get up.' He helped her back onto the seat. Then he caught sight of her bonnet. The left side of the brim was in tatters. He stared in horror and swore savagely. Penelope, still confused and uncertain about what had happened, was taken aback.

'What happened, George?' she asked in shaky tones.

'Someone shot at us. Or rather, at you!'

'Shot at me? Have you gone mad? What on earth for?'

George did not answer immediately. 'We'd better go home and tell Peter,' he said, and put the greys into a trot.

'George! Why did someone shoot at me? You must tell me!' Penelope was close to tears of fright and anger.

Resigning himself to the inevitable, George glanced at her and said, 'I suppose I'd better, but Peter isn't going to like it.'

'Did Peter know about it?'

'Well, obviously neither of us thought there could be any danger on the estate!' said George defensively. He continued, 'How much did Peter tell you about his heir, Jack Frobisher?'

'Not much. Peter told me that he doesn't like him. That was why he married me. To stop Mr Frobisher inheriting the title.' Penelope blushed as she said this.

'That is probably the explanation for this attack. Frobisher is in financial difficulty. He's counting on Peter's money. You, as Peter's wife, could be a danger to his plans. I warned Peter last night that the pair of you could be in danger, but we didn't think there could be any trouble here. Or that an attack would be so direct. Don't worry, Penny. We'll get home and Peter will sort it out.'

'He wasn't a very good shot,' said Penelope, trying gallantly to lighten the atmosphere.

George laughed shortly. 'If he'd been any better Peter would be a widower again! Feel the brim of your bonnet, Penny!'

Chapter Twelve

'Peter, may I speak to you for a moment?'

Darleston looked up from his desk, surprised at his wife's entrance and the note of distress in her voice. She rarely sought him out willingly. He looked at her closely. The slim hand resting on Gelert's collar was trembling slightly. He rose and went to her, taking her hand to lead her to the sofa.

'Come, sit down, Penelope. Something is upsetting you? Tell me what it is.'

She sat down obediently but remained silent, unsure how to begin. Would he rebuff her, or, worse, be very angry with George? Peter sat beside her, watching the play of emotion on her face. Yet again he cursed himself for setting her at a distance. If only she were not so reserved with him, he thought. Almost without realising what he was doing he took her hand in both of his and held it lightly, one thumb caressing the soft palm. She felt again the strange yearning that swept over her whenever he touched her. Why did she feel this way? He didn't really care about her, did he?

'Come, Penny, it can't be that bad, surely! Did George

overturn the curricle?' The gentle note in his voice almost
made her cry. Why couldn't he always be like this?

She smiled tremulously. 'No, Peter. George drives as
well as you do.'

'I'm glad to hear it, since they were my horses he was
driving! Tell me what it is. I promise I won't be angry
with you!'

'Or with George?'

The question startled Peter. What on earth did she
mean? Surely George had not made advances to her. He
stared at her. So that was why she was upset! He released
her hand abruptly and stood up, scarcely able to trust his
voice. 'Go on, you had better tell me.'

Penelope heard the suppressed anger and said bravely,
'You must not blame George. It was not his fault, Peter.'

'That I can well believe. I said you were being too
friendly.' Penelope blinked in surprise, unable to follow
his meaning at first. Then, as the reason for his anger
dawned, she blushed. Peter noted this cynically but made
no comment.

Penelope fought down the impulse to retreat, leave the
room without telling him. Only the realisation that if he
went to George in this mood it could destroy their friendship held her.

'George told me about your cousin, the threats he has
made and the money he has borrowed. Is it true that he
is trying to kill you, Peter?'

Peter was stunned. 'What? George must be insane to
tell you about that! It's little more than conjecture at this
stage.'

'He didn't have much choice, Peter. Someone shot at
us while we were out driving. Look!' She held out her
ruined bonnet. It was removed from her grasp by hands

that seemed to tremble. 'Peter, I'm sorry to interfere with your private affairs, but this involves me too.'

He didn't answer at once. He didn't trust his voice and simply stared at the bonnet, realising just how close the shot had come to killing Penelope. Then he dropped the bonnet, taking Penelope into his arms to hold her tightly. 'Oh, my God!' he whispered in a strangled voice. He did not try to analyse his feelings. All he knew was that the thought of Penelope lying dead due to his stupidity filled him with shame and horror.

Penelope gave an odd little sigh of relief as she rested her cheek on his shoulder. She could feel the strength of his arms and knew herself to be safe. They were silent for a moment before Peter spoke. 'I'm sorry, Penny, this is my fault. I should have warned you last night but all I did was insult you. I'm not a very good husband in any sense of the word.'

Her reply startled him. 'Don't be an idiot, Peter! George knew, but he still took me driving. He didn't think there would be any trouble if we stayed on the estate, and if I'd known I would have agreed. How could it possibly be your fault?'

Peter felt doubly shamed by her generosity and said bitterly, 'If I had taken the least thought for you as my wife I would have told you, forbidden you to leave the house and gardens until this mess was cleared up! Instead I lost my temper because I was jealous!'

Penelope gasped in amazement and struggled out of his embrace. 'Jealous? How can you possibly be *jealous* when you don't even like me! You made it quite clear after that first day. You avoided me, and every time I tried to talk to you at all you snubbed me! Then at other times you were friendly and…and kind. Peter, I don't know what to think!'

Peter was silent. What could he say? He had only himself to blame if she was confused about his attitude towards her. Eventually he spoke. 'Neither do I, Penny.'

'I'm sorry, Peter, but I'm not Melissa! Just because one woman betrayed you doesn't mean I will. I don't expect you to love me, but couldn't you at least trust me, even if I do disgust you?' Penelope was crying now. She fumbled for her handkerchief as Peter's arms closed around her again, gently rocking her back and forth.

Peter wondered if anyone else had ever made such a mess of a marriage as he had managed to make of his.

'How could you disgust me, Penny, you idiot? If anything I would have thought that my behaviour must have disgusted *you*.'

Her answer was barely audible through her tears. 'You k-kissed me that first day, and after that we went back to the house and you were different. You wouldn't talk to me, so I thought I must have done something you didn't like. All I could think of was that you didn't like it when I kissed you back. And the other time you kissed me, you...you pushed me away, so I thought I must be doing something wrong.'

He felt ashamed of himself. 'You didn't disgust me, Penny, I promise you, and I *did* like it when you kissed me. It was my fault for being so suspicious of you as a woman, but also I didn't want to force you into my bed, despite what I said initially.'

'But you said that you wanted an heir...and...that... you wanted me...' She stopped, embarrassed, then continued bravely, 'I do not want to be your wife in name only, but in...in truth, and I thought that was what you wanted.'

Peter took her face between the palms of his hands and kissed her gently on the mouth. 'It is what I want, Penny, and not just because I want an heir, but because I want you. That is what scared me so much and made me behave so stupidly. I'm sorry Penny, will you forgive me?'

Penelope nodded, unable to speak, with the tears still on her cheeks. Peter took the handkerchief and dried her eyes. 'Come along, Penny, bed for you. We'll discuss all this tomorrow. Sleep this afternoon. I'll bring your dinner to you on a tray and sit with you this evening. You've had a terrible shock and must rest. George can tell me exactly what happened He must be in quite a state!' Then, as the possibility occurred to him, 'My God, he's not hurt, is he?'

'No, I should have told you at once!' said Penelope rather indignantly. 'He saved my life, I think,' she continued. 'He must have seen the man, because he shouted and pushed me off the seat.'

'Thank God for George!' said Peter, and gathered her into his arms.

Late that night Peter woke with the odd feeling that someone had cried out. He sat up in the moonlight to listen but at first he could hear nothing. He was about to lie down again when it occurred to him that Penelope might have cried out in her sleep. She had slept all afternoon and he had had his dinner with her in her bedchamber. Knowing that she was still shaken by the attack, he had ignored her avowal that she was well enough to get up for dinner.

'Just remember that you promised to obey me and stop arguing!'

'But what about George? You can't leave him to fend for himself! He's a guest!'

'He's not a guest! He's my best friend, and I shudder to think what he'd say if I left you alone this evening, especially since you wouldn't let me send for Ellen! Besides, he's not fending for himself! The entire staff, and Meadows in particular, is treating him as a hero!'

Penelope had given up, and Peter was fairly sure she'd been grateful for his company. He had read to her until she fell asleep again. Then he had quietly blown out the lamp and retired to his own room, leaving the door open.

After a moment's hesitation he got out of bed and pulled on his dressing gown, a luxurious affair of deep red brocade. He moved softly to the connecting door and looked through. The moon was shining directly into the room. He could see that Penelope's bedclothes were tumbled and that she was very restless. As he stepped into the room she murmured his name in a distressed tone. Hesitantly he went to the bed to place a gentle hand upon her brow, wondering if she were ill. The cool skin assured him that she was not feverish, merely dreaming, and he attempted to straighten the covers for her.

As he did so, she cried out in fright at her dream. 'Peter, help me! Lost—can't see…where are you?' The note of anguish in her voice touched Peter's heart to the core. He wanted to comfort her but was reluctant to wake her.

Making up his mind quickly, he slipped into the bed and took her in his arms, whispering, 'It's all right Penny, it's just a dream, you're safe, shh.'

Waking, she turned in his arms murmuring, 'Peter?'

'Yes, little one. It's all right, go back to sleep.' With a relieved sigh she relaxed against him. He smiled to himself as he rested his cheek upon her hair, enjoying the faint smell of lavender that hung about it and the feel of her body pressed to him. Gently he caressed the curve of her hip and felt her quiver responsively.

Gazing down at her loveliness in the moonlight, he

wondered if he dared stay. He was agonisingly aware of his own desire and knew he would not be able to control himself for long. Reluctantly he gathered himself to go.

Penelope felt the withdrawal and, gathering all her courage, put her arms around him.

'Peter?'

'Yes.'

'Must you go? Won't you stay with me?'

He hesitated, then said quietly, 'Penny, you are a very lovely woman and I am only a man, not a saint. If I stay any longer I will make love to you. Do you want that?'

'That's why I want you to stay. Please, Peter, I…I want to be your wife…if…if you want me…'

He stared down at her. Her face was turned up to his pleadingly. Unable to deny himself any longer, he kissed her tenderly. His lips dwelt briefly on hers before travelling sensuously down the column of her throat, burning a trail of fire on the soft skin. He heard her gasp with pleasure at the sensation and began to undo the buttons on the front of her nightgown.

When he had dealt with them all he sat up, pulling Penelope with him. Restraining his urge to tear the filmy gown from her body, he slipped it off her shoulders, revealing the perfection of her creamy, rose-tipped breasts. Cupping one in his hand, he caressed it lightly before taking her mouth again. He felt her tremble as he kissed her and her mouth yielded under his. Dizzy with passion, he slid his tongue between her parted lips to explore the honeyed sweetness of her mouth. His hands moved possessively over her slim body, touching her with growing intimacy.

The nightgown was definitely in the way, he decided, and he felt himself to be distinctly overdressed for the occasion. He moved back from her to remove these impediments more easily, but she clung to him and begged, 'Don't stop. Please, don't leave me now!'

'I couldn't if I tried, Penny,' he said, his voice rough with desire. 'But I'm not going to make love to you in my dressing gown! Will you help me take it off?' He guided her hand to the cord which tied the garment. Her inexperienced fingers fumbled with the knot, finally releasing it. Free of the dressing gown, Peter removed Penelope's nightdress completely and pressed her back against the pillows.

She lay acquiescent in the moonlight and he drew a shaky breath at the sight of her loveliness. He lowered himself beside her to take her in his arms, pulling her against his aroused body. She was still shaking, and it occurred to him that she might well be frightened by his passion. He held her tenderly, stroking the dark red curls back from her flushed face. 'Don't be scared of me. I swear I'll be gentle. Trust me, Penny.'

For an answer she slipped her arms about him and pressed herself closer, lifting her mouth to his. Peter responded to the mute invitation, his lips moving demandingly on hers and then down her throat. His hands teased and caressed, drifting over the delicate curve of her waist, her stomach and on to her slender thigh.

At first she simply clung to him, trembling in ecstasy, still unsure of herself. Then her desire to give him as much pleasure as he was giving her took over. Instinctively she copied his actions, tentatively exploring his body. Her hands discovered the powerful muscles of his shoulders and chest, the flat plane of his stomach.

Her light caresses stirred Peter's senses nearly to madness. Gently he grasped her hand to lead it still lower, until she touched him intimately. The heated evidence of his desire was almost frightening.

'Peter?' She was a little scared, uncertain of what he wanted.

He heard the nervousness in her voice and was swift to reassure her. 'Like this, sweetheart. Don't be scared,' he murmured, and showed her.

Delighted with the results of her exploration, Penelope became bolder in her efforts to please him. His pleasure in her shy advances was intense. It was all he could do to keep himself under control and not take her immediately. He did not want to rush her. Instinctively he knew that she was still unsure of herself, knew that it would be only too easy to frighten her if he lost command of himself.

Groaning in pleasure, he lowered his mouth to her breast, circling and tantalising the rosy peak until she cried out in longing. Then, and only then, he slid his hand between her silken thighs to the very centre of her passion. He could barely restrain himself from possessing her at once when he discovered the tender flower of her virginity, already damp with the dew of desire. Not yet! He prayed for control. Dear God, don't let me hurt her or frighten her! He caressed her gently and took her mouth again, feeling it tremble as he acquainted himself with her sweetness.

Penelope moaned in total surrender as he stroked her intimately. She could not think, only feel, as he roused her senses to madness with his touch. His lips claimed hers again, passionate and demanding as he continued his exquisite assault on her body. Her delicate breasts were crushed against his muscular torso as she writhed against him in wordless ecstasy, her hips lifting instinctively.

Peter felt her hips move and knew that she was ready for him. Gently he pressed her legs further apart and slid one hard, muscled thigh between them. He moved his manhood suggestively against her, still fondling the sensitive core of her femininity as his tongue thrust deeply into her mouth in erotic anticipation. Releasing her lips momentarily, he gazed down at her face, flushed with passion, and whispered hoarsely, 'Shall I take you, little virgin? Do you want me?'

The answer was little more than a helpless sob of longing. He hovered over her, balanced on his elbows, stroking her face, and again asked softly, 'Do you want me, Penny?'

Wordlessly she nodded, her arms reaching for him urgently.

'Say it, little one,' he insisted, watching her face.

'You know I do!' she whispered. Her face was bathed in tears.

'I want you, little one, all of you!' he whispered passionately.

Unable to wait any longer, Peter parted her thighs and swung his other leg over so that he lay intimately cradled by her body. With gentle patience he pressed himself against her, throbbing with barely controlled desire as he moved back and forth, teasing her with the promise of his masculinity, his own senses reeling in expectation. Then, as her hips lifted in innocent invitation, he took her. He felt the resistance of the fragile barrier and steadied for a split second before broaching her maidenhead with infinite tenderness.

He felt her stiffen, heard her soft cry of pain mingled with pleasure as he possessed her, and stopped immediately, whispering endearments and encouragement, giving her time to get used to him. Feeling her relax, he withdrew slightly to thrust again.

This time she cried out. 'Oh, Peter, don't stop! Please don't stop!'

They were the last words she spoke for a very long time. She felt his lips come down on hers in absolute mastery, his tongue ravishing her mouth in an erotic counterpoint to the gentle rhythm of his loins. It seemed to Penelope that the darkness swirled around her and exploded as Peter increased the tempo, his thrusts lifting her to wild heights of joy.

Sensing that she was close to the edge, Peter slowed down and pulled back slightly, then, as she cried out in protest, he took her all over again. To Penelope it was as though the world shattered as he surged back into her, taking possession of her very soul.

Peter lay dozing in the early-morning light, listening to a song thrush with Penelope still cradled in his arms, just as she had fallen asleep after their lovemaking. He looked down at her peaceful face and smiled tenderly as he thought back on their belated bridal night.

She had been so responsive to him, but so endearingly innocent in her passion! It occurred to Peter with a jolt that he had never enjoyed a woman so much in all his experience. Furthermore, he knew that he had never cared so much about a woman's pleasure. It was oddly important for her sake, not just as a feather in his cap.

He caressed her shoulder through the silky auburn curls which spread in wild abandon over her and spilled onto his chest. So soft, so sweet! He couldn't believe that he had been stupid enough to distrust her innocence! His hand moved to stroke her cheek, the corner of her tender mouth which had melted in complete surrender to his desire. He longed to make love to her again, but told himself that to awaken her would be selfish.

At this point the thrush, perhaps aware of his feudal master's need, alighted on the casement, singing vigorously. The speckled breast swelled with ecstatic song, expressing Peter's mood perfectly. Penelope opened her eyes with a contented sigh. She wondered for a moment why she was lying in such an odd, yet comfortable position.

Then memory came flooding back as she realised that she was nestled very snugly in her husband's arms and that he was fondling her cheek. A blush stained her face as she recalled exactly why Peter was in her bed. Had she disappointed him? Or, worse still, disgusted him with her enjoyment?

'Peter?' It was little more than a whisper, but he heard the nervousness in her voice and, watching the emotions play across her face, had a very fair idea of its cause. He had to reassure her. It hurt him strangely that she should have any doubt of his delight in their union.

'Yes, little one, are you all right?'

She wondered at the concern in his voice. 'Yes, why do you ask?'

He gathered her still more closely in his arms and went on, 'You were so lovely, and I wanted you so much, that I thought I might have hurt you.'

The sincerity in his voice and the fact that one hand had found its way to her breast, where it was making it very hard for her to think straight, let alone speak, convinced her that he had not been *too* badly disappointed. Surely, too, he had not minded that she had enjoyed it if he was persisting in an action he knew she would respond to!

She was unsure how to answer him, finally opting for the truth. 'It only hurt a little, just at first, then...' She stopped, shyly.

'Then?' he prompted teasingly, enjoying her embarrassment.

'Then…it was w-w-wonderful!' Then, gaining confidence, 'And you, did you…? I mean, was it…? I didn't know what to do…'

'Are you asking if I enjoyed making love to you?' interrupted Peter. 'I must be a very bad lover if I could leave you in any doubt that you were beautiful in every way. And if you had any thought that I had finished with you, Madam Wife, get rid of it right now. I've wasted nearly two months of our marriage and I intend to make up for lost time!'

He then proceeded to demonstrate quite incontrovertibly how much he had enjoyed himself. His reassurances were wholly convincing to Penelope, who responded in a manner which left her husband in no doubt that his bride had no regrets about the belated wedding night.

When George entered the breakfast parlour he found Peter polishing off the remains of what had obviously been a hearty meal. Peter looked up as his friend appeared. 'Good morning, George.'

'Morning, Peter. How did you find Penny this morning?'

Now what the deuce was there in that, wondered George, to make Peter blush? He blinked in surprise as Peter disappeared behind the newspaper.

'She's very well, but I've managed to persuade her to breakfast in bed,' answered Peter. 'George, I don't think I really thanked you for what you did yesterday. There…there are no words. Penny told me that you saved her life…'

'Don't be an idiot, Peter, you would have done the same! So would anyone!' said George, flushing. 'I'm just glad that she's still alive and unhurt.' He noted with delight that Peter had dropped the rather formal use of his wife's full name. Without being precisely glad about the attempt to murder Penelope, he realised that it had permanently shaken Peter out of his mood of distrust.

The entrance of Meadows saved George from further embarrassment. The butler had been very much upset the previous day and it was obvious that he was still shaken. He poured a cup of tea for Peter and handed it to him, saying, 'I've sent Gelert up to Miss Penny, Master Peter, and her breakfast. Are you sure she's quite all right?'

'She's fine, Meadows. I'm going up to her after Mr Carstares and I discuss what's to be done. I'll tell her you were asking.' By avoiding George's eye Peter somehow managed to keep a straight face until his butler had left the room.

'Told you so!' said George smugly, '"Miss Penny"! D'you think he even noticed what he said?'

'Probably not!' said Peter with a grin.

Conversation revolved largely around how to deal with the previous day's attack. George was of the opinion that Peter should return to town with Penelope to let Bow Street deal with the affair, and Peter was inclined to agree.

'If it were just myself I'd stay here, but Penny will be safer in town. Here she would have to be confined to the house at all times. Obviously now we have to assume that the bridge was *not* an accident. At least in town it will be far more risky for anyone to make an attempt upon either of us.'

George nodded and said, 'But you can't deal with it alone, Peter. Even if only for Penny's sake, you must let the Runners know.' It was apparent to George that the attempt on Penelope's life had shocked Peter into a realisation of how foolish he had been. There was a note of tenderness in his voice when he spoke of her, making it plain to see that his determination to protect her did not stem merely from a sense of duty, but from affection.

Peter was silent for a moment. 'The last thing I want is publicity, but I think you're right. I'll send a message to Penny's sister and brother-in-law. They might be able to come up to town as well. Penny isn't very fond of town, and if we go it will mean attending some functions, or there will be gossip. She'll find it easier with family there.'

'Will you trust a letter like that to the post?' asked George.

'No, I won't. You're going to take it! Richard Winton's a decent chap, very fond of Penny, we can count on him in a corner. Besides that I suppose Carrington will be eager to assist, after Jack tried to elope with his sister?'

George shook his head. 'No doubt he would, but he and his mother have taken a house in Bath for several months. They have taken Amelia out of school and are introducing her quietly into society to take her mind off the whole business. Carrington feels it's best for him to stay close. Encourage the chit to confide in him a bit so he can guide her more easily.'

'Oh.' Peter thought about that. 'He's probably right. Well, I can't ask him to drop his own responsibilities to solve my problems! We'll manage with you and Winton to stand buff!' He got up and paced around the room. 'Blast Jack! If I get my hands on him he'll rue the day he was born!'

'No proof, old man. He'd deny everything even if we could get him arrested.'

'I wasn't thinking of getting him arrested! I had something far more personal in mind! And I wish to God Carrington *had* called him out! He'd have blown a hole in him and saved us all a lot of trouble!'

Chapter Thirteen

Three days later Lord and Lady Darleston, accompanied by Gelert, left Darleston Court for London. Penelope had been horrified by the thought of London society, but once the entire situation had been made plain to her she had been forced to admit the sense of going to London. The prospect of being with Phoebe had gone a long way towards reconciling her to the necessity, so she set out happily enough.

They arrived in London on a cold, wet evening. Dusk was falling and the cobbled streets shone wet in the lamplight. 'Nearly there, Penny. Are you tired?' asked Peter, concerned at her white face.

'A little,' she confessed, thinking to herself that it was worth being tired to hear the caring note in his voice. Since the night after the attack Peter had not slept with her, but his manner towards her had been consistently affectionate and protective. He had insisted that she recover completely from her shock and be properly rested before the long trip to London, and Penelope was instinctively aware that he needed time to adjust to the new intimacy of their relationship. Yet the door between their rooms had remained open, and when she was restless at night or bad dreams disturbed her sleep Peter always seemed to be there.

Shyly Penelope felt for Peter's hand and leaned against his shoulder. It was all so different from their last journey together in a chaise, she thought. Then she had been terrified of her unseen, unknown husband. This time she knew that even if he never loved her, at least he was her friend. Peter looked down at her and gently disengaged his hand, but only to slip his arm around her shoulders. She turned to him, smiling as she felt his hand under her chin, lifting it gently. Then his lips were on hers in a brief, tender kiss.

The chaise drew up before the Darleston townhouse in Grosvenor Square. Peter looked out at it through the pouring rain, noting the lights shining from it. Meadows had come up earlier in the day with the rest of the staff to open the house. A footman ran down the stairs from the front door to open the door of the chaise and let down the steps. 'Here we are, Penny. Let me help you out,' said Peter. He lifted her out and set her carefully on the pavement. Gelert frisked around them, delighted to be out of the confines of the chaise.

Meadows greeted them at the door. 'Good evening, my lord and lady. Refreshments are laid out in the library. I trust that your journey was not too tiring?'

'Thank you, Meadows. You're very formal all of a sudden,' said Peter.

'Mr and Mrs Winton, Mr Carstares and Miss Sarah Ffolliot are awaiting you in the library,' said Meadows with dignity.

An undignified shriek came from halfway down the hall accompanied by the sound of running feet. *'Penny!'*

Penny swung around and held out her arms to catch her little sister. 'Sarah! Whatever are you doing here?'

'Mama has gone to stay with Mrs Lacy in Bath because she's ill and begged Mama to come, so the house is shut up and I am staying with Phoebe and Richard. They weren't going to bring me to London but I told them I'd come on the stagecoach if they left me behind or sent me to Bath!' explained Sarah breathlessly. 'Oh, I *am* glad to see you!'

'Good evening, Darleston. I do apologise for springing this hoyden on you without warning.'

Peter turned to see Richard Winton and Phoebe watching the reunion in amusement.

'Richard!' gasped Penelope. 'Where's Phoebe?'

'I'm here, dearest,' said Phoebe, running to her.

The meeting was on the whole a noisy one. The three girls all talked at once, while Gelert signified his delight in having them all together by barking frantically as he leapt from one to another in a manner highly prejudicial to the safety of several chairs.

'Thank you for coming, Winton,' said Peter over the din, holding out his hand.

Richard took it in a friendly grip and said, 'No thanks are needed, Darleston. Penny is as dear to me as my own sister. Carstares explained everything.'

'Good. Will you stay for dinner? Where are you putting up?' asked Peter.

'We are at my sister's house, and we should be delighted to stay for dinner. Carstares has already informed your staff that we would be doing so,' said Richard with a grin.

'Good for him! By the way, where is he?' asked Peter.

'In the library, poring over your chessboard. Sarah has him very neatly trapped!'

'Good Lord, George is quite a dab at chess!' said Peter in amazement.

'Not as good as Sarah, I'm afraid!' laughed Richard. 'John Ffolliot was an expert and he taught all the girls. I avoid playing with Sarah. She's nearly as good as Penny. Phoebe I can at least beat three times out of five, but I suspect she gives me the odd game to salve my dignity. Sarah and Penny have no such delicacy, as you will doubtless find out!'

'Shall we rescue him, then? Meadows, when will dinner be ready?' asked Peter.

'In twenty minutes, my lord.'

'Excellent! Thank you Meadows.'

'You're not going to interrupt the game, are you?' asked Sarah indignantly, catching this conversation. 'Mr Carstares and I have been having such a good time. He has offered to teach me piquet after dinner.'

'At least that may give poor George a chance to salvage his pride after a game of chess with you!' said Penelope. 'Leave the chessboard set up, dearest. You can always finish the game later.'

At the end of dinner the ladies very correctly withdrew, leaving the gentlemen to the enjoyment of their port and brandy. The presence of the servants at dinner had precluded any discussion of the problem at hand, so the men did not linger but joined the ladies in the drawing room almost immediately. A fire had been lit and several lamps cast a warm glow over the room. It was a large apartment, furnished luxuriously but without ostentation. Most of the furniture was of an antique date, and dark wood gleamed with beeswax. Penelope and Phoebe were ensconced on a Queen Anne sofa, while Sarah sat on a rug before the fire with Gelert.

The three girls looked up as the gentlemen entered, and Gelert thumped his tail in greeting. It occurred to Peter that he had not seen this room appear so homelike since his mother's death. Somehow, he thought, Penny made it different. Phoebe had vacated her seat beside Penelope and gone to sit with Richard, so Peter, rather self-consciously, sat beside his wife.

She turned to him at once. 'Peter—Phoebe, Sarah and I have been talking, and we think it will be a good idea if Sarah stays here with us. That will give me a constant companion who will arouse no gossip. What do you think?'

Peter was taken aback. 'What do you think your mother would say? It is a good idea, but Mrs Ffolliot might conceivably object to me endangering two of her daughters. Besides, I was planning to look after you my-self!'

'If Penny's in it then so am I!' said Sarah.

Peter smiled at her and said, 'We're all in it, thanks to my unspeakable cousin. Your mother, however, might prefer you to be kept out of the firing line. I've little doubt Winton would prefer Phoebe out of danger!'

'I would, of course,' said Richard. 'But if we try to handle this without involving them we'll never know what they're up to. Much better to work with them, in my opinion. I sent a message to Mrs Ffolliot, telling her the situation. Her reply reached us at my sister's house. She can't come herself as her friend is ill and needs her. She wrote that if Sarah was a problem we were to send her to Bath but that she would be more useful in London. If she sends for Sarah I'll be very much surprised; this was probably the sort of thing she had in mind.'

'Very well, Sarah stays here. Penny can lend you what you need tonight. We'll send over for the rest tomorrow, Sarah,' said Peter. He was rewarded with a beaming smile from his young sister-in-law and a hug from his wife. 'What about George?'

'I can stay in my lodgings or here, whichever you think best,' said George.

'I think we need to consider our strategy,' said Richard thoughtfully. 'We can tackle this in two ways, as I see it. One, we can make it perfectly obvious that we are surrounding Penny and Darleston. You know, make Frobisher realise that we are on to him. Scare him off. Or, two, we can be a little more subtle, let him think we don't know and—'

'Try to smoke him out!' interrupted Sarah. 'Good idea, Richard!'

'Naturally if it were Sarah he wanted to relieve us of,' continued Richard, 'the second plan would be best. Since, however, we want to avoid any further danger to Penny, my first suggestion might be more appropriate.'

'Definitely!' said Peter with feeling. 'Sorry to seem disobliging, Sarah, but I have no intention of giving my cousin the slightest chance of harming Penny! It might be third time lucky for him! George, you're staying here, if you really don't mind.'

George nodded cheerfully. 'Much more comfortable than my lodgings!'

'Never mind, Sarah,' said Penelope consolingly. 'I dare say we can have a lot of fun scaring Mr Frobisher!'

Phoebe smiled. 'You will be able to play lots of chess, Mr Carstares!'

'Much obliged to you, ma'am!' said George dryly.

'What about Carrington?' asked Richard. 'He's a good friend of yours, Darleston. Where is he at the moment?'

'In Bath, unfortunately,' responded Peter. 'He's tied up with some family matters. I can't ask his assistance at the moment. Mainly because he would feel obliged to give it and I don't think he should!'

'Well, that's a pity, but obviously it can't be helped,'

said Richard thoughtfully. 'Meanwhile, how do we start our scare campaign?'

Peter thought for a moment and then said, 'I think, if Penny can stand it, that we launch ourselves into the autumn Little Season. We are bound to meet Jack, which will give us the chance to hint him off. Also George told me that Jack has been spreading unsavoury rumours about our marriage, so we'll take the opportunity to squash those as well!'

Sarah looked thoughtful. 'Of course I don't wish Penny to be hurt, but I don't think it will work. How are we going to know if he has been really scared off? He might just lie low for a while and then try later. You can't spend the rest of your lives wondering if your cousin is trying to kill you!'

The others were silent. Sarah had unerringly put her finger on the weakness in their strategy. Finally Peter answered. 'What concerns me is the threat to your sister. If Jack thinks that he can't get to her he will try for me…'

'*No!*' interrupted Penelope, 'You are not going to go around offering yourself as a target! I won't have it!'

The fear in her voice surprised everyone. Peter stared at her in wonder. Did she care for him that much? He knew she was fond of him, responded to him physically, but love? The thought made him uncomfortable, ashamed that he did not love her—whatever his heart might, on occasion, tell him to the contrary.

'Penny…' he began.

Penelope heard the constraint in his voice and knew she had betrayed herself. She tried to lighten the atmosphere. 'I'm too young to be a widow!' There was a general laugh at this.

'Very well,' said Richard. 'Let's start by seeing if we

can scare him off. I think we'll know if he's really scared or just lying low.'

Penelope nodded. 'That's a much better idea. I definitely do not fancy having any more pot-shots taken at me!'

Later, in the privacy of her bed-chamber, Penelope mentally kicked herself for being so foolish as to give Peter a clue to her feelings. Little fool! she thought. The last thing he wants is love! Sighing, she lay back against her pillows.

'At least he has come to care for me a little,' she whispered. His kindness and tenderness towards her were unfailing.

Her thoughts drifted back to the night he had spent in her bed. Never had she imagined that making love could possibly be so wonderful. Trembling at the memory of the fire he had ignited in her body, she wondered when he would come to her again. Briefly she considered going to him, but recoiled from the thought in fear of betraying herself any further. It was not just a matter of pride. She knew that to declare her love would make Peter uncomfortable, it might even cause him to withdraw from her again. He had never spoken of love and she was not naive enough to think that because he had bedded her with such tender skill he must needs love her.

A gentle knock at the door from Peter's room startled her from her thoughts.

'Come in,' she called, pushing back the covers to sit up.

Peter walked in, holding a candle. Shadows flickered on the walls from its dancing light. He gazed at Penelope, sitting almost lost in the shadows of her bed-hangings.

'Peter? Is that you?' she asked shyly, as his footsteps brought him close to the bed.

'Yes, I just wanted to make sure you were comfortable,' he said, looking down at her. He wondered if she had the slightest notion that Ellen always chose the most revealing nightdresses imaginable. Desire burned in his veins as his eyes rested on her, but he told himself firmly that she must be tired. Surely he could wait just one more night!

She smiled at him, saying, 'I'm very comfortable, thank you.' She held out her hand. Every fibre in her body cried out for him to stay, but somehow she said simply, 'Goodnight.'

He took her hand, kissed it, and then looked into her face. His heart lurched at what he saw there: love, desire, trust. Instead of releasing her hand he sat down on the bed, put the candle on a bedside table and took her in his arms.

'This is likely to be a very long "Goodnight", little one,' he whispered.

His mouth was on hers, wooing her tenderly, then more fiercely as he felt her ardent response. Her kisses inflamed him and he pushed away the covers to slide into the bed. Releasing her momentarily, he tore off his dressing gown, then lay down beside her, pulling her back into his arms. She yielded to him completely, her soft curves moulding to his hard, muscled contours. He groaned in excitement as he felt her mouth open under his like a flower. Never in all his life had he wanted a woman as he did now.

Much later, lying clasped in Peter's arms, Penelope found to her distress that she was crying silently. She did her best to hide it, but Peter felt the tension in her body. Startled, he lifted a hand to her cheek and found it wet.

'Why, Penny, you're crying!' he said in horror. 'Sweetheart, I didn't hurt you?'

She shook her head, tears still trickling down her cheeks, 'No, you didn't hurt me at all! It was wonderful! I…I'm fine…just a bit shaken.' How could she explain to him that she was crying because she loved him, because she knew he did not love her? How to tell him that every time he touched her, or spoke to her, her love increased? That when he made love to her it was an agony not to be able to say that she loved him?

Suddenly he understood. He had suspected that she loved him; her passionate response to his lovemaking told him a great deal. Now he realised just how difficult the whole relationship had become for her. No matter what he said or did he was going to hurt her unbearably. Tenderly he used the sheet to dry her cheeks, knowing that there was nothing he could possibly say to comfort her. To do so would be an intolerable wound to her pride, which would not allow her to accept pity. All he could do was hold her until she drifted off to sleep.

Chapter Fourteen

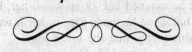

It seemed to Peter as he escorted his wife into the glittering, crowded ballroom that most of the Ton was present at Lady Edenhope's Ball. Two weeks had been spent in intensive shopping to outfit Penelope for the social whirl and this was their first appearance. He exchanged a glance with Richard Winton and said softly, 'This is going to cause quite a sensation!'

Penelope's hand trembled on his arm. The buzz of chatter in the room told her just how large the gathering was. She felt isolated, lost.

Peter looked down at her, understanding her nervousness. 'Don't be scared, little one. I will be with you all the time. Trust me!'

Penelope smiled up at him, reassured. The room was so ablaze with light that she could easily make out his tall figure beside her. 'I know. You wouldn't want me to trip over someone important and destroy your credit!' she teased.

'Nothing of the sort! *My* credit could withstand a dozen such scandals!' he replied with considerable aplomb. 'It is merely that I pride myself on being able to do just as good a job as Gelert. Think how mortifying for me if I had to admit publicly that your dog is more capable than I am!'

'Yes, I suppose we should keep that fact in the family!' answered Penelope with a laugh.

Phoebe, observing the look of shining confidence replace fear on her sister's face, murmured to Richard, 'Something tells me that this match is working very well. Not even Papa could have got Penny to a function like this!' She knew, without being told, just how much Penelope had come to care for Peter and trust him. Suddenly she was sure that Peter had come to care for Penelope. How else could he have understood, let alone banished her fear?

A footman announced them. 'Lord and Lady Darleston, Mr and Mrs Richard Winton.'

The hum of conversation ceased abruptly as the élite of society turned to inspect the unknown girl who had caught one of the richest prizes on the Marriage Mart. The marriage of Miss Phoebe Ffolliot to Richard Winton had surprised few. The marriage of Darleston to a girl whose very existence had been unsuspected was another matter.

Jack Frobisher had hinted at some sort of scandal, and despite his unpopularity the whiff of gossip had aroused curiosity. Most people knew of the row at Lady Bellingham's ball and they speculated on the probability that there was more to the situation than the bland announcement in the *Gazette* had told them.

The split second of silence was broken by a collective gasp of astonishment as society took stock of the twins. A babble of conversation broke out. Darleston and Richard were, as ever, immaculately turned out, but it was the staggering resemblance between the two women which was the topic of discussion. Penelope and Phoebe had taken a mischievous pleasure in dressing their hair alike and wearing very similar gowns of soft green silk, cut revealingly across the shoulders.

Odd scraps reached their ears.

'Good God! Peas in the pod ain't in it...'

'Which one did we meet?'

'Hope Winton and Darleston can tell 'em apart!'

Peter and Richard exchanged grins as this last remark drifted to their ears. Neither one had the slightest trouble distinguishing his wife, and the suggestion that they might struck them as ridiculous in the extreme.

Lady Edenhope came to greet them, 'Dear Peter, thank you so much for coming to me first! You have ensured that my party will be gossiped about for days! And Mr Winton, congratulations! Mrs Winton, I wish you happy!' She turned to Penelope, 'My dear, allow an old friend of Peter's to wish you very happy. I knew this wretch in his cradle. His mama and I came out together. We were the best of friends always.'

Penelope smiled and said shyly, 'Thank you, ma'am. I am so pleased to meet you. Peter has told me all about you.'

'Well, you must come with me to meet the sharks. I am sure they are all just dying to be presented to you! They all met your sister last year, but we had no idea there were two of you!' said Lady Edenhope merrily.

'For heaven's sake, Aunt Louisa, you'll be heard!' said Peter in amusement. 'I'll come with you, if I may. You may not have realised, Aunt Louisa, but Penelope is blind, so I have got used to warning her about steps and obstacles.' He knew as he said this that at least half a dozen people had heard him. The shock on their faces was mirrored in Lady Edenhope's eyes.

She made a gallant recovery. 'Oh, you poor girl! Fancy

being married to this handsome creature and unable to appreciate him fully!'

Penelope chuckled, 'Indeed, ma'am. I have been feeling most frustrated ever since my sister described him to me.'

'Never mind, my dear, he will have to be content with one less admirer. Very likely it will do him good! Come along!'

It was evident to Peter that his mother's closest friend, having taken a liking to Penelope, meant to make sure she was accepted by the Ton. It was also evident that Lady Edenhope's sympathetic response, tinged as it was with humour, had gone a long way towards setting Penelope at ease.

However, as she escorted them around the room the whispers sprang up in their wake. Amazement was the most common reaction. Everyone knew the story of the first Lady Darleston, and there were plenty of snide murmurs that Darleston had now picked a girl who would be totally dependent on him. Others, more shrewd, noticed the very obvious affection between the couple and discounted the idea. Some, like Lady Edenhope, who had known Peter well before his disastrous first marriage, were delighted to see him so relaxed and happy.

One of these was Lady Jersey, acknowledged Queen of the Ton. She came up to Peter with words of welcome. 'Darleston! How delightful to see you! And your bride! Please do introduce us!'

'Of course. Penelope, this is Lady Jersey, another old friend.' Peter stood back to watch his wife deal with the voluble peeress, who was living up to her nickname with a vengeance. She rattled on cheerfully but her inconsequent tongue did not prevent her from taking stock of the situation. Penelope responded to her chatter shyly, but with a humour that won approval from that notoriously high stickler.

'So difficult for you, Lady Darleston, not being able to see this den of lions you are flung into!' said Lady Jersey at last. 'I admire your courage. I vow I should not dare!'

'I did not dare last year,' admitted Penelope. 'But Lord Darleston has convinced me that you are not all ogres and that I must keep him company, at least some of the time.'

'Excellent! But do you know, Lady Darleston, at one time I feared that Darleston was becoming an ogre himself, and a bit of a recluse? I do think you must take some credit for halting the process. He is such a decorative addition to London!'

'So I have been told, Lady Jersey. But Lady Edenhope assures me it will do him good to have one admirer the less!'

A charming ripple of laughter greeted this answer, 'I'm sure it will! Lady Darleston, it has been delightful to meet you. I shall call on you in the near future and bring you vouchers for the, er…shark-pool, I think Lady Edenhope would call it!'

She moved away graciously to spread the word that Lady Darleston was quite delightful. A pity she was blind, of course, but if she and Darleston were happy there was an end to the matter. And, really, anything must be better than his marrying Caroline Daventry! Oh, good heavens! One would have had to receive her!

As Peter watched her go he said softly to Penelope, 'Well done! She means to give you vouchers for Almack's.'

'Was that what she meant?' asked Penelope. 'Goodness, I shall have to practise my dancing!'

'What an excellent idea!' said Peter. 'I shall be delighted to assist you!' Then, seeing George Carstares making his way through the crush towards them, 'Good God, here's George. What made you so late? We gave up and left without you!'

'My cravat. Matter of extreme importance! Hello, Penny. Enjoying yourself? Devilish squeeze, ain't it? Your cousin's here, Peter.'

'Jack? How charming!' Peter looked keenly around the room, and immediately spotted his cousin near the refreshment tables.

Jack Frobisher was looking straight at him. His face was mask-like as his eyes met Peter's icy glare and swung back to his companion. Peter recognised her at once. Lady Caroline Daventry! The voluptuous blonde turned to gaze across at him. He returned the look coldly, observing the scornful half-smile on her lips as her eyes raked Penelope. Deliberately he stepped in front of Penelope, presenting his back to his erstwhile mistress.

'Can't say I care for his choice of companion,' commented George in a thoughtful tone of voice, missing none of this by-play. He cocked a mobile eyebrow at Peter.

'Neither do I,' was the quiet answer. Peter was thinking furiously. Jack was one thing. He could probably be frightened off. But Lady Caroline was another matter. She had enough intelligence to be extremely dangerous. She had steered clear of open scandal but it was well known that she had been his mistress. Was Jack cultivating her assistance?

Peter could well imagine how angry she must have been that her plot to entrap him had failed. Her rage at his swift marriage must have been beyond belief, he thought sardonically.

'Who is it?' asked Penelope curiously. She could hear the edge in Peter's voice and feel the tension in his body.

He said lightly, 'No one that you would know, my dear.' Not to save his life could he have brought himself to mention his ex-mistress to Penelope. Penelope turned to him and he saw that she was wearing what he thought of as her 'second-sight look'.

He knew quite well that she was not fooled when she forbore to ask any further questions, merely saying, 'Oh, well, I suppose we can start our campaign to scare the skirter!'

'We can,' said Peter with a reluctant grin. 'But for heaven's sake don't use that sort of language in company! People will think George and I taught it to you!'

'More likely to blame my father, if they were at all acquainted with him!' said Penelope with a laugh.

Richard and Phoebe came up at that moment. 'Have you seen who's here?' asked Richard, jerking his head in the direction of the unsavoury pair.

'Of course,' answered Peter. 'George was just saying that the combination is not a pleasant one.' He looked at Richard evenly. Richard, of course, was perfectly aware of the earlier connection between Darleston and the lovely Lady Caroline. He knew something, too, of the lady's reputation for harbouring grudges, but correctly deduced that Peter would prefer to leave her out of the discussion at present.

Phoebe, being quite unaware of all this, said innocently, 'I don't think I know the lady with him.' She stared through a break in the eddying crowd, just as Lady Caroline turned towards them again. 'Oh! Yes, I do! It's Lady Caroline Daventry. Well, she's very beautiful but I don't like her much. She was rather horrid to me in a polite way after you danced with me at Almack's, Peter.'

'Which reminds me,' said Peter smoothly, 'that I have never danced with my wife, and I observe that the orchestra is beginning a waltz. May I have the honour, Lady Darleston? You did say that you wished to practise didn't you?'

'I didn't mean in public!' she protested. 'Are you sure you wish to, Peter?'

'Of course. We shall stay near the edge. Anyway, by this time the gossip that you are blind has been around the room half a dozen times. Trust Sally Jersey for that!'

He led her to the dance floor and swung her into the dance. At first Penelope was nervous, but Peter was very good at steering her away from possible trouble. Gradually, as she relaxed, she began to enjoy the dance.

Peter felt the change and said in a bantering tone, 'See! I am not such a bad dancer after all. It might interest you to know that lots of people are staring at us in the rudest way. You'd think they had never seen me dance with a beautiful woman before!'

'I'm sure you have danced with many, my lord,' answered Penelope, smiling up at him affectionately.

'Of course, it adds to my consequence!' said Peter laughing. They continued to chat easily throughout the dance, and Peter kept Penelope in a ripple of laughter with his at times caustic comments on the people they passed.

Richard watched the pair and said softly to George, 'I was against this marriage, you know. But it looks as if I was wrong. I haven't seen Penny this happy in company for years. And she is happy, isn't she, Phoebe?' He turned to his wife.

'Oh, yes!' said Phoebe. 'She could not appear so relaxed if she did not like and trust him.'

'I think it has been good for Peter too,' agreed George.

'Did my level best to talk him out of it, but it's the best thing he could have done. Oh, good evening, Lady Castlereagh.' He greeted one of the patronesses of Almack's.

'Good evening, Mr Carstares, Mr Winton, Mrs Winton,' said that stately lady. 'I have just been remarking to Lady Jersey how happy Lord Darleston appears. It must be a great pleasure to all his friends to see him look so much like his old self. Mrs Winton, allow me to wish you happy. I believe I have not seen you since your marriage.'

Phoebe blushed, smiling. Lady Castlereagh had always been very kind. 'I believe that you and Lady Darleston are twins! I do hope your mother and husbands can tell you apart, for I am sure that I should not be able to!'

'It is very easy, Lady Castlereagh,' said Richard. 'My sister-in-law, as you must have heard, is blind. She is generally accompanied everywhere by a very large dog who guides her every move!'

'But not at a ball!' said Lady Castlereagh with a twinkle.

'No, ma'am. Here she must rely on Darleston and her family,' agreed Richard gravely.

'Quite so. Ah, here they come. Darleston, I congratulate you! And Lady Darleston, I wish you very happy indeed. I have just been saying to your sister that I should find it impossible to tell the pair of you apart. But Mr Winton informs me that your dog attends you everywhere, so when in doubt I must depend upon that! Allow me to assure you that he will always be welcome in my drawing room if you are so kind as to call!'

Penelope stammered a confused thank-you. The thought of making morning calls without Gelert had been a source of worry to her. If Lady Castlereagh accepted him in her home every other lady of fashion would follow her lead.

She tried to convey her gratitude to Lady Castlereagh, who said, smiling, 'My dear, don't mention it. I should find it so very vexing to be blind myself that I shall be happy to assist you. Sally Jersey tells me she has promised you vouchers for Almack's. We shall all be pleased to see you there.' She made her farewells and moved away to greet other friends and comment on the charming bride Darleston had chosen.

At the other side of the ballroom were two people who viewed the social success of Darleston's bride with savage anger. Jack Frobisher felt cheated. He had counted his cousin's title and wealth as his own. To be supplanted by a second marriage was insupportable.

'Damn Peter!' he burst out.

Lady Caroline looked at him and said softly, 'Control yourself, my friend. You are not the only one who wants to scuttle this marriage. From now on we work together! If all goes well we can both enjoy the money and the title. Remember the price of my silence is marriage!'

Frobisher shrugged and nodded. 'You drive a hard bargain, Caroline, but if you can help me it will be worth it to get my revenge on the pair of them.'

Lady Caroline said curiously, 'You're not in this just because of the money and title, Frobisher. What else are you after?'

Frobisher gave an ugly laugh and said, 'I would dearly like the chance of a little chat with Lady Darleston, uninterrupted by her dog!' There was no mistaking his meaning.

Lady Caroline smiled evilly, saying, 'Done! She's all yours! Pay me a morning call in the next day or so to discuss ways and means. We had better not be seen too much together. Why don't you see if you can find out whether your cousin has any suspicion of your involvement in the shooting? For now, I'm off home. Louisa Edenhope's parties are such insipid affairs!'

'What you mean is that you can't bear to watch the prize you lost flaunting another woman under your nose,' said Frobisher.

Lady Caroline's colour rose at this taunt. It had already occurred to her that this was Lady Edenhope's sole reason for inviting her. She turned on her heel and left him.

Well satisfied with the progress he had made, Jack Frobisher helped himself to a glass of champagne from a passing footman. He drank a silent toast to his revenge on Penelope and Darleston. A pity his cousin had had the wench first, but doubtless he could think of any number of things Darleston would be far too gentlemanly to subject his wife to! An unpleasant smile came to his lips as he contemplated the future.

He moved off through the crush of people, nodding to various acquaintances, many of whom commented on his cousin's bride.

Frobisher merely smiled and said, 'Ah, yes, poor Ffolliot!' At this his listeners smirked knowingly. Frobisher observed the success of his efforts to stir up gossip. Already he saw himself as Earl of Darleston. Wrapped in this pleasant dream, he sauntered through the crowd towards the card room. A chance glimpse of Lord and Lady Darleston brought Lady Caroline's suggestion back into his mind. He stood irresolute, wondering if he dared greet his cousin.

The decision was taken out of his hands. Peter had already seen him. 'Here comes Jack,' he said softly to his companions.

Richard said fiercely, 'Good, let's give him a fright! Show him we know!'

'Good idea if it were just Jack involved, but the situation may be different now,' was the rejoinder. 'Better to draw him in, lull any fears he may have. That way we may be able to trap him. What do you think, Penny? Can you bear to meet him again after what has happened?' It sickened him to think of Frobisher being anywhere near her, and Penelope could sense his distaste for the whole situation.

'If it will help you, Peter,' said Penelope. Darleston could hear the constraint in her voice. Her fingers resting on his arm trembled. He laid his hand on hers and pressed it reassuringly.

'Here goes, then,' said Darleston, beckoning to his cousin with a friendly smile.

Jack approached in some trepidation. Surely Peter had glared at him earlier. Perhaps the glare had been for Lady Caroline. There was no trace of unfriendliness now, however.

'Good evening, Jack,' said Peter. 'You are already acquainted with my wife and her sister, Mrs Winton, but may I present Mr Winton? Winton—my cousin, Mr Jack Frobisher.'

'Good evening, Mr Frobisher,' said Richard politely. 'I don't believe we met when you visited the Ffolliots last spring.'

'Er…Good evening, Mr Winton,' said Frobisher uncomfortably.

He turned to Penelope. 'I heard you had been unwell. Took a toss from a horse, did you not? I hope my cousin is looking after you properly!'

'My lord has been very kind,' she replied steadily, wondering just how he had heard about that 'accident.'

He continued heartily, 'Must be difficult, being blind and all, having to find your way around that damned great barrack in Grosvenor Square. You just tell me if you need any help!' That, he thought, might be the ticket to get into the house and lull any suspicions.

'How kind of you, Mr Frobisher,' said Penelope. 'Lord Darleston has been so kind as to show me around already. But if you call I shall remember to have my dog under control.'

Darleston was startled to discover that he was torn between the urge to laugh at the infuriated expression on his cousin's face and the desire to plant him a facer on the mere suspicion that he had laid a finger on Penelope.

Somehow Frobisher managed to control himself, 'Ah, yes. Your dog has such an uncertain temper, fair Cousin!'

'Do you find him so?' asked Darleston in feigned surprise. 'Why, I find his behaviour quite predictable and logical!'

'No doubt he mellows on longer acquaintance,' said Frobisher.

Penelope listened carefully. He sounded nervous, ill at ease, and no wonder considering the turn the conversation had taken. The voice was over-eager to ingratiate but he seemed to gain confidence as Peter continued to be civil. Richard, however, sounded as though he were having difficulty containing himself at some of Frobisher's rather distasteful comments.

'Believe you live near the Ffolliots, Winton. Must have been a hard choice for you, choosing a wife. Could have just tossed a coin, eh?'

'I have never had the slightest difficulty distinguishing between my wife and her sister, even when they tried to fool us as children,' replied Richard in tones of utter boredom. 'Excuse me, please. I can see a friend I wish to speak to. Come, Mrs Winton.' He cast Peter a look of apology as he retreated.

'High and mighty, ain't he?' said Jack. 'Well, I must be going, Cousins. I shall pop in to see how you are going along. Evening, Carstares.' He moved away in the direction of the card room, confident that his formidable cousin had no idea of the plot against him.

His departure was much to the relief of Peter. Frobisher's blatant sizing up of Penelope had been almost too much for his self-control. 'What's your verdict, George?'

'Nervous, at least at first. Penny?'

She hesitated before saying, 'I agree. And he seemed over-hearty towards the end. A little over-confident.

'I've had enough of this business for one night,' said Darleston. 'I suggest we find Richard and Phoebe and repair to the supper room. Then we can dance some more before going home!'

The rest of the evening passed pleasantly, and Lord and Lady Darleston arrived home at about three in the morning. When Meadows opened the door accompanied by Gelert Peter stared in amazement. 'What the devil are you doing up, Meadows? I said you were not to, didn't I?'

'Begging your pardon, my lord, but with all this nasty business going on I preferred to know you were safe home. I did go to bed but I couldn't sleep,' replied the butler with dignity.

Peter stared at him helplessly and then turned to Penelope, saying, 'See what sort of a demoralising effect you are having. Even Meadows doesn't trust me to look after you. Up to bed with you, my lady, while I deal with this insubordination.'

Penelope laughed. 'Goodnight, Meadows! Thank you. I shall give you a little bottle of laudanum next time we are out late!'

She went upstairs to find Ellen waiting for her, also contrary to instructions. 'Why, Ellen, you and Meadows are as bad as each other!'

'His lordship's valet, Fordham, is up too,' said Ellen, grinning at her mistress unrepentantly. 'Now stop fussing, milady. I had a little nap on the day-bed. See how pleased Gelert is to see you safe!'

'Oh, Ellen! What could possibly happen to me at a ball?' asked Penelope, petting Gelert, who was jumping around her like a puppy.

'I'd have said nothing could happen down at Darleston, but I'd have been wrong!' was Ellen's grim rejoinder. 'We did make Miss Sarah go to bed. She went off to sleep like a baby!'

'Thank goodness someone did!' said Penelope, as she submitted to being undressed and arrayed in a very pretty nightgown. When Ellen sat her down at the dressing table and produced the hairbrush, however, she rebelled, sending her off to bed with dire threats of being sent back to the country.

No sooner had Ellen left than Peter walked through the connecting door in his dressing gown, saying expressively, 'Our servants! Did you know Fordham was up? I haven't let him stay up for me in years!'

Penelope chuckled as she continued to brush her hair. 'Never mind. At least they care about us!'

Peter watched her for a moment before walking over to remove the brush from her grasp. 'May I, Penny?'

'If you wish,' she answered shyly.

He brushed her hair in silence, enjoying the feel of the silken curls, gazing at her in the mirror. Firmly he told

himself that she was probably tired, that he should leave
her alone, that his lovemaking only increased the pain of
the relationship for her. He told himself this every evening when he came to her room, ostensibly to bid her
goodnight. And every night he found himself unable to
return to his own bed. She never asked him to stay, he
understood that her pride would not permit it, but always
she responded to his advances passionately.

Now his eyes kept straying from her face to the delectable curves so temptingly revealed by the nightgown.
Those soft curves which fitted so miraculously to his own
body. His gaze lingered on her lips, such a sweet mouth
which yielded to his demands in total surrender.

Unable to help himself, he put the hairbrush down,
grasped her shoulders and pulled her up to stand against
him. One arm slipped around her waist as he bent his
head to kiss her neck. She could feel the heat of his
mouth and turned in his arms, pressing herself against
him. Her breath came unevenly. She wondered just how
long her legs would be able to support her.

'I want you, Penny, you're so lovely!' said Peter shakily. She simply lifted her mouth to his and kissed him.
Then his hands were at her breast, undoing the buttons
of her gown. Gently he pushed it off her shoulders. As
it slid to the ground with a silken whisper he stepped
back to feast his eyes on her loveliness. Swiftly he removed his robe and took her in his arms again, his mouth
tender and seductive. His hands ranged over her trembling body, delighting in her response.

Penelope could feel the hard strength of his body and
then felt him lift her into his arms, his mouth still locked
to hers. She nestled in his arms as he crossed the room
to deposit her gently on the bed.

He stood looking down at her for a moment and then
joined her. 'Penny, sweet little Penny,' he whispered, before his mouth came down on hers.

Chapter Fifteen

Two days after Lady Edenhope's ball Penelope sat alone in the cushioned luxury of her drawing room wondering just how many members of the Ton were going to pay bride visits. Admittedly some of them were friends of Peter's, but many, she was well aware, had come out of sheer curiosity. Lady Castlereagh and Lady Jersey had been among the earliest visitors. They had called together, bringing the promised vouchers for Almack's. Their visit had been extremely pleasant.

The presence of Gelert had not bothered them in the slightest. Lady Jersey had everyone so far as to say that all women of consequence should have one to discourage unwanted callers, 'Just think how useful! Lady Darleston, you will be setting a fashion. I don't suppose you would consider lending him to me?'

'Nonsense, Sally! Lady Darleston will have enough unwanted callers in the next few days to keep him busy. As for you, if your butler does not know by now whom to admit you should replace him!' Lady Castlereagh had replied, and continued kindly, 'I dare say you will receive a great many callers, Lady Darleston. Most of them will only call once, out of curiosity to see Darleston's bride.

We had all quite given up hope that he would marry again, you see!'

Penelope was turning this tactful warning over in her mind when Sarah came in and said, 'Can I go to Hatchard's to buy a book? Ellen will go with me if you say yes.'

Penelope stood up and stretched. 'Give me twenty minutes to change into a walking dress and I'll come too. Peter won't be back for some time and I haven't been out all day. I'm tired of visitors. We'll take a walk in the park afterwards. Gelert needs one.'

Half an hour later they set out with a footman in attendance to carry the parcels, for, as Sarah said, 'It's no good going to a bookshop and expecting to only buy one book! Besides, Roger will probably enjoy the walk because he likes Ellen so much!'

Sarah was full of energy and skipped along, laughing at Ellen's remonstrances which were the more forceful due to her embarrassment at Sarah's wholly accurate observation of the regard in which Roger held her.

'It's no good, Ellen!' said Penelope in amusement. 'We're not used to London and having to be so terribly well-behaved. I'm not sure who is in more need of exercise, Sarah or Gelert!'

'Well, there's no doubt who's the better behaved!' said Ellen bluntly. 'Give over, Miss Sarah! You'll never get a husband if you're not more ladylike!'

'Pooh! Who wants a husband? I'm not going to get married until I meet someone who can give me a good game of chess! Why, Phoebe says she actually *lets* Richard win occasionally just so that he can feel superior. I won't do that!' said Sarah in disgust.

'I'm sure you won't!' said Penelope. 'What is the book you want to buy?'

'Peter told me about it. It is called *Northanger Abbey*, he thinks I would enjoy it. What are you laughing at, Penny?'

'Nothing, Sarah!' said Penelope unconvincingly. 'It is nice to see you have enough respect for Peter to take his advice on the choice of a book!'

'Oh, well, he plays chess properly, even better than George, and he said he'd pay for the book if I didn't like it,' said Sarah ingenuously. 'But I think I shall because it is by the same person as *Pride and Prejudice*, and we liked that excessively. Actually, he offered to buy me the book as a present, but I didn't think I should let him. I wouldn't like him to think I was *sponging* off him. Even if he was like Montoni in *The Mysteries of Udolpho*, which doesn't seem very likely.' This last in tones of infinite regret.

'Did you tell him that?' enquired Penelope with a grin.

'Yes. He said he could see my point but that he ought to be prepared to back his advice, and that was why he said he'd buy the book if I didn't like it.'

Amusement at Peter's tactics made it difficult for Penelope to maintain her gravity. Obviously he was determined to win over her suspicious young sister! Equally obviously Sarah's vivid imagination was having a hard task in the face of Peter's kindness and good nature. What she would say when she started to read this book Peter had recommended was anybody's guess. No doubt, thought Penelope, it would be distinguished by a certain directness of expression!

They continued along South Audley Street, discussing books and music happily. The conversation was not limited to Penelope and Sarah only. Ellen's opinion was frequently sought, since she often read aloud to her mistress, and she swelled with pride to think that her thoughts and

ideas were valued. Even Roger, a young man who knew
his place to a nicety, was dragged into the discussion of
music.

'It's no good saying, "I don't know, I'm sure, miss!"
You hear us playing all the time and you must know
which bits you like, Roger!' said Penelope firmly. Roger
gave in and admitted that although he quite enjoyed
Mozart, Beethoven held more appeal for him. More stirring, if they took his meaning.

'Hmm. I can see we're brewing a revolution below
stairs, Sarah!' said Penelope in amusement. 'No more
Beethoven when Roger is about. A straight diet of Haydn
and Mozart with perhaps a little Handel should curb these
dangerous tendencies!'

Roger blushed and disclaimed any revolutionary tendencies, saying that Ellen and Mr Meadows would bear
him out. In this fashion they beguiled the walk to
Hatchard's in Piccadilly. The sheer noise of the traffic in
this thoroughfare smote on their country-bred ears with
stunning effect. Penelope was hard put to it to make any
sort of sense out of the jumble of sounds and maintained
a firm grip on Gelert's collar.

On her other side Sarah pressed close, sensing her sister's confusion. Upon reaching the shop they stood outside for a moment while Sarah gazed through the bow
windows at all the latest publications.

'It is nice,' she said, 'to be able to walk here as a
matter of course, change books at Hookham's and so on,
but I think on the whole I prefer the country. Town is so
dreadfully noisy!'

With this comment she led the way into the shop. This
was Penelope's first visit to Hatchard's, and an assistant
at once rushed forward to protest at the entrance of a
large dog. However, his outrage was transformed into

fawning obsequiousness when he realised that his new patroness was none other than the Countess of Darleston, whose dog was already an accepted presence in Tonnish circles.

He assisted them to find the book they sought and diffidently suggested that they might also enjoy the latest works by the author of *Guy Mannering*, if these had not previously come their way. Penelope was entranced at the suggestion. Papa had read *Guy Mannering* to them all with great success, so she unhesitatingly invested in *Rob Roy* and *The Heart of Midlothian*, commenting that Peter would probably be reading aloud for a year!

Sarah was struck speechless at this extravagance, especially when Penelope told her to choose an extra book for herself. 'And if you dare to say a word about *sponging*, Sarah, I'll slap you!'

By the time they left the shop Roger was laden with parcels, for Penelope had been struck by the happy thought of buying a present to send off to Mrs Ffolliot in Bath, as well as Southey's *Life of Nelson* for Peter.

It also struck her that Roger might not relish a walk in the park thus burdened. 'Roger, if you would prefer to take the parcels straight home rather than walk in the park you may do so,' she said with a smile.

Roger, however, had no intention of being sent home, and stated his complete willingness to carry twice as much before he would even consider deserting his mistress.

Accordingly the entire party set off towards Hyde Park Corner. It was drawing close to the hour of the fashionable promenade and many members of the Ton were converging on the park. A great number of people greeted Penelope with pleasure, among them Lady Edenhope and her friend Lady Wickham, who promised Penelope a card for her ball the following week.

'Such a pleasure that Darleston is back in such good spirits, Lady Darleston. We are all delighted! And this must surely be a younger sister. Charming, quite charming!'

Penelope laughed and said, 'Indeed, this is my sister Sarah. She is staying with us at the moment while my mother is nursing a sick friend. I hope you will visit us soon, Lady Wickham.' They parted merrily, with Lady Wickham promising to visit and bring the invitation card personally the very next day.

A waft of powerful scent announced another presence, and a cooing voice said, 'Dear Lady Darleston, you must forgive me for presenting myself in such an informal way! I am Lady Caroline Daventry. I saw you at Lady Edenhope's the other night. Such a squeeze, was it not? But you and dear Peter were surrounded. I vow there was no getting near you! Permit me to wish you happy! What a conquest you have made! We all thought Peter would remain single.'

Penelope's mind worked swiftly. The name was familiar. Surely this was the woman who had been with Jack Frobisher the other evening! Peter had changed the subject as soon as her name was mentioned. He and George had both seemed somewhat embarrassed.

Lady Caroline managed to insinuate herself between Sarah and Penelope. For days she had walked in the park, hoping for just such a chance as this to get into the Countess of Darleston's good graces. Well did she know that she stood not the slightest chance of being admitted to the house, but she was counting on Darleston's fastidious nature to have recoiled from warning his bride against her.

Lady Caroline seethed with suppressed fury as she stared at the slender girl who held the position she had counted as hers for the taking. She could not for the life of her understand what Peter saw in the chit. Red hair, for heaven's sake, although the generous might call it auburn. A bit on the thin side, and blind, if you please! Yet she could have screamed in vexation as she recalled the way Darleston had gazed at his bride, the pride in his bearing as he presented her to high society. Damn the wench! She had stolen Darleston!

'How kind of you, Lady Caroline. You are an old friend of my lord's?' asked Penelope politely. Her hand gripped Gelert's collar warningly as she heard the faintest of growls from him.

'Very old friends, Lady Darleston. Indeed, I am quite wounded that I was not invited to the wedding. But I understand your father and brother…so sad! No doubt Darleston could not bear to wait to carry you off! Quite a romance, is it not?'

All this was said in tones of great good humour, but Penelope was quick to detect the smirk in her voice as she claimed long friendship with Peter. Also she was aware of enmity behind the dulcet accents and wondered at it. What reason could the woman possibly have for allying herself with Jack Frobisher? And why was Peter so reluctant to discuss her? Then Phoebe's remark about Lady Caroline's behaviour to her flashed into her mind and everything fell into place.

The conviction that she was conversing publicly with her husband's mistress—well, ex-mistress, she hoped— did not have quite the effect on Penelope that one might have expected from a delicately bred girl. Sensible enough to realise that her husband's past amours were no concern of hers, she found the situation extremely funny, and it was only with great difficulty that she managed to control her features as she listened to Lady Caroline. It occurred to her that in this case the whole situation must be of the greatest interest to all of society, and that a public set-down would only exacerbate the situation. Besides, she might be quite wrong in all her suspicions!

'Dare I hope, Lady Darleston, that you might join me for a drive in the park tomorrow afternoon? I should be delighted to present you to my friends.'

'How very kind of you, Lady Caroline, but I have already accepted an invitation to drive with Mr Carstares,' said Penelope, resolving to inform George of his kind invitation the minute she reached home.

'No matter. Another day, perhaps!' replied her ladyship carelessly. To be sure it would have been too good to be true if the chit had accepted her invitation! Anyway, it would be far safer for all of them if she were to vanish without any tangible evidence of complicity on the part of Lady Caroline Daventry.

'Lady Caroline, may I make my youngest sister, Sarah, known to you? She is staying with us at the moment.'

'Goodness, is this another sister? No doubt we may look to see her make her début and catch a husband!' The thinly veiled sneer suggested that there was something rather curious about the swift marriages of Penelope and Phoebe.

Penelope merely smiled and said, 'At the moment the only use my sister has for an eligible bachelor is to learn to drive and beat him at chess. She is not quite fourteen.'

'Ah, well, time enough, then!' said Lady Caroline, with a patronising glance at Sarah. She blinked slightly as she met that damsel's steady regard.

Sarah had swiftly come to the conclusion that she did not like Lady Caroline at all. Furthermore she had shamelessly overheard a conversation between George and Peter which suggested that there was some connection between Jack Frobisher and Lady Caroline. It was also plain even to her inexperienced gaze that the conversation between Lady Caroline and her sister was, for an unknown reason, occasioning some shocked looks from various quarters. Obviously Penelope could not extricate herself without an embarrassing scene.

Unobtrusively she dropped back to walk with Ellen and Roger. 'Ellen, is it just my imagination or should we do something about this?'

Ellen nodded vigorously. 'That we should! But what? The gossip that it will cause if the mistress openly snubs her ladyship! Though why she should be called "lady" is beyond me!'

Sarah, however, had already made a plan. 'Roger, his lordship is probably still at White's with Mr Carstares. You must go at once and tell him to meet us here. If necessary we'll pretend you have taken the books home. Take this money for a cab and run!'

Roger grinned at her, said to Ellen, 'She's got a head on her shoulders, for all she's gentry!' and obeyed.

Lady Caroline, quite unsuspecting, continued to chat sociably, and Penelope responded in a friendly but dignified fashion, stifling the urge to bury her nose in her handkerchief. Listening carefully, she decided that Lady Caroline was under some stress. Something was making her nervous.

Finally, a seemingly innocent question gave her the answer. 'I suppose you see little of Darleston during the day? In his club, no doubt? Will he be joining you here?'

'I shouldn't think so,' said Penelope, wishing to herself that Peter *would* appear. No sooner had she thought this than her quick ears heard a carriage draw up beside them.

Gelert uttered a blood-curdling snarl and Penelope could feel the fur on his neck rise up, bristling. She could only think of one person likely to bring that response from the dog. She knew a moment's fear, but fought it down and said calmly, 'How do you do, Mr Frobisher? I believe you are acquainted with Lady Caroline and my sister.'

Jack Frobisher was stunned. How the devil had she known? He could see from the look of shock on Caroline Daventry's face that she had not told Lady Darleston who was approaching.

Sarah mentally applauded this stroke. Gelert's reaction had not been lost on her, and she could see that Penelope's confident identification of Frobisher before he had even spoken had momentarily shaken the man. Determined to make her presence felt, she moved up beside her sister and said, 'Good afternoon, Mr Frobisher! I see that your arm is better.'

Jack Frobisher stared at her in acute dislike but said politely, 'It is indeed, Miss Sarah. I hope you are enjoying the sights of London.'

'Oh, yes. Of course one sees so many odd things, and people!' said Sarah sweetly.

Jack's eyes narrowed. 'Your sister has not altered by a hair's breadth, Lady Darleston. But you! Allow me to inform you that I have never seen you looking so well. Your new station in life seems to agree with you!'

'Such a welcome addition to your family, is she not, Frobisher?' said Lady Caroline.

'Indeed she is! And will you not honour me by taking a turn around the park in my curricle dear Cousin? I am sure Lady Caroline will be only too happy to chaperon Miss Sarah.'

Penelope's stomach turned over. Common sense told

her that he could not possibly kidnap her in full view of the Ton, but a carriage accident…? Besides, the thought of being alone with Frobisher under any circumstances terrified her. How to get out of this politely and avoid scandal! She wondered desperately just how many people were listening. What would happen if she let Gelert go?

'How kind of you, Mr Frobisher, but I must decline. It is time that my sister and I were returning home.' She hoped that would do the trick.

'But, Cousin, I should be only too happy to drive you to Grosvenor Square!' said Frobisher suavely.

'Oh! I would not dream of expecting Sarah to walk while I am driven home!' said Penelope firmly, breathing a mental sigh of relief. Surely this excuse was unexceptionable!

Frobisher pressed on. 'But Miss Sarah could not be so churlish as to deny me the pleasure of your company!'

'Of course not!' said Sarah with alacrity. 'Especially as here come Darleston and Mr Carstares, who will doubtless escort me home!' For there *were* Peter and George, a hundred yards away, striding towards them purposefully.

Penelope, whose breath had practically stopped at Sarah's first words, recovered her self-possession and said innocently, 'No doubt Darleston has come to escort us home. Perhaps another day, Mr Frobisher!'

Frobisher bit off an exclamation of annoyance, changing it to a sneeze. Lady Caroline was far more successful in concealing her disgust.

'How delightful!' she exclaimed. 'I declare I've not seen Darleston for an age.' Her mind worked fast. Curse the man! How like him to appear just when one would wish him not to! Had he been tipped off? Or was he merely doting on his insipid bride!

Peter approached the little group swiftly, mentally schooling himself to hold his temper in check. Fury that his ex-mistress should have had the effrontery to approach his wife almost choked him. Leaving aside his suspicions of Lady Caroline's motives, the thought of Penelope having anything to do with the woman was unbearable.

And Penelope, how much had she guessed? He knew how quickly her mind worked, how sensitive she was to people's moods and thoughts. She frequently read his thoughts with unnerving accuracy. Could she possibly have divined the situation? Even at this distance he could see that Penelope was frightened: something in the way she was gripping Gelert's collar and holding herself. At this point he saw who was in the curricle beside the three ladies.

George spotted Frobisher a split second later and spluttered, 'Good heavens! D'you see who's with them? Thank God for Sarah!'

'As you say, George. What an impossible situation for Penny! She can't administer a snub to either of them in public without causing a scandal. Hurry up, George, before she's tempted to let the dog go! For some reason apart from this business she is scared of Jack!'

He saw the party turn towards him and raised his hand in greeting with a polite smile firmly affixed to his face. A strong odour of scent assailed him; it was with difficulty that he bit back an exclamation of disgust. One look at his wife's face informed him that she shared his distaste.

She was turned towards him, a welcoming smile mingled with heartfelt relief. 'My lord, and Mr Carstares, how lovely! I was just telling Lady Caroline that you would not be joining us here! And here you are, making a liar out of me. You are acquainted with Lady Caroline, I believe? And your cousin, of course. He was so kind as to offer to drive me home, but now you are here he need not trouble himself.'

Peter nearly exploded! No wonder she had looked so upset! Well did he know the gossip that would have ensued had Penelope allowed the Ton to see her distaste and fear.

'Of course. Lady Caroline, what a surprise to see you.' He bowed as he spoke. 'Cousin. I trust you are well?'

'Never better, Darleston. Believe me, conveying my new cousin home would have been an undiluted pleasure!'

Lady Caroline responded archly, 'Why, Darleston, you cannot have supposed that I would be the least backward in any attention to your wife!' Her tone was sweet but there was an edge to it which warned Darleston that the woman was up to something.

'Not at all, Lady Caroline. I am sure if I had given the matter a moment's thought I should have expected to see you!' The implicit suggestion that he had *not* considered her worth a moment's thought was wasted on neither lady. Penelope, however, was far more successful at concealing her reaction.

Lady Caroline's eyes blazed suddenly but she managed to respond with an artificial titter. 'My dear Darleston, I do not expect to be remembered among so many! And now I really must go. Mr Frobisher, you may escort me home.'

'With the greatest pleasure, dear Lady Caroline!'

Lady Caroline left with her escort and Peter turned to face his wife. Before he could say a word, she asked, 'Does Lady Caroline always wear that much scent, Peter?'

'Frequently. Perhaps we had better discuss this at home.' Penelope could hear the suppressed anger in his voice and decided to drop the subject. Sarah, who had intended to ask her brother-in-law to explain everything, took one look at his face and came to the conclusion that she could just as well ask George later on.

George looked solemn, but not nearly as grim as Peter. She peeped at him from under her bonnet and caught his eye.

Involuntarily his expression lightened, and he flicked her nose with a careless forefinger. 'Well done, brat!' he said softly.

Sarah's heart rose at the knowledge that she had done the right thing.

They walked home without much conversation. Penelope was very subdued to think that Peter was angry, although she could not think what she could have done to have avoided the situation. She was also curious as to how Peter had known what was afoot. That Sarah had something to do with it she was certain.

Upon reaching the house, Peter said, 'Come to the study, please, Penny. I need to speak to you privately.' Then, turning to his sister-in-law, 'Thank you, Sarah! I'm buying that book, so let me hear no more rubbish about *sponging*! See you at dinner, George.'

They went into the study together and Penelope immediately asked, 'How on earth did you know, Peter? I've never been so glad as I was when Sarah said you were there! What did she do?'

'She sent Roger around to White's,' he replied shortly.

She waited patiently for Peter to speak again. He was silent for a moment, and then said, 'I would prefer you to take steps to avoid any further conversation with Lady

Caroline. If she approaches you again, refuse to acknowledge her.' His voice sounded flustered.

Penelope considered her reply. 'Won't that cause gossip?'

'Not as much as if you recognise her,' said Peter shortly. He felt uncomfortable, even hypocritical.

Penelope's next question took him totally by surprise. 'Why, Peter? Because she was your mistress?'

Outraged that she would dare to question him, he turned to her, saying coldly, 'You forget yourself, Lady Darleston. It is no concern of yours if she was, or is still, my mistress!'

Penelope was fully aware that she had gone too far. She did not resent his past involvements, or his remonstrance, but the suggestion that he might still be involved with Lady Caroline made her feel physically sick with jealousy. Close to tears, she did not trust her voice for a moment.

Then she said carefully, 'I beg your pardon my lord, please excuse me. I...I... have something to attend to.' She rose to her feet, knowing that she was going to cry, preferring, in her pride, to conceal her pain.

Accompanied by Gelert, she left the room for the privacy of her bed-chamber. Even there she tried very hard to hold back her tears. 'Watering pot!' she said angrily. 'I won't cry! I won't!' But the sudden thought of Peter making love to Lady Caroline as he did to her was too much for her precarious self-control. She sank onto the day-bed, buried her face in her hands and wept despairingly.

When Peter walked quietly through the open connecting door ten minutes later she was still crying. Gelert was snuffling at her desperately, pawing at her gown, whimpering in sympathy. Peter was already feeling the lash of his conscience, and had come to apologise, but the sight of Penelope weeping so bitterly shocked him. He hesitated in the doorway, wondering if he should go away. Then he remembered the terrible night before the attempt on her life down at Darleston. He had left her to cry herself to sleep then, after hurting her. He couldn't do that to her again.

Gently he spoke her name. 'Penny?' She started up in shock. The pain he saw in her face told him just how great was his power to wound her.

'Go away!' she said furiously. He ignored that. Three quick strides took him across the room and he was beside her, holding her tightly.

'Sweetheart, you mustn't cry! I'm not worth it! All I seem to do is hurt you. I'm sorry, Penny, you had every right to ask that question. Caroline Daventry *was* my mistress. She is not now. I swear it.' He could feel her shaking in his arms and cursed himself for the cruel thing he had said. He knew that Penelope felt more for him than mere affection. He also knew that she would cut out her tongue before admitting to anyone that she loved him. Tenderly he stroked her hair, holding her until her tears at last abated.

'Better now, Penny?' She nodded, still not trusting her voice. He continued with difficulty. 'You had better know the whole story. Lady Caroline considered herself as a likely candidate for the role of Countess of Darleston. She tried to have an advertisement of our engagement inserted in the *Gazette*. Fortunately the editor had the sense to check it with me first. It was that coupled with the proximity of Jack to the title which prompted me to marriage.'

'Why didn't you wish to marry Lady Caroline?' The

question was little more than a whisper and Peter took his time in answering it.

Finally he said, 'Because, even if I didn't know it, I wanted my wife to be like you. Not a second Melissa. Caroline only wanted to marry me for my money and title. She does not care for me in the slightest, nor I for her.'

'But you married me without love,' said Penelope.

Peter was silent. What could he say? He knew she loved him, but would never say so. His own feelings were still confused. He was fond of her, she roused him physically as no other woman ever had. But did he love her?

At last he said, 'There has never been any pretence between us. Lots of misunderstandings, but no pretence or lies, and we have come to care for each other. I doubt that you could lie to anyone, and I know that I could never lie to you. Penny, I am glad I married you. You have made me feel whole again.' He wished he could say more, but he knew she would not believe a declaration of love even if he could bring himself to lie to her.

'Now, tell me all about it. Did you get any hint that she might wish you harm?' he asked.

Penelope described the whole incident while Peter listened carefully.

'Do you think she is really in league with your cousin?' finished Penelope. 'She wanted me to drive with her tomorrow but I said I was driving out with George.'

'Good, I doubt she would dare try anything when you were known to be in her company, but it would certainly raise some eyebrows if you were to be seen with her again. She may well be in league with Jack. Certainly I have given her reason to hold a grudge, and if she is working with him then Jack is no longer in complete control. That makes the situation far more dangerous.

Caroline is much smarter than my cousin. Besides which
we could probably make Jack alone back off. I don't
think his desire for money would make him risk his
neck.'

'What about Lady Caroline?' asked Penelope.

'I'm not sure of her involvement,' answered Peter
slowly. 'She has a tendency to hold grudges and I have
known her to go to extreme lengths to pay one off. Jack
by himself would be more likely just to demand money
from me, as he has done in the past. He has no real
quarrel with me apart from the fact that we dislike each
other!'

'He has a quarrel with me,' confessed Penelope. 'Remember I told you that Gelert bit him? It…it was because
he…he tried to kiss me once and I hit him in the face.
It was awful. When he wouldn't stop I screamed, so
Gelert came in and attacked him.' Peter could feel her
distress. She was shuddering at the memory as she continued, 'He told me then that he wasn't finished with me,
so maybe he would help her to get back at me.'

She felt Peter's arms tighten around her. When he
spoke there was icy rage in his voice. 'If Frobisher dares
to touch you again, Penny, I swear I'll kill him.' The
murderous fury in his heart was a total surprise to him.
It was not mere jealousy. The thought of Penelope frightened and helpless in the power of a man like Frobisher
aroused a protective instinct in him.

Penelope touched his face gently, tracing the strong
line of his jaw. He relaxed suddenly and kissed her.
'Never mind, Penny. We'll sort it out somehow!'

Greatly daring, she said, 'Perhaps we should simply
have lots of babies. Then they might think there were too
many of us to get rid of!'

Peter chuckled. 'Well, I'm doing the best I can, Penny,

but I think it might take too long! Not that I object to trying, of course!' The vision of Penelope nursing his children was immensely satisfying, somehow. Not merely a son, but daughters as well, preferably just like Penelope.

Lady Caroline Daventry was in a dangerous humour when she returned home. The encounter with Darleston's bride had infuriated her. Insipid wench! she thought furiously. The prospect of turning her over to Jack Frobisher appealed to her greatly. But how to achieve it? Had Darleston's appearance been a coincidence or had he been somehow tipped off?

Not for a moment did she suspect Sarah! That a child could have taken action was beyond her comprehension. All she could think was that someone in the park had consequently met Darleston and mentioned seeing his wife.

As she entered the house with Frobisher she caught sight of her butler and said, 'Bring suitable refreshment to the drawing room when I ring. Otherwise do not disturb us! I am not at home to anyone!' She went upstairs with Jack Frobisher and shut the drawing room door behind them with a bang.

Frobisher flung himself into a chair and asked abruptly, 'Was that coincidence?'

'God knows! Possibly someone who saw us subsequently met him and tipped him off. He was not pleased to see either of us, I fancy.'

'He most certainly was not!' agreed Frobisher. 'Do you think he suspects us, or did he merely take exception to his ex-mistress having the effrontery to approach his bride?'

'I should think the latter. I doubt not that his appearance was chance. How could he have known? Nevertheless, this is going to require some careful thought, my friend. Her ladyship was scared for some reason…'

There was a faintly questioning note in her voice, but Frobisher merely smiled enigmatically. He said thoughtfully, 'It all hinges upon us getting the girl, of course. That will bring Darleston after her and we can trap him easily enough.'

'You fool! The last thing we want is Darleston right on our heels!' exclaimed Lady Caroline. 'He'll be ripe for murder! No. We lay a false trail to give us time to prepare for him.'

Frobisher considered this carefully.

Lady Caroline added, 'That will give you more time for whatever you have planned for the bride, of course.'

Frobisher's eyes narrowed. 'Very true, Caroline. I wouldn't want to go to all this effort for nothing, after all. But where do we take the wench?'

'France. I have an old friend there who will help us readily enough. We will be able to conceal the girl in his château near Dieppe. The place is shut up, with no one there at all, so we can take her there with no one the wiser. My friend the Marquis will deny all knowledge, suitably bribed. He prefers Paris and never goes near the château. Listen. We still have to work out how to take her. That's the hard part. Once you have her it's easy. I have the house in Scotland, so I'll set off in my chaise the same night. They are bound to try to find out where we are so we'll make it easy for them. Make it look as though we've both taken her to Scotland. By the time they catch up with my chaise, it will be too late to catch you.'

'I'm impressed, Caroline. Then do I let Darleston know somehow?' asked Frobisher.

'You let the girl get a message to him. One of the villagers can be duped somehow into revealing her whereabouts but not who has her,' said Lady Caroline. 'That will fetch him, but he'll have no proof of who holds her. Furthermore, fear of scandal will prevent him making the affair public! He and the girl can simply disappear.'

'Hmm. It might just work, you know. It will have to. As you say, Darleston will be ripe for murder, and I don't fancy being in his way.'

'I don't advise it,' said Lady Caroline grimly. 'After a reasonable period, you can reappear. There will be no proof except my knowledge, and once we are married you are safe!'

Frobisher looked amused, 'Charming,' he murmured. 'Absolutely charming! I can't imagine why we mere males persist in thinking of your sex as weaker! Now, do you have a scheme for actually kidnapping the girl?'

Her ladyship was silent for a moment, then she smiled and said, 'I think I've hit on something.'

'Excellent. Caroline, I make you my compliments,' said Frobisher. 'Why don't you ring for something with which to toast our success!'

Chapter Sixteen

Lady Wickham's ball was destined to be recalled in the mind of the Ton as the most startling social event of the year. The excellence of the refreshments and the attendance by all of consequence did not suffice to make it memorable. It was the scandal occasioned by the mysterious disappearance of the Countess of Darleston and the language used by her husband which ensured that it would live in the minds of all as an entertainment of no mean order.

The evening started in the most unexceptionable way possible. Lord and Lady Darleston arrived slightly late, with the Honourable George Carstares and her ladyship's sister and brother-in-law. They were observed to be in the cheeriest of moods. A number of people who had openly suggested that Darleston had remarried for convenience and an heir were obliged to reverse their opinion.

The look of adoration on the Earl's face as he waltzed with his lovely wife left no one in any doubt that he was head over heels in love with the chit. Nor could anyone in their right mind, observing the Countess of Darleston, possibly believe her to have been coerced into marriage to clear her brother's debts! The idea was ludicrous! It was patently obvious that she adored her husband! More likely the engagement had been the reason for Darleston's forbearance with the young fool!

Peter himself was no longer in any doubt. For the past week the realisation that he had fallen very deeply in love had been borne in on him. Finally, that very evening, as Penelope had come into the drawing room arrayed in a silver gauze ballgown, he had admitted to himself that he loved her. But the presence of Sarah and George had made any declaration impossible.

Sarah, however, had seen the look of adoration on her brother-in-law's face and had wondered. She knew, of course, that Penelope was very deeply in love. The fact that she said nothing about it told Sarah that she did not wish anyone to know. Sarah understood why, her love for Penelope providing an understanding beyond her years. She had grieved for Penelope's problem, and see-ing Peter gaze at her sister with undisguised love in his eyes had given her hope.

When Peter and Penelope had been leaving for the ball with George, Sarah had done something she had never done before. As a matter of course she had hugged Penelope, but had also given Peter an impulsive hug, then stepped back, blushing.

Peter had been a bit startled, but he had flicked her cheek with one finger, saying with a grin, 'Don't stay up too late, brat!'

Nothing happened to mar the evening until the arrival of Lady Caroline Daventry. A few whispers ran around the ballroom when Lady Caroline was observed dancing very close to Lord and Lady Darleston. Naturally the in-telligence that she had actually approached the young bride and been acknowledged had got about. Darleston's outraged intervention had lost nothing in the telling. There had been some chuckles at this, but many were shocked that the woman had dared.

Those who were charitably inclined and too far away to see said afterwards that Lady Caroline must have been extraordinarily clumsy. Others who were closer swore that she stepped on Lady Darleston's gown on purpose. Peter led his wife from the floor immediately, totally ignoring Lady Caroline's fulsome attempt to apologise.

'Is it ruined, Peter?' asked Penelope.

'I think it might require more than mere pinning up,' he replied.

Their hostess came bustling up. 'Dear Lady Darleston, come with me at once. You can't possibly pin that up. I shall take you upstairs where my maid shall mend it for you. Such clumsiness, *most* unsubtle! We shall not be long, Darleston.'

Lady Wickham swept Penelope upstairs to her boudoir and summoned her maid. 'Clara, please find a needle and thread to mend Lady Darleston's gown. When you have mended it you may escort her ladyship back to the ballroom. She cannot see, so you must be very careful. Tell her about steps and so on. Do you understand?'

'Yes, milady,' answered Clara.

Lady Wickham said, 'I must return to the ballroom, Lady Darleston. Do not, I beg of you, refine too much upon this little episode. Caroline Daventry has gone entirely too far!'

Jack Frobisher had observed the episode from a sheltered alcove. Silently he applauded his accomplice's ploy. He watched Lady Wickham take Penelope upstairs and smiled fiendishly when she returned alone. 'Well done, Caroline.' He produced a small phial from his pocket, emptied the contents into a glass of champagne and unobtrusively made his way upstairs.

Clara had not got very far with her repair job when a voice at the door said, 'Your mistress wants you immediately, Clara.'

'She asked me to do this,' protested Clara.

'Well, she wants you downstairs for a moment. In the library. You'd better hurry.'

'Oh, very well. Excuse me, milady. I'll be as quick as I can.'

'No matter,' said Penelope cheerfully.

The maid left. A moment later the door opened. Penelope swung round. She could make out a figure moving towards her. 'Clara?' she asked. There was no answer. Suddenly frightened, she opened her mouth to scream for help, but it was too late. She was taken in a powerful grasp, a glass forced to her mouth, the contents tipped ruthlessly down her throat. Then a hand was clamped over her mouth as she tried to scream again. Her frantic struggles grew weaker as consciousness slipped away.

Frobisher dropped her and ran to the door. He looked out but saw no one. Swiftly he went back to pick up his senseless victim. A footstep at the door startled him.

Lady Caroline said, 'Hurry, Frobisher, the chaise will be waiting and you don't want to miss the tide at Newhaven. That drug may not last long either. It works fast, but sometimes it wears off easily. I must leave now and head for Scotland. Enjoy yourself! The maid is locked in the library.' She was gone on the instant.

Frobisher made his way to the back stairs. A curious footman accepted the explanation that the lady had taken too much champagne and was being taken home to avoid scandal. He also accepted the coins pressed into his hand with the injunction to keep his mouth shut.

Clara waited ten minutes in the library and then discovered that the door was locked. It took her another twenty minutes to attract the attention of a footman. When she reached Lady Wickham's boudoir she was shocked. An overturned chair and broken champagne glass told her that she had been duped. Terrified, she raced downstairs to the ballroom. Swiftly she pushed her way through the startled guests, with little regard for their consequence, until she found her mistress.

'Milady,' she gasped into a startled silence, 'Lady Darleston's gone. A man came and said you wanted me in the library, so I left her. When I went back she was gone, a chair turned over and a champagne glass broken!'

'What?' shrieked Lady Wickham. 'Foolish girl! I sent no message!' She shook the hapless Clara, who was nearly in tears.

Peter, standing nearby with Phoebe, Richard and George, wondered if his heart had stopped, for it gave such a sickening lurch. He never remembered much about the next few moments, except for grabbing the maid and racing upstairs with her. George assured him later that the language with which he cursed Caroline Daventry and Jack Frobisher would have shaken an infantryman, and that a number of ladies had actually fainted.

He regained some measure of control as he surveyed the evidence of Penelope's struggle. He sniffed the champagne glass, wrinkling his nose at the sickly odour.

Richard, George and Phoebe had followed him upstairs with Lord and Lady Wickham. The latter was weeping and wringing her hands.

Lord Wickham said, 'I'll try to find out which way they went.' He left the room.

'Drugged?' asked George tersely.

Peter nodded. Phoebe gave a cry of horror and clung to Richard.

'I'll kill them,' said Peter softly. 'I swear I'll kill them.' He swung around and his gaze fell on the sobbing Clara. Even in his own agony, his heart went out to the girl. 'Don't blame the maid, Lady Wickham. I should have stayed with Penny. It's my fault. We knew there was danger, but Caroline and my cousin were too clever for us.'

'The question now,' said Richard, 'is where the devil are they going? They haven't much of a start. We may be able to find out by questioning their servants.'

'Caroline has a place in Scotland,' said Peter. 'They might take her there, but it's a long way. They must know I'll be on their heels.'

'That's what they want,' said Phoebe suddenly. 'Don't you see? By taking Penny, they can trap you.'

'But if we're too close behind the whole thing could backfire on them,' said George. 'If I were them, I'd want a good lead so that I could prepare a decent trap. Caroline Daventry may be a bitch, but she's smart enough to think of that.'

Lord Wickham returned. 'Caroline Daventry left alone by the front door, but a man carrying a woman left via the back of the house. One of the footmen saw him, but he was cloaked and hooded and the back stairs are so ill-lit that he wouldn't recognise the fellow, so we have no proof of who was involved. Charles said he heard a carriage of some sort in the mews.'

A puzzled little voice from the doorway asked, 'Is something wrong, Mama?' They turned around to see

Miss Amabel Hartleigh, the six-year-old daughter of the house, clutching a doll.

'No, sweetheart, go back to bed,' said Lady Wickham.

'Was the lady very sick?'

The grown-ups stood as though they had been turned to stone.

Peter went to the child, dropped to one knee and asked, very gently, 'What lady was that, my pet?'

'The red-haired lady. The man carried her out and there was another lady.'

'Was there? Did you hear anything they said?'

'Yes. I was going to come down the stairs a bit, to watch the dancing, but I heard their voices so I hid behind a door.'

'What did they say?'

'The red-haired lady didn't say anything. I think she was asleep. The other lady said something about a chaise.'

'Anything else?'

'Yes. Something about the tide at Newhaven and going to Scotland. Oh, and she called him Frobisher.'

Peter hugged her. 'Good girl! What do you want most in the world?'

'A pony.'

'Well, you shall have one. I'll keep you mounted for the rest of my life!' He turned to the others. 'We've got them! Obviously we were meant to think of Scotland— probably if we went to Caroline's house we would discover that she *has* left for Scotland. Frobisher won't be expecting us this close behind, so we've an advantage. We go back to Darleston House and collect horses, as well as my chaise to bring her back. Phoebe, will you come with us in the chaise?'

'Just try to leave me behind!' was the answer.

* * *

The reaction at Darleston House when they arrived was one of horror. All the servants loved their mistress, and the white agony of the master's face was pitiful to behold.

Sarah was still up. She dragged a warm cloak from her wardrobe and along with Gelert presented herself to George and Phoebe in the hall. 'I'm coming too.'

'The devil you are. It's too dangerous!' snapped George.

'Shut up, George! If you try to leave me behind I'll saddle a horse myself and follow you anyway! If Phoebe's going, so am I!' was the uncompromising answer.

Phoebe nodded and said firmly, 'Of course she's coming!'

Richard came in. 'The chaise and horses will be round directly. What are you doing Sarah?'

'Coming with you! Don't bother to argue about it!'

'Where's Peter? He may have something to say about this!' said Richard.

'Fetching his pistols,' answered George. 'Dammit, Sarah! You can't come. Your mother would be furious with us for taking you! I warn you, people are likely to be killed tonight! Peter is out of his mind!'

'Good!' said Sarah. 'Maybe now he'll stop being scared to admit that he loves her!'

Peter arrived in the hall with his pistols just in time to hear this outburst.

Sarah met his eyes defiantly and said, 'Don't you start, Peter. I'm coming with you and that's all there is to it!'

He looked at her gravely. 'If we left you I suppose you'd come after us, wouldn't you?'

'Of course.'

He simply nodded and said, 'I've ordered my racing

curricle as well. We have to take Gelert, and he can't possibly run the whole way. Fortunately I have cattle stabled on the Newhaven Road. We can change as often as necessary.'

Meadows ran in. He thrust a greatcoat at Peter. 'Brandy flask in the pocket, Master Peter. For God's sake, bring her back!'

Peter gripped the old retainer's shoulders. 'Trust me, Meadows, we'll catch them!'

A clatter of hooves announced the arrival of the curricle, chaise and horses.

'Who is on the chaise?' asked Peter.

'Your coachman,' said Richard. 'He insisted. George and I are riding with you. That way if we have to leave the main road to follow them one of us can wait to give the chaise directions.'

'Let's go, then. They're an hour ahead of us. Tide's not till nine, but I want to catch them before they can reach Newhaven!' He met George's eyes, unable to voice his fears for Penelope's safety in Frobisher's hands.

Sarah and Phoebe were handed unceremoniously into the waiting carriage. 'Newhaven, John,' said Peter. 'Spring them and change horses as often as necessary. All that matters is speed. Check at all the usual posting inns for instructions; we'll leave messages.'

The coachman nodded and cracked his whip. The restless team sprang into motion, thundering over the cobbles.

'Let's ride, gentlemen! Come on, Gelert!' Peter swung himself into his curricle, followed by the dog, and smiled grimly at his companions. Without another word they galloped after the chaise, swiftly passing it. Sarah was looking out to watch them go by. George saw her and raised his whip in salute, then they were gone.

*   *   *

Penelope regained consciousness slowly. She had a splitting headache, no memory of what had occurred, and the rocking of the chaise confused her. Waves of nausea threatened to overcome her, made worse by the motion of the carriage. Gradually, as the after-effects of the drug wore off, she realised that she was lying along a seat in a carriage. Instinct warned her to keep quiet and listen. Gradually she became certain that she was not alone. A faint sound of breathing and small movements told her there was someone on the opposite seat. Who was it?

The carriage slowed slightly, and immediately her unknown companion moved to the window, leaned out and yelled, 'Put 'em along! I can't risk missing the tide at Newhaven! We'll change teams at the next posting station!'

Penelope recognised Frobisher's voice instantly, and with increasing terror she slowly pieced together what had happened. The tearing of her dress had been a clever ploy to separate her from Peter, and they had fallen for it! Now she was on her way to Newhaven and Peter had no way of knowing where they were going. She shuddered at the implications of what she had just heard. Stay calm! she ordered herself, but it took every bit of self-control she possessed not to give in to her fear. It occurred to her that if she continued to feign unconsciousness she might be able to take him by surprise at the posting inn and call for help.

Desperately she clung to that faint chance, schooling herself to remain as limp as possible, even when a hand grasped her chin and forced it up. 'Still out cold, are you?' came Frobisher's voice. He released her chin, but his fingers slid down over her throat briefly. 'By God, I'm looking forward to this!'

It was all Penelope could do not to recoil, screaming,

from his touch and the brutal note of lust in his voice. She lay still for what seemed an eternity, trying to convince herself that Peter would somehow be able to follow her or that she would be able to escape when they changed horses.

A sudden slowing down of the galloping horses warned her that they were nearly at the posting station. Wait to see if he gets out, she thought. All chance of escape vanished, though, when she felt those dreadful hands grasp her again. Casting all pretence and caution to the winds, Penelope struggled in futile desperation. She was flung to the floor of the carriage and held there. One powerful arm gripped her, holding her helpless, while a hand smothered her nose and mouth in a cloth. Unable to breathe, Penelope lapsed into unconsciousness.

She came to her senses with her hands tied behind her back. The horses were again thundering on at a steady gallop. Weakly she tried to sit up, but was instantly grasped and dragged back.

'We are quite alone, Lady Darleston. And this time we won't be interrupted by your dog.'

Frantically Penelope fought to free herself from that cruel hold, but gradually she was forced down by his superior weight and strength. She could feel Frobisher's hands tearing at the bodice of her gown, feel his hot breath on her face. Terrified, she tried to evade his mouth, but one hand came up to grip her throat while the other fumbled at her exposed breast. Then, as she screamed in terror, his lips were on hers, choking her screams as he forced his tongue into her mouth. Finally, in absolute desperation, she bit him.

She had a brief moment of satisfaction as he jerked back from her and swore. Quickly she tried to roll away, but he grabbed her again, saying savagely, 'You'll regret that Lady Darleston. Scream as much as you like. Nothing can help you now!'

Peter and his companions thundered along the Newhaven road, leaving a trail of dust in the moonlight. George was beginning to wonder if they would ever catch up when they came to the last posting station and heard that the chaise was only fifteen minutes ahead of them. They galloped out of the village with fresh horses. Peter's mouth was set in a grim line. His fears for Penelope had grown with every mile, until he was nearly insane with them. The chance comment let fall by the hostler about Frobisher's dishevelled appearance horrified him. He had prayed desperately that Frobisher would at least keep his hands off Penelope until the chaise reached Newhaven.

Finally, half a mile ahead, they saw the lights of a carriage just before it disappeared around a bend in the road.

'There it is!' called Peter. 'Slow down a bit. We have to plan this.'

'How do we tackle them?' asked Richard.

'You take them from the front!' was the answer. 'The road winds a lot just here. Take to the fields at the side of the road, get around ahead of them, behind that hill to cut off the last bend, and then charge. With a bit of luck their horses will panic. You and George take the nearside and deal with the postilions. I'll hold back until I can see you, then Gelert and I can come up on the other side and tackle anyone on the box. Then we can deal with whoever's inside.'

'All right, let's do it!' said Richard.

'Look! There's a gap in the hedge!' called George, and angled his mount towards it. He sailed over, closely followed by Richard. Together they raced across the fields, swinging up over the shoulder of the hill. As they tore down to rejoin the road they could see that they were going to be well ahead of the chaise. The bends in the road had slowed it down considerably.

They reached the road while the coach was still out of sight and pulled up. The horses' flanks were heaving. George cast a glance at Richard and said, 'If any harm has come to Penny, I don't fancy Frobisher's chances. I've never seen Peter like this!'

Richard shook his head. 'It won't just be Peter he has to deal with, George!' he said, then, listening sharply, 'Here it comes!' They could hear the thunder of the horses. The chaise swung into view around the last bend and suddenly, mingled with the noise of the hooves, came an agonised scream.

In the curricle, fifty yards behind the chaise, Peter went berserk. Gone was his plan to check that George and Richard were in position. A cold fury took possession of him and his team felt the lash of the whip as he dropped his hands and sprang them into a full gallop. Then, beyond the chaise, he could see two horses charging down the road at a breakneck pace. Gelert stood on the seat, barking at the voice of his mistress. Peter could not spare a glance for the dog, but he said, 'Penny. We're going to find Penny!' Gelert redoubled his barking.

The chaise horses were terrified at the approach of George and Richard. Desperately the post-boys tried to control the team and avoid the attackers, but the nearside wheels slid into the ditch, violently tipping the chaise at a drunken angle. One wheeler was down and the other horses plunging and rearing.

The horsemen were upon them! The servant on the box, thinking he had to deal with highwaymen, raised a pistol, but it was struck out of his hand by Carstares's whip and the shot went wild. He dodged, and then heard the thunder of the curricle on their offside. He turned in terror as Gelert launched himself from Peter's side onto the box. His weight hurled the hapless guard to the ground, knocking him unconscious, just as Richard dragged the lead post-boy from his seat. Gelert managed to roll clear of the frantic horses. He staggered to his feet and leapt, barking madly, at the door of the chaise. Peter, his team well in hand, brought them to a plunging stop and jumped from the vehicle. George flung himself from his horse, grabbing a pistol from the saddle holster. Peter joined him, pistol in hand, and together they tore open the door to the chaise.

'Stand back if you want her alive, Darleston!' snapped Frobisher. He sat in the corner of the carriage, one arm gripping the unconscious Penelope and a knife in his other hand. Peter grabbed Gelert's collar and hauled him back.

'Put your pistols down and get back, but stay in sight of the door! And keep that dog under control!'

Peter and George obeyed, watching helplessly as Penelope was dragged from the chaise. Her ripped gown and bound hands horrified them. She hung so limply at Frobisher's side that for one dreadful moment Peter thought she was dead. A faint moan, as Frobisher shifted his hold, reassured him, and he tightened his grip on Gelert's collar as the dog struggled to get loose, snarling fiercely.

'Right back, Darleston. You! Winton! Bring a horse around!'

'Do it, Richard,' said Peter between clenched teeth.

Richard brought his horse forward wordlessly.

'Fine. Now join Darleston and Carstares!' Frobisher hoisted Penelope up across the horse's withers and turned to the others. 'If you try to follow me you'll regret it. I'll leave her for you a few miles down the road. I'm sure the horse will be much faster with a lighter load. But if I so much as suspect pursuit, she dies. I've nothing to lose, so don't risk it.'

He bent down to pick up one of the pistols. As he did so Peter released Gelert. The dog attacked with a blood-curdling roar of fury, and went straight for the throat. The pistol went off as man and dog rolled together under the belly of the startled horse. Peter leapt forward, catching Penelope's limp body as she was flung from the rearing animal.

'Gelert! Back!' yelled Richard as the horse descended, screaming in fright. The dog saw the danger and twisted clear, but Frobisher's shriek of terror ended abruptly as the steel-shod hooves crashed down. Sickened at the sight, George and Richard turned away.

Peter was kneeling in the road, cradling Penelope in his arms. Desperately he fumbled at her throat for a pulse, unable to breathe until he felt it, steady under his fingers. Tears of relief slid down his cheeks. Next he untied the cord binding her hands, cursing softly when he saw the scoring on her wrists. Whimpering in pain, Gelert limped over. He snuffled at Penelope, and licked Peter's face. Blood dripped from a long shallow wound on his shoulder.

'Put this around her,' said Richard, removing his great-coat. 'We've got to keep her warm until the girls arrive. We'll go on to Newhaven and find a doctor there.' Carefully they wrapped her in the garment, checking at the same time to see if anything was broken. All they could find was a great bruise on her left temple. She moaned softly when Peter gently probed the bruise, but he could feel no evidence of a crack.

George came over, looking rather sick. 'Frobisher is dead. The horse smashed his head in.'

'What about the servants?' asked Peter.

'One with a broken leg. They claimed not to know what was afoot, but I tied them up anyway. What do we do with them? Not to mention Caroline Daventry! What about her?'

'Leave them here with one of you on guard. I gave Meadows a note for the Bow Street Runners. They can collect them and sort it out. As for Caroline, with Jack dead we can't prove her involvement to the satisfaction of a court. But you can take it from me that she's finished in society!'

'Is Penny all right?' George asked anxiously.

'I don't know,' said Peter unsteadily. George looked at his white face. Never had he seen Peter so totally devastated. Not knowing what to say, he gripped Peter's shoulder hard and they waited silently for the arrival of the other chaise.

Chapter Seventeen

Somewhere, a long way off, there was an appalling headache. It seemed to be away at the end of a long dark tunnel, a tunnel which swung sickeningly about her. Someone was moaning. Dimly Penelope realised it was herself. Then she could feel a hand holding hers. A very familiar voice was saying something terribly important. Desperately she tried to hear, despite the fact that the effort brought her closer to that headache.

'Penny, sweetheart! Oh, Penny, my darling, it's all right. You're safe now! Little love!'

The long wait had been agonising for Peter. Despite the doctor's assurances that she would recover, he had just spent the longest day of his life. Now, as Penelope finally stirred, he could no longer hold back the words of love he had been longing to speak. He had no idea whether or not she could hear him, but he had to speak. All day he had sat with her, his eyes fixed on her white face. Phoebe and Sarah had sat with him in turns, their faces almost as pale as Penelope's. Shortly after midnight he had insisted they both go to bed, promising to call them if there were any change.

With a huge effort Penelope opened her eyes. The

dimly lit room was completely new to her. All the light was coming from a fireplace on the opposite side of the room. Puzzled, Penelope concentrated on the strange man leaning over her. Anguish stared from his dark brown eyes, a normally olive complexion was drained of all colour and his dark curly hair was dishevelled. I'm dead, thought Penelope in total confusion. Who is this man?

'Penny? It's me, Peter. It's all right, you're safe.' It was Peter's voice, tender and beloved. Was this what he looked like?

'I'm dreaming,' she said weakly.

He stroked her cheek tenderly. 'No, dearest, you're awake. I'm really here.' The strange look on her face frightened him. 'Penny, darling, what's wrong?'

'Don't wake me, Peter. It's such a wonderful dream. I can see you in it…and you said you loved me.' Her voice trailed off and her eyes closed as she drifted back to sleep.

Stunned, Peter stared at his sleeping wife. She could see him! Could the blow to the head have restored her vision? It must have done! Swiftly he made sure that she was comfortable and went to the door. He opened it and looked out into the corridor. A gleam of light shone from under the door of Sarah and Phoebe's room. He ran to it and knocked softly.

'Come in.' He opened the door. Both girls were sitting up in the same bed. Phoebe had her arms around Sarah, who had obviously been crying. They blinked at Peter's wild eyes.

'Peter, is something wrong? Why have you left Penny?' cried Phoebe, throwing back the bedclothes.

'She woke up,' said Peter in a choked whisper, 'and she could see me! She thought it was a dream, but it wasn't!'

The two girls stared at him, unable to believe their ears. 'She…she could see you?' stammered Sarah. 'Are you sure?'

'She said she was dreaming, because she could see me, then she went back to sleep,' said Peter.

Phoebe said in tones of wonder, 'That bruise, it's exactly where the bruise was when she fell off her horse and lost her sight. At the time the doctor could find nothing wrong with her eyes. He said there must be some damage, interfering with the messages going to her brain. The blow on the head must have reversed the damage! Oh, Peter, how wonderful!' She jumped out of bed and snatched up a dressing gown. 'Go back to her, Peter. I'm going to wake Richard! Come on Sarah!' She rushed from the room.

'I'll get George,' said Sarah excitedly. 'I can't believe it's true! Can we see her?'

'When she is a little stronger, Sarah. I think she still has a dreadful headache. She is asleep again now. I'd better go back.' He suddenly found himself being enthusiastically hugged by Sarah. He returned the embrace and said, 'Go on, hoyden! You'd better tell George!'

He went back to Penelope's room. She was still sound asleep. Very quietly he crossed the room to her and settled himself beside her on the bed. A deep contentment had come over him. All the confusion he had felt was gone. This was his wife and he loved her more than life itself. It was as simple as that. Nothing else really mattered any more. Completely relaxed, he leaned back against the bed-head, dreaming of all the things he and Penelope would do together. Children, he thought. That would be wonderful!

Towards dawn he felt Penelope move beside him, then her eyes opened. She looked dazed.

'Better now, love?' he asked softly.

Penelope stared at him in disbelief. What had happened to her? Suddenly she remembered the chaise, the brutal strength of her abductor. Had it all been a nightmare? Despite the pain in her head she tried to sit up, but was gently restrained.

'No, dearest. Just lie down and rest. I won't leave you, I promise.'

'Peter?' She was shocked at how weak her voice sounded. 'Is this a dream? Is that really you?'

'Yes, it's really me. Go back to sleep. I'll be here.'

'My head hurts, but I can see you!'

'I know, darling. You must have hit your head when the chaise overturned. The doctor will be back again later this morning. He said that you'd have a headache when you woke up. It's nothing to worry about, especially if you can see again.'

'The chaise? Then it wasn't a nightmare? Oh, Peter, I was so scared!' She began to weep uncontrollably. 'He w-wouldn't stop…tried to stop him, but my hands were tied…kept tearing at my gown…oh, God! His hands! He said…scream…no one to hear! He must have… Oh, Peter, I couldn't stop him!'

Convulsive sobs racked her slender body. Tenderly Peter lifted her and cradled her in his arms. He realised in horror that she thought she had been raped.

He said urgently, 'Penny, stop it! We did hear you, darling. We were close enough to the chaise then, just about to stop it. It ended up in the ditch. Frobisher is dead, Penny. He'll never hurt you again.'

'Then he didn't…? I thought…you'd hate me!'

'Stop thinking it, Penny. We heard you screaming just as we attacked the chaise.' His cheek rested on top of her head. Lovingly he put one finger under her chin and brought her face up to his. 'Penny, even if Frobisher had done that to you, it would not have made the slightest difference to the way I feel about you.'

'The…the way you feel about me?' she faltered, hardly daring to hope.

He looked deeply into her wide grey eyes, bright with tears. 'I love you, Penny. I've known it for a long time, but I was too scared to say it. I knew it the day you told me Frobisher had attacked you and I didn't feel jealous, simply protective and murderous! The thought of you being in his power sickened me! A man who would take advantage of a blind girl! But even before that—the first night I made love to you…and you gave yourself to me so sweetly… Penny, I loved you then. I was just too stupid to realise it.'

Her face was transfixed with joy as she gazed at him. She couldn't believe what she was hearing, what she could see in his eyes. 'You l-l-love me?' she asked in amazement. 'You don't just mean you're fond of me?'

His arms tightened around her. 'Oh, Penny, darling Penny, I couldn't even begin to tell you how much. You're mine. I'll never let you go! When we caught up to the chaise and heard you screaming. I was ready to commit murder! And George and Richard weren't much better!'

Tears of happiness slid down her cheeks. 'You really love me? Oh, Peter, I've loved you so much! I tried not to let you see. I thought you wouldn't want that and I didn't want to bother you!'

'I did know, Penny,' he admitted. 'Remember I told you once that you wouldn't know how to lie? Everything about you told me, but I also knew why you said nothing.'

'You knew that I loved you? How?'

He smiled. 'You told me with your body every time I made love to you!'

'Oh!' She blushed furiously as she met his gaze.

'Dare I hope, dearest Penny, that you will continue to tell me that you love me?' he asked teasingly.

Shyly she nodded, unable to speak. Her eyes told him all he needed to know. Later there would be a time to tell her that the others were here, that they had all come after her. Later they could plan the rest of their life together, a life of love and joy which he knew could only increase with the coming years.

THE MARRIAGE TRUCE
by
Ann Elizabeth Cree

Ann Elizabeth Cree is married and lives in Boise, Idaho, with her family. She has worked as a nutritionist and an accountant. Her favourite form of day-dreaming has always been weaving romantic stories in her head. With the encouragement of a friend, she started putting those stories on to paper. In addition to writing and caring for two lively boys, two cats and two dogs, she enjoys gardening, playing the piano, and, of course, reading.

Chapter One

Devin St Clair, the fifth Marquis of Huntington, stood at the window of his bedchamber in Henslowe Hall and watched the Earl of Monteville's carriage come to a halt in the circular drive below. He let the curtain fall and turned, a scowl on his brow. The prospect of the forthcoming ball was about as appealing as a stay in Newgate. Particularly now he knew the party from Monteville House had arrived. He had no desire to spend an evening under the same roof as Sarah Chandler.

'Dev?' His younger sister Jessica stood in the doorway. She was dressed for the ball in a pale pink gown, her thick dark hair pulled back in a knot, a few tendrils framing her pretty, delicate face. He felt a little tug at his heart. She looked much too young to be going to her own betrothal ball.

She smiled at him. 'Are you ready? I thought perhaps you would not mind escorting me down.'

'Of course not. Although I am surprised Adam is not fighting me for the honour.' A smile lit his usually cool face. 'You look lovely, Jess.'

'And you look extremely dashing.' She eyed his

black coat and black silk breeches. 'Oh, Dev! I am
so glad you are here. I know it cannot be at all easy
for you.'

He raised a brow. 'I will own it was a trifle inconvenient of you to fall in love with the man whose
future estate runs with Monteville House, and a
cousin of the Chandlers to boot.'

A chagrined expression crossed her face. 'I tried
very hard not to.'

He moved forward and looked into her face. 'I am
only teasing you a little.' He took her gloved hand
in his. 'Don't look so worried, Jess. I quite like your
young man, and I never would have consented to the
match if I didn't think he would make you happy.
And I promise to behave myself.'

She tried to smile. 'I am hardly worried about that.
You have never done anything wrong, no matter
what anyone says. It is entirely Lord Thayne's doing!' Her hazel eyes clouded with a touch of anger,
before filling with concern. 'It is only—I don't want
you to be hurt again.'

He pressed her hands lightly before releasing
them. 'There is nothing to worry yourself about. It
is in the past.' Which was precisely where he intended to keep all of it, especially the Chandlers.
'Come, we must go down or Adam will think you've
changed your mind.'

She gave him another little smile as he held out
his arm. She placed her hand lightly on the sleeve of
his coat.

But as they descended the winding staircase of
Lord Henslowe's country seat, the sounds of laughter
and chatter drifting up from the ballroom below, his
mouth curved in a bitter smile. It was going to prove

devilishly difficult to keep the Chandlers where he wanted them. He had found it impossible to completely avoid Sarah Chandler a month ago in London, and now she was going to be under his nose again for an entire evening. It should be no problem, he would just make certain to stay on the opposite side of the room.

Sarah Chandler stood in one corner of Lady Henslowe's ballroom, partially hidden by a Grecian column entwined with ivy and silk flowers, and wished, not for the first time this evening, that she could go home. Pleading a headache and quitting the ball would, however, be all too obvious.

The only redeeming factor was no one had quarrelled, at least publicly. But the air was thick with unspoken tensions. It hardly helped that the ballroom had somehow become divided into two sides which resembled nothing as much as two armies preparing for battle. The Chandler relations stood on one side near the tall double doors leading into the hallway, and the St Clairs on the opposite side near the doors leading to the garden. The rest of the guests chose the other two walls with a few brave souls meandering between the two. The only thing that would make it worse was if her brother, Nicholas, was present. Thank goodness, he was safely in Scotland.

She looked over at the dancers and picked out Adam, her second cousin, gracefully executing the steps of a quadrille with his betrothed. From the way they gazed into each other's eyes, it was apparent they were deeply in love. How unfortunate that Lady Jessica's brother undoubtedly detested the Chandlers more than anyone on earth. At least Adam was only a cousin. It would be much worse if Lady Jessica was marrying into Sarah's own family. But of course, Lord Huntington would probably send his sister to a convent before he would allow such a thing.

She glanced over at the St Clair wall. For once he wasn't staring at her, thank goodness. He leaned against the wall, arms folded over his chest, regarding the company with a faintly amused look on his darkly handsome face as if he found the ball a source of sardonic amusement. Of course, he had had a similar expression on his face nearly every time she saw him in London last month, so that was nothing unusual. Certainly the tensions seemed to affect him not at all. But neither had the speculations and stares cast his way in London.

Sarah would have thought him completely indifferent except that once or twice she caught an expression on his face that was oddly vulnerable, despite his cool stance. And then had experienced the most insane desire to approach him. But of course, he would only have walked away from her.

As if sensing her interest, he turned his head and looked at her. His mouth curved in a slow, rather wicked smile that made her feel vulnerable. She flushed and forced her gaze to a spot over his left shoulder, trying to pretend she found something there quite fascinating before looking away. For not the first time, she wondered why Adam must fall in love with Lord Huntington's sister. She only prayed Huntington wouldn't feel obligated to visit the Henslowe estate very often.

'Sarah, are you hiding again?'

Sarah started. Her cousin, Amelia, Lady Marleigh, appeared at her side. She was tall and blonde with a slender graceful figure, and a pair of lively blue eyes. 'Not that I blame you. 'Tis the most dreadful ball I have ever attended. I've never seen a group with such dismal faces.'

'I know. It's rather like the air before a thunderstorm. The clouds are gathering and the air is still and sticky and one is just waiting for the storm to break and clear the air.'

'What do you think the storm will be? A duel, perhaps?'

Sarah made a face. 'No, please not that! I don't think I could bear another duel!'

'Well, perhaps we should go and stand with the St Clairs. That would certainly create a diversion. Perhaps by Lady Beatrice. She looks extremely displeased. Or...' Amelia's vivid blue eyes sparkled with sudden mischief. 'We could have Lord Henslowe present you to Huntington as his next partner.'

'No, thank you!' Sarah nearly shuddered at the thought. 'He'd probably just look at me in his odious way and walk off.' Or, worse, accept and she'd be forced to spend an entire set with his sardonic gaze and confusing remarks. Such as the time in London when Lady Ralston made the grave error of seating her next to him at dinner. Or the time she'd backed into him at a rout where he'd looked down his arrogant nose at her while she stammered an apology. She still cringed at the memory.

'Are you certain? He's been staring at you all evening. Just as he did in London. Even John said something and he is so terribly dense at noticing such things.' A mischievous smile crossed her face. 'I sometimes wonder if Lord Huntington has a *tendre* for you.'

'That is the most ridiculous notion,' Sarah snapped. 'In fact, he quite detests me. Not that I can fault him.'

Amelia rolled her eyes. 'How perfectly idiotic! I will admit, I find this whole quarrel tedious. Certainly the affair was very dreadful, but it happened nearly two years ago. I can understand why he wants nothing to do with Nicholas, but with you? You had nothing to do with it.'

Sarah looked away. Amelia was wrong, she had everything to do with it. If she hadn't invited Mary to stay with her, if she hadn't been so worried about Mama, if she hadn't been so naïve, perhaps things would have turned out differently. As it was, every time she saw Huntington, she felt the same regret and guilt all over again.

Amelia shut her fan. 'Well, you would be better off with Huntington than with Cedric Blanton. I fear he's about to ask you for another dance. If you stand up with him one more time, everyone will consider you practically betrothed.'

'Oh, dear.' She turned and saw that Amelia was right, Cedric Blanton was heading in their direction.

A rather florid man in his early thirties, he had recently bought a small estate nearby nearly a year ago. From the first time she met him at a dinner party, he had made his interest in her quite clear. He had even appeared in London when she had been there for a month visiting Amelia and her husband John. She found his conversations annoying. She did her best to avoid him, but tonight had been difficult.

'Since you cannot bring yourself to snub him, I think you should make your escape,' Amelia said.

'Go. I will keep him occupied with my witty conversation.'

Sarah cast her a grateful look and started around the edge of the ballroom. The best route of escape looked to be towards the double French doors leading to the veranda. Unfortunately, it was also the St Clair wall, but perhaps if she hurried past no one would notice her, or at least she wouldn't notice them. She had just arrived at the enemy wall when a plump elderly woman stepped in front of her.

Sarah side-stepped in order to avoid standing on the lady's foot. Instead, she landed squarely on a masculine shoe fastened with a shiny buckle. She glanced quickly up at the tall figure standing before her. 'I beg your…' The words died on her lips when she saw the man's face.

Lord Huntington looked as startled as she felt and then his brow shot up in his arrogant fashion. 'Miss Chandler, I am beginning to think you desire a more intimate acquaintance with me.'

'You are quite wrong,' Sarah snapped.

'Then why do you persist in stepping into me?'

'I could ask why you persist in standing in my way.'

His gaze roved over her face in a careless fashion that made her flush. 'Perhaps because I desire a more intimate acquaintance with you.'

He was doing what he always did, making some sort of suggestive remark that erased any sympathy she might have felt, and flustered and irritated her at the same time.

She gave him her most quelling look. 'I fear you are merely attempting to annoy me, my lord.'

'Why would I wish to do that?'

'I've no idea. Perhaps you could let me pass.'

'I could. However, are you certain it is safe?'

'Now what do you mean?'

His smile was most annoying. 'This appears to be the St Clair side of the room. Perhaps you should retrace your steps and take the, er…safer route. Not to mention that our host seems to disapprove of your conversing with me.'

She glanced around and saw that Lord Henslowe was indeed watching them with his most thunderous look. She turned away, feeling even more impatient. 'This is the most ridiculous….really, there is no reason why anyone shouldn't take whichever side of the room they want. Or speak with whomever they choose.'

His brow rose again. 'Does that mean you are here because you wish to talk to me?'

'No! Must you…' Over his shoulder she saw Cedric had broken away from Amelia and was peering around the room. He caught sight of her and started in her direction. 'Please excuse me, I cannot stand here trading nonsense with you.'

Huntington still watched her in that lazy way that made her want to hit him. 'Then perhaps you would consider continuing the, er, nonsense while we danced.'

Her mouth fell open and hot colour rushed to her cheeks. 'I…I pray you will not tease me in such a fashion.' She backed away. 'I…I really must find my…my grandfather.' She dashed away towards the open doors leading to the veranda and had no idea whether it was Huntington or Blanton that she wanted to escape most.

* * *

Dev watched Sarah Chandler brush through the double doors that opened on the veranda. She was looking for Lord Monteville in the garden? She would do better to try the card room.

He frowned. What the hell came over him every time he saw her? He had no idea why he wanted to tease her out of the wary disapproval with which she regarded him. Or bring a blush to her lovely cheeks. If he had an ounce of sense, he'd stay out of her way. Certainly, from the horrified look on her face when he suggested she dance with him, she fervently wished he would.

'At daggers drawn again, I see. Now, what devilish thing did you say to Miss Chandler to cause her to run off?' His cousin Lord Jeremy Pennington, appeared at his side.

Dev quirked a brow. 'I merely asked her to stand up with me.'

'Not quite the usual reaction to such a request from you. Not that I blame her. You seem determined to needle her.'

'I cannot help it if she regards me as the devil incarnate.'

Jeremy glanced at him. 'She has nothing to do with her brother's sins.'

'No.'

'I don't suppose you would consider some sort of reconciliation? It's bound to make things a trifle awkward now with Jessica and Adam.'

Dev shrugged. 'Even if I should wish that, I doubt if Miss Chandler would agree.'

Jeremy looked at him, a little smile at his lips. 'I was not speaking particularly of Miss Chandler.'

Dev frowned, and then his attention was caught by Cedric Blanton who stood at the doors leading to the garden. He seemed to be looking at something outside. And Dev had a good idea what it was. His fawning after Sarah Chandler in London had been obvious to any fool. It made Dev exceedingly uneasy, particularly after a houseparty Dev had attended last summer where Blanton had also been a guest. Blanton had pursued the Duke of Wrexton's daughter in the same fashion. Like Sarah, Lady Alethea had attempted to avoid the man as much as possible. She'd been successful until the picnic two days before they were to leave. And then Dev had caught Blanton almost ravishing the girl near a thicket of bushes by the lake. Dev had stopped him, barely restraining himself from mowing the man down. Only the knowledge of the certain scandal and insult to Lady Alethea's name that would be the certain result kept him from doing so. Instead, he'd threatened to ruin Blanton if a word of it leaked out.

The music had stopped and a footman appeared to announce the supper. Jeremy glanced at him. 'Coming? Aunt Beatrice has commanded that I escort her. I've no desire for a scold if I don't appear on time.'

'Not yet.' He shifted his attention back to Blanton, who still stood in the doorway.

Jeremy gave him a curious look. 'Later, then.'

Dev watched Blanton disappear through the French doors. He frowned. Was Sarah Chandler still foolish enough to be outside? A quick search of the guests milling towards the doors and out of the ballroom revealed no sign of a slight figure with a crown of rich auburn hair in a cream-coloured gown. And surely he'd have noticed if she had come back in.

He stalked towards the terrace doors, wondering

what sort of a fool he was about to become. If she were there, she would probably stare at him with her calm, collected look as if he was partially invisible.

The garden was cool and dark. A veil of wispy clouds covered the moon. He walked to the edge of the terrace and looked down into the garden. At first he saw nothing, then he heard voices coming from the shrubbery. He moved down the steps with a light tread. He rounded the edge of the circle of shrubs, just in time to see a woman struggling in Blanton's arms. She suddenly yanked away and Blanton grabbed for her. There was an ominous sound of ripped fabric. And Dev caught a glimpse of Sarah Chandler's frightened face.

'Let me go!'

'No, my dear, I must speak to you,' Blanton said smoothly.

Without a second thought, Dev stepped forward. 'I suggest you do as the lady asks.'

The two froze. Blanton's head whipped around and he stared at Dev, his eyes unfocused. Then he glared, hatred shooting across his face. 'What do you mean by interrupting a private conversation, my lord?'

Dev regarded him coolly. 'If you wish to hold a private conversation, I suggest you find somewhere less public than this. Particularly during a ball.' His eyes briefly swept over Sarah. She stared at him, her arms crossed over her breast, trying to hide the damage to her bodice. She looked dismayed, shocked and completely miserable. He fought to keep his fury at bay. 'Although the lady does not appear to particularly enjoy your conversation.'

Blanton took a step towards him, his chin trembling with anger. 'What do you mean by that?'

'It should be obvious. Miss Chandler wished to go and you attempted to detain her by force,' he said indifferently.

Blanton tugged at his stock. 'It was hardly by force. And she is my fiancée.'

Sarah gasped. 'I am not!'

Blanton turned to her. 'But you will have to marry me. It will hardly do to have it spread about that we were alone together and you were allowing my embrace. Your reputation will be ruined.'

'No,' she whispered.

'Such lengths are unnecessary.' Dev folded his arms across his chest, regarding Blanton with contempt. 'I've no intention of mentioning this particular conversation.'

'I have no reason to trust your word.' Blanton looked as if he held a trump card. 'You detest the Chandlers. What better method of revenging yourself than by destroying Miss Chandler's reputation? It would bring disgrace down upon her entire family.'

'You are mistaken. I would no more enact revenge by ruining a lady's reputation than I would force her into marriage by the same means.' Dev took a step towards him. 'So, unless you wish to meet me tomorrow, I suggest you keep such speculations to yourself.'

Blanton stiffened, fury distorting his features. Dev took another step in his direction and Blanton tugged at his cravat, backing away, and then scurried off.

Dev watched his portly figure retreat through the ballroom doors. Then he looked over at Sarah. She stood motionless as if she'd gone into shock. 'Are you all right?'

She nodded. 'Yes.'

He found himself half-wanting to shake her and half-wanting to take her into his arms, and erase the misery and shame from her face. The unexpected thought made him scowl. 'What the devil were you doing out here with Blanton?'

'I…I wasn't out here with him. That is, I was here alone and he…he followed me.'

'I don't suppose it occurred to you that wandering around in dark gardens alone is not only improper, but highly dangerous? Unless, of course, you wish to encourage behaviour such as Blanton's.'

That seemed to jolt her out of her trance. 'I most certainly do not! And I was not wandering around— I…I was merely standing here.' Her voice quivered and she suddenly looked utterly defeated. 'I…I know it was quite improper to come here, but I…I wanted to escape for a few minutes and it was nice to be alone and I did not want to go in and suddenly he…he appeared…'

She looked away from him for a moment as if trying to collect herself. When she spoke, her voice was calm. 'So, I suppose it was my fault. If you will excuse me, my lord, and thank you for…for rescuing me.' She started to move past him, still clutching her bodice.

'Wait.'

She glanced up at him, a question in her dark eyes.

He frowned. 'How bad is the tear?'

'Not very bad. A small rip in the lace, I think. Nothing that cannot be mended with a needle and thread.'

'You cannot go into the ballroom with a rip in your bodice.'

'I have little choice. At least everyone has gone into supper.'

'We can only hope,' he said drily. His glance fell to the small brooch she wore. 'Your brooch. Can you use that to repair the tear?'

She looked down also. 'Perhaps. I…I think so.' She fumbled with the clasp, but her fingers were trembling and he realised that, despite her collected manner, she was very badly shaken.

'I'll do it.' He stepped forward. She went very still as his fingers brushed her breast. His fingers suddenly seemed as clumsy as hers and he was finding it difficult to concentrate on the task at hand. Her scent was soft and sweet and feminine and the fact she seemed to be trying very hard not to breathe was making his own breath come far too fast.

'My lord, I…I think I should go in.' Her voice was faint.

He scowled. 'In a moment.' He'd just about extricated the pin from the soft silky fabric of her dress when he heard a screech from behind them.

And then, 'Oh, my! Oh, my goodness!'

He spun around, the brooch in his hand. Lady Henslowe stood behind them, a hand clasped to her breast. Even in the faint moonlight, he could see her eyes were wide with shock. And with her was Lord Henslowe, a murderous look on his normally placid face.

'Damnation.' He was beginning to think fate fully intended to make him pay for every one of his numerous sins.

Chapter Two

Never, even if she lived to be a hundred and one, would Sarah forget the shocked expressions on the faces of Lord and Lady Henslowe. She closed her eyes and prayed she could vanish. Or die on the spot.

But she did not. She opened her eyes to find Lord Henslowe advancing on Huntington. He fixed him with an icy stare. 'I trust this means there is to be a betrothal, my lord.'

'Yes,' Huntington said coolly.

'No,' Sarah replied at the same time.

'But, my dear, you cannot allow such…such liberties and not marry him!' Lady Henslowe exclaimed. 'And, oh my! Your gown!'

Henslowe's gaze swung to Sarah's torn bodice. He stared and then glowered at Huntington. 'So this is how you repay my hospitality! By attacking my guests! It is too late to forbid the marriage between my son and your sister but, damn you, you will not set foot in this house again!' He advanced on Huntington as if he meant to thrash him.

Huntington seemed to be frozen to the spot. Sarah ran forward and caught Henslowe's hand. 'No! Stop it! He…he did nothing wrong! He is not responsible for this!'

Henslowe shook off her hand. 'You are defending this rogue?' he demanded. 'The devil! Has he seduced you already?'

'No, of course not,' Sarah said.

'But, my dear, how did your gown become torn? And why are you in the garden and with him?' Lady Henslowe asked. Her gaze was fixed on Sarah's bodice with horrid fascination.

'I…I went to the garden for a few minutes…I wished to be alone and then…'

Huntington's cool voice cut in. 'This is neither the time nor the place for this conversation. Miss Chandler is shaking. I suggest, Lady Henslowe, that you take her in and see she has some brandy.'

'Oh, yes.' Lady Henslowe bustled to Sarah's side. 'My dear, such a shock…you must come with me.'

'I don't want brandy,' Sarah said.

'You will remain with me, Huntington,' Henslowe said, ignoring Sarah. 'No use thinking you're going to run off until this affair is settled.'

'I wouldn't think of it,' Huntington drawled. His arms were crossed and his eyes held the faintly amused indifference Sarah was so accustomed to.

Sarah felt wretched. 'Please, you must listen. Lord Huntington did not do this. You see, I was…'

'Go in, Miss Chandler.' Huntington's eyes held a warning which Sarah completely planned to ignore.

'No! Not until I explain the matter.'

The indifference left Huntington's face. If anything, he looked as if he wanted to strangle her. 'There is, Miss Chandler, nothing to explain. Lady Henslowe will take you in.'

Lady Henslowe tugged on her arm. 'Come, my dear. You cannot stand here with your gown in such repair! Oh, Sarah, how could you do this? Whatever will Monteville say?'

Sarah stared at her. 'Oh, no! Not Grandfather! You cannot tell him about this. He…he will probably murder me!'

'My dear child, I hope I have done nothing to put such fear in you.'

Lady Henslowe stiffened and made a little moaning sound. Sarah froze, her gaze going to the man who had silently appeared behind them. For the second time that night, she wished she might vanish from the face of the earth.

The Earl of Monteville's cool, impersonal gaze travelled over the group for a moment. It was only when his gaze fell to Sarah's bodice that it hardened. He looked at Huntington. 'I trust there is an explanation for why my granddaughter should be standing in a darkened garden with a rather large tear in her gown.'

Huntington's own gaze was equally hard and direct. 'I believe, my lord, we had best meet in private.' He did not look at Sarah.

Sarah shook off Lady Henslowe's arm. 'No, there is no need, I can explain…Lord Huntington has done nothing…he only wished to help me!'

'The rogue tried to seduce her!' Henslowe said.

'It is not true!' Sarah glared at him. His mouth fell open.

The look Lord Monteville turned on her was not unkind. 'My dear child, it is best that you go in. You are undoubtedly cold. Penelope can take you in and find your shawl.'

'Oh…oh, yes!' Lady Henslowe, who had been watching in stunned silence, sprang to life. 'My dear, come with me.'

Sarah allowed Lady Henslowe to take her arm without protest. It was no use arguing with her grandfather. She had seen that look too many times to know that any sort of resistance was in vain. She only prayed that he would talk Huntington out of the ridiculous notion he must marry her.

Dev stepped past Monteville into Henslowe's private study. A candle on the massive mahogany desk cast a dim light in the dark panelled room. Monteville closed the door and moved to the sideboard. He poured two glasses of brandy and held one out to Dev. 'I believe this might be in order.'

Dev accepted the glass. Apparently Monteville had no intention of calling him out, at least not yet. Despite the Earl's age, he was reputed to be a master with a sword. Although Dev possessed no mean skills in that regard, he had no desire to duel with a man several decades his senior. He took a neat shot of the liquor, its warmth burning down his throat, then turned his gaze on the Earl.

Monteville watched him without touching his own drink. Although in his mid sixties, he was still a formidable presence with a lean, upright figure and a pair of piercing grey eyes. Now they were fixed on Dev. 'So, Lord Huntington, perhaps you will explain the little drama in the garden and Lord Henslowe's rather confused desire to either evict you from his house or run you through.'

Dev set his glass down and looked directly at Monteville. 'He believes I tried to ravish or seduce your granddaughter. I am not certain he's yet decided which.'

'And did you?'

Dev scowled. 'No.'

'Then perhaps you will enlighten me as to what did happen.' He looked merely curious, a sign Dev found more disconcerting than all of Henslowe's blustering.

'Lord and Lady Henslowe found us alone in the garden,' Dev said.

Monteville raised a brow. 'And was that all? Although secreted alone in a dark garden is somewhat improper, I cannot quite fathom how the position could be described as damnably compromising. I would imagine a man with your intelligence could come up with a plausible explanation for your, er, situation.'

'My hand was at her breast,' Dev said bluntly.

Monteville's brow shot up further. 'Ah, I can see that might present a more delicate dilemma. I trust you had a reason for doing so?'

'I was attempting to remove a brooch. She needed it to repair a tear in her bodice.' He would not have been surprised if Monteville demanded satisfaction. Even to his own ears the explanation sounded feeble.

'And precisely how did that tear come to be in her bodice?'

He had no intention of revealing Blanton's role. 'I haven't the damnedest idea. I did not do it if that is what you wish to know. I have every intention of marrying her,' he added stiffly.

'Why?'

'Because I've no desire to be held responsible for seducing your granddaughter.' He gave a short laugh.

'There's enough tension already between our families—it would probably make the Battle of Waterloo look like a tea party.' He fixed Monteville with a hard look. 'Nor do I intend to let my damnable sins interfere with my sister's happiness. Henslowe has not only made it clear I'm not welcome here, but he would stop the marriage if he could.'

Monteville moved towards the sideboard and set down his glass and picked up the decanter. 'More, my lord?'

'No.'

He set the decanter down. 'I am still at a loss to know exactly why you were in the garden with Sarah?'

'I saw her quit the ballroom, and when it was time to go into supper, she still had not returned. I decided to look for her.' He undoubtedly sounded like a complete fool or a liar.

'I see.' Monteville looked at him. 'Tell me, my lord, do you hold any fondness at all for my granddaughter?'

Dev nearly staggered back. It was the last question he'd expected from the man. 'I hardly know her.' He gave a short laugh. 'I fear our relationship could best be characterised as an armed truce.'

'Quite understandable under the circumstances,' Monteville said. He looked at Dev carefully. 'You see, I have had a rather interesting evening. Shortly before I joined your little party in the garden, another gentleman, who, er, claimed he had also been alone with my granddaughter, accosted me, saying they had been interrupted by a witness who would have no scruples in spreading the tale about that he'd seen my granddaughter and this gentleman locked in an embrace. Under the circumstances, the gentleman seemed to feel I was obligated to give my consent to a match between himself and my granddaughter.'

Cold fury rose in Dev. 'You may rest assured that his witness would sooner sell his soul to the devil than spread such tales about. Nor was the embrace willing, at least not on your granddaughter's part.'

'I thought not,' Monteville said. He continued to regard Dev with his bland gaze. 'I am concerned for her happiness. I would not want her marriage to you, for instance, to be a notch better than a marriage to this other gentleman.'

Dev had the sudden image of her struggling in Blanton's embrace. He took a step towards Monteville. 'If you want her happiness, then keep her away from Blanton. I wouldn't allow a dog in his care, much less a woman. He would make her miserable. At least, I would not—' He realised Monteville was regarding him oddly. It would not do to let anything but cool logic show. He frowned. 'I will not make her unhappy,' he added stiffly.

'I trust not,' Monteville said. 'She has a kind and generous heart. I would not want that changed.' His eyes had lost their bland indifference and Dev suddenly knew why Monteville could be such a formidable enemy.

'No.' Dev understood. He would not hesitate to strangle any man that dared to hurt his sister Jessica.

'Good,' Monteville said softly. He glanced at the clock on the mantelpiece. 'It is late. I suggest we continue this conversation in the morning. By the way, did you give my granddaughter any indication of your intentions?'

'Yes. She was not pleased.' An understatement.

She had looked as if he'd said he was going to imprison her.

Monteville's mouth lifted in a ghost of a smile. 'I imagine not. You will need to pay your addresses in the more conventional manner. You will call tomorrow.' He moved towards the door, indicating the conversation was finished. He paused and looked back at Dev. 'And if you are wondering where you are to sleep tonight, I can assure you Lord Henslowe will be quite amenable to having you remain under his roof.' He departed, silently closing the door behind him.

Dev stared after him, wondering if he'd lost his mind. Had Monteville just commanded him to properly offer Sarah Chandler marriage? He'd hardly known what to expect when he'd entered the study with the man—Monteville calling him a libertine and a liar, perhaps even a threat to his life…but never such ready acquiescence.

He knew the Chandlers had no more love for him than he had for them. No matter that it had been Nicholas who had been his wife's lover, the Chandlers had blamed him as well. Rumours had circulated that it was Dev's own cold treatment of Mary that had driven her into Nicholas's arms.

And then there was the duel between himself and Nicholas. He smiled grimly. There had nearly been another duel tonight. From the look on Henslowe's face, he had no doubt it was still a possibility.

He stalked to the sideboard and picked up the decanter. What the devil had he done? He should have followed his instincts and stayed away from Sarah

Chandler. But if he hadn't—Blanton might be the man who was calling on Sarah tomorrow. He set the decanter down, the thought making another shot of brandy unpalatable.

Chapter Three

Sarah attempted to force a piece of toast down her throat and finally gave up. She fell back against her pillows. Morning sunlight streamed across the patterned green quilt covering her bed. Usually on such lovely days she looked forward to spending a few happy hours painting or drawing in the magnificent gardens surrounding Monteville House.

But not today. She wanted nothing more than to crawl back under her covers. Or wish herself back to yesterday, when the sky had been leaden and grey, a day when it had still been possible to plead a headache and forgo the Henslowe ball. No matter that it would have upset Lady Henslowe and insulted the St Clairs. At least she wouldn't be awaking today with the events of last night fresh in her memory like a bad dream.

Lady Henslowe's expression of horrified shock, Lord Henslowe's threats, her grandfather's cool, impersonal assessment. And, worse of all, the cold look on Huntington's face.

Even Blanton's declaration of love and his repugnant kiss had dimmed compared to the subsequent events. She'd had no chance to speak to her grandfather. Lady Henslowe had led her to a small private saloon and bustled off to find a servant. And then her aunt, Lady Omberley, had appeared, Amelia in her wake. The worried look on their faces had been almost too much to bear. Lady Omberley had insisted that Sarah must leave immediately and had routed John, Amelia's husband, from his card game to escort them home. His face was grim, although he said nothing. In fact, none of them had said a thing and instead treated her with a solicitude which was more frightening than if they had scolded her.

It wasn't until Sarah was in bed that Amelia finally spoke. She still had that careful concerned look on her face, as if Sarah was some sort of porcelain figure that might break any moment. 'Sarah, are you all right? I do not wish to overset you, but what did happen? Mama and I had just finished supper when Cousin Penelope sent for us. She was quite hysterical and moaning about vipers in her bosom and said we must go to you right away as Lord Huntington had tried to seduce you! And then Grandfather sent word we should bring you home.' Her face momentarily lost its worried look, and she suddenly looked fierce. 'And if Huntington has harmed you, I vow I will call him out myself!'

'No, he…he did nothing wrong.' Except come to her rescue. She took a deep breath. 'He was trying to help me. When Lord and Lady Henslowe found us he was trying to remove my brooch. I…I wished to use it to pin my bodice. It had a tear.'

'Yes, my dear,' Amelia said in patient tones. 'But, Sarah, how did it come to be torn? And why ever were you in the garden with Huntington?'

'I wasn't. I went out by myself and then Cedric Blanton came. He started saying the most ridiculous things about how I was a vision of loveliness in the moonlight and when I said I must go in, he…he grabbed my wrist.' She bit her lip and looked away, ashamed at the memory. 'And then he…he kissed me.'

'Oh, Sarah, how awful!'

It had been. Blanton had had a most peculiar look in his eye, almost as if he'd enjoyed her struggles. She had felt a clutch of fear that he meant to ravish her. And then Huntington had stepped in. She had felt such relief until she realised how the situation must look to him and then she had felt nothing but shame.

'Sarah?'

She forced her mind back to Amelia. 'He wouldn't let me go and when I tried to break away, he…he tore my gown. And then Lord Huntington came. Mr Blanton said I was his fiancée because Lord Huntington would undoubtedly tell everyone I was ruined out of revenge. Lord Huntington became very angry and said he would not, and finally Mr Blanton left. And Lord Huntington thought I could use my brooch to repair my tear and he tried to help me remove it. That was when Lord and Lady Henslowe came.'

'Oh, Sarah!' Amelia repeated. She looked stunned. 'When I suggested we create a diversion, I hardly expected this!'

'No.' Sarah hugged her knees. She shuddered. 'It was horrible. Lord Henslowe said that Lord Huntington would never set foot in his house again.

That was after he demanded to know if there would be a betrothal.'

'And what did Huntington say?'

Sarah flushed. 'He said there would be. But, of course, there will not be.'

'But, Sarah, I do not think you will have a choice! When this gets about...'

'But why must it? Only Lord and Lady Henslowe know and you and Aunt and Grandfather, of course. But no one else need know and once I explain it to Grandfather...'

'Oh, Sarah, I fear it is far too late! Cousin Penelope has already told Serena and, although she means well, she can never keep a secret!'

'Oh, no,' Sarah said faintly. It might as well be announced in front of the entire neighbourhood. Lady Henslowe's only daughter was kind-hearted in her own way, but she was an incessant talker and could never keep a confidence. And, unfortunately, Lady Henslowe always told her daughter everything. Sarah had realised that there was no hope of keeping anything secret.

Even now, in the sanctuary of her bedchamber, she felt the same helplessness. And worse, she had no idea what Huntington had said to her grandfather. The thought had kept her awake much of the night. She only prayed he had not felt obligated to offer marriage again. In fact, she could think of no conceivable reason why he'd taken the blame for a situation which was none of his doing. Despite the rumours that he had driven his wife into the arms of another man, he had every reason to desire revenge upon her family.

But his behaviour last night had been that of a gentleman.

Her only hope was that her grandfather would see there was no need for an offer after he understood Huntington was innocent of all wrong. Her grandfather had a strong sense of justice. Surely holding Huntington responsible for any of last night's disaster was anything but just?

Which was why she must speak to him as soon as possible. She had already learned from the maid that Lord Monteville had gone out for his customary morning walk. Surely he would be back by now. As soon as she dressed she would go to his study. Her stomach churned at the thought. He had never been anything but kind to her in the three years she had lived with him since her mother's death, but she still found him intimidating. He did not tolerate fools or foolish behaviour. And her behaviour last night had been nothing but foolish.

She had just put her nearly untouched tray aside and climbed out of bed when the door opened. Amelia peered around the corner. She looked fresh and pretty in a dress of pink sprigged muslin. She came into the room and looked at Sarah, her face worried.

'Sarah? Are you well?'

'Yes, of course.'

'You look terribly pale.'

'I am just rather tired.'

Amelia looked sympathetic. 'I daresay you did not sleep well.'

'Not particularly.' Sarah managed a wan smile. 'But I've had worse nights.' Not many, however. 'I thought I would see Grandfather.'

'That is what I came to tell you. He wants to see

you as soon as you are presentable. And, Sarah, Lady
Beatrice is here.' She knotted her hands together and
looked as if she was about to deliver news of a death.
'With Lord Huntington.'

Sarah stood outside her grandfather's study and
took a deep breath. It was all she could do to keep
from turning tail and scrambling back to her room.
But that would be of little use. She had to face him
some time, unless she planned to disappear forever.
She only prayed Lord Huntington and his formidable
aunt, Lady Beatrice, were not with him.

She stepped inside and her stomach leaped to her
throat. Heaven had not seen fit to answer in a fa-
vourable fashion. Her grandfather stood near his desk
with Lady Beatrice seated in a wing chair in front of
it. And Huntington stood near the mantelpiece. His
cool, unfathomable gaze met hers before she tore her
eyes away.

She looked at her grandfather and forced herself
to speak. 'You wished to see me, sir?'

'Yes. However, you may come forward, my dear.
I assure you none of us will bite.' There was nothing
in his face that indicated any sort of disgust of her.

'No, sir.' She moved across the room, taking care
not to glance Huntington's way, although every
nerve in her body tingled with awareness of him.

She stopped tentatively in front of the cherrywood
desk. Lady Beatrice rose. 'Miss Chandler, I trust you
are well.' It was more of a statement than a question.

'Yes, thank you,' Sarah replied. She managed to
meet Lady Beatrice's sharp blue eyes. 'And you, my
lady?'

'Well enough.' She looked at Sarah closely. She

was a large, imposing woman with a forthright manner and a reputation for outspokenness. 'I will be much better as soon as this affair is settled. I wish, however, that you and my nephew had chosen a more suitable time to discover your mutual affection for one another.'

Sarah started. 'I beg your pardon?'

Lord Monteville moved forward in a leisurely way. 'I imagine it came as a shock to both of them to discover the feelings they had tried to keep suppressed were reciprocated. I believe they can be forgiven for their lapse in discretion.' He looked at Lady Beatrice. 'I am certain many of us have had a similar experience.'

Lady Beatrice actually looked taken aback. 'I assure you I never have,' she snapped.

'No?' Monteville turned his gaze to Sarah. 'My dear, Lord Huntington is here to properly pay his addresses. I hope you will not let the unfortunate circumstances of the past influence your answer. I have given my consent to the match and I have hopes it may serve to heal the breach between the families.'

Sarah stared at him, wondering if she had taken leave of her senses. Whatever were they talking about? Mutual affection? Between her and Lord Huntington? She realised he was waiting for her to say something. 'You…you have given your consent?'

'Yes.' There was the slightest warning in his cool eyes.

She stepped back. 'Oh, dear.'

It was obviously not the correct answer. Lady Beatrice's sharp, suspicious gaze swung to Sarah's face. 'You are not pleased?'

'She is just shocked. As I was.' Huntington had stepped to Sarah's side. 'We had never expected that Lord Monteville or you would consent to the match so readily.' His hand came to rest on Sarah's shoulder, his fingers exerting a slight pressure as if he warning her to say nothing. 'I would like to speak to Miss Chandler alone.'

'Very wise,' Monteville said. 'Come, Lady Beatrice, we will repair to the drawing room. Perhaps some refreshment would be in order.' He moved towards the door and held it open. Lady Beatrice had no option but to follow. However, when she reached the doorway, she paused and looked back.

'I trust there will be no repeat of last night. I should not want to find you have been engaging in such indecorous liberties again before you are properly wed.' She stared at Sarah as if she suspected Sarah would throw herself at Huntington's person as soon as the door was closed.

'Miss Chandler will be quite safe,' Huntington said drily. 'I generally do not ravish ladies before dinner.'

Lady Beatrice frowned at him. 'This is not the time for levity.' She followed Monteville out, leaving the door open.

Huntington moved to the door and shut it firmly, then leaned against it as if he thought Sarah planned to escape. His handsome face had that unsmiling, remote expression she was so accustomed to; if it weren't for the slightly dark shadows under his eye, as if he'd slept no better than herself, she would have thought he was completely unaffected.

Sarah finally spoke. 'Would you please tell me what is going on, my lord?' At least her voice was cool and steady, despite the feeling she had wandered into a strange dream where nothing made the least sense.

'It seems we are betrothed, Miss Chandler,' he said, his voice equally cool. 'And in love.'

She stared at him. 'In love? What…what sort of ridiculous notion is that?'

He folded his arms across his chest. 'It was the only thing I could think of to explain last night's débâcle, particularly after my aunt accused you of trying to seduce me.'

'She thought I tried to seduce you?' Had she even heard correctly? The sensation that she was in a bizarre dream only increased.

'Yes.' He gave a short laugh. 'Ironic, isn't it? Your family thinks I tried to seduce you and mine is equally convinced you tried to seduce me.'

'How…how odd.'

His brow shot up. 'That is one way of putting it.' He uncrossed his arms and moved from the door, coming to stand on the other side of the wing chair from Sarah. 'I decided the best way to defuse the mounting storm was to confess we have been harbouring a secret but hopeless passion for each other and finally last night in Henslowe's garden our finer feelings overcame our reservations. Unfortunately, my aunt insisted on accompanying me over here. Thank God, your grandfather asked no questions and went along with the scheme.' His gaze swept over her face. 'And you did not swoon or run shrieking from the room. I must compliment you, Miss Chandler.'

'I never do those things.' She suddenly felt rather breathless, for he had never said anything remotely complimentary to her before. Unbidden, the memory of his dark head bent towards her, his hand fumbling with the pin at her breast, sprang to her mind and she felt almost shaky.

She forced her gaze away. 'So…so how long must we pretend to be betrothed, my lord?'

'Pretend?' His sharp tone made her look back at him. His eyes bored into hers. 'My dear, there is no pretence. We are betrothed and we will be married as soon as I procure the special licence.'

'No!' She jumped back. 'That is, I…I don't want to marry you.'

His eyes cooled. 'You don't have a choice. We don't have a choice. Not after last night. You, my dear, are ruined.'

'I…I really don't care about that.' She would just go live with Great-aunt Charlotte in Northumberland, who was always hinting she wanted a companion. Anything would be better than marriage to a man who detested her.

'But I do.' His expression was grim. 'I've no intention of living with that on my conscience. I've enough scandal attached to my name as it is, without it being said I attempted to seduce you for some sort of revenge.'

'But, surely no one would think that.'

'They already do,' he said shortly.

'But how can they? It is so terribly unfair and so…so wrong!' Sarah wrung her hands together, completely distressed. 'What did you say to Grandfather? Surely, if they knew the truth, that it was Mr Blanton…' The dark look he turned on her nearly made her quail.

'What truth? That you went to the garden and

Blanton accosted you? My dear, they will wonder
what sort of young woman you are if it comes out
you were compromised by not one, but two men in
one evening. They will think I was coward enough
to cast the blame on Blanton. Then there is my sister.
I will not have her hurt by this. And she would be.'

Sarah stared at him as she remembered Lord Hens-
lowe's words. And in her mind, she saw Jessica and
Adam dancing, the obvious happiness in their faces.
Would such a thing really affect them?

He read her mind. 'Yes, my dear Miss Chandler,
she would be hurt. Her in-laws might tolerate her,
but she would not be accepted. It is not a pleasant
situation. You see, my mother was never accepted by
my father's family. She was Irish and they thought
he had married beneath him.' He was silent for a
moment, a bitter twist to his mouth, before focusing
back on Sarah. 'So, we will be married.'

'I am so sorry, my lord,' Sarah whispered. She
turned and walked to the window, not wanting him
to see the sudden tears that pricked her eyes. Through
the window she could see the gardener trimming the
hedge. The ordinary, familiar sight suddenly seemed
to belong to another world.

She started when Huntington spoke.

'It won't be quite as bad as a death sentence.'

She turned and looked at him, taken aback to find
him standing behind her. 'What won't be?'

'Marriage to me.'

He was too close. She forced herself to speak
lightly even though she wanted to cry. 'Then only as
bad as imprisonment in Newgate, my lord?'

'No. I have no intention of being your gaoler. Our
dealings together will be minimal. Only as necessary

to quell the gossip.' His eyes rested on her face. 'Nor will I expect you to share my bed,' he said indifferently.

Colour mounted to her cheeks and she turned away. 'I see.' Such a thing had never even occurred to her. She could not even feel relieved, only confused.

He still stood next to her. She forced herself to look at him. He was watching her, a slight frown on his face, almost as if he was concerned about her. 'Are you well?'

The thought he might actually care was so unexpected she found herself saying, 'Yes. I...I promise I will not go into a decline, my lord.'

'I hope not,' he said softly. He stared at her, and she felt her heart begin to hammer in a most uncomfortable fashion. He suddenly backed up a few paces as if he wanted to put distance between them and went to stand near the mantelpiece. 'There is one more thing, Miss Chandler.' His drawl had returned.

'What?'

'We had best behave as if we are in love with each other.' He folded his arms across his chest again.

'As you are now?' Sarah retorted, stung by his retreat into his usual indifferent shell. Anger had begun to fill the void she'd felt earlier.

'I beg your pardon?'

The startled look on his face was most gratifying. Sarah stared pointedly at him. 'You are standing across the room from me and staring in that...that odious way. And besides that, my lord, I have never accepted your offer. In fact, you have never made me an offer.'

He uncrossed his arms and straightened. 'Exactly what do you want?'

'Since you have no particular sentiments for me, I don't expect you to declare any fond feelings, but you could at least ask me, instead of assuming I would be delighted to marry you.'

'Believe me, that assumption never crossed my mind.' His gaze swept over her face. Then, without warning, he stepped forward and came to stand in front of her. He caught her hands, faint amusement in his expression. 'My lovely Miss Chandler, will you do me the honour of becoming my wife?'

'I am not your lovely Miss Chandler,' she said crossly. Why must he always sound as if he was mocking everything?

'No?'

'Most certainly not.' She stared into his eyes with the vague realisation they were not brown at all but a deep mossy green.

'You've not answered my question,' he said softly. His fingers tightened on hers.

'What?' she blinked. 'I…I suppose so.'

He continued to look into her face, his expression slowly changing. Her heart was beating too fast again. 'Not exactly an unqualified yes, Miss Chandler.' His voice held an odd huskiness.

'Well, no…'

'You have had more than enough time to settle this!' Lady Beatrice's voice cut through the air.

Huntington dropped her hands as if he'd been burned. He backed away and retreated towards the door. 'Yes, the matter is settled.'

'Good.' She strode into the room, followed by Lady Omberley. 'Helen quite agrees that the marriage will take place as soon as possible. However, an announcement must be made straight away.'

'At dinner tonight,' Lady Omberley added. 'Since most of the families are still here for Lady Jessica's betrothal.' She smiled, but it looked more than a little strained. 'The dinner will be here.'

'Although I would have preferred it at Ravensheed,' Lady Beatrice said. 'It might have been possible if you had behaved in a more decorous manner.' Her eyes fell on Sarah, and Sarah had the uncomfortable feeling Lady Beatrice held her completely responsible for last night's disaster.

Which of course she was. She had managed not only to ruin her own life, but Lord Huntington's as well.

Chapter Four

Dev followed Lady Beatrice into the cool hallway of Henslowe Hall. His hopes of escaping to the stables were quickly dashed when Lord Henslowe popped out of his study just as they passed the door. He fixed Dev with the same suspicious stare he'd had since last night.

'So, my lord, I trust you've settled the matter.'

'Yes.' Dev had no intention of elaborating further. His patience at being treated like a pariah was evaporating. He started to move past Henslowe, who stepped in his way.

'There will be a wedding, my lord?' It was almost ·a snarl.

Lady Beatrice, who was halfway up the staircase, suddenly turned around. She gave Henslowe one of her most quelling looks. 'I hope you are not accusing my nephew of dishonourably compromising Miss Chandler. He is, of course, to marry her. However, may I point out, her own behaviour is hardly above reproach.'

Henslowe swung his bushy-eyed stare to Lady Beatrice. 'May I inquire exactly what you mean by that, madam?'

'I mean…'

'I fear my aunt is rather shocked by the fact that once Miss Chandler and I discovered our—er—feelings were mutual, we could no longer resist the temptation to express those feelings in a more bold manner.' He was rapidly becoming an adept liar as well as a diplomat.

At least this round appeared to be diffused. Lord Henslowe looked taken aback. 'Er, I see.'

Dev smiled coolly. 'Yes. If you will excuse me, then, I must take my aunt to her bedchamber. She is rather fatigued after the morning's events.'

'Er, of course,' Henslowe said. He backed into his study.

'Fatigued? I most certainly am not!' Lady Beatrice snapped. 'And this nonsense about expressing your—'

'But you are.' He mounted the steps and took her arm before she could say anything else. He finally managed to get her safely to her bedchamber and then retreated to his own.

The quiet was welcome. He walked to the window and looked out at the rolling park spread before him. In the distance he could make out the grey roof of Monteville House.

What the devil had happened? He rubbed the back of his neck in an attempt to ease the knot he could feel forming. The last place on earth he'd ever expected to set foot in was Monteville House.

But it was no more bizarre than contemplating marriage to Sarah Chandler.

He had first seen her at the ball celebrating his

betrothal to Mary. Mary had spoken of her dearest friend many times before, but he'd hardly been prepared for a pair of expressive brown eyes in a heart-shaped face and a smile that lit her face from within. He'd taken her hand, and a jolt of recognition shot through him, almost as if she was the woman he had been waiting for. The sensation had scared him and set his carefully ordered world reeling.

Up until that moment, he had accepted his betrothal to Lady Mary Coleridge as a matter of course. Beautiful, cool and reserved, Mary had seemed to expect no more from marriage than he did. Nor did she appear affected by his less than pristine past. Or the fact that he'd scandalised most of society by a rash affair with one of the most dashing and notorious widows in London.

He had avoided Sarah Chandler as much as possible at the ball and the picnic the following day. He had been relieved when she'd left. Her own hesitant friendliness towards him had quickly turned to puzzlement at his brusque manner, and finally to cool politeness. The next time he expected to see her was after he was safely wed to Mary.

The last thing he had anticipated was that his cool, proper wife would run away a fortnight after their wedding. And that he would find her three weeks later with another man, a man who happened to be Sarah's brother.

Undoubtedly, Sarah held him responsible for Mary's death as did a good half of society. Rumours had been rampant that he'd done away with Mary until she was found. And then the gossip had turned to speculations on what he must have done to his wife to cause her to flee his house so soon after her marriage.

They were only wrong in the details. For he had, without doubt, driven Mary to her death.

And now he was about to again undertake marriage with a woman who did not want him. Except this time, he planned to stay as far away from his wife as possible.

'Dev?'

He swung around to find his sister had quietly entered the room. 'You are not out riding with the others?' he asked.

'No.' She came towards him. 'How could I until I knew what had happened? Besides, I was worried about you.'

He gave her a slanted half-smile. 'There is no need.' He moved away from the window and rubbed the back of his neck. 'All is well.'

'So, you are to marry Miss Chandler?'

'Yes, and I fear I will beat you to the altar,' he said lightly. 'I hope you do not mind.'

'Mind?' To his surprise, her face lit up and she dashed forward, and threw her arms around his neck. He staggered back a little at the impact. She pulled away. 'Never! You don't know how much I feared leaving you alone. Now, you won't be.'

'You approve?' he asked stupidly.

'Oh, yes! I have always like Miss Chandler, she has such a nice face, but I did not wish to say anything because you always look so cross when you see her. And then I had wondered if perhaps you had a *tendre* for her, but did not wish anyone to know because of her brother! And then to find it is true after all! And even more astonishing, that she is in love with you!'

'Certainly it is,' he said faintly.

'Adam says that she has a very kind heart, so I know you will be safe with her.'

'Safe?' He was losing track of the conversation. 'Wouldn't it be more proper to worry more about Miss Chandler's person in my safekeeping?'

Jessica smiled. 'Oh, no. Because I know you will take care of her, just as you have cared for me. No, it is you I fear for. I never want you to hurt so much again. And I do not think Miss Chandler will hurt you at all.'

Amelia touched Sarah's arm. 'Come, we cannot stay in your bedchamber forever.' She ran a critical eye over Sarah's person. She had helped Sarah dress, pulling out one gown after another before deciding on the pomona green silk. It had a round, low-cut bodice, the hem trimmed with rows of matching ribbon. 'You look very lovely. Lord Huntington will be enchanted.'

'I really don't want him to be enchanted.' Sarah snatched up her gloves from the dressing table. What she really wanted was for him to go away and leave her in peace.

Amelia arched a brow. 'My dear, you need to look a bit more enthusiastic if you're to convince everyone you've conceived a mad passion for his lordship.'

Sarah scowled. 'That was his idea, not mine.' As the dinner approached she had found herself in more and more of a horrid mood. The last thing she felt like doing was pretending to be in love with Lord

Huntington. She could feel the beginning of a headache and her stomach was churning. At this point she would be quite fortunate if she made it through dinner without being sick.

'Yes, you have made that very clear. But you will need to do better than that. Such a sour look will hardly persuade anyone you're in ecstasy over finding your hidden love reciprocated.'

'I would prefer that it had remained hidden,' Sarah snapped. She heaved a sigh. 'I am sorry, Amelia. I have a slight headache and I wish I was anywhere but here.'

'I quite understand.' Amelia picked up a fan from Sarah's dressing table and pressed it into her hand. 'But we do need to put in an appearance or everyone will think you decided to escape through the window.'

'I still might,' Sarah said. She trailed Amelia down the staircase, wishing it truly were possible to run away. She had finally decided to lie down before dressing for dinner. It had not helped; instead of resting, her mind had replayed the events over and over. She had tried to tell herself that she should be noble and accept marriage to Lord Huntington to save his reputation as well as to ensure his sister's happiness. But instead she felt resentful and trapped. And, underneath, more than a little despairing.

And the headache gnawing at the back of her neck hardly helped.

He was the first person she noticed when she entered the drawing room. He stood near the window engaged in conversation with Adam, Lady Jessica, and her grandfather. He looked elegantly masculine.

His tight pantaloons fitted over well-muscled legs and he wore a bottle green coat moulded to broad shoulders which obviously had no need of artificial aids.

He looked over when she entered with Amelia. His cool eyes met hers and she felt her heart slam alarmingly against her ribs. Worse, the room fell silent and everyone else turned to look at her as well. She wondered how she was ever to make it through the evening.

Lady Omberley bustled over, her expression relieved. 'My dear, we had quite wondered where you'd gone to. That is, we had hoped nothing was amiss.'

'Sarah couldn't find her fan,' Amelia said brightly.

'Oh? If that was all… Come—' Lady Omberley took Sarah's arm in a firm grip '—we must greet Lord Huntington. But first, here is Lady Beatrice and I believe you have met Lord Pennington.'

'Yes, how do you do?' Sarah managed to smile although she feared it was probably strained.

'Well enough,' Lady Beatrice snapped. She wore a remarkable gown of purple satin trimmed with lace and silk flowers, a matching turban on her head. The effect with her broad, double-chinned face was quite intimidating.

Lady Omberley gave her a wary look, then her face brightened. 'I see the Misses Waverly have arrived. If you will excuse me, I must greet them.' She hurried off, leaving Sarah to cast about in her mind for something to say.

Lord Pennington smiled. He was tall and lean with light brown hair and a pair of humorous grey eyes. 'Congratulations, Miss Chandler. It is quite amazing.

Only last night I suggested to Dev that he might consider repairing relations between himself and your family. However, I will confess I hardly expected he would take it to such lengths.'

'Nor did I,' Lady Beatrice said, giving Sarah a suspicious look as if she still suspected Sarah had managed to bring Huntington to heel by less-than-honest methods.

'Take what to such lengths?' Huntington materialised at Sarah's side.

'Your method of effecting a reconciliation between the two families,' Lord Pennington said.

'So far I can't see it has had much effect,' Huntington said drily. His fingers closed lightly around Sarah's arm. 'If you will pardon me, I would like to speak with Sarah alone.'

Sarah? Had she heard correctly? She glanced up into his face, but his expression was bland. He escorted her over near the window before she could say a word. He looked down at her. 'Should we make a stab at some sort of conversation? I'd hate everyone to think we have quarrelled already.'

'But then we'd have an excuse to break our... our...'

'I believe the term is betrothal.' His mouth curved in a humourless smile. 'No, it would only give Henslowe an excuse to put a bullet through me. Although that might solve your problem.'

His drawling words made her scowl. 'That is really an extremely stupid remark! I certainly would not consider that a way to solve anything.'

His brow shot up. 'Wouldn't you? Should I be flattered?'

'No, you should not. Besides, Cousin George is a

very poor shot. His eyesight is quite dreadful although he would never admit it.'

A hint of amusement crossed his face. 'I am relieved. However, my dear, I suggest you cease to look at me with such blatant disapproval. I fear no one will ever think you were in the throes of a violent passion for me.'

'No more than they think the same of you,' Sarah retorted. 'If you think I intend to…to cast sheep's eyes at you while you stare at me in that sardonic fashion, you are quite wrong.'

His eyes glittered. 'I fear, my lovely Sarah, if I was to truly pretend that I was in love with you, you would run as far and as fast as you could. And I've no intention of scaring you away.'

'Oh.' She took a step back, suddenly a little frightened. For the first time, the realisation sank in that she would soon be bound to this dangerous stranger.

His brow snapped together. 'There's no need to look so fearful. I've no intention of abusing you,' he said coolly.

'No.' She shivered and looked away. Most of the guests had arrived and she again experienced the odd sensations of being in a bad dream. She rubbed the back of her neck, which by now ached.

'What is wrong?'

She looked back at him, startled to see an odd concern in his face. But it vanished so quickly she thought she must be mistaken. Thrown off, she said, 'I merely have the headache, but it is nothing.'

'I hope not.' His eyes roved over her face, a little frown on his brow. 'Try not to worry too much. I'll make certain this damnable mess doesn't hurt you any more than necessary.'

Again he surprised her. She bit her lip. 'You are very kind, considering this entire affair is all my doing.'

'Hardly,' he said curtly.

'Dinner has just been announced.' Lord Pennington's voice broke the odd tension between them. He raised a brow. 'So perhaps you should cease gazing at each other and join us.'

Sarah blushed and turned away, only to find Amelia regarding her with amusement.

Her grandfather spoke. 'Perhaps, Lord Huntington, you will escort my granddaughter to dinner.'

'Of course. Miss Chandler?' Huntington held out his arm, his voice polite. She lightly placed her hand on his coat sleeve, avoiding his eyes. So, they were back at daggers drawn. At least it felt infinitely safer than his concern.

Dev put down his scarcely touched wineglass. His gaze drifted across the table to where it had been most of the never-ending dinner. On Sarah Chandler.

She was listening to something Adam said, a polite smile on her face, but he suspected from her pallor that her headache had increased. She had barely touched her dinner, mostly pushing the well-prepared food around her plate. He hoped she would make it through the dinner without collapsing.

At least some sort of truce seemed to be in effect. Lady Beatrice sat next to Lord Monteville, whose presence served to keep her more outrageous remarks in check. The rest of the guests were making an effort to carry on conversation and the room hummed with the usual sounds of a normal dinner party, quiet conversation punctuated by laughter, the clink of covers laid and removed. If anyone noticed his terse silence, they gave no sign.

Which he must give Sarah credit for. She seemed determine to carry on some semblance of conversation, showing her innate good manners. And, in spite of his reluctance to admit it, he found her completely lovely. Her auburn hair curled softly around her face in a manner that made her dark eyes more luminous. Her gown, a pale green, clung enticingly to her slender curves. She had matured from the rather uncertain girl she had been at nineteen to a beautiful, composed and extremely desirable woman. The thought was frightening.

As if sensing his regard, she turned to look at him, slight colour rising to her cheeks. Her brown eyes met his and an uncomfortable bolt of awareness shot through him. It was not exactly desire, but something much more disturbing.

He tore his gaze away, only to meet his cousin's amused eyes. He took a sip of wine, wondering what the devil was wrong with him.

He set his wineglass down with unnecessary force. A few drops sprayed out.

'My lord, I can certainly understand why your preoccupation with my cousin might cause you to forget your manners, but I must draw the line at being drenched with wine.'

He turned to Lady Marleigh, who was seated next to him. 'I beg your pardon.'

A little smile touched her lips. 'Sarah is quite lovely, isn't she? I cannot blame you for wanting to marry her.'

His brow shot up. 'I take it that means you approve?'

'Not quite,' she said carefully.

'And what are your reservations?' He leaned back a little, watching her.

Her blue eyes were direct. 'She has the kindest heart of anyone I know. I hope you will remember that.'

Monteville had said much the same thing. As had Mary. He smiled sardonically. 'And you fear I intend to trample it.'

'Not intentionally. But your reputation does concern me.' All archness had left her manner.

'Ah, I see you've heard the rumours. Set your mind at rest. I do not intend to lock your cousin away or beat her so she finds it necessary to run fleeing from my house.'

'I was not speaking of your first wife, but of your other liaisons.'

'You are blunt, Lady Marleigh.' His fingers closed around his wineglass. 'I will be blunt in return. There are no other liaisons at the moment. Nor am I contemplating one. Amazingly enough, you see, I believe in fidelity in marriage.'

Her brow arched in surprise as she searched his face. For the first time an actual smile lit her countenance. 'Very good, my lord. I think there might be hope for you and for Sarah after all.'

This time it was his turn to feel surprise. Before he could speak, Monteville stood.

The Earl waited until everyone had quieted down. 'As most of you know, we are gathered here for a most important occasion, to announce an alliance, an alliance that I hope will serve to eradicate the unfortunate fissure between the Chandlers and the St Clairs.' He paused for a moment, a rare smile touching his lips. 'I am most pleased, then, to inform you that there is to be a marriage between Devin St Clair, the Marquis of Huntington, and my granddaughter, Miss Sarah Chandler.'

There were a few exclamations of surprise. And then the dining room doors were flung open behind Monteville. He turned. A man swept into the room with firm, purposeful strides and then stopped. In the silence that followed, Sarah's faint, 'Oh, no!' was audible.

And then Dev's own blood ran cold.

Nicholas Chandler, Viscount Thayne, stood in the doorway, drops of rain glistening on his golden brown hair. His cool gaze surveyed the room and then fell on Dev. Surprise flicked in his eyes, before they hardened. 'How very interesting. Pray, Lord Huntington, whatever has induced you to step foot in my family home?'

Dev rose, the anger he'd thought long dead sparking to life. He smiled coldly. 'A very happy occasion. I am glad you have arrived in time to celebrate.' He looked at the nearby footman. 'A glass of wine for Lord Thayne.'

The footman stepped forward and quickly proffered a glass. Thayne took it, his eyes never leaving Dev's face. Dev raised his glass. 'Shall we have a toast, gentlemen?' The others, who'd sat in stunned silence, hastily stood. Dev looked at Thayne, a devilish smile curving his lips. 'A toast to my upcoming marriage to Lord Thayne's sister, Sarah Chandler.'

He raised the glass to his lips, downing the contents in a single swallow accompanied by a chorus of well wishes. The satisfaction of watching the colour leave Thayne's face was worth a thousand such announcements. Until he saw Sarah.

Her face had gone completely white, as if someone had just dealt her a death blow. The quick rush of heady pleasure evaporated and he wondered what the devil he had just done to her.

It wasn't until the guests had left and Sarah had finally escaped up the stairs that Nicholas cornered her. She was just about to enter her bedchamber when he appeared at her side.

'Sarah, what the devil do you think you're doing?'

'Going to bed,' she snapped. The rest of the evening had been a disaster, which had left her head hurting worse than ever. Nicholas's presence had cast a pall over everyone and the company had quickly divided into two opposing camps. Angry and hurt, Sarah had made no effort to speak to Huntington and instead had aligned herself firmly on the Chandler side. She cared little what anyone thought.

'Not that.' He took her by the shoulders and turned her to face him. 'I don't know what the devil has happened, but you can't marry Huntington.'

'I am.'

'Why? Damn it, Sarah, it is more than apparent he only wants you out of revenge. He looked as if he'd just swallowed a cream pot when he announced you were to be wed.'

Sarah tried not to flinch. The memory still burned. 'None the less, we are to be wed. There is no choice.'

'Why?' His brows snapped together. 'What did he do to you?'

'Nothing at all.' She opened her door. 'If you will excuse me, I am extremely tired.'

'Not until you tell me why.' He had that stubborn look on his face, which meant he planned to persist until she was forced to answer. 'You can't fob me off, Sarah.'

She sighed and rubbed her temple. 'If you must know, Lord and Lady Henslowe found us together in their garden last night. I had gone out to be alone for a moment. And then I saw my gown had a tear in the bodice. My...my brooch had torn the cloth and Lord Huntington tried to help me repair it. If we do not marry, I will be ruined.'

Nicholas's fist tightened. 'I will call him out,' he said softly.

'No! Please, Nicholas! It was not his doing. And I couldn't bear another scandal! Or more pain! Do you understand?'

He stared at her in disbelief and then gave a short laugh. 'Much more than you think. He purposely tried to compromise you.'

He was always so stubborn, particularly when it came to someone he disliked as intensely as he did Lord Huntington. 'No, he did not. I told you, it happened even before he came. He saw me leave the ballroom and wanted to assure himself of my safety.' It was no use trying to pretend they had met in a lovers' tryst. Nicholas, like her grandfather, had the disconcerting habit of ferreting out lies. So she might as well give him as much of the truth as she could without revealing Blanton's role.

'Assure himself of your safety? I find that impossible to swallow. Why should he care what happens to any of us?'

'I don't know,' Sarah whispered. His behaviour last night and even up to Nicholas's arrival had seemed to indicate some concern for her. But after tonight, she could only think it had been false.

Nicholas's expression hardened. 'Neither do I. But if he hurts you, he'll have me to answer to.'

Chapter Five

Sarah sat cross-legged on the grass next to the lake and looked down at her sketch. She frowned. No matter how she tried, her pencil refused to cooperate and produce the soft, graceful curves which were needed to convey the peaceful scene before her. Instead, the quick, angry strokes made the lovely swans look as if they were gathering for an attack.

She threw down her pencil and glared at the water. Usually she loved coming to sit next to the small lake in the park behind Monteville House. Today, she felt extremely out of sorts. No, she was furious. Furious at Nicholas for showing up in his brash arrogant way, furious at Huntington for making it clear he regarded their marriage as a way to avenge himself on Nicholas and, most of all, furious at herself for caring a whit.

She hugged her knees to her chest. She had left the house as early as possible, wanting to escape before anyone, especially Nicholas, was up. The conversation still left a bitter taste in her mouth. Not only because Nicholas might be right about Huntington's motives, but because she feared the marriage would drive a greater wedge between herself and her brother. She had always loved her charming, sometimes irresponsible brother, but she had not been able to accept his running off with another man's wife, no matter what the circumstances were. She had tried her best to understand and forgive him since Mary's death in a remote Yorkshire inn had nearly destroyed him.

She had never thought her rakish brother would fall so deeply in love. Or that raven-haired Mary with her cool, untouchable beauty would return his love with an equal passion. Mary had seemed to accept her family's wishes that she marry Devin St Clair, then Lord Warwick, without a qualm. She'd once told Sarah that a marriage of convenience suited her very well for falling in love seemed such an uncomfortable business. She had dismissed all Sarah's arguments for a love match as hopelessly romantic.

And then Sarah had met Mary's handsome, charming fiancé with his rather wicked smile and wondered if he would be willing to let Mary remain detached after all.

In the end it was not Mary's husband but Sarah's brother who had fanned her passion to life. And if Sarah had not invited Mary to stay at Meade Cottage, Mary might still be alive.

She shivered a little as a cool gust of wind brushed her arms. She'd scarcely noticed the ominous grey clouds gathering overhead. Reluctantly, Sarah gathered her sketchbook and pencils and stood.

'Miss Chandler.'

She whirled around, nearly dropping her notebook. Cedric Blanton stood behind her. She felt a sudden lurch of fear, even though it was broad daylight. 'What are you doing here?' she asked.

'I must speak to you.'

'I would rather not. I must go in.' She turned and started to walk down the gravel path.

To her dismay, he caught up to her and fell into stride beside her. 'You cannot marry Lord Huntington.'

She kept her eyes fixed on the path and increased her pace. 'That is none of your concern.'

'But it is. You were with me first. If he hadn't interfered, you would be betrothed to me.'

'That is ridiculous. If you hadn't behaved so…so ungentlemanly then I would have no need to marry anyone.'

'You would do better to marry me.'

'It is too late. I am to marry Lord Huntington in a few days.' Thank goodness the house was only a short distance away.

'We could elope.'

'No!' This time she stopped and stared at him. 'I could never do that.'

His mouth tightened. 'You will be sorry if you marry him. As will he.'

Was he threatening her? But she could not tell from the expression in his pale blue eyes. A drop of rain recalled her to the fact she was about to be caught in a rainstorm. 'I…I must go in.'

'What the hell are you doing with my fiancée?'

Huntington's icy voice cut through the air like a whip. Somehow, he'd managed to come up behind them, the wind obscuring his approach. He was dressed in a dark coat and breeches, the wind ruffling his dark hair, his expression grim, like some sort of avenging angel. Sarah resisted the urge to cower.

Blanton looked at him, unruffled. 'I was merely offering Miss Chandler my services if she should need me.'

Huntington took a step forward, his face full of icy contempt. 'I will see you to the devil before she needs your services.'

Blanton's smile faltered and then returned. 'I hope not, my lord.' He looked over at Sarah, his eyes filled with a cold fury that made her shudder. 'Goodbye, Miss Chandler.' He turned and walked away.

Sarah forced herself to look at Huntington. His face looked as stormy as the sky. She shivered. 'I was just about to return to the house.' She started to move, only to find him blocking her way.

'What were you doing with him?' he demanded.

His arrogant tone, along with the implication that she had actually sought Blanton's company, set her back up. She lifted her chin. 'I was not with him.'

'Then he was an apparition?'

'Of course not. I only meant...' Several large drops of rain hit her squarely on the forehead. They were swiftly followed by several more. 'This is not the time to engage in idiotic conversation, my lord. We are about to become extremely wet.'

He glanced up at the sky. 'You are right.'

'There is a small temple over there,' Sarah said. He looked up in the direction she indicated, then grabbed her hand and started hauling her towards the summerhouse. By now, the rain was coming faster and faster.

The skies burst open just as they stumbled up the steps of the small Grecian temple. Rain dripped from

Huntington's hair and he looked as if someone had dumped a bucket of water over his head. Sarah had no doubt she looked every bit as bad. She shivered a little in her thin muslin gown.

He brushed the water from his coat, then shrugged out of it. He held it out to her. 'Put this around your shoulders.'

She shook her head. ''Tis very kind of you to offer, but…'

He scowled, and stalked to her side. 'You're shivering. Don't argue.' He draped it around her shoulders, the warmth from his body penetrating her skin.

'But won't you be cold?' She glanced over at him and then quickly away, the sight of his broad shoulders under the fine linen of his shirt making her uncomfortable.

'My waistcoat is enough. I generally tend to be warm.'

'Do you? I am always cold.'

'I am glad we have that settled. Why don't you sit down, Miss Chandler?'

She was about to argue and changed her mind. She sat down on the small stone bench near the wall and pulled his coat more tightly about her.

He had retreated to the other side of the building and leaned against a column, arms folded across his chest, his booted legs crossed as well. 'What did Blanton want?'

'Nothing, really.' How many times had she said those words in the past few days?

'I find that difficult to believe.'

She sighed. He had that implacable expression she was beginning to dread. She wrapped his coat more firmly about her shoulders. 'Must we discuss this? It matters little.'

He scowled. 'But it does. You are betrothed to me.'

'That does not mean I must answer to you in every matter.'

'It does in this matter. Stay away from him.'

His tone indicated the matter was closed. 'Yes, my lord.'

'Nor are you to go anywhere on the grounds without a footman.'

'No, my lord.'

He shot her a suspicious glance. His scowl deepened. 'There is one more thing.'

'Yes, my lord?'

'Will you cease to address me as "my lord"?' he snapped.

'Very well, sir.'

The next thing she knew he had stalked over to stand in front of her. She resisted the urge to cower and merely looked at him, her hands clasped in her lap.

'Perhaps, Miss Chandler, you could tell me what the devil is going on,' he said.

'With what?'

'I am very close to strangling you,' he said softly.

'I see.'

'And the prospect does not frighten you?'

'No. I suppose it might save quite a bit of trouble in the long run,' she said complacently.

He suddenly laughed. 'Hardly. I would have murder added to my long list of sins.' He paced away from her. The rain was starting to ease up. He turned and looked back at her. 'Can we try for some sort of civility? I know I've a damnable temper and I've been told more than once I'm dictatorial, but there's no need for you to defer to me like some sort of lackey. I'd rather you argue with me than persist in those blasted "yes, my lord, no, my lords".'

She sighed. 'I fear I was rather angry with you. And when I do disagree, you immediately ply me with a thousand questions.'

'I apologise.' He ran a hand through his dark hair. 'But I don't want you out walking alone. I don't trust Blanton.'

'I am certain there is nothing to worry about,' she said with more confidence than she felt, remembering Blanton's words. But surely there was nothing Blanton could do.

He raised a brow. 'On this point, I don't want you to argue. I am responsible for you.'

'But we aren't married yet. And even when we are…'

'Sarah.' His voice held a warning.

'Yes, my lord.'

He suddenly grinned, the harshness leaving his face. 'I've changed my mind. You may defer to me after all, particularly in this instance. Although you will eventually need to address me by my given name.'

She stared at him, her breath caught in her throat, hardly hearing his words. She'd never really seen him smile before, never seen his face light up without a hint of its usual cynicism. He looked almost boyish and immensely attractive. A peculiar warmth centred in her stomach.

'Sarah?'

She blinked. 'I beg your pardon?'

'Do you always disappear into such trances?'

'No.' She flushed and rose, her knees shaky. 'The rain has stopped. Perhaps we should return to the house.' She removed the coat from her shoulders, the loss of its warmth making her feel almost bereft. 'Thank you for your coat.' She held it out to him.

'You may wear it until we reach the house.'

'Th…thank you.' Whatever was wrong with her? There was no reason for her to stammer like a schoolgirl just because he had smiled in such a way. It was unlikely to happen again. In fact, she hoped it would not, it was too unsettling.

She started to move past him, only to find him blocking her way as he had earlier. He took the coat from her hands and draped it around her shoulders again. 'It will hardly do you any good if you carry it.'

'No.' She gave him a swift smile, moved away as quickly as possible and descended the two steps leading from the temple. She stumbled a little in her haste.

He was instantly at her side, his hand cupping her elbow, steadying her. His touch burned her skin and she jerked away.

'Now what the devil is wrong?' he demanded.

'N…nothing.'

'You are acting as if I'm about to ravish you. If you recall, my dear, I told you I had no intention of forcing you to my bed.'

Her face heated even more. 'It is not that.' How could she explain that his touch completely unnerved her, made her heart beat too fast, her stomach tighten and disoriented her thinking, shattering her usual cool composure.

'Then what is it?' he asked impatiently.

She held her sketchbook tightly against her chest. 'I am rather tired. Perhaps we should go in.'

'Very well,' he said coolly. He fell into step beside her.

They said nothing as they made their way to the house. He had retreated into a cool shell and Sarah's mind had gone completely blank.

They finally reached the steps leading to the back terrace. Sarah removed his coat from her shoulders and gave it to him. 'Thank you, my lord.'

'Of course.' He looked down at her, his expression impenetrable. 'I came to tell you I am leaving today to procure the marriage licence. I will see you tomorrow. The wedding will take place the day after.'

She bit her lip, her stomach hollow. 'Is this really necessary?'

'Yes.' His eyes were cool. 'And don't even think of trying to escape me.'

'Most certainly not, my lord,' she said coldly. The sudden flash of anger in his eye was quite satisfying.

But when he turned on his heel and strode off, her brief spurt of victory was replaced by despair. In two days, she was to be married to a man who did not want her and she had no idea how she would ever bear it.

Cedric Blanton crumbled the not-quite-polite request for settlement of his account at Stultz's. He tossed it in the fireplace and flung himself down in the chair behind his expensive mahogany desk. Not even the sight of the ornate snuffbox he'd paid a small fortune for calmed his fury.

If it weren't for Huntington's interference, he

could send off the announcement of his betrothal to Sarah Chandler, the Earl of Monteville's grand-daughter. Instead of sending him increasingly less courteous demands for payment, his creditors would fling open their doors and beg for his patronage.

Instead Huntington himself was to have the prize.

How could his plans have gone so far awry? He'd meticulously thought it out. He would persuade Sarah to accompany him to Henslowe's study. And then a carefully worded note to Lady Henslowe, say-ing that Sarah needed help, would bring her to the study just as Sarah succumbed to his kisses. Lady Henslowe with her rigid morality would see to it that Sarah would become engaged as quickly as possible.

He hadn't quite worked out the excuse to lure Sarah to the study, but had no doubt he'd come up with one. Ladies, particularly when someone was in distress, were likely to forget about propriety in order to render service. But when Sarah left the ballroom alone, he realised an excuse was not needed. His op-portunity had been handed to him.

But his nemesis had interfered again. Just as he had a year ago when Cedric had nearly compromised the rather stupid Lady Alethea, the Duke of Wrex-ton's daughter. Her frightened screams had brought Huntington to her aid.

Huntington had listened to him in his cool, arro-gant manner as Cedric explained why he must marry the chit. And then Huntington had threatened to ruin him if a word of it ever leaked.

Cedric had no doubt that Huntington would do so. Just as he had no doubt Huntington had had him blackballed from Whites' when old Stanton had sponsored him for membership.

Even now he was filled with a helpless burning fury.

He stared out the window at the lush green lawn spread before him. This was what he had wanted, had been born for, a country estate, fine food and furnishings, the best tailors and bootmakers. If his mother hadn't been so stupidly proud, he could have been the heir to Baron Ruckston's riches, mixing with the best society, welcomed into the best circles. Instead, his mother had refused to agree to his uncle's terms that she was to never see her son again once Cedric became his heir. And so Cedric remained a poor clergyman's son raised with five whining sisters while he watched an insipid cousin take his rightful place. And Cedric was forced to scheme, gamble, scrape and bow, and steal when necessary, for everything he had.

His mouth curled. He had no intention of allowing Huntington to interfere any more. Nor would Huntington have everything handed to him. It was time to upset Huntington's plans.

And Sarah Chandler's. Her rejection of him still rankled. He'd cultivated her acquaintance, flattered and cajoled her and then she dropped him for a bigger prize. Perhaps the prize would not be hers after all.

He smiled. Sometimes his less-than-desirable acquaintances could prove quite useful. And the wedding was the day after tomorrow. There was still time.

Dev returned from London in the early afternoon of the following day. Most of the house party had gone off on a picnic and Henslowe was closeted with his agent, which suited him. He had no desire to speak with anyone, not even Jessica.

Not that he'd had a problem procuring the licence. He yanked off his leather gloves and tossed them on the dressing table. No, the damnable document was safe in his pocket. The document he'd never intended to see his name on again.

He dropped his coat on the bed and paced to the window. The sun shone brightly, the hills rolling away. In the distance he caught a glimpse of Monteville House. His stomach lurched with a nervousness he had not felt for an age.

He turned away. What the devil was wrong with him? He'd marry Sarah Chandler and then have as little to do with her as possible. The sooner they began their separate lives, the better.

It would hardly surprise him if she did decide to bolt. It was quite apparent she had no liking for him. However, he'd been deadly serious yesterday—he would hunt her down and force her to the altar if necessary. He suspected Blanton had no intention of giving Sarah up until she was safely wed. And he had no intention of letting Blanton near her.

'My lord?'

Dev jerked around to find a footman standing behind him. 'What is it?'

'This has arrived for you.' The man stepped forward and held out a letter.

'Thank you.' Dev took it. The footman silently departed. Dev looked down at the unfamiliar but rather feminine writing. Frowning, he tore open the seal.

His frown only increased after he read the short note. He had no idea what to make of it. He had not thought Sarah was the sort of female who would send vaguely worded letters requesting an assignation. Certainly he was one of the last persons she would ever desire to meet privately, so why she would want to meet him in the summerhouse on her grandfather's property hardly made sense.

He looked down at the note again. But then, he did not know her very well at all. And the thought of her waiting for him alone and at the possible mercy of Blanton was hardly appealing. He folded the note and laid it on his dressing table and glanced at the clock on the mantel. He had nearly an hour before he was to meet her there. Of course, he could ride to Monteville House and demand to see her in a more conventional place. But by the time he reached the house, she would already be on her way to meet him.

A half-hour later, he pocketed the note, then picked up his gloves and quit his room.

But there was no sign of Sarah at the Grecian summerhouse where they had sheltered from the rain. He glanced at his pocket watch. He was five minutes early, but he saw no slender figure coming up the gravel walk. He dismounted and caught the chestnut's reins.

The first assailant caught him from behind. He dropped Gawain's reins and instinctively shoved his elbow into the man's gut. The man groaned and abruptly released him. He jerked around, intending to land a blow to the man's jaw, but a second pair of arms yanked him back. Before he could react, his first opponent hit him in his stomach. The pain nearly sent him reeling, but he managed to slam his foot back into his captor. He grunted and Dev used every trick he knew to break free.

But, despite the hours spent at Gentleman Jackson's boxing saloon, he was no match for his two bulky assailants. The last thought before he lost consciousness was of Sarah Chandler. He prayed she'd changed her mind. He did not want her to meet his assailants. Or find him dead.

Chapter Six

'Sarah!' Amelia's frantic voice made Sarah jump. She had just returned to the music room from the side garden where she'd spent most of the afternoon, nerves on edge, half-expecting Lord Huntington to call any moment. The book she had carried with her remained nearly untouched and she had done nothing but ruin two sheets of paper with unsatisfactory drawings of flowers.

She turned and her pulse leaped. Her usually un-flappable cousin looked horrified. 'Amelia? What is wrong?'

'It is Lord Huntington! He…he is badly hurt! They have brought him in. I have been looking for you everywhere! You must come!'

'Lord Huntington? I don't understand. He is hurt?' Sarah slowly put down her sketch pad.

'Yes.' Amelia grabbed her hand. 'Nick and John found him by the summerhouse. He was barely conscious and so Nick went for help. John came to tell me and said I should fetch you immediately. He asked for you.'

A cold pit of fear had formed in her stomach. 'Where is he?'

'Upstairs in one of the bedchambers.'

Sarah followed Amelia up the stairs, feeling as if she were in some sort of nightmare. And when she entered the panelled room and saw him lying on the bed, his face bruised, eyes closed, her heart slammed into her throat. She watched, horrified, as her aunt bustled around giving orders while one of the maids pressed a cloth to Devin's face. He groaned.

John looked up and saw them. He came to their sides, his normally pleasant face grim. 'Nick has gone for the physician,' he said in a low voice.

Sarah clutched his arm. 'John, what has happened?' she whispered.

His face was grave. 'He was beaten near the summerhouse.'

'Beaten? Who would do such a thing?' The thought made her physically ill.

'We don't know.' He glanced over at the bed and back at Sarah. 'Can you speak to him for a moment? He seems worried about you.'

'Yes, of course.' She had no idea why he would be worried about her. She moved to the side of the bed and knelt down. 'My lord. De…Devin, can you hear me?' Her voice shook.

He slowly opened his eyes and focused on her face. 'Sarah.' His voice was slurred. 'You are not hurt?' It was obvious he was in a great deal of pain.

'No, of course not.'

He struggled to speak. 'Good. Your note. I thought…'

'Note?' She stared at him, increasingly puzzled. Was he delirious?

'In my coat. You wanted to meet me.'

'I sent no note.' She felt a sliver of apprehension.

'No?' His gaze sharpened for a moment.

'No, my lord.' He closed his eyes. She looked up as the door opened and then rose. Nick entered, followed by the physician and her grandfather. Both Nick and Monteville wore expressions that were as grim as John's. Lady Omberley took Sarah's arm. 'Come, we must leave him to Dr Hampton. He will be in good hands.'

'Yes.' She glanced once more at Huntington, but the physician was already bending over him. She followed her aunt out of the room.

Amelia stood outside, her blue eyes filled with worry. 'Sarah, perhaps you should rest.'

'No.' She was still worried. 'Amelia, where is Lord Huntington's coat?'

'I suppose it is in the room. Why?'

'He said there was a note in his pocket. Please, could you have John look for me?'

'Yes, but why do you care about a note? Surely it can wait?' She touched Sarah's shoulder. 'You've had a terrible shock. At least come and sit with me.'

Sarah scarcely heard her. 'But he said the note was from me.' She looked at Amelia, a vague fear beginning to take shape. 'You see, I sent him no note.'

Dev stirred and finally forced his eyes open, despite the fact that his head felt as if it had been kicked by a herd of horses. His ribs felt no better. At first he had no idea where he was—the room with its pale green walls and green and gold hangings bore no resemblance to any room he'd slept in lately. From the light falling across his bed, he judged it to be morning.

He slowly turned his head towards the window, the movement making him groan. His sister sat in a chair, her eyes closed.

'Jess?' he said, puzzled. And then his memory returned. He was at Monteville House and someone had beaten him unconscious.

Her eyes shot open. She stared at him and to his amazement, her eyes filled with tears. 'Dev? You are awake, thank goodness!' She rose from the chair and came to him, then knelt by his bed. 'How…how are you feeling?'

'As if I'd been mowed down by a mail coach.' He attempted a grin, which was probably more of a grimace. 'No need for tears, I'm still here.'

'Yes.' She caught his hand, trying to return his smile although hers was rather watery. 'I was so worried, all of us were. We took turns sitting with you last night.'

'We?'

'Yes, Lady Omberley and Lady Marleigh, and me, and, of course, Miss Chandler. Even Aunt offered to come, but we feared she would fall asleep.'

Miss Chandler spent part of the night at his bedside? The thought was almost too incredible to contemplate. He closed his eyes for a brief moment and then remembered something else. He opened them and looked at Jessica. 'I believe today is my wedding day. Perhaps you would send for someone to help me dress more appropriately.'

Her mouth fell open. 'Dev, you cannot possibly think of a wedding. Not when you are so terribly hurt.'

'I am fit enough to say the necessary words. Please inform Miss Chandler that the marriage will go on as planned.'

'Dev, I really do not think this is wise.' Jessica looked at him as if he'd run mad.

'But it is.' He struggled to sit, despite the pain in his ribs. 'And if you do not, I will be forced to tell Miss Chandler myself.'

The look of resigned disapproval that crossed her face suddenly reminded him very much of his mother. Jess rose and looked down at him. 'Very well, then. I just hope someone can talk you out of this completely idiotic scheme.'

The abigail had just finished helping Sarah dress when there was a knock at her door. She opened it and was stunned to find her grandfather on the other side. He rarely came to her room. Her first thought was that Lord Huntington had taken a turn for the worse. 'Is there something wrong?' she asked, fearing the answer.

'No, at least nothing new. May I come in for a moment?'

'Of course.' She stepped aside to allow him to enter. Her eyes went to his face, but as usual he was impossible to read. 'Lord Huntington, is…is he better?'

'Apparently so.' A slight smile touched his mouth. 'I have just come from his bedchamber. He is at least well enough to insist your wedding take place today as planned.'

She stepped back in shock, her hand going to her breast. 'He…he still wishes to marry me?'

'Very much so. He is in the process of dressing and shaving.'

Her head was beginning to spin. 'I cannot marry him, not after yesterday. Not after that note.' She felt ill every time she thought about it. It had been clear then that someone had used her name to lure him to the isolated spot where he'd been deliberately beaten.

Lord Monteville's expression held mild surprise. 'My dear child, he hardly holds you responsible for yesterday,' he said gently.

'Perhaps not, but there is everything else.' She took a deep breath and twisted her hands together in distress. 'How can he bear to marry me? Not only is he forced into marriage with me because of my own foolishness, but I am the sister of the man who…who seduced his wife. He must completely detest me.'

He smiled a little. 'I hardly think he detests you at all. In fact, he is quite determined to protect you. I agree with him, however, that the ceremony should not be delayed. It will only make this marriage more difficult for you.'

'But how can he even go through with a ceremony? He is not well!'

'Apparently he disagrees. I do not think we can dissuade him. You will be married in the chapel as planned.'

She glanced at his face. His eyes held a trace of sympathy, but she also knew argument was useless. 'Yes, sir.'

His hand rested on her shoulder for a moment. 'Good. I will send Amelia in to help you.' He walked to the door and then turned. 'I believe, my dear, you will be quite safe with him. He is honourable and will treat you well. But you will need a great deal of patience, particularly at first. And, as always, if there is anything you need you may come to me.'

'Thank you, sir.' Sarah managed a shaky smile, but her stomach churned. She sat back down on her bed, her mind in a complete turmoil. Perhaps she should have taken up Blanton's offer after all. Then at least Huntington might have been spared, not only marriage to her, but his beating as well. For she had no doubt Blanton was behind it.

She had given the note to her grandfather as soon as John had retrieved it for her. Her grandfather had read the note and then she had haltingly told him of her encounter with Blanton. He'd not seemed the least bit surprised by her suspicion that Blanton was behind the attack. His assurances that they would discover the truth had given her little comfort. Neither had the news that Huntington's injuries were no more severe than bruised ribs, a swollen face and a nasty bump on his head. She had no doubt he probably rued the day he'd even heard of the Chandlers, for her family seemed to bring him nothing but disaster.

The light knock roused her from her unhappy thoughts. Amelia entered, a rather stunned expression on her face. 'Grandfather has just told me you are to be wed after all,' she said. 'John has gone to fetch Mr Tuttle from the Rectory and a note has been dispatched to Henslowe Hall to inform them the wedding will take place. We must leave as soon as you are ready.'

Sarah rose, feeling as if she was about to go to her own execution.

'Sarah?' Amelia looked more closely at Sarah's face and went to her side, catching her hands. 'Sarah, please don't look like that. Everything will be fine,

I promise you. Lord Huntington may be rather difficult, but he is not unkind.'

Her grandfather had said much the same thing. 'I know. I...I will be all right.' At least she hoped so.

Amelia squeezed her hands, then released them. 'You will be. Come, let me help you look more bride-like.' She ran her eyes over Sarah's cream muslin gown. 'Your gown is very nice. You can wear your pearls and carry your best fan.'

Sarah waited in a daze while Amelia found her necklace and then fastened it around her neck. After that she found a fan and pressed it into Sarah's hand, then stood back to observe her. 'You look very lovely. I've no doubt Lord Huntington will be pleased. Come, Sarah.' She took Sarah's arm in a gentle but firm grasp. 'I think we'd best go or your bridegroom will think you have changed your mind.'

The chapel occupied half of the north wing of the house and rose two floors. The day was overcast and grey morning light spilled through the high narrow windows and across the marble floor and carved altar. Sarah stopped inside the door, and her stomach leaped to her throat when she saw the pews were filled with people. She vaguely registered Lady Jessica in one of the front pews. And then her heart nearly stopped when her eyes fell on Huntington, who already stood near the altar with Lord Pennington and Mr Tuttle, the thin, stooping vicar. His eyes, dark and intense, met hers; then she looked away, the reality of what she was about to do hitting her with shocking force.

Lady Omberley bustled forward and caught her arm. 'Oh, Sarah! You are here, thank goodness! I really do not think Lord Huntington can remain on his feet much longer.'

Lord Monteville suddenly materialised at her side. 'Are you ready, my child?' And then he was guiding her up the short aisle to join Huntington in front of the vicar.

Huntington looked down at her. 'So you are here,' he said.

'Yes,' she whispered. The bruises on his cheekbone were still visible and he was dreadfully pale. She only prayed he would not faint before the end of the ceremony.

Mr Tuttle cleared his throat. 'Shall we begin?'

'Yes,' Huntington said. His eyes were still on her face, his expression unreadable.

Sarah scarcely heard the words of the brief ceremony. She must have made the correct responses, although she had no idea what she said. She barely registered Huntington's cool, brief replies. Not even the plain gold band he slipped on her finger seemed quite real.

She blinked when Mr Tuttle pronounced them man and wife.

'Sarah,' Huntington said.

She looked up into his face. His gaze drifted to her lips and he started to bend his head towards her. And then he swayed. Pennington rushed forward and caught him just as he fell.

Sarah stood outside the door to Huntington's bedchamber and forced herself to lightly knock. When she heard his curt 'Come in', she stepped into the room. He was in the tester bed, propped up by pillows, gazing out the window. He turned his head and looked at her, his expression unreadable. 'You may come further into the room, Sarah. I promise I won't eat you.'

'Of course not.' She moved to the side of the bed, her heart thudding again. She had not seen him since the brief ceremony a few hours ago when he had swooned. Pennington and her grandfather's valet had helped him to bed and then Sarah had been occupied with the wedding breakfast. The last of guests had left a few minutes ago and Lady Jessica had come down from Huntington's chamber and whispered to Sarah that he wanted to see her.

She looked down at the man who was now her husband. He was dressed only in a loose-fitting white shirt and dark breeches. She could see the outline of the bandages under his thin shirt. His ribs must still hurt him terribly. She moistened her lips. 'How… how are you?'

A smile touched at his mouth. 'I've been better.'

'I am sorry,' she whispered.

'There's no need. You're not at fault.'

His words did not keep her from feeling that she was. 'Do…do you wish to see me about something, my lord?'

His eyes flickered over her face. 'First of all, you are to cease addressing me as "my lord". My name is Devin, although I prefer Dev.'

'Very well, D…Dev.' Her tongue tripped in an embarrassing manner over his name. 'Is there anything else?'

'I want to leave tomorrow for Ravensheed.'

She stared at him. 'Tomorrow? That is impossible!'

'Why?' His mouth curved in a cynical smile. 'I

suppose you dread going away with me. Do not worry. As soon as we have spent a reasonable amount of time residing together you may go where you please.'

'No, that is hardly what I meant.' She felt angry and hurt that he wanted to be rid of her so soon. She tried to shove her hurt aside. 'You are not well at all. How can you think of travelling?'

'I'll manage well enough. I've travelled in worse shape.' His eyes strayed over her face. 'So, will you come with me?'

'Yes, of course.' Although the thought of leaving her home so soon filled her with something akin to dread.

'Of course,' he repeated softly. 'You've taken vows to obey me, so I suppose you feel you have no choice.'

'No, I do not,' she said coolly. He seemed to be baiting her and she had no idea why. 'Although I think it would be extremely foolish of you to think of travelling. You have been very badly injured and bouncing over rough roads will hardly do you any good. Doctor Hampton said you should remain in bed another few days.'

'I prefer my own bed. And it will hardly do me good to remain here.'

She bit her lip. He undoubtedly wanted to escape from a place that held nothing but bitter memories. She could not blame him at all. 'I...I can quite understand. If you wish to leave tomorrow, I will, of course, go with you.' She clasped her hands in front of her. The pallor in his face was increasing. 'I should leave you to rest, then. Is there anything else you would like?'

'There is, actually.' His gaze had drifted down to her mouth. 'A kiss.'

She nearly leaped back. 'A…a what?'

'A kiss. It is not a very unusual occurrence when one has just married.'

'No, but you said…' The heat rushed to her cheeks.

'I am not demanding we consummate our union. Merely that you kiss me.'

Perhaps he was delirious. His eyes held a peculiar glint that could be termed feverish. She briefly closed her eyes. Surely she could manage a simple kiss. 'Very well.'

She bent forward and brushed his cheek with her lips. His cheek was rough and warm and she heard his quick intake of breath. She straightened, the brief contact making her light-headed. 'Perhaps I…I should leave you.' She had no intention of asking if he wanted anything else.

'I think that would be wise.' His voice sounded rather thick. She backed out of the room and closed the door, her knees shaking. She leaned against the wall, trying to calm herself before she met anyone.

Perhaps it would be best after all if they lived apart. Particularly if he had such a devastating effect on her. Or maybe once she grew used to him she would no longer feel so shaky and peculiar in his presence.

Somehow, she rather doubted it.

Chapter Seven

Sarah carefully wrapped the small portrait of her mother in a clean handkerchief and placed it on top of the ribbon-wrapped packet of letters in the small valise. She had packed them last and intended to take them with her today along with one trunk of her clothing. The rest of her belongings would be sent in one of her grandfather's carriages.

Sarah sat down on her bed and looked around. All her personal belongings were gone. Her fans and gloves, the small blue and white vase given to her by her mother, her favourite quilt, and the small watercolour of the garden she had painted ages ago had been packed away. Her room now looked rather sad. Sarah felt as if she had no courage at all to leave her home. In fact, she was seized with the cowardly desire to run and hide and hope Huntington would simply leave without her.

In less than an hour, she would step into the carriage that would take her from her home.

'Sarah?' Jessica stood in the doorway. She looked rather hesitant. 'May I call you Sarah? I would feel rather odd to call you Lady Huntington. But perhaps you would prefer that.'

Sarah stood and smiled. 'Of course you may call me Sarah. Please come in.'

Jessica moved into the room and looked around. 'It must be so difficult for you to leave your home. I know I shall feel such pangs when I must go from Ravensheed. As much as I want to be with Adam.' She gave Sarah a tentative smile. 'Is it not odd? I shall be moving near your home and you shall be moving into my home.'

'I know.' Sarah already felt homesick. 'Will you soon be returning to Ravensheed?' Perhaps it wouldn't be so difficult if Lady Jessica was there. Considering everything, she had been exceedingly kind to Sarah.

'I hope to. Aunt has demanded I spend at least a fortnight with her, but I will attempt to escape as soon as possible.' She looked at Sarah and her expression was suddenly sympathetic. 'Really, you need not be afraid of my brother. He is not nearly as black as he is painted. Or as black as he wants everyone to think him. He is actually rather nice.'

'Is he? That is, I am certain...' Sarah felt heat course through her cheeks. She hardly sounded like an adoring bride. She tried again. 'Certainly his behaviour has been most...most honourable since he has been here.'

Jessica suddenly giggled. 'Well, there are a few points with which I might disagree.' Her face sobered. 'Please don't let him keep you at arm's length. He will try, you know.'

Sarah knotted her hands together. 'I think he already has.'

'Promise me you won't let him. He needs you,' Jessica said. Her eyes begged Sarah to agree.

He needed her? Sarah stared at Jessica in astonishment. She could hardly think of anything more unlikely. 'I don't think…' Sarah bit her lip, unable to hold out against Jessica's plea. 'I will try my best.'

'Thank you.' Jessica's smile was tremulous. And then she stepped forward and gave Sarah a hug. 'I will see you very soon.' She released Sarah and quietly left the room.

Sarah stood in the middle of her room. There was nothing left to do. She picked up her kid gloves and stepped into the corridor. She slowly closed the door.

'Sarah.'

She spun around. Nicholas stood behind her. 'It is time to leave,' he said. 'I thought it would be proper of me to escort you to your carriage.'

Tears pricked her eyes. 'I would like that.' She tried to smile at him. 'I will miss you, you know.'

A wry smile touched his lips. 'Will you? I've been devilishly difficult. It is only that I want you to be happy. And marriage to Huntington hardly seems the way.' His face sobered. 'Despite everything, I don't think he'll treat you badly.' He looked away for a moment and then back at her. 'Mary told me he bore none of the fault for her leaving.'

'Thank you,' she said softly. It could not have been easy for him to tell her that.

She hugged him then. His arms came around her and he patted her awkwardly. And then it was time for her to leave.

The carriage rumbled to a halt in the yard of the posting inn where they were stopping for dinner.

Sarah glanced over at Dev. He was sprawled in the
opposite corner of the carriage, eyes closed as they
had been most of the journey. His face was pale and
a lock of dark hair hung over his brow, giving him
a rather rakish look. Although he'd said little, she
had no doubt that, despite his well-sprung carriage
and padded seats, the trip was exceedingly uncomfortable.

They had been travelling for nearly five hours with
only one stop. The weather had been pleasant and
they had encountered only one minor delay behind a
herd of sheep.

She should probably wake him. As if sensing her
regard, he opened his eyes. For a moment he looked
startled, as if he hadn't expected to see her, and then
he sat more upright, grimacing a little. 'We have
stopped.' He appeared rather dazed.

'Yes. At an inn.'

'The White Pigeon, to be exact.' He rubbed his
shoulder. 'The food is tolerable. I trust you are hungry?'

'Very much so.' Which was surprising, but somehow on the journey, watching the passing scenery,
she had begun to feel calmer. Her maid, Liza, like
Dev, had slept most of the way. Sarah had spent the
time thinking about nothing in particular.

Dev climbed down from the carriage, his movements stiff, and then helped her down. They crossed
the busy inn yard, the early evening air cool on her
cheeks.

They entered the inn and the proprietor, a heavy-
jowled man, hustled forward, pleased recognition
lighting his features. 'My lord, a pleasure. You will
want your private parlour, of course. We have a fine

cut of mutton…' Then his eyes fell on Sarah. He stopped, the curiosity only thinly veiled.

'Mr Henwick, may I present my wife,' Dev said.

This time he looked startled and then a smile broke across his face. 'My felicitations, my lord. I wish you all happiness, my lady.'

'Thank you,' Sarah said. She cast a worried glance at Dev, who had that white look around his mouth again. 'If the parlour is available, perhaps we should sit. Lord Huntington is not very well.'

Dev levelled a scowl at her, which she ignored. Mr Henwick's expression immediately changed to one of sympathy. 'Of course, of course. I trust nothing serious? You must come this way.'

He led them to a small cosy room and, after promising to send their dinner straight away, quit the room. Sarah looked at Dev. If possible, his face had paled another degree. 'You should sit,' she said gently.

The scowl returned. 'There was no need to inform Henwick of the condition of my health. Nor am I "not very well".'

'You look as if you are about to collapse and I feared Mr Henwick meant to keep offering his felicitations. I suggest you sit.'

He continued to stand and folded his arms. 'I had no idea you were so managing.'

'Probably not,' she said calmly. 'The wing chair looks not uncomfortable.'

'You are still standing.'

'Yes.' She resisted the urge to heave an exasperated sigh. Certainly he was much less trouble asleep. She plopped down on the small settee. 'Now I am sitting, so you may do the same.'

To her consternation, he strode over and took the seat beside her, his leg brushing hers as he sat. 'I believe this looks more comfortable.'

'Perhaps.' She stared straight ahead, trying to ignore the peculiar sensations his nearness wrought. She had no idea whether she wanted to leap up or press closer to him.

'So, tell me, Sarah, are you really concerned about me?' he asked softly.

She turned her head and found his dark eyes locked on her face in a way that made her blush. 'Of course,' she said, as calmly as possible. 'I should hate to have you taken seriously ill, particularly since I have no idea where we're going. That is, I've never been to Ravensheed and would poosibly become horribly confused.' Just as she probably sounded now.

'Even in the unlikely event I should collapse on you, my coachman is quite capable of getting you there,' he said drily. He rose. 'I believe you are right, the armchair is probably more suitable.' He stalked over and sat rather heavily. They said nothing more until a buxom woman, followed by a slender pink-cheeked girl, entered with the dinner. Unlike the loquacious Mr Henwick, his wife seemed disinclined to say more than a few words and, after laying the covers with efficiency, departed.

They took their places at the table. The food smelled and looked appetising. Sarah tasted the mutton, which was quite delicious. As were the peas. In fact, she was really very hungry. She had eaten a good quarter of her meal when she looked up. Dev was not only staring at her, but had hardly touched his food. 'Are you not hungry?' she finally asked. After watching most males in her life eat, it seemed peculiar to have one in front of her who seemed to have little appetite.

'No, not particularly.' The bruises on his cheek were even more pronounced under his pallor and he'd begun to look rather sickly.

'What is wrong?' she asked, concerned.

'Nothing.'

'Then you should eat something. The food is quite good.'

A smile flickered at the corner of his mouth. 'I can see that. Or else I have badly starved you most of the trip.'

She flushed a little. 'Oh, no. Grandfather's cook sent a very well-stocked basket. I ate very well.'

'And you still have an appetite?'

'I always am very hungry when I travel.' Sarah felt rather defensive, although she suspected he was teasing her.

'I must remember that for future journeys.'

She looked away, suddenly uncomfortable, a stab of homesickness darting through her. She was not on a mere holiday, but a journey to a new home. She forced herself to look back at him. 'How far is Ravensheed?'

'Less than two hours. When you are finished, we can continue on.'

'Are you certain you are well enough?' She did not like his pallor or the weariness in his face. She glanced at the clock on the mantelpiece. By the time they reached Ravensheed it would be dark.

He scowled. 'Yes. Nor am I an elderly invalid whose health you must continually inquire about.'

'I beg your pardon.' She pushed her chair back and rose. 'I am finished, if you wish to go.'

'I did not mean we must leave at this very moment,' he said stiffly. He stood and then swayed, his face going quite white.

'Dev?' She rushed to his side. 'What is it?'

He had a peculiar look around his mouth. 'I fear I am about to be quite ill. I suggest you move.'

'Oh, dear.' She looked around and grabbed the nearest useful item at hand, which happened to be a half-full pitcher. She thrust it at him just as he started to retch. She turned away, not wanting to make it worse for him by staring. When he was through, she held out his handkerchief.

He took it without looking at her. 'I beg your pardon,' he said stiffly. 'I fear I have not played the role of attentive husband.'

'I hardly expected you to.' He still looked quite unwell, although not as white. She took a breath, knowing he was certain to dislike her next suggestion. 'I think we should stay here for the night.'

He cast her a swift frown. 'We are going to Ravensheed.'

'Then you may go without me. I've no intention of travelling with a man who is likely to become sick in the coach.' She plopped down on the sofa.

His brows snapped together. 'I am not planning another such episode.'

'No one ever does.' She folded her hands and looked at him. She had no doubt he intended to attempt to ride roughshod over her. 'And you look quite dreadful. I imagine you must feel even worse.'

He gave a short laugh. 'Thank you. I am highly complimented. Do you have any more arguments to put forth?'

'Yes. It is growing dark and I dislike travelling when it is dark.'

'Is that all?' To her surprise he suddenly sat down in the nearest chair. 'Very well, we will stay if it pleases you.'

'Then I will speak to Mr Henwick.' She rose and quickly left the room before he could change his mind.

Dev fell back on the pillows with a groan. He'd managed to remove one boot and his coat but his other boot, waistcoat and cravat seemed too much effort. His ribs ached and his stomach still felt uneasy. As much as he was loathe to admit it, Sarah had been right to demand they stay the night. If he hadn't been so determined to get Sarah away from Monteville House and Blanton, he would have stayed there for another day or two. The only consoling thought was that he'd soon be in his own bed. If he survived the trip.

He roused himself when he heard the light knock on the door. 'What is it?'

He did not look up right away when the door opened, but when he did he first thought he was dreaming. Sarah stood in the doorway, dressed in a white gown with a large paisley shawl around her shoulders, her hair hanging in a braid down her back. He sat up, his eyes on her face, half-fearing she would disappear. He caught his breath and this time it had nothing to do with the pain in his rib. 'Sarah?'

Her eyes took in his half-dressed appearance and widened. She took a step back. 'I…I came to see if you were all right. Or needed something.'

'I am well enough.' He slowly swung his legs over

the edge of the bed and stood, trying to ignore the pain in his ribs and head. 'Come in and shut the door.'

She did, with her eyes on him the entire time as if she would bolt at any unexpected movement from him. 'If…if you don't need something, then perhaps I should go.'

'There's no need to worry, I've no intention of ravishing you.' He sat down rather abruptly as a wave of dizziness overtook him. 'I fear I am hardly capable of doing so at any rate.'

'Oh, dear!' Her expression quickly changed to concern. She crossed the room to his bed and looked down at him. 'You are in pain.'

'A little.' He grimaced, the genuine concern in her face throwing him off. He had not expected that from her. 'Nothing to worry about, my dear.'

'How did you manage to get your boots and coat off?' she asked.

'Very slowly, I assure you.'

She leaned forward a little and her shawl fell opened and he realised she was not in proper dress at all. He levelled a frown at her. 'What the devil are you doing wandering about an inn in your night-dress?'

Even in the dim light he could see the quick flush that stained her cheekbones. 'I am hardly wandering around the inn,' she informed him. 'I merely walked from my room to yours.'

'That's dangerous enough. Where's your maid?'

'She is sleeping. At any rate, there is only one other family here and one single gentleman who is quite elderly. They seem quite respectable. I did not come to discuss the occupants of the inn, but to see if you are in need of assistance.'

'I appreciate your concern, but I need nothing.' He had no intention of allowing her to stay in his room any longer than necessary. Not with her dark, expressive eyes and soft inviting mouth and the candlelight making the room far too intimate.

'But don't you wish to remove your other boot and the…the rest of your clothing?' Her colour increased as she stumbled over the words. 'That is, your waistcoat and stock?'

He raised his brow in his most sardonic fashion. 'Are you offering to help me?'

'Well, yes.' She bit her lip. 'Unless there is someone else in the inn.'

'Unfortunately not. Mr Henwick is too busy and I hardly wish his wife or daughter to play valet. I will manage, my dear. If I need to, I'll sleep in my clothing. Go to bed.'

'But that is hardly comfortable.' She seemed to make up her mind. 'I can at least remove your other boot and help you with your other items.' She sat down on the bed. 'I will start with your boot.'

He was too stunned to protest when she reached for his booted foot. Her grasp was surprisingly strong for such delicate hands and she somehow managed to pull the boot from his foot. She set it on the floor and then moved closer to him. 'I think your cravat next.'

'I think not—' he began but she was already leaning over him.

Her fingers fumbled with his cravat. He closed his eyes as her arm brushed his cheek and her soft scent enveloped him, and then bit back a groan as his body reacted with a desire that was hot and swift.

He must have made some sound for she sat back, his cravat in her hands. 'Did I hurt you? Are you in pain?' Her voice was soft and full of concern.

His eyes shot open, which was a mistake, for he was looking into her lovely, heart-shaped face. His eyes fell to her lips and he wanted nothing more than to pull her on top of him and kiss her until she lay soft and wanting in his arms. He forced himself to speak. 'No, there's no pain.'

'Then let me help you with your waistcoat. You will need to lean forward. Can you do so?'

'Yes.' He shifted and she gently eased the garment over one arm and then reached around him to pull it down his other arm. The feel of her body against his was akin to torture. By the time she was done, his body was throbbing with more than the pain due to his injuries. She finally sat back, his waistcoat in her hands. 'Is there anything else?' Her own voice was rather faint.

He tore his eyes away from her lips. 'No, I think you'd best go.' Before he did something he would regret.

She stood. The shawl slipped from her shoulders. She quickly retrieved it. 'Then I…I will bid you goodnight.' She didn't quite look at him.

'Goodnight. Lock your door.'

'I will.' She laid his waistcoat on the chair over his coat and backed out of the room. Then closed the door swiftly behind her as if she'd just escaped from imminent danger.

Which perhaps she had. He fell back against the pillows, stunned at the force of his desire. Perhaps he was merely delirious, as he surely had been the day of their wedding when he'd asked for a kiss. He realised his mistake as soon as her soft lips brushed his cheeks.

He closed his eyes with a groan. The last thing he wanted was to lust after his wife. He'd best put as much distance between them as quickly as possible.

Chapter Eight

'We should be at Ravensheed within the next few minutes.'

Dev's voice aroused Sarah from her contemplation of the gentle, green countryside, something she'd been engaged in most of the two-hour journey from the White Pigeon, despite her now stiff neck. Her other choice had been to contemplate Dev sitting across from her in the carriage; after last night, the prospect seemed too alarming.

She forced herself to look at him now. He looked better than he had yesterday, although she could tell he was still far from recovered. He had dressed himself today, although he'd omitted his cravat and waistcoat and wore his shirt open at the neck under his bottle-green coat. He had not bothered to shave and the dark shadow of beard around his mouth gave him a dangerous masculine aura.

Whatever had possessed her to insist on helping him undress? She had only gone to his room in the first place because she had promised Jessica she would look after him. And then he had looked so tired and rather helpless as he lay there with one boot on. It wasn't until she actually sat next to him that she realised she was about to perform a very intimate task. By then, it seemed too late to back down. The feel of his strong muscles, his masculine scent and her fingers contacting his strong cheekbones burned in her memory. She had experienced the most odd desire to brush a stray lock of dark hair from his forehead and tangle her hands in his thick hair.

A desire she had no business feeling, especially for him.

She realised from his expression that he was waiting for her to say something. 'The countryside looks very nice,' she stammered.

His brow arched. 'I am glad you think so since you have spent most of the journey watching it. Have you been to Kent before?'

'Only once.' She clasped her hands together, trying hard not to notice his long muscular legs stretched out in front of him. Whatever was wrong with her? She'd never felt so peculiar around a man before. She was grateful Liza was with them even if she had spent most of the trip sleeping, soft snores issuing from her slightly open mouth.

He glanced out the window. 'We have just turned into the drive. Ravensheed is around the next bend.'

Sarah looked back out the window in time to see the house. Her stomach knotted as she saw the place that was now to be her home.

It stood on a slight rise, a square house of red bricks with two symmetrical wings. In front of it spread a rolling green lawn. In the late afternoon sun, the house had a peaceful, mellow appearance. Ordinarily she would have thought it appealing, but at the moment it had all the appeal of a prison. A wave of homesickness washed over her. She moistened her lips and glanced back at Dev. 'It…it is very lovely.'

He fixed her with one of his penetrating looks. 'I am glad you think so. However, I can see you are less than pleased at the prospect of stepping foot in it.'

Was she really so transparent? She glanced down at her hands. 'It is just everything seems so strange. I imagine that once I am used to it, I shall like it very much.'

'I hope so.' His voice held an odd note.

She looked quickly back at him and caught an expression that could almost be sympathy cross his face. But it was gone too quickly and then the carriage had rattled to a halt.

Liza roused herself and looked out the window with sleepy eyes. The footman flung open the doors and Dev stepped down. He helped Sarah down. She stood for a moment, looking up at the house and then Dev took her elbow. 'Come, it's time to go in.'

Her heart thudding, she went with him up the steps. The door was opened by a footman and she stepped into a spacious entry hall. A thin, middle-aged woman came out of one of the doors that opened into the hall. Her eyes widened in surprise and then she hurried forward. 'My lord, Lady Jessica, I did not expect you.' Then she peered more closely at Sarah and her face stiffened in shock.

'This is my housekeeper, Mrs Humphries. May I present my wife, Lady Huntington?'

'Your wife?' Her mouth fell open and then she recovered herself. 'How do you do, my lady?'

'Very well, thank you,' Sarah said awkwardly.

Dev dropped his hand from her elbow. 'Perhaps

you could show Lady Huntington to the bedchamber in the family wing. We've had a long journey and she is undoubtedly tired.'

'Very well, my lord.' Mrs Humphries's face was impassive. 'This way, then, Lady Huntington.'

'I will see you at dinner, Sarah.' His voice was clearly dismissive.

She followed the housekeeper through a door that led into a long gallery with paintings on one wall. At the end of the gallery was a small square hallway with a door on either side. Mrs Humphries opened one and Sarah followed her into a large bedchamber with pale blue walls and a large tester bed against one wall.

Mrs Humphries crossed the room and opened another door. 'The dressing room is here. Lord Huntington's own dressing room opens into it.' She returned to the door of the bedchamber. 'I will send your maid to help you unpack. Perhaps you would like to rest before dinner. His lordship generally dines at five, although tonight he will undoubtedly wish to dine later. Is there anything else you wish, my lady?'

'No, I think not. Thank you.' Sarah watched the housekeeper leave, and then she slowly removed her pelisse and bonnet and laid them on the bed, wondering what to do next.

She finally sat in a *chaise-longue* near the bed and looked around the room, which was now to be hers. The blue walls and white curtains and bed-hangings gave it a light airy atmosphere, but the room had a curiously impersonal feel to it as if it carried no impression of any previous occupant. The dressing table was bare except for a small looking glass; the fireplace, with its white carved mantelpiece and iron grate, was clean and neat as if it had not seen a fire for an age. The only bit of life was a small painting of a large manor house set in a rolling, green park.

This had undoubtedly been Mary's room for the few brief weeks she had been Dev's wife. Before she ran away with Nicholas. The thought of Mary made Sarah feel an intruder, almost as if she were appropriating Mary's home, Mary's place and worse, her husband. Except Mary had not wanted any of them. And it seemed almost that fate had had somehow decreed that Sarah was to take her place.

Sarah took one last look at herself in the looking glass and squared her shoulders. There was no need for such apprehension, she was merely going to dinner, not an inquisition. Despite his impatient temper and dark scowls, the last two days had taught her that Dev was a gentleman. And, she reminded herself, she had dined with him alone last night so she had no reason to dread eating with him tonight.

Except she did. And tonight was different. This time she was alone with him in his house.

Liza had helped her dress in one of her favourite gowns, a pale peach silk with matching ribbon around the hem and rounded neckline. It was over a year old, but she had hoped wearing it would give her courage. Perhaps if they had a real marriage she would be concerned with trying to impress her husband but, under the circumstances, that was the last thing she wanted to do.

She opened the door and nearly jumped when Dev stepped out of the door across the small hallway that separated them. He was also dressed for dinner in a black coat and dark pantaloons. He glanced up, an equally startled look on his face. 'We seemed to be of a similar mind,' he said.

'Yes.' She willed herself to meet his eyes and managed to force a smile to her lips. 'And quite fortuitous as well as I was not exactly certain where I was to go.'

'I hardly expected you to, although I would have sent a servant for you.' He held out his arm. 'Shall we proceed to the dining room, then? Since we have no company tonight, we can dispense with the formalities in the drawing room.'

She gingerly placed her fingers on his coat sleeve, careful to avoid any more extensive contact with him. Not that he seemed to desire it any more than she did. He held himself stiffly away from her as they passed down the picture gallery and through a small square hall where a staircase rose to the next floor, then crossed the entry hall to the dining room.

The room was elegant with dark red walls and drapes. Dev dropped her arm and she moved to the window that framed a view of the park at the back of the house. An expanse of smooth green grass sloped gently away to a wooded area. She caught a glimpse of a small lake in the distance. It was quite different from Monteville's formal gardens and well-planned paths.

'The park was designed by Capability Brown,' Dev said, coming to stand behind her. 'However, my mother insisted that she must have a flower garden. So there is one at the side of the house outside your room. You can see it from the south window and, of course, you may use it as much as you like.'

'I will. Thank you.' She kept her eyes on the view, his words reminding her she was more than a guest.

There was an awkward silence between them. 'Perhaps we should eat,' Dev said.

He sat at the head of the large mahogany table and Sarah was seated to his right. The footman brought the first course. The soup smelled delicious, but the now familiar shaky nervousness in her stomach made it impossible to do more than take a few sips.

She finally gave up after the cheese course. She glanced at Dev, who had been as silent and preoccupied as she had most of the meal. Occasionally she would catch him watching her, an impenetrable expression on his face that only served to unnerve her more.

She had just reached for her wine when he spoke. 'You are not eating much.' She started. Her hand hit the glass and, in horror, she watched it spill across the tablecloth.

'Oh, dear.' She jumped up and reached for the glass and managed to knock her fork to the floor. Her hands went to her flaming cheeks. 'Oh, drat! I…I am sorry.'

'Drat?' His mouth suddenly quirked. He stood and righted the glass. 'Sarah, it is hardly a disaster. Sit down.'

She quickly obeyed, feeling completely idiotic. She watched in mortified silence as the footman mopped up the spill and then placed another fork at her place.

Dev waited until the footman finished before speaking. 'Usually, I don't frighten my dinner guests quite that much. Although,' he added softly, 'you are not a guest.'

She looked quickly at him, still flustered. 'I fear I was daydreaming. I am sorry.'

'I will own the fault was mine,' he said wryly. 'If I had been a more attentive partner then you would not have found it necessary to retreat. I beg your pardon.'

'Please don't,' she said quickly. 'I imagine you must be very tired after the trip. I really did not expect you to entertain me with witty conversation.'

His dark eyes fastened on her face, his expression unreadable. 'Are you always this generous, Sarah?'

She looked at him, puzzled. 'I have no idea what you mean.'

'Only that, instead of taking me to task over my lack of manners, you find an excuse.' His voice held a self-mocking edge.

She frowned a little. 'Is it an excuse? But I can see for myself that you are not quite well. I cannot think that travelling over the roads in a coach with injuries such as yours would be very comfortable.'

'No.' His hand tightened around his wineglass, his eyes still on her face. 'Mary once told me you had a propensity for rescuing strays, whether animal or human.'

'Did she?'

'Yes.' His expression was forbidding. 'I hope, my dear, that you do not see me as one of your strays. For I've no desire to be rescued and most certainly not by you.'

'I…I have no intention of doing so.' She stared at him, stung by the anger in his words.

'Good.' He suddenly rose. 'But you are right about one thing, I am damnably tired. If you will excuse me, I am going to retire. I'll send Mrs Humphries to you. If you need anything you may apply to her. Goodnight, Sarah.'

'Goodnight,' she whispered. She watched him stride out of the room and thought she had never felt so alone in her life.

Chapter Nine

The next morning, Sarah stood at one of the tall windows of her bedchamber and watched the rain stream down the windowpane. The small private garden Dev had mentioned was outside the window, the lady's mantle and gillyflowers looking rather forlorn with their heads hanging from the force of the rain. She turned away, not certain what she should do next. A maid had already brought her a steaming cup of chocolate and toast and then Liza had helped her into a long-sleeved gown of fawn muslin.

As much as she might like, she could not hide in this room all day. She supposed she should inquire after Dev, but after last night she almost dreaded to do so. He'd made it quite clear he wanted nothing from her, most certainly not her concern. No matter what she had promised Jessica, she could not force herself on him. It would only serve to give him a greater disgust of her than he already had.

Perhaps she could at least see some of the house. She opened the door to find the housemaid who had brought her tray on the other side. The maid squeaked. 'Oh, 'tis a scare you gave me, my lady! I did not expect—I beg your pardon!'

Sarah gave her a kind smile. 'It is quite all right…Sally, is it not?'

'Yes, my lady.' She still looked a little breathless. 'His…his lordship wishes to see you in his study.'

'Does he?' Sarah's heart leaped to her throat. She'd hardly expected to be summoned for an audience with him so early. If anything, she had expected him to avoid her. 'Perhaps you could show me the way to his study.'

'Oh, yes! That is, certainly, my lady. 'Tis right next to the library.'

Since Sarah had no notion where the library was, she was happy to have Sally for a guide. His study turned out to be a room off the main entrance hall. She stepped inside.

He sat at a large desk, his head bent over a sheaf of papers, pale light from the nearby window spreading across the desk. He looked up immediately when she entered and then stood. 'Please, come in,' he said politely.

He came around to the side of his desk. He was dressed in buckskin breeches, top boots and a brown coat and looked the complete country gentleman. 'I trust you slept well,' he said in the same polite tones. 'You may come here.'

'Very well.' She came to stand in front of her desk, her hands clasped in front of her, feeling as if she had been summoned by her grandfather.

'Please, sit down.' He indicated a chair near his desk. She took it and perched on the edge, folding her hands in her lap.

'Is everything to your satisfaction?'

'Most certainly everything,' she said with some acerbity. Really, she'd had more personal conversations with a horse. She might as well be a stranger he barely remembered.

He finally looked at her, his face expressionless. 'You will undoubtedly want to see the house. Mrs Humphries will show you the rooms.' He glanced back down at his papers as if he could not wait to get back to them.

As if he intended to keep her firmly out of his way like an unwanted poor relation. She was seized with an uncharacteristic desire to shake him out of his indifference. 'I would prefer that you show me the house, my lord,' she said.

His head shot up. 'Why?'

'Otherwise I shall feel as if I'm taking a…a country home tour. I did once, when I was sixteen. We visited Laurelhurst and the housekeeper most obligingly took us through the house. And then, because it was raining and she felt sorry for us, we were given refreshments before we left.'

He frowned. 'I wasn't exactly planning to have Mrs Humphries provide you with refreshments before sending you off.'

'Weren't you?'

'Hardly.' He stared at her. 'I would have thought you would prefer having Mrs Humphries for a guide.' He glanced at his desk again. 'And I have business I must attend to.'

A twinge of hurt mixed with anger shot through her. It was obvious he wanted nothing to do with her. Well, she had no intention of begging him to accept her company. 'Of course, my lord. Then I will leave you.' She whirled around and walked towards the door, head high as if it didn't matter a whit.

She'd just reached the door when he spoke. 'Sarah!'

She paused and looked back at him. 'Yes, my lord?'

'Damnation!' Now he had a scowl. 'Give me an hour and I will be with you. I've business with my steward first.'

She lifted her chin. 'There is no need to put yourself out, particularly if you plan to swear at me. I am certain Mrs Humphries will do an admirable job.'

He fixed her with a dark stare. 'You will be waiting for me in an hour. In the library.'

So now he was back on his high horse again. 'Yes, my lord.'

His look darkened. 'And if you continue to call me my lord, I will give serious consideration to locking you up. Do you understand, Sarah?'

'Quite. My lord.' She fled from the room, taking grim satisfaction from the black scowl on his face. And then wondered what in the world she had done now.

Dev jerked his mind back to Thomas Dalton's words. He was a stocky man with a pair of intelligent grey eyes in a weatherbeaten face. He'd been at Ravensheed for nearly twenty years. Dev's parents had died of influenza when he was barely seventeen. Since then, Dalton had been his mentor as well as employee.

He realised he hadn't a notion of what his steward had said. Something about the north field. 'I apologise, but I was not attending.'

Dalton gave him one of his slow smiles. 'I imagine not, my lord. Not with a new bride waiting for you. Perhaps you would rather discuss this later.'

'That might be best.' Dev rose, cursing himself for behaving like an idiot. He'd spent most of the hour trying to keep his mind focused on the business at hand. Instead, his thoughts strayed to Sarah…almost as if he actually was a besotted bridegroom.

'We wish to offer our most sincere felicitations,' Dalton said. 'And Nancy looks forward to the honour of making Lady Huntington's acquaintance.'

'Of course. As soon as there is a day suitable for riding.' Dev stifled a groan. He had forgotten all the duties associated with bringing home a new wife, such as making her known to his tenants. He could hardly hide Sarah away and pretend she did not exist.

He left Dalton with a heavy book of accounts and quit the room where he conducted most of the business of managing the vast estate. He strode more quickly from the servants' wing than he usually would have, despite having cut short his meeting with Dalton.

His footsteps slowed and he scowled. The last thing he'd wanted was to spend time with Sarah. Every encounter he had with her managed to overset his equilibrium. He couldn't even sit through a dinner without feeling confused. Worse was her obvious concern for his health and comfort, something that he'd rarely experienced from any woman outside his family. It threw him completely. As did the unwelcome thought that she regarded him as nothing more than a hurt stray that needed her pity.

After last night, he vowed that he would keep away from her. Treat her with polite indifference and hope he would recover from the unwelcome effect she was having on his well-ordered world.

So why he was now entering his library to show her around his house was a complete mystery. Except she had looked so forlorn standing in front of his desk that he had felt an unexpected twinge of conscience. And then, when she walked away, her chin tilted as if it mattered not at all, his vow was shot to hell.

He walked into the library. She sat at one of the tables, her head bent over a book. She looked up and smiled. 'You have a wonderful library. I always thought my grandfather's was superb, but I must own, I think yours is superior.'

He caught his breath, taken aback by the first genuine smile she'd ever directed at him. Its warmth lit her face and nearly sent him reeling with its impact.

She was waiting for his response. 'I collect books, or rather my father and grandfather did, and I've added to them,' he finally managed to say.

'What sort of books do you have?'

He shrugged, trying to remain indifferent. 'Philosophy, history, geography, some scientific works.'

'What? No novels?' Her voice held a teasing note that threw him off even more.

He arched a brow. 'I hate to crush your expectations, but I do have an extensive collection of novels. Including some put out by the Minerva Press.'

Her smile deepened. 'But the question is, do you ever read them?'

He smiled. 'Yes, my dear, I do.'

'Really?'

He moved to stand in front of her. 'Really. In fact, I have read all of Mrs Radcliffe's works, and a few with such fascinating titles as *The Horrors of Oak-endale Abbey* and *Spectre of the Turret.*'

'Indeed,' she said. She could hardly look more stunned if he had announced he habitually robbed homes. 'Did you like them?'

'They were fascinating, to say the least. I broke my leg two summers ago and Jessica decided I needed something less dry than my usual reading. So she brought me an armload of novels. I was actually quite entertained. If I recall correctly, one had a ghost who dripped blood.' His brow shot up at her amazed expression. 'I see I have surprised you.'

'It is just that men in general, that is, my brother—' She suddenly looked stricken. 'I beg your pardon.'

'There is no need. I am not about to explode in a rage at the mention of your brother.'

'I would hardly fault you if you did,' she said in a small voice. She looked away, the animation drained from her countenance.

Now what was going on? With a sense of shock, it hit him that for some incomprehensible reason she seemed to think he cast some of the blame on her. 'Sarah.' He braced his hands on the table in front of her. 'The whole damnable affair had nothing to do with you.'

She looked back at him, her eyes large and unhappy. 'But it did.'

'No. It did not.' His eyes held hers. 'I've no idea why you think that. I doubt very much that you encouraged your brother and Mary to fall in love with each other.'

'No, I did not, but…' She bit her lip.

'But nothing. I have never blamed you for any of it, no matter what you seem to think.' He straightened up and backed away. 'I believe you said you wished to see the house. Shall we go?'

'Yes.' She rose slowly, but he could see she was still distressed. The anger he'd managed to quell threatened to rise to the surface. No matter how he tried to keep the affair in the past, it seemed determined to surface. He wondered if any of them would ever be free from it.

He realised Sarah was regarding him with an odd expression. He mentally shook himself. 'Where shall we start? The drawing room?'

'Yes, if you please.' Her voice was subdued, as if she thought he was about to strike her.

Did she really fear him that much? 'There's no need to sound so afraid. I don't know what damnable tales you've heard about me but I haven't touched a woman yet. At least not in anger.'

'I…I did not think that.'

'Good. So there's no need to defer to my wishes or fear expressing an opinion contrary to mine. In fact, I prefer that to cowed agreement.' He stalked to the door. 'So, is it agreeable to you if we start by looking at the drawing room?'

She looked completely taken aback. But when she finally spoke, her voice was calm. 'Yes, I would like that.'

His mouth lifted in a slight smile. 'That is much better.'

Sarah glanced over at Dev and realised she'd missed half of what he had just said. She forced her attention back to his words and away from the rich timbre of his voice as he explained something about the mantelpiece.

They stood in the saloon between the dining room and drawing room. She vaguely recalled Dev had said the large room was used as a ballroom. Now he moved towards the window, which, like the other two rooms, faced the back of the house. 'You might have noticed that most of the ground-floor rooms lead directly to the garden.'

'Well, yes.'

He turned to look at her. 'My grandfather built this house in 1766, two years after the original house burned down. My grandfather had visited Edinburgh with my grandmother and saw a house designed by Sir Williams Chambers. My grandmother was so taken with the idea that one could step directly from the drawing room to the garden that she insisted this house be built in the same style. Of course, now this style is not quite so uncommon.'

'Well, no. I suppose it would be nice to step directly into the garden.' Had she ever realised that his eyes were really a fascinating mixture of browns and greens? Or that he had a slight indentation in his chin?

What was wrong with her? She yanked her thoughts back to architecture. It was only that she had never seen him this relaxed. As he took her through the rooms, he had lost his rather guarded look and his voice held none of the drawl she was so accustomed to. He suddenly appeared a great deal more approachable, which was proving extremely distracting.

'Particularly when it is not raining. I do not think we will attempt that exercise today.' He turned away from the window. 'We've seen most of the ground floor. The upper floor has a sitting room directly above this room and more bedchambers. Is there anything else you'd like to see?'

There was not, but she did not want to quit his company yet. 'Perhaps the long gallery that we must pass through? The one with the paintings. If I am not taking you away from your other duties.'

'Not at all,' he said politely. 'Then we can have some nuncheon, if you'd like.'

She saw he was beginning to look rather tired. She bit back the urge to suggest he sit down. 'A short visit, then. I am really quite hungry.'

His mouth quirked. 'I'm not surprised. You ate very little last night, which very much disappointed Cook. Perhaps you'll do more justice to this next meal.'

She smiled at him. 'I will certainly try.'

A quarter of an hour later Sarah had nearly finished walking through the gallery, Dev beside her. He had started out by identifying the subject as well as the artist of most of the paintings, but as they progressed he'd become more silent. A glance at his pale face told her he was not particularly well, but she feared another one of his sardonic comments if she suggested they leave before she completed at least a cursory look at the wall.

She was about to tell him she was through when she spotted a series of exquisite landscapes. From their execution, they appeared to be by the same artist as the one in her bedchamber. She turned to Dev. 'These small paintings. Who is the artist?'

'My mother.'

'Your mother?' She looked at him, amazed. 'I had no idea. They are beautiful. She did the one in my bedchamber, did she not?'

He nodded. 'That one is of her home in Ireland. She painted these on a trip she took with my father to Italy. She was an artist. I scarcely remember seeing her without a sketch pad or pencil in her hand.' He glanced down at her. 'I believe you also like to draw. Do you paint as well?'

She made a face. 'Yes, but I can hardly lay claim to such talent.'

He smiled. 'She learned under some very excellent artists. After her marriage, my father continued to encourage her talent. He built a studio for her upstairs on the attic floor. Some of her works are still there.'

'How very kind of your father.'

He looked away from her. 'He was very much in love with my mother. He wanted her to be happy, particularly since her own family was not close at hand.'

They had something in common. And perhaps as she did, he hoped for love in marriage. She spoke without thinking. 'My parents were in love also. I always thought such a marriage would be the most wonderful—' She stopped, stricken by what she was about to say. For a moment, she had quite forgotten they were trapped together in a marriage neither one of them wanted.

'Pray continue.' His voice was cool. 'Your habit of leaving unfinished thoughts is disconcerting. The most wonderful what?'

'The most wonderful thing in the world,' she said quietly.

His eyes hooded. 'A dangerous notion.'

'And probably very foolish.' She forced herself to

look at him calmly as if the conversation had nothing to do with them.

'No, not for…' He stopped, the colour mounting in his cheek. 'Mrs Humphries will have a cold nuncheon laid for us. Perhaps we'd best eat.'

She nodded. They walked to the dining room in silence, both were careful to avoid the least contact with each other.

Sarah glanced over at Dev, who was seated across from her. They had eaten the cold meats and fruit in a silence that neither one seemed incline to break. Her appetite had fled again, but she had forced some of the meal down her throat, worried that, if all her meals went like this, she'd probably waste away within the month.

Dev put down his fork and spoke. 'When the weather improves my steward, Dalton, can show you the estate. I trust that you ride?'

'Yes, I do.' She kept her voice as cool as his.

'If there is nothing in my stable that suits you, I will instruct Dalton to procure a more suitable mount,' he said indifferently.

'I doubt if you need to do that. I can ride almost anything.'

He raised a brow. 'Almost anything? I find that hard to believe.'

There was no need for him to be so cynical about it. She considered riding one of her best accomplishments. 'Yes, almost. Except for my brother's half-broke colt. He shied at a squirrel and I fell and broke my arm. Although,' she added, 'I probably would not have fallen if I had used a saddle.'

A hint of a smile appeared at his mouth. 'Undoubtedly not. How old were you when you undertook this adventure?'

'Nearly fifteen.' And too old for such unlady-like pranks, as her mother had scolded her when Sarah was brought in.

'I hardly imagined you a hoyden.' He started to look faintly amused.

'I wasn't, really,' Sarah said. 'Nicholas claimed no mere girl could possibly manage such a horse.'

'And, of course, you set out to prove him wrong.' His amusement had increased.

'Well, yes.' She blushed a little.

'My lord, my lady.' A footman appeared in the doorway. 'You have a visitor. Lady Coleridge.'

'I can show myself in, if you please.' A tall, elegantly dressed woman stepped past the footman into the drawing room. Sarah's heart slammed to a halt. Dev half-rose and muttered, 'Hell.'

The visitor's sharp glance took them in at once. 'I see the rumours are true. I must admit I could hardly credit them, as I could not fathom a more unlikely coupling. However, Devin, I would have preferred to have the news directly from you rather than through a rather confusing letter from Beatrice.'

Dev stepped forward. A slight flush stained his cheeks. 'I beg your pardon, Maria. I fear it was all done rather quickly.'

'I see.' Her tone implied she did not see at all. She glanced at Sarah and her eyes softened a touch. 'My dear, I will own I hardly expected to see you again under these circumstances.'

'I am sorry,' Sarah whispered. She had risen and regarded Lady Coleridge with a mortified expression.

How could she have forgotten that Mary's mother still lived at Lacey Manor, not far from Ravensheed?

'I have no idea why,' Lady Coleridge said. Her gaze swept over Sarah's flushed face. 'How are you, my dear?'

'I…I am fine.'

'You have met Sarah?' Dev asked. He moved closer to Sarah's side.

Lady Coleridge smiled a little. 'If you recall, I have known her from before. She stayed with us for a week before your betrothal ball. And, of course, Mary spoke of her very often.'

'Yes.' A shadow passed over his face.

Sarah glanced away, feeling an interloper. How could Lady Coleridge bear seeing her in Mary's place? And to hear of such news through a letter rather than directly from them! She must feel they had both betrayed her daughter's memory.

But there was nothing in her face that indicated any such feeling when she spoke to Dev. 'And you had an accident before your wedding. Hardly the way to start a new marriage.'

'It was nothing to signify,' he said stiffly. 'Will you be seated? You are welcome to take nuncheon with us.'

'I cannot stay. I am on my way to Kentwood to call on Caroline, but I wanted to assure myself of your well being. I couldn't quite make out what Beatrice said about your injuries. She crosses her lines dreadfully.' She turned to Sarah. 'What did happen, my dear?'

Dev spoke before Sarah could open her mouth. 'A few bruised ribs, that is all.'

'And a rather nasty gash across your head from

the looks of it,' Lady Coleridge said. 'I wonder that you returned home so quickly. But then, you have never been reasonable. However, that's not what I came about.' She fixed a stern look on Dev. 'There is bound to be a great deal of talk over your rather hasty marriage. Particularly in this case. You will need to introduce your wife properly. Perhaps a small dinner party.'

Dev looked taken aback, as if the thought had never occurred to him. 'That is not necessary.'

She snorted. 'Nonsense. It will be considered most odd if you do not. Unless, of course, you plan on hiding your wife away.'

'Hardly, ma'am.'

'We will discuss this as soon as you are recovered,' she said firmly and then looked over at Sarah. 'I really cannot stay long. Perhaps you would not object to walking with me for a moment.'

'No, of course not.' Sarah followed her from the room, not daring to look at her husband. She would not be the least bit surprised if Lady Coleridge meant to reproach her for her hasty marriage.

She accompanied Lady Coleridge to the hallway. Lady Coleridge paused in front of one of the carved tables. There was nothing in the gaze she turned on Sarah that suggested censure. 'So, my dear, perhaps you will tell me now what happened to Devin?' She smiled a little. 'He is my godson as well as my son-in-law, so I feel a certain responsibility towards him. His mother was my dearest friend, you see.'

'Yes.' Mary had told her that, something that made Sarah feel even more wretched. Under the circumstances she felt she had no choice but to be honest. 'He was assaulted the day before the ceremony by two men who beat him. His ribs were badly bruised, as was his face.'

Lady Coleridge was clearly shocked. 'Beatrice said something, but I thought I had misread…oh, heavens! A robbery?'

'We are not certain,' Sarah said cautiously, not wanting to alarm Lady Coleridge more than necessary. 'Nothing was taken.'

'And you still were wed?' She appeared incredulous.

'Yes,' Sarah said unhappily. 'He insisted, although he was far from well. And then he would not stay in bed and decided we must come to Ravensheed yesterday. I could not stop him.'

'Of course not,' Lady Coleridge said. She covered Sarah's hand with her own. 'Oh, my dear, I fear you will not have an easy time of it. I understand Jessica is with Beatrice and that makes it more difficult for you. But you may apply to me if you need any sort of assistance.'

Tears sprang to Sarah's eyes. 'You are too generous.'

'My dear, I am not. Mary always spoke of you so highly—you were the dearest friend she had ever had.' Her face softened.

'And she was mine.' Sarah's guilt only increased. How could Lady Coleridge treat her so kindly?

But there was no blame in her blue eyes, only kindness. 'I will leave you for now.' Her voice had returned to its normal briskness. 'Perhaps you will be so good as to take tea with me soon. And then we can speak of Mary, if you would not object.'

'No, I would very much like that.'

'Very well.' She took Sarah's hand. 'And you may

tell me how you came to be wed to my godson if you wish.'

Sarah watched as the footman opened the door for Lady Coleridge. She stepped out into the rain where her carriage waited in front of the door. Sarah remained motionless for a moment and then slowly returned to the dining room. Dev stood at the window, his back to her. He turned. 'I apologise. I had no idea my mother-in law would come to call so unexpectedly. I hope she said nothing to distress you.'

'No. She was so very gracious. Much more than I would ever expect her to be.'

He frowned. 'Why would you expect otherwise?'

'Because how could anything be more dreadful than seeing—?' She stopped.

'You're doing it again. Leaving your sentences unfinished. Than seeing what?' he asked softly.

''Tis nothing.'

'Not if it makes you look like that. What were you going to say?'

She attempted a smile. 'It really was nothing at all.'

'Sarah.' He took a step towards her, his expression dangerous. She knew he would not let her go without an answer.

She took a breath. 'I can't think of anything worse than seeing me here.'

His brows crashed together. 'What the devil makes you say that?'

'Because…because I am not Mary.'

He stared at her for a moment. 'No. You are not,' he said shortly. And she saw the pain in his eyes.

'I am so very sorry,' she whispered.

He looked at her blankly. Then said, 'I've no idea why.' He turned away, his shoulders bowed.

He had completely shut her out. And Sarah could do nothing but walk from the room.

Chapter Ten

Sarah sipped her chocolate and gazed out of the window of the sunny pleasant morning room. The sun was shining for the first time since she had arrived at Ravensheed a week ago. After the first day she had decided to take her breakfast in this small room with its cheerful green and white wallpaper and a sweeping view of the front drive.

For the first time since her arrival, she felt almost hopeful. For what, she had no idea. She'd seen little of Dev for the past few days. If not in his study, he was closeted with Mr Dalton or riding somewhere on the estate. Their only contact was at dinner where they attempted a semblance of polite conversation.

He treated her with exquisite formality and Sarah had given up trying to shake him out of it. So she answered his questions in a voice as coolly civil as his. She had no idea how she was to keep her promise to Jessica. Not when he made it so clear he wanted nothing to do with her.

Last night he had announced he was leaving for London today. She had suddenly been gripped with a sense of panic, the same sort of panic she had experienced as a small child when her mother had left her for a few days with an aunt. But she'd forced herself to smile at him and pretend that she did not mind at all being left in a house where she knew no one. Perhaps if she had some role to play in his household she would feel more at home. But he had said nothing and Mrs Humphries seemed to run the house with a grim efficiency.

She finished her toast and eggs and shoved her plate away. She supposed she would become used to dining by herself and keeping her own company. But it didn't keep the thought of years ahead from stretching out into loneliness.

She must stop this. She should find something to do. She had thoroughly explored the house and spent numerous hours in the library. The rest of her belongings had arrived and yesterday she had arranged her room. The day before she had sat in the garden for a few hours when the rain had let up and had done a watercolour of one corner of the garden. She had not found it very satisfactory but Mrs Humphries had admired it and so Sarah had given it to her.

She rose. Perhaps she could explore the estate. From one of the upstairs windows she had caught a glimpse of an intriguing-looking tower in the distance. She could not, absolutely would not, give in to despair.

Several hours later, Sarah realised she was hopelessly lost. The sloping lawn had given way to a patch of woods where she'd found a stream. She had sketched for a bit and then started walking again. She followed the stream and then veered off in the direction of the tower she had spotted from the house.

And now she stood at the edge of a pasture and realised she had no idea in which direction Ravensheed stood.

It hadn't helped that her thoughts had wandered completely away as well so she had not made note of any landmarks.

'Good day.'

She gasped and spun around. Behind her was a man mounted on a grey horse. 'I beg your pardon. I did not mean to startle you.' He smiled, a pleasant smile that crinkled the corners of his eyes. He was dressed in the clothes of a country gentleman, but their perfect fit and elegant cut proclaimed their London origins.

'I fear I was not paying any attention.'

'You appeared to be quite lost in thought.' He leaned forward, his gaze impersonally assessing her, a little curious. Then comprehension dawned in his eyes. 'You must be Lady Huntington.'

'Yes.' She lifted her chin. Although he looked the gentleman and had an open, trustworthy face, she felt at a distinct disadvantage. 'And you are…?'

'Charles Kenton. My property runs next to Ravensheed. Which you are on,' he added quite kindly.

Sarah coloured. 'Oh, dear. I…I am very sorry. I was walking and wanted to find…' She bit her lip. ''I fear I am rather lost.'

'There is no need to apologise. I doubt very much you wish to poach anything. And not often do I come across such a lovely trespasser.'

Her colour deepened, even though there was nothing at all suggestive in his gaze. 'Perhaps you could tell me the way back to Ravensheed.'

'I will do even better. I'll take you myself.' With

a graceful movement, he dismounted, and caught up the reins in his hand.

'That is really not necessary,' Sarah said, not wanting to put him to the trouble. 'I am certain you must be quite busy, Mr Kenton.'

'Not at all. Actually, I was on my way to Ravensheed to deliver an invitation to dine with us tomorrow night.' He smiled at her. 'How did you come? Through the trees? Then it's no wonder you were lost. There's a path along the edge of the pasture. It leads directly to your husband's property and then continues on towards the stables.'

His kind, impersonal manner was reassuring. She finally relaxed and smiled tentatively back at him as he fell into step with her, the horse ambling along behind. 'Thank you.'

They walked along the pasture, the sun warm and friendly on her face and arms. Her companion talked easily about his own property, Kentwood Hall. He informed her that the tower she had looked for had been part of the original Ravensheed manor. It had burned down nearly half a century ago. And she started to feel a little less lonely and for a moment nearly forgot she was married to a man who did not want her. Until Charles Kenton suddenly stopped. 'We are nearly at the stables.' The smile left his face. 'I do have one question, Lady Huntington.'

'Yes?' Her stomach was starting to knot again when she realised she was nearly home. Which was ridiculous.

'Why is your husband allowing his new bride to wander around on her own?'

* * *

Dev frowned at the housekeeper. 'What do you mean, Lady Huntington has gone out?' he snapped.

Mrs Humphries pursed her lips. 'She left the house, my lord. By herself.' She looked at him with clear disapproval.

'When?'

'Nearly three hours ago.'

Three hours ago? A shaft of fear pierced him. Where the devil could she have gone that would keep her away for so long? His gardens were extensive, but hardly a three-hour walk. Surely she would not have gone much further. Or had she decided to run away?

'She had a paper and pencils,' Mrs Humphries added grudgingly.

So, she had gone to sketch. Common sense reasserted itself—she would hardly have been planning to run away with only her drawing implements.

But what if she was hurt?

He took his leave of Mrs Humphries and quit the house, then headed towards the stables. He would find her if it took all morning. He had no intention of leaving for London until he did.

He had meant to depart at least an hour ago, but had been delayed by a problem that could not wait until his return. He had spent most of the morning in his study as he had every day since the second day of his return. However, his damnable conscience wouldn't let him depart without bidding her goodbye. Not that it would matter to her.

He had been avoiding her. He had no idea why, except there was something about her quiet politeness that unnerved him. She'd retreated from him completely. He tried to tell himself that was what he wanted. It was a marriage of convenience, after all, a forced marriage, and there was no reason that they needed to be more than civil to each other.

Except it made him feel a stranger in his own home. And he thought of her constantly.

He rounded the corner of the stable and stopped short.

Sarah stood with Charles Kenton, a smile on her face. Then Kenton said something that caused the smile to fade from her face. Jealousy, sharp and possessive, shot through Dev.

He stalked forward. 'I see you've met my wife, Kenton.' It took all his discipline to hang on to his temper.

They both started, obviously too engrossed in their conversation to have noticed him. Sarah paled. Kenton merely looked at him in his calm manner. 'Yes, I have had the pleasure of making Lady Huntington's acquaintance. I found her on my property. She had lost her way. So, I brought her back.'

On Kenton's property? She must have walked more than four miles. He fixed her with his most formidable look. 'What were you doing so far from the house?'

He was startled to see brief anger flash in her eyes, but she lifted her chin and stared back at him, her expression defiant. 'I merely wished to see the property and I went too far, my lord.'

My lord? He reined in his temper. Aware that Kenton was observing them with more than a little interest, he turned to Kenton. 'Thank you,' he said dismissively. 'I will see to her.'

'I trust so.' Kenton's gaze held a touch of censure that suddenly reminded him of his housekeeper's. 'If she was my wife, I do not think I would be quite so careless.' He smiled at Sarah and pulled a note from his pocket. He gave it to Sarah, his hand touching hers and lingering far longer than Dev thought proper. 'Lady Huntington, I will see you tomorrow evening. My mother and sister look forward to making your acquaintance.'

'Thank you, Mr Kenton.' She smiled back at him, but it faded as soon as he was out of earshot.

'If you will pardon me, I believe I will go to the house,' she said coolly without looking at Dev.

Dev caught her arm. 'What did he mean, he will see you tomorrow evening? And what is in that note?'

'It is an invitation to dine at Kentwood.'

'You're not going,' he said flatly. 'Furthermore, we are going to discuss this matter now.'

She looked up at him. He nearly reeled under the anger in her face. 'Discuss what matter? The invitation? Very well, I will not go. And will you release me? You are hurting my arm!'

He dropped her arm. 'You are not to leave the house again without a proper escort.'

She merely looked at him. 'So I am to be kept a prisoner, then.' Her voice had that remote calm that made him want to strangle her...or kiss her.

He thrust the thought away. 'Hardly. As long as you have a footman or a maid with you, I have no objections. And as long you stay within the confines of the park.'

'A prisoner, then. Very well, my lord.' She glared at him, clutching her drawing pad to her chest as if it was armour. 'If that is all, I shall return to my cell!' She whirled around and stalked off.

He started to reach for her again and dropped his hand. 'Sarah!' She paid no heed and he caught up with her in a few long strides. 'Listen to me!'

She stopped and stared at him. 'Why? I suppose you wish to tell me I cannot leave the house! Or perhaps my room without suitable escort!'

'No! Damn it all! Do you think I am so unreasonable?'

Her eyes flashed with barely suppressed fury. 'Yes! And will you please refrain from…from swearing at me?'

'I beg your pardon. It is only…' He paused and glared back at her. 'I hadn't the least idea where you were when I returned to the house. Mrs Humphries said you'd been gone nearly three hours and I thought…'

'Yes?' She raised her chin in challenge. 'Perhaps you would finish your sentence, my lord!'

He took refuge in his scowl. 'You were lost.' He was hardly going to admit he feared she had decided to run away.

'I was, but Mr Kenton kindly brought me home.'

The mention of Kenton irritated him more. 'That is the point. You are not fit to take off on these damnable rambles. Nor do I want you consorting with Kenton.'

'Oh? I am not fit? Are you accusing me of insanity?'

'Hardly, my dear,' he ground out.

'And what is wrong with Mr Kenton? He seems perfectly respectable.'

'He is.' Except the thought of him escorting Sarah home made Dev want to run his respectable, well-mannered neighbour through. He would have to be nearly senile not to notice Kenton's interest in her. He ran a hand through his hair. What the hell was happening to his iron control? He was beginning to feel as if his own sanity was in danger of slipping. 'Next time Kenton may not be around to rescue you. What if you met someone less respectable?' The flicker of uncertainty in her eye made him press forward. 'Nor do you know the area. What if you were hurt? And every time you've gone off by yourself in the past few weeks you've ended up in some sort of trouble.'

The militant light extinguished. 'Very well, you have made your point. I will not go out unattended.' Her voice was subdued and she looked utterly defeated.

That wasn't what he wanted either. In truth, he was beginning to feel like her gaoler. 'Why did you walk so far?'

'I wanted to see some of the estate. And the old tower,' she said quietly.

'If that's it—' he frowned '—Dalton can take you.' And then he had a sudden vision of Kenton meeting her there. The tower sat on the line of the two properties. 'I'll take you,' he said shortly.

She stiffened and looked away. 'There is no need to trouble yourself.'

'I'm not. And we'll both dine at Kentwood tomorrow evening.'

She glanced at him, a little frown on her brow. 'Are you not leaving for London today?'

'My business can wait. I'll show you the estate tomorrow.' He had no intention of leaving her to wander around on her own. The prospect suddenly seemed too dangerous. And he had no idea why.

* * *

Nicholas threw down his cards and rose, too restless to sit. Adam glanced at him and quirked his brow. 'Finished al- ready? You've not yet relieved me of my purse.'

'I make it a practice to leave my relations with something,' Nicholas said lightly.

Adam's brow inched up. 'A recent practice, I take it. Can't remember you've concerned yourself with that before.'

'I am attempting to reform.' He gave Adam a half-grin and wandered out of the small room and towards the assembly hall where a ball was in progress. He watched for a moment, ignoring the coy glances cast his way by a trio of giggling young ladies. Since Mary's death, he'd experienced little desire to do even the minimum social niceties. He walked through the French windows and out on the balcony overlooking the dark drive below.

Someone stepped out behind him.

He turned to find Blanton at his elbow. Blanton smiled. 'Ah, Lord Thayne. I have not seen you since the Henslowe ball.'

'I've been away,' Nicholas said briefly. Cedric Blanton was not a man he wished to converse with at any length.

'Have you? I am soon to leave myself in a few days. To attend a houseparty at Harrowood, Sir Ralph Filby's estate in Kent. Very near the house where your unfortunate sister now resides.'

Nicholas glance sharpened. 'Why do you say unfortunate?'

Blanton smiled in his bland, ingratiating way. 'Why, the circumstances of her marriage. To be coerced to marry a man, particularly one she must detest, because he forced his attentions upon her.'

'And how did you come to that conclusion?' Nicholas asked tightly.

If Blanton noticed the dangerous light in Nicholas's eyes, he ignored it. 'I must own I was there. Even now, I berate myself for not coming to your sister's aid, particularly when I saw her bodice was torn as she struggled in Huntington's grasp. Alas, Lord and Lady Henslowe arrived before I could make myself known.'

Nicholas stared at him, barely containing his urge to shove Blanton against the wall. 'I should throttle you if what you've said is true. If not, you're to keep your damnable speculations to yourself.'

'Of course, my lord. I should not wish to harm your sister's reputation.' But his eyes held an odd satisfaction that roused Nicholas's suspicions.

None the less, he intended to find out the truth of the matter. He quit the balcony and left the assembly. If what Blanton hinted was true, he'd kill Huntington.

Lord Monteville was in his study, seated behind his desk. He removed his spectacles when Nicholas stalked into the room and regarded his grandson with mild curiosity. 'The assembly has finished so soon?'

'No.' Nicholas strode towards the desk and stood looking down at his grandparent. 'I met Blanton tonight. He told me Huntington forced his attentions on Sarah during Henslowe's ball. He claimed he was a witness. I'd hardly believe the man except he said her bodice was torn. And no one knew that except our family.' He gave a short laugh. 'Damnation, I've no idea why I accepted Sarah's explanation that she had ripped her bodice with her brooch.' His mouth tightened. 'If this has a hint of truth to it, I will put a bullet through Huntington.'

Monteville rose, still calm. 'Save your bullet. It is true in part, although Blanton has reversed the roles.' He raised his hand. 'My dear boy, before you rush away to avenge your sister's honour, hear me out.'

Nicholas forced himself to listen. When Monteville finished, he swore. 'I wonder you did not call Blanton out yourself. I nearly went for his throat tonight. I regret I did not.'

'I find violence rarely serves a purpose, and in this case, Blanton was quite neatly thwarted. However, I do not trust him. He has a deplorable habit of attempting to wed heiresses by foul methods. I was informed by the lady's parent himself that Huntington foiled another such plot of Blanton's last year. I rather suspect Blanton does not wish Huntington well. Which perhaps explains why he decided to tell his tale to you.'

Nicholas gave a short laugh. 'In hopes I'd shoot Huntington, I suppose.' His brow snapped down. 'Do you suspect him of the attack on Huntington?'

'I am certain of it, although I do not yet have positive proof.'

'He also informed me tonight he will be at Sir Ralph Filby's for a houseparty.'

An arrested look appeared in Monteville's eye. 'Will he? I did not know that.' He frowned. 'I wonder what his purpose is.' He looked at Nicholas. 'Have you an invitation to Sir Ralph's?'

'I may have, but I've no intention of going. I have

yet to meet a worse set of toad-eaters under one roof.'

'I think, however, that you will overcome your aversion to toad-eaters and go to Kent.'

Nicholas stared at him and then laughed shortly. 'Will I? Very well, sir. Although I doubt if Huntington will exactly welcome me into the neighbourhood with open arms.'

'You may be surprised. I suspect your sister may wield more influence over Huntington than you think.'

Nicholas smiled grimly. 'That remains to be seen.'

Chapter Eleven

$\mathbf{S}$arah smoothed down the skirt of her drab riding habit. It had been made shortly before that fateful ball. The ball that divided her life into two radically different halves. She picked up the matching hat from her bed, wishing she did not feel so much trepidation. It was not precisely the emotion she'd imagined feeling at the prospect of meeting her husband. But then, she had always thought she would be in love with her husband, and her love would be reciprocated.

She put on her hat and tied the ribbons. There was nothing to fear. He would probably be his usual high-handed self and make it perfectly clear she was nothing but a bother. Which hardly explained why he'd suddenly decided to show her the tower instead of his steward. Perhaps he thought she would try to escape Mr Dalton and lose herself again.

She started at the knock on her door. She opened it. Her pulse leaped when she saw Dev.

'I thought I would see if you were ready,' he said with studied indifference.

'I…yes. Except for my gloves.' She stepped back,

her pulse fluttering, and hoped he would not see how flustered she felt. 'I just need to find them.'

She went to her dressing table and finally located her kid gloves. When she turned, she saw he had stepped into her room and was looking around.

'The room is different,' he said slowly. 'It looks very comfortable.'

'Perhaps you mean untidy,' Sarah said, even more disconcerted that he would find her room in such disorder. She had not put all her paints away and a book lay open on her bedside table. At least her blue and white vase was filled with fresh flowers.

He slanted a smile at her. 'Not at all. Comfortable and very nice.' He moved to inspect one of the watercolours she had hung on the wall. 'Is this one of yours?'

'Yes. It is a picture of the garden of our house in Lancashire. We…Nicholas and I, grew up there.'

'It is very good.' He glanced over at her. 'When did you go to live at Monteville House?'

'Shortly after my mother died, three years ago. My grandfather kindly offered us a home with him.' It no longer hurt as much to speak of her mother's death.

'Why ''kindly''?' he asked.

'My father had severed all connections with my grandfather after he married my mother. My grandfather did not approve of the match. My mother was only a vicar's daughter and my father had nearly been betrothed to the daughter of a duke when he ran off with my mother. It was a horrible scandal at the time, I believe.' At least according to her mother's eldest sister, who had taken great delight in regaling Sarah with the details. Her mother had never spoken much of it, or of her husband's highborn family, even after his death when Sarah was twelve. What little she had heard about her grandfather had made her dread the prospect of meeting him. But, despite his formidable appearance, he had turned out to be quite kind and regretted the years of estrangement from his only son's family.

'We have something in common, then,' he said. 'I believe I told that you my father's family did not approve of my mother.'

'Yes,' she said a little sadly. 'It seems rather a waste, does it not? I cannot think of a kinder, more loving or wise person than my mother. She was a lady in every way that matters. I think my grandfather would have liked her very much.' She glanced at him. 'And I think that you held your mother in a similar regard.'

'I did.' He looked away for a moment. 'Shall we go, then?'

'Yes, perhaps we should.' She moved past him into the hall.

The groom had already saddled two horses. One was a chestnut Sarah recognised as Dev's and the other a slightly smaller bay. The groom, Jerrick, was a middle-aged man with grey hair and a long, lined face. However, a quick smile lit up his rather sober features when he spoke to Dev. Sarah could see the evident fondness and respect he held for his employer. As, she was beginning to discover, all his servants did.

'I have saddled Perceval for you,' Jerrick told her. 'He's not too difficult to handle, but has a bit of spirit so he won't rock you to sleep.'

Sarah smiled. 'I am certain he will be fine.' She patted the gelding's neck, liking the intelligent expression in his fine dark eyes. Her spirits lifted a little. The day was slightly overcast but warm and she found she actually looked forward to a ride through the countryside.

They left the stable yard and started along the lane that ran along one side of the property. When the lane widened enough to accommodate two horses, Dev slowed his mount down until she was alongside.

He looked over at her. 'Mrs Dalton would like to make your acquaintance. Would you object to calling on her first?'

Sarah smiled at him. As usual, he was hatless, the breeze ruffling his dark hair. His face appeared relaxed today, as if he also looked forward to the outing. 'Of course not. I should like to meet her. They have a new baby, do they not?'

He looked surprised. 'How do you know that?'

'Sally told me.'

'Sally?' One brow quirked.

'She is one of the housemaids.'

'I see.' He frowned.

He probably disliked her gossiping with the servants. Half-expecting him to take her to task over it, she was startled by his next words. 'Are you finding everything to your comfort?'

She hesitated. 'Yes.'

'But not everything. What troubles you?'

She decided to plunge ahead. 'I have no idea what you expect from me.'

'What do you mean?' He looked at her sharply.

'I feel rather like a barely tolerated houseguest. Do you wish me to do anything useful?'

'Useful?' His expression was startled. 'Such as?'

'Well, the sort of things a…a wife usually does. Household things, that is.' In case he thought she was hinting at something else. 'I have done nothing at all. Mrs Humphries has everything running very smoothly and I know Jessica will soon return, but I dislike being so idle. Not that I am complaining, for you have an excellent library, and I have been drawing, but I feel rather useless.'

He pulled his horse to an abrupt halt. Perceval obligingly stopped as well. Dev leaned forward, his expression incredulous. 'You are saying you wish to run my household?'

She flushed, feeling as if she'd just demanded that he hand over the family jewels. 'Well, no. That is, I hardly wish to impose, but…' Her voice trailed away and she fervently wished she'd never brought the matter up.

'You are not.' He looked at her oddly. 'It never occurred to me. Jessica has managed most of the household in the past few years and, as you have noticed, Mrs Humphries is extremely efficient. Perhaps too much so at times.' He considered her for a moment and a brief smile touched his mouth. 'So, if you're game, my dear, you may take over. I will inform Mrs Humphries she is to report to you.'

'Are you certain?' She had not expected it to be so easy.

His brow shot up. 'Cold feet now, Sarah?'

'No.' She lifted her chin and looked at him.

'Good.' One of his rare, unexpected smiles crossed his face, causing her to catch her breath. 'And if you can persuade Cook to serve something besides fowl in some form, I'd be most grateful.'

'I…I will.' She found herself smiling back at him. She heard his sharp intake of breath as his smile faded and his gaze locked with hers. She knew, at that moment, he felt the same awareness of her that she had of him.

He looked away first. 'We'd best go,' he said and for once she was glad of his abrupt manner.

Sarah followed Nancy Dalton's plump figure around the corner of the neat, thatched cottage. Sarah held a grey tabby cat that had been weaving around her feet since their arrival at the cottage. Now he was snuggled into Sarah's arms, his eyes half-closed and his purr the most rumbling one she had ever heard.

'I dare say his lordship is out here,' Mrs Dalton said over her shoulder. 'Hannah and Will, they had some kittens to show him.'

'How nice,' Sarah said faintly, trying to imagine Dev viewing kittens. Of course, she'd hardly expected the two young Dalton children, six-year-old Hannah and her four-year-old brother, Will, to launch themselves at him with shrieks of delight despite their mother's embarrassed admonition to 'show his lordship the proper respect'. Nor to allow Hannah to take his hand and drag him out of the cottage, Will happily babbling away at his other side.

And Sarah had found herself on a wooden bench, holding a two-week-old baby while Mrs Dalton chattered about everything and nothing in particular and Sarah learned more about the parish in a quarter of an hour than she had in the week since her arrival. The baby had fallen asleep in Sarah's arms and Mrs Dalton then announced he could be laid in his cradle and they'd best find his lordship before the children talked him to death. 'They adore him,' she explained. 'He sometimes brings them sweets and the like, but more than that he pays heed to their nonsense. Men often do not.'

The sight of Dev with a black kitten climbing up his elegant coat, the children bouncing around him, hardly helped her equilibrium. Hannah spotted them first and clapped her hands. 'Mama! Look! Patience likes him!'

He turned, his eyes meeting Sarah's with an almost helpless expression. 'I can't get the thing off.'

'How…how dreadful!' She nearly laughed but instead she walked over to him. She set down the grey cat who gave her a reproachful meow.

'It is really very simple.' She gently tugged on the kitten, which mewed in protest and sank its tiny claws in further. She looked up at Dev. 'I am afraid Hannah is right, it likes you. You may be forced to wear a kitten as an ornament.'

'Sarah,' he said warningly, 'I don't like cats.' His eyes glinted down at hers and she suddenly felt rather dizzy.

'Oh, very well.' She gently disengaged the little creature's front claws and pulled the kitten away, careful not to hurt its tiny paws. She handed it to Hannah.

Her grey friend meowed and stared up at her. She picked him up and he began to purr again. Dev watched her, his brow arched. She smiled a little and stroked the cat's head. 'He reminds me a little of a cat I had when I was a girl. She was my best friend.'

A smile tugged at his mouth. 'He seems to regard you in the same light. However, we'd best go,' he said.

The children flung themselves at him for a final farewell. Over their heads, Mrs Dalton gave him a sly smile. 'I expect you will soon be setting up your own nursery, my lord.'

Sarah's face heated. Dev froze, the expression on his face dumbfounded. 'I…yes,' he said. Faint colour stained his cheeks.

If it weren't that the topic was so uncomfortable, Sarah would have laughed at his discomfort.

Instead, they made their farewells and left the cottage in awkward silence. He finally looked over at her, his expression stiff. 'I hope Mrs Dalton's speculations did not overset you too much. I, of course, do not intend to…er, set up a nursery.'

'I suppose it is a natural assumption when two people are married.' At least her voice was calm and logical despite the fact that her insides felt as heated as her cheeks had been earlier.

'Yes.' His voice had a peculiar note. She glanced at him and was surprised to see he still looked embarrassed. 'We're nearly at the tower,' he said, the relief evident in his voice.

They had come to a pasture where a flock of sheep peacefully cropped the grass. The grey stones of the tower stood at the opposite end of the field. She was surprised to see there was a good portion of remaining wall attached to the tall structure.

The sheep paid little heed as the horses cut across the green field, one or two lifting their heads to look at them curiously. As they drew closer, she could see the wall was actually part of a small building.

They halted near the tower. Dev dismounted and came to Perceval's side. He looked up at her. 'Come down.'

She gazed down into his dark green eyes with the sudden awareness they were completely alone. She hesitated and then slid off. Her skirt caught a little in the saddle and she fell against his chest. Her hat slipped to one side. His arms closed around her and, for a moment, she could hear the strong beat of his heart and smell his unique scent. And then it occurred to her he was making no effort to release her, nor was she making any effort to free herself.

She yanked away, hot colour rising to her cheeks. 'I…I beg your pardon.'

'Not at all.' His eyes were hooded, hiding his expression.

But he'd retreated back behind his wall. He gathered the reins of both horses in his hand. 'We can secure the horses at the back. And then eat.'

He waited for her to fall into step beside him. 'Eat?' She still felt a little dazed.

'Yes. There's a picnic.'

'A picnic?'

He slanted an amused look at her. 'Perhaps you've heard of them? Food and drink taken outside, often in a rural setting.'

'I was merely inquiring how a picnic came to be here. But perhaps you have some exceptional sheep.'

His mouth twitched. 'Was that your question? I fear I misunderstood. And, no, my sheep are quite ordinary. The picnic was brought in a very unexceptional manner by my groom.'

At least they were back on familiar ground. They skirted around the side of the building and came to a wall. A gate led into a small enclosed garden, which seemed to be surprisingly well tended. Dev secured the horses to a ring in the wall and they stepped through the gate. Dev turned to her. 'There is a bench near the wall. You may sit while I see to the food.'

'Do you need any assistance?' she asked.

'No. I'll return in a moment.'

She found the iron bench located next to the wall and by a small patch of fragrant lavender. She watched Dev cross the paved courtyard to speak to a groom who had appeared from the other side, while her thoughts returned to Mrs Dalton's comment.

She had been mortified, but her mortification was due to much more than the modesty of a new wife. The entire hypocrisy of their marriage had struck her with full force. The hypocrisy of pretending there was a marriage where none existed. Of allowing others to believe there might be a child when there never would be. And had Dev ever considered that, by marrying her under those terms, there would be no heir?

She sighed and leaned against the wall. She could not see how this sham of a marriage had solved anything. They had both been thrust into a sort of purgatory with no possibility of redemption.

Dev watched Sarah pick at her apricot tart. They sat on a cloth under a spreading tree, the remains of the lunch between them. She had appeared distracted during most of the meal, saying little. Not that he'd been much better, except his distraction had to do with her. Ever since Nancy Dalton's unfortunate remark about setting up a nursery, he had thought of little else. The image of her holding a child, their child, was unexpectedly erotic.

His eyes took in the soft curve of her cheek, the tendrils of auburn hair that escaped from under her hat, the delicate line of her nose. Her severely cut riding habit only emphasised her slender curves. He could still feel the way her delicate body felt against his when she fell against him. He'd wanted nothing more than to crush her to him, moulding her body to his, possessing her mouth until she surrendered to him.

He stood abruptly, needing to move before he gave in to his unwelcome desire. 'When you are finished we can return to the house.'

She glanced up at him. 'Very well.' Her voice was as carefully civil as his, her expression schooled into indifference. Then she laid her napkin aside and rose. 'Actually, I have finished. Shall we go?'

'We could.' His glance fell to a small orange speck near her mouth. 'However, you are still wearing some of your tart.'

'I am? Oh!' She coloured and dabbed at her mouth with the back of her hand, missing the crumbs entirely.

'Allow me.' Without thinking, he reached over and with his thumb gently brushed the offending remainder of tart from her cheek. Her skin was as soft and silky smooth as that of a rose petal. His eyes fell to her slightly parted lips, which seemed to invite his kiss.

Her breath caught, her brown eyes widening, but she didn't move. 'Is it gone?'

'Not quite.' He stepped closer, unable to stop himself. 'There is a little more, just to the right.' He lightly circled the spot with his thumb and forefinger, feeling as if he was playing with fire.

'Is…is it gone now?' Her voice was barely above

a whisper. Her eyes were on him, almost as if she were mesmerised.

'Yes,' he said, his voice husky. He started to cup her cheek and then jerked his hand back. He would be violating the terms of their marriage. 'We should go,' he said curtly.

When they returned to the house, he was astounded to find the entry hall filled with an assortment of trunks and portmanteaus. Before he could say anything, Jessica stepped out of his study, wearing a dark green carriage dress, a delighted smile brightening her face when she saw them. 'I am so sorry I did not write that I was coming! It was rather impulsive, I fear. I suddenly had the most urgent need to return and see how you were getting on! I hope it is not too inconvenient!'

'Oh, no!' Surprise crossed Sarah's face. 'This is your home. It could never be inconvenient.' She went forward and took Jessica's outstretched hands. 'I am so very glad to see you.' Her voice shook a little with some emotion Dev could not quite identify. But he had no doubt she found Jessica's arrival very welcome.

And the damnable thing was, he had no idea if he felt the same way or not.

Chapter Twelve

Jessica had declared herself quite fit to dine at Kentwood that evening. Now, she smiled across at Dev from her place beside Sarah in the coach. Sarah was amazed she could look so pretty and fresh in her rose gown and not at all as if she had spent a good four hours in a coach. 'It was not as difficult to escape from Aunt as I had feared,' Jessica said. 'I told her that Sarah undoubtedly needed me to instruct her on managing Ravensheed and Mrs Humphries. And when I said that Mrs Humphries was probably riding roughshod over Sarah, she insisted I must leave at once.' She flashed a smile at Sarah. 'She and Mrs Humphries quite dislike each other and Aunt could not bear the thought that she might get the upper hand over you. I hope Mrs Humphries has not been too difficult.' Jessica had been chattering in an artless manner since they had left Ravensheed, something Sarah was grateful for as Dev had lapsed into one of his abstracted silences.

'No, at least not yet,' Sarah said. Probably because she had not yet interfered with Mrs Humphries much. She had no idea how Mrs Humphries would react when Dev told her she was to take orders from Sarah, although the housekeeper's demeanour had softened a trifle towards her since being presented with the painting.

The carriage halted in the drive in front of Kentwood Hall, a square red-bricked house. They alighted from the carriage and, after being admitted to the house, were shown to a pleasant drawing room. Several others were already present, Lady Coleridge among them. Charles Kenton broke away from the group and, after greeting them, turned to Sarah. 'My mother and sister wish to make your acquaintance.'

She caught a quick glimpse of the frown on Dev's brow before introductions were made to Mrs Kenton, a slender middle-aged woman with a pleasant air, and his sister Caroline, a pretty girl whose grey eyes and quick smile looked very much like her brother's.

Sarah liked both of them very much. She smiled at Mrs Kenton. 'You have a lovely home.'

Mrs Kenton looked pleased. 'Why, thank you. 'Tis not as grand as Ravensheed, but we are very comfortable here. Do you like gardening? I have a conservatory of which I am very proud.'

'Mama is always in there, her hands quite dirty while she tends to her plants. Sometimes I think she cares more for them than her pug,' Caroline said teasingly. She smiled at Sarah. 'She is hoping you will ask to see it.'

'I would be delighted to do so,' Sarah said.

'Then perhaps after dinner.' Charles smiled at her. She returned his smile, wondering why he should be so easy to talk to and her husband so difficult.

She glanced over at Dev, who stood with a thin young man whose elaborately tied cravat and elegant dress proclaimed the dandy. Dev met her gaze, a look of displeasure on his face.

Oh, dear. Now what was wrong? She hurriedly looked away. Did he really object to her conversing with Mr Kenton so much? But it made no sense unless he was jealous and that was hardly possible. Another, more disquieting, reason occurred to her. Did he mistrust her? Think that she, too, would seek solace in another man's arms?

The thought hurt. She turned away, trying to attend to what Mrs Kenton was saying.

Mrs Kenton paused at the sound of footsteps outside the drawing room. She looked over expectantly. 'That must be Mr Branley's friend. He is staying with us tonight before he goes to a house party at Harrowood tomorrow. I think you will be glad to see him, Lady Huntington. He is from your neighbourhood.'

Sarah turned so that she could see the new guest…then froze as Cedric Blanton entered the drawing room.

Dev returned to the drawing room with the rest of the men. They had just finished a tedious discussion about the Prince Regent's latest extravagances and then gone on to argue over the best shooting spots in the neighbourhood. Between Blanton's presence and his impatience to see Sarah, Dev had paid scant heed to the conversation.

He glanced around and spotted his wife standing with Mrs Kenton and Lady Coleridge. Sarah wore a sky blue gown that draped enticingly over her slender curves and he'd barely been able to keep his eyes off her during dinner. As he watched, her lips curved in her warm smile at something Mrs Kenton said.

To the devil with his decision to stay away from her. He started across the room, only to see Kenton reach her first. He spoke to her and she nodded. And then the three of them left the drawing room.

Jealousy, pure and hot, seared him. No matter that a third person was with them. Where the hell was she going with Kenton? And what the devil did he mean by making eyes at another man's wife?

Every instinct he possessed shouted he should go after them, shove Kenton up against a wall and yank Sarah to him, kissing her until she wanted nothing but him.

The violence of his emotion brought him up short. What was wrong with him? He rubbed the back of his neck. He could hardly behave like a savage, thrashing his neighbours, forcing his lust upon his wife. She would grow to detest him even more than she probably did.

Better to think of something else. Such as why Blanton was suddenly here. He shifted his attention to where the man stood with Caroline Kenton, smiling at her in his ingratiating way. With her usual good manners, Caroline listened to what he said, although it was clear from the glazed expression in her eyes she would prefer to be elsewhere.

Dev frowned. Blanton had greeted Sarah in an overly polite manner, which Dev did not trust. More than once during dinner and in the dining room after the women had withdrawn, Dev had caught Blanton observing him with ill-concealed malice. He strongly suspected Blanton's presence here was no mere coincidence.

Lady Coleridge appeared at his side. 'There is no need to look so grim. This is a social engagement, not a hanging.'

'I beg your pardon,' he said stiffly.

She laid an elegantly gloved hand on his sleeve. 'Come and walk with me for a moment. I thought perhaps the veranda.'

A smile quirked his mouth. 'If you wish, although I fear you have something of a serious nature to discuss.'

She smiled back at him. 'Yes, rather. But not a scolding,' she added.

'I am relieved to hear that.'

They proceeded to the veranda overlooking the dark garden. She dropped her hand away and went to stand near the iron railing. He folded his arms and looked at her. 'What is it?'

'Your marriage.' She smiled a little at his expression. 'My dear Devin, I wish you all happiness, I always have. You have, indeed, been as a son to me.'

He glanced at the garden for a moment. 'You are far too kind. Particularly in light of all that has happened.' He could not understand why she had not reproached him for Mary's death, why she seemed to hold him blameless.

She sighed. 'No, I am not. I am actually quite selfish. If I knew you were happy, then I could perhaps forgive myself a little.'

He looked at her, not understanding what she meant.

She touched his arm. 'I think, if you will allow it, your marriage could be your salvation.'

'My salvation? I had no idea I was such a desperate case.' He kept his voice light.

'Not yet. But I don't want you to retreat any more than you have. Or to drive Sarah away from you.'

When he said nothing, she made an exasperated sound. 'I can see you intend to be stubborn about this. Very well, I won't press you now.' She glanced toward the doors. 'Shall we go in? Perhaps it is time we retrieve Sarah from Charles.'

His mouth curled cynically. 'I somehow doubt she wants that.'

'I am quite certain she would rather be at your side. But I will give you a warning—you must be careful you do not inadvertently push her Charles's way. He is offering her friendship and she is lonely. And that is dangerous.'

'And this is the conservatory,' Charles said. He stepped aside and allowed Sarah to proceed past him into the circular room attached to the rear of the house. They had looked at the library first and then Mrs Kenton had been called away to address a minor problem with the guest bedchambers. She had insisted that they go on to the conservatory without her.

The conservatory was filled with potted trees and flowering shrubs, the air heavy with unfamiliar sweet, spicy scents. Although it was now dark, a few lamps had been lit and the room had the appearance of a moonlit garden. 'How magical,' Sarah said, gazing around.

Charles smiled. 'It is. And very romantic. At least that is what my sister tells me.'

'Oh.' Sarah felt a little uncomfortable, although his voice was light. Somehow it seemed rather improper to talk of such things with a man not her husband. And she felt a vague disappointment that it was not Dev with her in this lovely room.

But that was ridiculous. Dev had no desire to spend any time with her in such a place. Even if he had touched her face in such an intimate way at the tower, his eyes darkening with some emotion that left her breathless. She shoved the thought away. It had undoubtedly been some sort of aberration on his part.

She realised Charles had spoken. 'I beg your pardon, I am afraid I was not attending.'

'I merely asked if you want to see some of my mother's more exotic plants?'

She smiled at him and shook her head. 'Perhaps another time. I think perhaps we should return to the others.' As kind as he was, she did not feel comfortable alone with him for very long.

'Of course.' He looked down at her. 'I have enjoyed your company very much.' He hesitated. 'Perhaps I should not speak, but I sense you are not all together happy.'

Sarah attempted a smile. 'I am fine.'

His eyes searched her face. 'If you need a friend, I am here.'

'Thank you. You are more than kind.' But his kindness only served to make her more aware of the enormous gulf between Dev and herself.

She started and flushed at the sound of footsteps, feeling as if she'd been caught in an indecent act. And then her cheeks burned when she saw Lady Coleridge with Dev behind her. His face wore the same unreadable expression it had all evening.

Lady Coleridge smiled as if nothing was amiss. 'Prudence told us you had gone to view the conservatory, so we thought we'd join you as well.' She laid a hand on Charles's sleeve. 'However, I must own I am rather fatigued. Charles, would you mind taking me back to the drawing room?'

'Not at all,' he said politely. He glanced at Sarah, but obediently held out his arm. They left the room.

The silence was tangible. Sarah finally stole a look at Dev, half expecting him to take her to task over going away with Charles Kenton. Instead he asked, 'Did you enjoy your tour with Kenton?'

'Yes. We really only saw the library and then came here.'

'I see.' He paced away from her and then turned to look at her. 'You seemed to get on well with him.'

'I suppose so.' She had no idea what he was getting at. 'Although he is barely an acquaintance. I've only seen him but twice.' She sighed. 'Is there something you wish to say to me?'

He frowned and folded his arms. 'I suppose if you weren't trapped in this marriage he would be the sort of man that would interest you.' His voice was carelessly indifferent.

Her mouth fell open. And a surge of pure hot anger shot through her. 'If you must know, he is not.' Her voice shook, but she looked squarely at him. 'I would like, my lord, to return to the drawing room.' And she whirled away, not caring if he followed or not.

Chapter Thirteen

Jessica smiled over at Sarah from across the breakfast table. 'You did very well. Mrs Humphries is not too terribly difficult to manage if you just remember to always ask her advice on a matter while at the same time suggesting what you want. She will almost always agree with you. She merely wants to feel important!'

'And she almost smiled,' Sarah said with no little astonishment. It was the first time since her arrival that a movement had touched the lips of the dour housekeeper which could possibly be termed a smile.

Jessica reached for a piece of toast. 'She quite approves of you.'

'Whatever makes you say that?' Although Mrs Humphries had dutifully appeared at the door of the library nearly a week ago to tell Sarah that 'his lordship says I am to take orders from you,' there had been nothing in her demeanour that suggested approval. Since Sarah had spent most of the time quizzing Jessica on the intricacies of running Ravensheed, she probably thought Sarah was incapable of doing so herself.

'She told me so.' Jessica buttered her toast. 'Yesterday. She owned that, although she experienced severe misgivings the day he arrived with you on his arm, she thinks you've been an influence for the good on his soul.'

Sarah nearly choked on the tea she had just sipped. Perhaps Mrs Humphries was delusional as well as dour. 'I...I see.' Since Jessica's arrival, he had been even more distant than before. Except for meals, she rarely saw him.

Which was just as well. His remark at the conservatory at Kentwood had hurt her deeply. He had made it very clear he did not trust her.

'Sarah?'

Jessica's voice recalled her to her surroundings. 'I am sorry, I was daydreaming.'

'Again?' Her eyes held a hint of teasing. 'You are as bad as Dev. Since my return, I've noticed he fades off into the same sort of trance in the middle of a conversation.'

'Does he?' Sarah tried to keep her voice indifferent.

'Yes.' Jessica's smile faded. 'I've tried to persuade him to come riding with us, but he says he is too busy. I think it's merely that he is afraid.'

'Afraid? What would he be afraid of?'

'You.'

This time Sarah nearly knocked her teacup over. She withdrew her hand. 'Me? But why?'

'He likes you. It scares him.'

Sarah tried to smile. 'I should hope he likes me a little. We...we did marry.' Any pretence of being in love had gone badly by the wayside. It was difficult to keep up when one of the parties was absent.

'Oh, Sarah.' Jessica's voice held sympathy. 'After the wedding, I began to suspect that you were forced to marry him. I know it cannot be easy—I dearly love Dev, but he can be so difficult. He wasn't always like this. Oh, he could be quite provoking—he was rather wild and could be so terribly stubborn. But at least he seemed to care about things! And then Mary died and he shut himself away for months. I have sometimes worried he does not intend to care about anything again!'

'But he cares about you,' Sarah said softly. The pain in Jessica's face tore at her heart.

'He does. But it is not enough.' She looked swiftly at Sarah. 'I have worried terribly about leaving him here. Which is why I told Adam I did not wish to marry right away.' A little smile crossed her face. 'And then Dev told me he was to marry you and I knew he would be safe.'

'How can you possibly say that?' Sarah asked unhappily. 'He is always so excessively polite except when he is dictating to me. Most of the time I feel rather like a…a stray kitten he's been forced to take in. And he said he does not like cats.'

Jessica giggled. 'I don't think he regards you as a stray kitten at all. I knew he liked you, even when we were in London. But he doesn't want to.'

'I see. He likes me against his better judgement.' The thought was hardly comforting.

'Oh, Sarah! You are as bad as my brother.' She giggled and then sobered. 'I think it is because of…of your brother, but more than that, he is afraid of being hurt again.'

Sarah was puzzled. How could she possibly have any power to hurt him? Such hurt could only come from a strong attachment. 'He must have loved Mary very much.'

Jessica's brow puckered. 'I don't know. Perhaps.' But there was a doubt in her voice that puzzled Sarah. 'Their marriage was arranged. My father and her father had wanted the match since Mary was born so it was expected they would wed as soon as Mary had her first season. I do not think either one of them ever thought about falling in love.'

Sarah said nothing more. Somehow, prying into the relationship between a husband and wife seemed wrong, as if she trod on sacred ground.

Jessica finished her toast and shoved her plate away. She glanced outside. The sky was a lovely cerulean blue with only a few lazy clouds floating overhead. 'Shall we ride today? Perhaps to the tower. Did you climb up inside when you went with Dev?'

'No. We did not have time.'

'Then we will today. The view is magnificent, Sarah. You can see everywhere.' She grinned. 'And Dev will come with us.'

'I doubt if he'll agree.' He would probably rather be dragged behind a runaway carriage than spend an unnecessary minute in her company.

'Oh, he will, particularly when he discovers we're planning to climb the tower.' Jessica's eyes sparked with mischief. 'He planned to spend the day with Mr Dalton going over accounts. We'll send him a note just before we leave the stables. He will be there almost before we will.'

'Jessica, I really don't think that is wise. He'll probably be furious.'

'Well, yes, a little. But he is leaving for London tomorrow. How else will we ever see him? And how will he ever realise there is no need to be afraid of you?' She looked mischievous again.

'Jessica,' Sarah said weakly, 'I really have no desire to put myself in his way.'

'I see. You're afraid of him also.'

'I really am not.'

'Then why don't you want to see him?'

'I do see him. At dinner.'

'But that is not properly seeing him,' Jessica said. She pushed back her chair. 'Come, Sarah, he's really not so dreadful and it will be fun. Besides he knows all the history. He can tell you all the most boring details about all of our very dull ancestors. I suspect you like that sort of thing.'

'Yes, but, Jessica…' Sarah heaved a sigh. Her sister-in-law's sweet countenance had a stubborn expression that was remarkably like her brother's when he wanted something.

'Don't worry.' She patted Sarah's arm. 'Nothing bad will happen.'

Dev tore open the note the footman had just delivered. He perused it quickly and then swore.

Dalton glanced over at him from his place across the table. A large book of accounts lay between them. 'A problem?'

'My sister has decided to take Sarah up the old tower. She knows better, it's damably dangerous unless you've done it a dozen times. I've no idea why she wants to risk Sarah's neck.' However, he strongly suspected Jessica was using it as a ruse to obtain his company. Otherwise, she would have kept quiet.

'Then perhaps you'd best go with them,' Dalton

suggested mildly. 'There is no significant change since we last went over the figures two days ago.' He looked faintly amused as if he knew why Dev had developed a sudden passion for reviewing numbers every day.

Dev scowled. It was bad enough that Jessica had noticed he avoided Sarah, but now his employees did too. He rose, loathe to give into his sister's blackmail, but his concern for Sarah overrode his misgivings. 'I'll return as soon as I sway them from their folly.'

'Of course,' Dalton said, obviously not believing a word he said.

Dev caught up to them just as they were crossing the pasture near the tower. He rode up next to Sarah. 'I am sorry for the delay.'

She gasped and looked at him, a delightful blush rising to her cheeks. 'I…I did not hear you.'

'But weren't you expecting me?' His eyes roved over her face under the becoming hat she wore. The lively colour in her cheeks made her eyes sparkle.

'Not…not exactly.'

His brow shot up. 'No? But I suspect my sister was.' He glanced over at Jessica, who rode on the other side of Sarah.

Jessica merely grinned at him.

They halted the horses near the old wall and tethered them to the rings. He helped Jessica down and then turned to Sarah. She hesitated and then slid into his arms. Unable to resist, he pressed her closer than necessary, the softness of her breast against his chest. His arms tightened around her and then he quickly dropped them away. What was he thinking of? This was why he was trying to avoid her, otherwise he forgot their marriage was nothing but a sham.

She backed away, her cheeks heated. 'Th…thank you.'

'Not at all.' He turned to find Jessica watching them, a quizzical look on her face. He stalked towards her. 'Well, what is it you wanted me for?'

She giggled. 'I never said I wanted you. Only that we were going to visit the tower.'

'Which was tantamount to saying you wanted me since you know you've no business climbing it without me or someone else who knows it well.'

She cocked a brow. 'I thought you'd rather escort us than have me ask Charles Kenton.'

It was all he could do to keep from swearing. He looked down at Sarah, who had come up beside them. 'Well, do you wish to see the tower?' he snapped.

'Only if you wish to show us,' she said politely.

'Since I am here, I might as well.'

Her face closed. 'I really do not want to take up your time. Perhaps Jessica and I can walk by the stream.'

'I will take you,' he said impatiently.

She looked at him, a touch of anger in her face. 'It is very clear that it is quite against your will. I have no intention of forcing you.'

And it was obvious it was against her will to have him do it. He ground his teeth together. 'Very well, then I will return to my business.'

'But…' Jessica began in a subdued little voice.

They both turned to look at her. Her smile had disappeared. She had the same crushed look on her face she would get as a young child when she suffered a bitter disappointment. He suffered a stab of guilt.

He met Sarah's eyes and saw the same guilt cross her face. She lifted her chin and gave him a tight smile. 'I believe I would like a tour after all.'

'Of course. I would be more than delighted.' He held out his arm. It had never occurred to him that the awkwardness…no, the tension between himself and Sarah was affecting Jessica so badly.

Sarah laid her gloved hand lightly on his arm. 'Jessica? Shall we go?'

'Oh, yes.' Jessica's voice was still subdued.

She trailed after them through the gate in the wall and then through the garden. The door to the tower was inside one of the few remaining rooms that had survived the fire. He dropped Sarah's arm and pulled a key from his pocket. He shot his sister a grin. 'This was the other reason you needed me. You forgot the key.'

Jessica had the grace to blush. 'I remembered when we were halfway here, but I thought we could climb through the drawing-room window.'

'We? I trust that does not mean you expected Sarah to climb through a window as well. Not everyone is the monkey you are.'

Sarah shot him a challenging look. 'I assure you that task is not beyond me.'

'It had better be, my dear. I've no intention of carrying your prone body back to the house.'

'So, you would just leave me here, then? I suppose it would not be such a bad place to haunt. Or perhaps you already have a ghost in residence.'

His mouth suddenly quirked in a smile. 'Not that

I know of.' He unlocked the heavy wood door and pushed it open. 'Come in.'

Sarah stepped into the old drawing room, comfortably furnished with a sofa, a table and chairs. She looked up at him, surprise on her face. 'I had no idea it would be so well preserved. It is rather like a small cottage in here.'

'My grandfather had it enclosed. These two rooms were damaged very little except for the smoke. There is one room upstairs that survived although the floor needs repair.'

'How lovely.' She crossed to the fireplace with its elaborately carved wooden mantelpiece and ran her hand over the wood. 'What beautiful carving. When was this house built?'

'In 1698.'

'How sad it burned down.'

'It was. But, fortunately, my grandfather and his family were in London at the time and all of the servants managed to escape unharmed. A very timely rainstorm helped put out the fire before it completely destroyed everything.'

She smiled up at him. 'That was indeed timely. Does anyone ever use the house?'

'Sometimes. My parents often came here when they wanted some privacy. There is a bedchamber connected to this room.'

'Oh.' She flushed. 'It would be very nice for that.'

'Yes.' He looked down at her flushed face and slightly parted lips. An image of her alone with him, shut away from the world together, sprang to his mind. They would dine in this small, cozy room and then he would take her to the heavy bed and...

'Shall we climb the tower now?' Jessica's voice interrupted his lustful thoughts.

'Er, yes.' He glanced at Sarah. 'Are you game?'

'Yes.' She didn't quite meet his eyes. Her face flushed as if she had guessed his less-than-proper thoughts. He nearly groaned. The last thing he wanted to do was let her know how much he wanted her. She'd probably run like the devil himself was after her.

The staircase to the tower was located in a small hallway off the drawing room. Sarah and Jessica waited while Dev went up a few steps. He looked back down at them, his face partially in the shadows. 'Come on,' he said. 'But be very careful.'

'You go first, Sarah,' Jessica said.

Sarah took a tentative step. The wood creaked but seemed solid enough. She held her skirt up and started the climb up the steep, winding staircase. Light filtered down from some sort of window above. On the second turn, Dev stopped and looked back at her. 'Watch the next step.'

She could see where the wood had partially rotted. She carefully stepped over it. The next turn brought them to a small landing. Dev stopped abruptly and she smacked into his back. 'I beg your pardon.'

'Not at all.' He shot her a rather wicked grin. 'You may run into me any time. I rather liked it.'

'Oh.' His unexpected teasing threw her off balance completely. She stared at him and he stared back, his expression slowly changing as it had when they had ridden together.

'Shall we show Sarah the upstairs room?' Jessica

came up behind them, breaking the sudden tension between them.

'There's not much to see, just a small room that was once used as a bedchamber.' Dev opened a door on one side of the landing. He stepped aside so Sarah could peer in. She brushed against his chest, the contact sending an unwelcome spark of awareness through her. She was hardly aware of the small shuttered room.

They continued up the stairs, Dev in front of Sarah. She had no idea why she should suddenly be so aware of his broad shoulders and narrow hips and the curl of his hair over his collar. It was extremely disconcerting. She hoped they would look at the tower and then leave so she could escape him as quickly as possible.

At the top of the staircase was a small hallway with two narrow windows that let in the light. On one side was a heavy wooden door with a key in the lock. Dev turned the key and then frowned. 'The key is nearly worn in half. Another reason why you've no business coming here on your own.' He shoved open the heavy door and entered first. Sarah followed. Jessica peered around Sarah and shuddered. 'Ugh. Cobwebs! There are probably mice too.'

Dev shot her an amused look. 'Probably.'

'Well, I have no desire to see any mice. I will wait downstairs while you show Sarah the view.' She turned on her heel and left, her footsteps echoing down the stairway.

Dev glanced at Sarah and shrugged. 'Do you wish to brave a possible encounter with a mouse?' His voice was carefully nonchalant.

'As long as we are here I would like to see the

view.' It would probably be too obvious if she were to turn tail and run. She looked around the room. It was round and small, the only furnishing a wooden bench. Faded shutters covered the narrow windows.

Dev opened the shutters on one of the windows. Brilliant sunlight poured across the room, transforming it from a rather shabby hole to an enchanted tower. 'Come and see the view,' he said.

She gathered her skirts to keep from brushing against the dilapidated wood bench and moved to the window.

Jessica was right, the view was stunning. The countryside spread out below, the green fields and hedgerows and trees, and pastures dotted with sheep. The sky and the clouds rolled away into the distance where she could see the spire of the village church.'

'What do you think?' He had moved closer to her.

She jumped a little, his nearness making her heart skip. She half-turned and tried to interject a note of lightness in her voice. 'It is beautiful. I don't think I would mind haunting this at all.'

A smile flickered at his lips. 'I hope you are still not offering yourself as the resident ghost. I've no intention of seeing you in that role.'

'I suppose it would be rather confining.'

'Among other things.' He was watching her in a way that made her feel rather light-headed. 'And I much prefer you in the flesh.'

'Do you? I have sometimes wondered.'

His gaze sharpened. 'What do you mean?'

'It is just that…'

The sudden click of the door made them both jump. Dev broke his gaze away. 'What the devil?' He strode to the heavy door and tried the handle. It refused to turn. 'We are locked in here,' he said. His voice held incredulity.

Sarah crossed to his side. 'Are you certain? Perhaps it is merely stuck.'

'We shall see.' He pushed against the door with his shoulder but it refused to budge. After another two tries, he finally looked over at Sarah, a wry twist to his mouth. 'We'll have to hope Jessica soon decides we've been here too long and comes to look for us. Then we'll send her for help.'

'I imagine she will.'

He strode to the bench and pushed it with his foot. It rocked on unsteady legs. 'I doubt if I could use this to batter the door down. It'd probably splinter at the first try.'

'Perhaps we should call for her,' Sarah suggested.

'We can try. Unfortunately, the door is as thick as a castle wall.'

But a round of shouting and pounding brought no results. Dev finally leaned against the door. 'I refuse to believe she's forgotten we are here.' He grimaced. 'I am beginning to feel like one of the idiotic characters in one of Jessica's Gothic romances.'

'As long as we do not see any spectres that drip blood.'

He grinned. 'I certainly hope not. We must hope Jessica comes before it grows dark and we seriously start worrying about such things.'

Sarah smiled and then sobered as a thought struck her. 'Do you suppose she is hurt?'

He frowned. 'It's unlikely. She's more agile than a...' He broke off, a peculiar expression crossing his face. 'Nor does she generally go up in the boughs over mice or cobwebs. She deliberately shut us in here.'

'Why ever would she do that?'

'To force us into each other's company.' He folded his arms across his chest, his mouth curving in a sardonic fashion. 'The other day, in no uncertain terms, she informed me that I do not spend half enough time with you.'

'Did she?' With a sinking heart, she recalled her conversation this morning with Jessica.

'Yes.' He gave a short laugh. 'Apparently I have not been properly fulfilling my role as adoring bride-groom.'

'There is no need to berate yourself,' Sarah said crossly. 'It would not have made much difference. She has already guessed we were forced into marriage with each other.'

He stared at her. 'How do you know that?'

'She told me.' She stared back at him. 'So you see, my lord, there is no need to pretend you have the least affection for me.'

'I am not pretending I have the least affection for you.'

Unexpectedly hurt, Sarah snapped back, 'No, you most certainly are not. In fact, you make it quite clear you dislike me intensely.'

He moved away from the door and stalked towards her. 'What the devil are you talking about?'

She resisted the urge to back away. 'Nothing.'

'Nothing?' He towered over her. 'Nothing? This is the second time today you've hinted that I hold you in some sort of dislike. You will do me the cour-tesy of explaining yourself.'

'I...' Why ever had she brought this stupid topic

up? What did it matter how he felt about her? It was only a marriage of convenience and she had no reason to care what he thought.

'Well?' He looked impatient and demanding, and Sarah felt like throwing something at him.

'Very well. You make it quite clear that spending time in my company is akin to….to having a tooth pulled. You showed me the tower with the greatest reluctance. If Jessica had not looked so stricken, you would have done anything in your power to avoid me!' She glared at him. 'Do you deny that?'

'So you assume that means I dislike you?' he asked softly.

'Yes!'

He took two steps towards her and this time she stepped back, unfortunately finding her back against the wall. She stared at him, her heart pounding at the wild, reckless look in his eye as if his careful control had snapped. His hands came down on either side of her shoulders. 'So you think I dislike you?' he repeated.

'Well, yes,' she whispered. His eyes were dark green pools and she felt as if she could fall into their depths. Her gaze fastened on his strong lips, the faint outline of his beard around his mouth. Her knees trembled.

His laugh was short and not at all amused. 'Shall I show you how much I dislike you?'

Before she could answer, he yanked her to him and his mouth took hers. His lips were hard and demanding, his arms bands of iron moulding her to his hard chest.

Her senses were spinning and her world consisted of nothing but him. His heart beat strongly under her ear, his male scent overwhelmed her and his mouth commanded her surrender. Instead of feeling afraid, she pressed closer to him. It was only when his tongue probed her mouth and then slipped inside, touching her own tongue, that she gasped in surprise.

He released her so abruptly that she nearly stumbled. Her eyes shot open. He stared at her, a stunned look on his face as if he had no idea what had happened. Then he stepped back and ran a hand through his hair.

'I beg your pardon,' he said, his voice stiff. He could have been apologising for stepping on her foot. The only consolation was that his breathing was as hard as hers.

''Tis nothing.'

'Nothing?' He stared at her. 'I just violated the terms of our marriage agreement.'

'Was that what you did?' Sarah asked stupidly.

'Yes, dammit. I said I would not touch you!'

'Oh, then if that was the case you…you have violated it before. You kissed me after our wedding.'

'Not like this.' He took a step towards her and stopped. 'At any rate, you kissed me.'

'Yes.' What was his point? A thought struck her. 'Was it such a dreadful experience?'

He stared at her. 'Was what dreadful?'

'Kissing me.' The look on his face made her feel as if she was speaking Greek. 'It is only that you do not look as if you found it very pleasing.'

'Not very pleasing? My God! I suppose this is along the lines of whether I dislike you or not.' He glared at her. 'Very well, I found kissing you pleasing. In fact, too damnably pleasing.'

'There is no need to sound as if you are confessing

under torture! I did not ask you to kiss me,' Sarah said, affronted by his angry tone.

'No. You asked if I liked you or, more accurately, if I held you in dislike. What do you think now?' His voice was dangerously soft.

'I have no idea.'

'Don't you? Then perhaps I should kiss you again. Obviously I did not make my point clear.'

'No!' She pressed herself as flat as possible against the wall, although he had backed several paces away from her.

His smile was grim. 'Don't worry, I was only teasing you.'

'Indeed.' She tried to make her voice cool, but inside she felt as if she was on fire.

A small shape scuttling across the floor made her gasp. For a brief moment she'd nearly forgotten they were shut up together in an old bare tower. She shivered.

He started. 'One of Jessica's mice. Are you cold?'

'No.'

'Come here.'

'Why?'

'I am going to give you my coat.'

'Thank you, but I don't need your coat.' She had no intention of allowing him to do her any favours. Not when it was so very apparent that anything he felt for her was strictly against his better judgement. The next thing she knew he was in front of her and had shrugged out of his coat. He draped it around her shoulders in an impatient movement. 'Better?'

'You'll be cold now.'

'I believe we have had this discussion before in

your grandfather's summerhouse. We decided that you are cold and I am rarely ever cold.'

'Oh.' That seemed ages ago.

He stalked over to the bench. 'Come and sit. I've no idea how long Jessica plans to keep us here. We might as well make ourselves comfortable.'

From the dark look on his face she knew any sort of protest would only result in another ridiculous argument. Not that she cared. It was just she had no desire to sit next to someone who kissed her in such a way and then acted as if it had been a gross miscalculation. Miffed, she plopped down next to him, careful to shift as far away as possible from him on the bench.

He seemed to be doing the same thing except she had the unnerving feeling his eyes were fastened on her face. She finally turned to meet his dark, intense gaze. She frowned. 'Must you stare at me like that? Is there a speck on my face?'

'No.' He scowled. 'Did you find my kiss at all enjoyable?'

She started. 'I beg your pardon?'

He folded his arms. 'I merely asked if you found my kissing you completely objectionable.'

'Not completely. That is, I…I have not been kissed very often so I really have no basis for comparison.' Whatever did he want to know? 'I think it was a very nice kiss,' she finished lamely.

'Very nice? Does that mean you would not object if I were to kiss you again?'

She pulled his coat more firmly around her. 'I…I don't know.'

'Shall we find out?' he asked softly.

'I don't think it would be such a good idea.'

Though in truth she half-wanted to have his lips on hers, to experience his arms around her again.

'Perhaps not. But we are married, so there would be no impropriety.'

'Would it not violate your…our agreement?'

'Undoubtedly.' But he had already shifted so his leg pressed against hers. He tilted her chin towards him with a gentle finger. 'But sometimes agreements should be violated and the terms changed.'

Her body already felt soft and pliant in anticipation. She tried one more time. 'I don't think…'

'You think too much.' He lowered his head and, for the second time that day, his lips covered hers.

This time his kiss was gentle and warm, exploring her mouth, coaxing her surrender instead of demanding. His lips were firm and strong, his taste intriguing. His hands crept under the coat still draped over her shoulders and he pulled her firmly against the hard warmth of his body. She scarcely noticed when the coat slipped from her shoulders.

This time, when his tongue probed her mouth she opened to him. His tongue slipped inside, strange and intriguing all at once. She shyly touched his tongue with her own. He made an odd sound, almost a groan and pressed her closer, his kiss more demanding. And then his lips left her mouth and trailed down her neck, and his hand cupped the softness of her breast. A warm pit of feeling was growing in her stomach, making her want to press closer.

Suddenly he lifted his head and swore.

Her eyes snapped open, the sudden loss of his warmth devastating. 'Is something wrong?'

His breathing was hard, his eyes heavy and dark. And he looked as if he'd just committed a crime.

'Nothing is wrong. You are right, we should not be doing this. It's too dangerous.'

'I see.'

'I don't think you do at all.' He gave a short laugh. 'I doubt very much that next time I will want to stop at a few kisses.'

'Oh.' She flushed, the desire in his eyes making her feel shaky and vulnerable.

'So, you see, my dear, there is a reason I wish to stay away from you. I doubt very much if you'd like the consequences.'

He was staying away from her out of the desire to avoid seducing her? She felt more confused than ever. Had he loved Mary so much that any tug of attraction he experienced for another woman was a betrayal of her memory? It was obvious he found any desire he had for Sarah unwelcome. She tugged his coat back up around her shoulders tightly as if trying to block out the hurt she felt.

A tear trickled down her cheek. She swiped at it with the back of her hand and tried to hold back a sniff. She'd rather die than have him think she was crying over him.

'Are you crying?'

'No!'

'You are!' She felt him shift closer to her. 'I did not mean to make you cry. The whole situation has become so damnably complicated.' For once he sounded completely at a loss.

'It really is not. Tomorrow you will leave for London and then when you are…are back, I will go. You…you said I could live anywhere I want. That way we can avoid each other.'

'That is hardly what I want. Sarah, will you at least look at me?'

A pounding at the door startled them. Then it burst open, crashing against the wall. Jessica rushed in followed by Mr Dalton.

'Sarah, Dev!' she cried. 'Are you all right?'

Dev rose. 'What did you mean by locking us in here?' he demanded.

Jessica stopped near the door. She clasped her hands with consternation filling her face. 'I...I really only meant to keep you in here for a while, but when I came back to let you out the door would not give. So I went to fetch Mr Dalton. It was just I thought that perhaps, if you were here alone together, you might...' Her voice trailed away at her brother's black expression. 'I am very sorry.'

'You should be. We will discuss this later.' He looked at Sarah who had also stood. 'Come, Sarah.' His voice was cold and clipped.

She slipped past him. Jessica touched her arm. 'I am sorry, Sarah.'

Sarah managed a smile. ''Tis no matter. I am fine.'

Jessica hardly looked reassured. 'I hope so.'

Sarah started down the winding steps. Her head was starting to hurt and she wanted nothing more than to escape. She felt miserable and confused. To her dismay, tears filled her eyes and she had the lowering feeling she was about to burst into tears.

She reached the small landing. She stopped to catch her breath. A noise from the room caught her attention. It almost sounded as if someone had stepped away from the door. But that couldn't be. She started down the steps again and then something struck her with such force she stumbled.

Her foot met nothing but air. She vaguely heard Jessica's cry and then another cry, which she realised was her own. Then her head hit the cold stone wall. The last thing she heard, as darkness descended, was Dev's agonised shout.

Chapter Fourteen

'Sarah, Sarah, can you hear me?'

The urgent feminine voice penetrated Sarah's hazy consciousness. She fought against the urge to drift back into the embracing foggy twilight. She moaned a little, trying to shift her position, and found her left shoulder and arm ached. Her wrist felt awkward and constrained; with vague surprise, she thought she had broken it. She forced her eyes open.

Jessica's worried face floated above her. She stared at Sarah for a moment and then tears filled her eyes. 'Thank goodness. Oh, Sarah, I feared you would never awake! How…how are you?'

'I…I am fine.' Jessica looked so stricken that Sarah wanted to reassure her.

Jessica made a little choking sound that was half-laughter and half-tears. 'How can you say that! Your shoulder was wrenched and your wrist broken and your poor head! When you fell…I thought… Oh, Sarah, you cannot know what terrible things flashed through my mind! But I am talking too much! Do…do you need anything?'

'Water, please.' Her throat was parched and there

was a peculiar taste in her mouth she thought must be from the laudanum. She had the vaguest memory of someone forcing the liquid down her throat and voices drifting above her head before the agonising pain in her shoulder sent her into blessed unconsciousness.

Jessica returned with a glass and helped Sarah take a few sips. Then Sarah fell back against the pillow and winced as her head made contact. Jessica knelt next to her. 'Will you see Dev now? He is so terribly worried. He spent the entire night by your bed and it was just a mere half-hour ago that Lady Coleridge and I persuaded him to sleep. I doubt very much he is doing more than pacing his room.'

Dev was worried about her? He had spent the night in her room? And why was Lady Coleridge here?

'Sarah, will you see him?' Jessica looked anxious.

'Of…of course.'

But her heart pounded uncomfortably when the door closed behind Jessica. And when Dev stepped into the room, she had the most insane desire to bury herself beneath the covers. He stared at her for a moment. With more than a little confusion, she saw he looked as if he'd slept in his clothes. His breeches and white shirt were rumpled. Even from across the room she could see the shadow of his beard.

'You are awake.' He came towards her, his eyes still on her face.

'Yes.'

He stood over her and she was taken aback to see how weary he looked. 'Are…are you all right?' she asked.

He appeared startled and then a brief smile lifted

the corner of his mouth. 'I believe that is the question I am to ask you.' His face sobered. 'How do you feel?'

'I don't know.' The gentleness in his voice confused her as did the concern in his eyes. He almost appeared a stranger. Perhaps she was still delirious. She closed her eyes for a moment.

'Sarah? Sarah, damn it! Don't fade off again!' His voice was rough and commanding.

At least she knew she wasn't dreaming. She opened her eyes. His face hovered over hers, so close she could see the dark stubble of his beard. Her gaze fastened on his strong mouth and she suddenly recalled the feel of his mouth on hers. As if he read her thoughts, his own eyes suddenly darkened and then he straightened as if he'd been shocked. 'I should leave you,' he said abruptly. 'You're probably tired.'

He looked as if he were about to move towards the door. For some reason she did not want him to leave her. 'You did not go to London?'

He stared at her. 'No. I would hardly leave you in this state. Not when—' He stopped. 'My business can wait.' He hesitated, then asked, 'Do you need anything?'

'How long have I been here?'

'Since yesterday. Do you remember much?'

'A little.' Just the sensation of falling through space. And pain and voices as she drifted in and out before falling into a deep sleep. A vague memory of something else tugged at her, something before her fall. She was beginning to feel tired again and the effort of talking was too much. Her eyes fluttered shut. But she had the oddest notion that before she drifted away again, she felt Dev's lips on her fore-head.

Dev watched her for a few minutes more, her face peaceful as she slept. He would never forget his stark terror when he heard her scream and then saw her still body lying at the foot of the stairs.

He had run to her, numb with fear and knelt beside her. She was breathing, although her arm was twisted under her and she was barely conscious. He stayed with her while Dalton left for the carriage and on the interminable trip to Ravensheed. She was uncon-scious by then, only waking briefly while the phy-sician eased her shoulder back into position and bound her wrist and then the laudanum took its ef-fect. He'd sat with her the entire night, and only when his godmother had arrived did he finally retire to his own room.

He realised as he kept vigil that he couldn't bear to lose her. And through his own arrogance, just as he had with Mary, he'd nearly sent Sarah to her death. For he had no doubt it was his kisses and words that had sent her fleeing down the tower steps.

When Sarah woke again, she could see from the way the sun fell across her bed that it must be late afternoon. She turned her head a little, the movement making her wince.

Lady Coleridge sat near the window, reading a book. She looked up and put her book aside and smiled. 'Hello, my dear,' she said, rising. She came to Sarah's side. 'I'm glad you are awake. Are you in much pain?'

'A little, but it is not bad.' She did not want more laudanum.

'I hope not. We have all worried so much about you.' She touched Sarah's hand, concern and affection in her eyes. 'And there is someone else here who is waiting anxiously to see you. Your brother.'

'Nicholas?'

'Yes. He is staying at Harrowood. As soon as he heard of your accident, he rode over. He will dine with us tonight, but first he wants to see you.'

Nicholas was to dine at Ravensheed? It was almost beyond her comprehension. And when he walked into her bedchamber, his tall, broad-shouldered figure so very familiar, she could scarcely believe it.

He came to stand next to her bed. 'What do you mean by falling like this?' he demanded, his voice gruff. 'Huntington should be taking better care of you.'

'Oh, Nick! It was hardly his fault.' She tried to smile at him, but felt tears dangerously close. 'What are you doing here?'

'I am at Filby's house party. Just came yesterday and then discovered my sister was injured the very first thing today. So, of course, I rode over and demanded entry.' His grin was wry. 'Amazingly enough your husband actually let me in.' His face sobered. 'So, what happened, Sarah? Did you trip?'

'I must have.' It had all happened so fast. She had reached the small landing and then had fallen. Except there had been the other thing. And then she remembered. 'I think that someone pushed me.'

Dev walked to the sideboard. 'Brandy?' he said to Nicholas. They had dined early. Jessica and Lady

Coleridge had left the men to themselves. Their mutual concern for Sarah had forced them into an uneasy truce, but it was quite apparent Nicholas would rather be any place than here.

'If you please.' Nicholas leaned back in his chair.

He poured one for Nicholas and then himself. Nicholas accepted the glass, the same brooding look on his face Dev had glimpsed more than once during dinner. Dev suspected it was more than the irony of finding himself at Ravensheed.

He sat across from Nicholas. 'What is it?' he asked abruptly.

Nicholas took a swallow, then set the glass down. 'She said she was pushed. Down the stairs.'

Dev stared at him, cold fingers gripping his heart. 'Who?'

'She has no idea. There is a small landing with a room, I believe. She thought she heard footsteps inside and then felt a blow to her back. She never saw her assailant.' His face was grim. 'Do you have any idea who would want to harm her?'

Dev rose. 'The door to the old house was left open when Jessica went for help. So anyone could have come in and hid in the room.' He paced to the window and half-turned. 'But I can think of only one person who might wish her harm.'

'Cedric Blanton.'

Dev whipped around. 'What do you know about that?'

'I met Blanton over a week ago. After informing me he was invited to Filby's house party, he hinted you had forced yourself on my sister that night. I demanded the truth from my grandfather. Consequently I found myself ordered to spend a few nights under Filby's roof as well.' He polished off his brandy and slammed his glass down. 'And then I'm too late.'

'No, damn it! I am the one who should've protected her. I let her go down the staircase by herself. She was upset. It was my fault. We had argued.' The memory would haunt him for the rest of his days. 'When I saw her there, lying so still, I thought—' He stopped. 'I thought I had lost her.'

Nicholas regarded him with a curious expression. 'So you care for my sister?'

'Yes.' His mouth curved in a cool smile. 'I care for her and I'll go to the devil before I'll allow Blanton or anyone else to harm her. And as soon as I've proof of this he'll rue the day he laid eyes on me.'

Nicholas met his eyes. 'I think, Huntington, we may have something in common after all.'

Sarah put her book aside and sighed. She lay on a sofa which had been drawn near the window in the drawing room so that she had a view of the park. A week had passed since her fall. Already she was tired of spending her days reclining on the sofa. Despite the visitors—Lady Coleridge, Mrs Kenton and Caroline, and Nicholas every day—she was quite bored. Although her left wrist was the injured one, she still found it difficult to do much drawing. And Dev had insisted she was to strictly follow Dr Milton's orders to remain in bed or on the sofa.

Her brow creased into a frown. Dev visited her for a few minutes each day, inquiring about her health with polite formality. He paced around the room and acted as if he hardly knew what to say. Then he would leave. It was very peculiar. She would almost prefer his sardonic remarks to such uncomfortable civility.

She wondered if she dare leave the sofa to steal to the library without Mrs Humphries or Jessica bustling in to scold her. She swung her legs over the edge of the sofa and was about to stand when she heard very familiar footsteps in the hall.

She quickly resumed her prone position and looked up just as Dev stepped into the room. And then her mouth fell open.

Dev stood in the doorway, a large grey tabby cat in his arms. They both regarded her with similar expressions, as if they could hardly wait to escape their predicament.

'You…you have a cat,' she said faintly.

'A correct observation. I'd rather hoped you would relieve me of it.'

'Yes, but…' She watched, completely astonished, as he walked across the room, an iron grip around the cat. The animal struggled as Dev approached the sofa and then leaped out of his arms, landing neatly at Sarah's feet. He stared at her for a moment with huge yellow eyes. Purring, he made his way up to Sarah's chin and rubbed against her face.

She scratched behind his ears and looked at Dev. 'Is this not Hannah's cat? What is he doing here?'

'She insisted he should be yours. She thought it might make you feel better.'

'How very kind of her. But, Dev, do you not mind?'

'No.' He shrugged. 'I agreed with her.' But she sensed he was not as indifferent as he appeared.

She bent her head towards the cat for a moment

and then looked back at him. Tears pricked her eyes. 'Thank you. You are very kind as well.'

'Not at all.' He shifted uncomfortably. 'If it proves to be a decent mouser, Cook will undoubtedly be extremely grateful.'

'So you will not banish him to the stables?'

'Why would I? I've no intention of having you visit it there.' A swift frown crossed his brow. 'I assume you want it for a pet?'

'Oh, yes.' She smiled through the tears. 'I do. He is the nicest present I have ever been given.'

His brow shot up. 'Surely not?'

'But he is.' She looked down at the cat, which had settled on her lap and started washing his face. 'Did you bring him all the way here?'

'Yes.' He grimaced. 'Hardly an experience I wish to repeat. He started out in a basket in my curricle and protested most of the way before he managed to escape. He then crawled out and decided my lap would make the most appropriate seat. I fully expected him to jump out, but he did not. Probably because he used me as a foothold. And my coat is covered with fur.'

He sounded so affronted by the latter, that she couldn't help the bubble of laughter that escaped. 'How very dreadful for you! I know how much you adore cats! Jessica is right, you really are very nice, you know.'

'Hardly.' He moved to the mantelpiece and leaned against it, something she realised he did when he was uncomfortable.

'So you don't consider yourself nice?' she asked, wanting to tease him a little. 'I do, even though you try your best to hide it.'

'No, I do not.' A hint of colour stained his cheeks. He shifted from his position. 'I had best leave you.'

'Must you?' She felt disappointed. 'Cannot you stay and talk?'

'Perhaps later.'

'Very well.' So, despite his gift, he really didn't wish for her company after all. 'Thank you again for my present.'

'Of course.' He glanced at the cat. 'I suppose you know what it needs. Mrs Humphries can help you.'

'Yes. And it is really not an "it". It is a "he". Does he have a name? I never asked Hannah.'

He frowned a little. 'I believe she said it was Merlin.'

'Merlin.' She stroked the animal's head. 'It suits him quite well.'

'How can you tell? All cats appear remarkably alike to me.'

'They aren't really. No more than people are.' He looked sceptical. 'I can see you've never been personally acquainted with a cat. How unfortunate,' she added with a smile.

'Something I don't intend to remedy.'

'No?' Despite his earlier words, he seemed in no hurry to leave.

'No.' A slight smile curved his mouth as he looked down at her.

'My lord.' The footman appeared behind them.

Dev turned. 'Yes?'

'You have a visitor. Lady Marleigh.'

Amelia stepped into the room, a blue cloak over her fawn gown. Her gaze took in Dev and then fell on Sarah. 'Good heavens. I thought I'd best come and see for myself how Sarah is.' She looked at Dev, a slight arch to her brow. 'But I can see I have arrived rather too late.'

Chapter Fifteen

Amelia glanced over at Sarah. 'So, my dear Sarah, what exactly is going on between you and your charming husband?'

They were sitting in the small flower garden at the side of the house. This was Sarah's first excursion from the house since her accident. Dr Melton had examined her the previous day and pronounced her healing well, although she was to continue to wear a sling until her wrist was completely healed. However, he allowed that short visits to the garden would be beneficial.

Sarah flushed a little and stroked Merlin, who had jumped up beside her on the bench. 'Nothing. That is, nothing to signify. We are very amiable together.'

'I can see that,' Amelia said drily. 'You carefully avoid the least contact with each other, you speak as if you're bare acquaintances and then pretend you are not staring at each other over dinner every night. Really, Sarah, I had hoped that by now you'd have everything resolved.'

'We'd have what resolved?'

Amelia rolled her eyes. 'The fact that you are both very attracted to each other.'

'We aren't.' Sarah looked away, praying Amelia wouldn't see the truth in her eyes. No matter how hard she tried, she couldn't put the memory of his kiss from her mind. Neither did telling herself it was some sort of reaction to being locked up together in a cold tower help.

Thank goodness, he'd finally left for London two days ago and she would no longer have to worry that he would see her feelings in her face.

'You are,' Amelia said firmly.

Sarah turned to look at her and Amelia fixed her with a little smile. 'I knew it even when we were in London. A man doesn't spend his time staring at a woman like that unless he's developing the most violent *tendre* for her.'

Sarah scowled. 'If he has, it is completely against his will. He told me he must stay away from me. And if you must know, our marriage is nothing but a…a business arrangement.' There, she had said it. She waited for the look of shock on Amelia's face.

Amelia did not appeared the least bit surprised. 'I have quite suspected that. Although I must own I am surprised it has remained a business arrangement for this long. So, my dear cousin, what are you planning to do about it?'

'Nothing at all,' Sarah said stiffly. 'He does not want anything done about it and neither do I.'

Amelia smiled and patted Merlin. 'I somehow doubt that. Any man who brings a woman a cat when he dislikes them must be truly head over ears.'

'Amelia! Will you stop this?' Sarah snapped. Then

she sighed. 'I am sorry, but I would prefer to discuss a different topic.'

'Oh, very well. If you both wish to remain miserable.' She gave Sarah a sidelong glance. 'Of course, I would be more than happy to help you bring Dev to heel, if you wish.'

'No!' Sarah's cheeks heated. 'I've no intention of throwing myself at him.'

'Well, it wouldn't be throwing yourself at him. There are very subtle ways. Seducing one's husband can actually be quite fun.'

Sarah stared at her cousin. 'Have you done so?' She had never asked about the intimacies between Amelia and her husband. Although on more than one occasion she had seen the unspoken but very apparent desire pass between them and, once, the look on John's face as he closed the door to their bedchamber. She had felt curious and slightly embarrassed, and envious all at once.

'Oh, yes.' Amelia's eyes danced. 'It is quite satisfying and gives one such a heady sense of power.'

'Amelia!' She was shocked, but not half as shocked as she should be. What would it be like to hold such power over Dev, to have him look at her across a room with a hot flare of passion in his eyes instead of his dark scowl? She felt almost weak at the thought.

Whatever was wrong with her? Even if she was inclined to do such a thing, he'd probably give her one of his stiff looks and back away. 'I doubt if it would work,' she told Amelia.

Amelia grinned. 'You will never know until you try. If you change your mind, let me know.'

Sarah stood, her cheeks still heated. 'Perhaps we should return to the house.'

They entered the drawing room and found Lady Coleridge seated there with Jessica, taking tea. Lady Coleridge rose when Amelia and Sarah entered. She greeted Amelia warmly and took Sarah's hand. 'You look much better, my dear. A little more colour in your cheeks at last. You must sit, however. And I will tell you my proposition.'

They each took a wing chair and Lady Coleridge resumed her seat. She smiled at Amelia. 'I had intended to throw a dinner party for Sarah to formally introduce her as Devin's wife but, with all that has happened, I fear it had to be postponed. However, we hold a midsummer's eve ball each year. I had a sudden thought that perhaps it could be held in Sarah's honour. I have discussed it with Jessica and she quite agrees, do you not?'

'Oh, yes!' Jessica said with great enthusiasm. 'I thought it a splendid idea!'

Lady Coleridge took a sip from her china cup and set it back on the saucer. 'The invitations have already gone out. My son and daughter-in law have just returned from Scotland and Jane agrees that Sarah should be the guest of honour. Sarah has only to show up properly attired. And with Devin in tow, of course.' She turned to Sarah. 'So, my dear, what do you think?'

'You are very kind, but I don't think…a ball is too much work.' She felt more than a little stunned and completely unworthy of such a thing.

'Not at all. We hold the ball every year, it is only a matter of introducing you as the guest of honour.

It will be in a fortnight. Your arm should be much better by then.'

'I...'

'And I would very much like to do it for you. If you please.' For the briefest instant, something vulnerable and sad flashed across her face. And Sarah knew she could not say no.

'Thank you. I would be very honoured.'

Lady Coleridge cleared her throat. 'Then it is settled. I wondered if it would be possible for me to talk to Sarah alone for a moment.'

'Of course,' Jessica said. 'Amelia and I can look at the latest *Belle Assemblée*. We can find a gown for Sarah. Mrs Remington is quite expert at copying the latest fashions and she will fall over herself in delight to make one up for the new Lady Huntington.'

'An excellent idea,' Amelia said. She cast Sarah an amused glance and followed Jessica out of the room.

Lady Coleridge finished her tea and patted the place next to her on the sofa. 'Come and sit by me, Sarah.'

She waited until Sarah had seated herself next to her before speaking. 'So, tell me, my dear, how are things between you and Devin?'

Sarah managed a smile. 'They are fine.'

'Are they?' Lady Coleridge asked, her gaze direct. 'I would like to think that, but I sense not all is completely well. It is quite apparent he has strong feelings towards you, but I am not certain he knows what to do about them. And you, my dear, I fear are trying your best to keep from falling in love with him. Is this true?'

Sarah folded her trembling hands in her lap. 'Yes.' She looked at Lady Coleridge, the guilt she never failed to feel in her presence rising to the surface. 'I am sorry.'

'Why?'

'Because I am certain it must be so difficult for you…to have me at Ravensheed. I…my family has caused so much unhappiness. He should be married to Mary. Not me.'

Lady Coleridge regarded Sarah for a moment, sudden understanding in her eyes. 'My dear, I had no idea. Is this what is stopping you?' She leaned forward and caught Sarah's hand. 'You had no part in the whole affair.'

Dev had said much the same thing. Sarah bit her lip. 'But I did. You see, when Mary came to visit, I…I sent her off with Nicholas. Mama was so ill and I could not leave her side very often, and they seemed to deal so well together. And I never thought, never dreamed that they would…would…'

'Fall in love. For that is what happened.' Lady Coleridge released Sarah's hand and sat upright. 'I knew when Mary returned that something was different. She rarely revealed her emotions, but I could see something troubled her. And she asked, no, begged to call off the wedding. And I said no.' She looked away. 'I thought her sudden reluctance was due to the doubts that all brides experience. She had accepted that she would marry Dev all her life. And my husband, like your mother, was ill and he wanted the alliance, wanted to see them settled. He had promised Dev's father, you see, that they would marry. And so I forced her to go through with it. I made certain she was busy and had no chance to speak with Dev alone.' A bitter smile crossed her face. 'She could be very stubborn and I feared she would break off the betrothal directly with him.'

Sarah twisted her hands together. 'But if Mary had never met Nicholas, there would have been a chance for her and Dev.'

'Perhaps. Dev was never in love with Mary. Nor was Mary in love with him. Neither one of them had ever indicated a strong desire to marry elsewhere. Dev had his liaisons as men do, but there was nothing serious. As for Mary, I sometimes wondered if she was capable of passion.' She spoke almost to herself. She looked back at Sarah. 'She was. But it was not for her husband. And it was not you who was at fault, but me. I ruined the lives of two people…no, three people, if I am to be honest. For I've no doubt your brother suffered as well.'

'He did,' Sarah said softly. 'He loved her.'

Lady Coleridge nodded, her eyes unhappy. 'I lost my daughter. And my godson has been lost as well. He, too, carries the burden of Mary's death. He feels he should have let her go. She wanted to annul the marriage and he refused. And that is when she ran to your brother.'

Her pain was raw. She looked away and then back at Sarah. 'So, you see, when I heard of your marriage I had hopes it might bring some happiness to Dev, some healing for his soul and perhaps even my own.' She reached over and took Sarah's hand. 'And I see that you need it as well.'

'Yes.' Sarah bowed her head. 'Thank you,' she whispered.

'My dear.' Lady Coleridge's fingers tightened around Sarah's hand. 'I think we must go forward.

You must not be afraid to love Dev. He needs you very much.'

Sarah looked up. 'He doesn't want to need me.'

A ghost of a smile touched Lady Coleridge's lips. 'He is also afraid. I think you must help him see there is no reason to fear loving and being loved in return.'

'I do not know if I can.'

'But I do know. Mary spoke of you often, how kind and generous you were. How she could confide in you. In fact—' her smile was ironic '—she once said she thought you and Dev might be very well suited.'

'Did she?' Sarah flushed.

'Yes.' She smiled at Sarah, her expression warm and encouraging. 'So I think Mary would quite approve. As do I.' She released Sarah's hand and rose. 'So, my dear, I think you must go and do your best to bring your husband around. And a child of his own would undoubtedly help. I shall, of course, expect to stand in as a surrogate grandparent.'

'Of…of course,' Sarah said.

Lady Coleridge picked up her bonnet. 'I will leave you now. I expect you need to rest.' Sarah started to rise and she shook her head. 'No, you may remain seated. I will show myself out.' She clasped Sarah's hand for a brief moment. 'Thank you again, my dear.'

Sarah watched her leave and then sank back on the sofa, her thoughts and emotions in complete confusion. For some reason, the two people who cared the most about Dev seemed to hold the erroneous idea that Sarah somehow held the key to his salvation.

And even it if were true, that was the last thing he wanted from her.

Chapter Sixteen

Sarah picked up her fan from her dressing table and wished she could quell the nerves in her stomach. There really was no reason for such apprehension—they were only going to a ball, and she had Jessica and Amelia with her.

And Dev. The thought made her feel shaky. He'd returned last night from London with Adam. She had tried very hard to greet him with calm politeness as if her heart hadn't nearly come to a standstill at the sight of him. He'd been equally formal, which had made her even more unnerved, as she was quite aware that Amelia watched their every move with sharp interest. At least her cousin hadn't made any more disconcerting comments about their attraction for each other.

Merlin leaped to the top of the dressing table and mewed. Sarah stroked his head and then managed to gently lift him down with her good arm, careful not to let his claws tangle in the silk of her balldress. Unfortunately, she was left with a fine smattering of grey hair on her gloves. He'd been a welcome companion; his only shortcoming was that he shed more hair than any cat she'd known.

Well, it was too late to look for another pair of gloves. It was nearly time to leave. At least her sea-green ballgown was unlikely to show his grey hairs. She took one last look at herself in the looking glass. The gown was lovely, a soft greenish-blue silk with a square neckline, the hem trimmed with several rows of lace and small creamy silk roses. Amelia had loaned her a silk scarf in a green that nearly matched the gown to use as a sling.

The others were already gathered in the drawing room by the time Sarah entered. She knew almost without looking that Dev stood near the mantelpiece with Adam. Instead, she kept her gaze on Amelia and Jessica who were looking out of the window. 'I am sorry I am late.'

Jessica turned, a smile lighting her face. 'You are not. Oh, Sarah, how lovely you look! Does she not, Dev?'

'She does.'

Sarah forced herself to look at him. Her heart leaped to her throat. He looked devastatingly hand-some in his black evening coat and black silk breeches. Masculine and elegant and completely un-nerving. His gaze locked with hers and the expression in his eyes made her breathless. She looked away.

'Before we go, Dev has something to give you,' Jessica said with great excitement.

'Oh.' Sarah's mind was blank. 'Now? Perhaps it can wait.'

'It cannot.' He had moved and came to stand in front of her. She saw he held a small box. 'Jessica has informed me that it is quite necessary I present it to you tonight. She will give me no peace until I do.' He glanced at her arm. 'Should I open it for you?'

'If you please.'

He lifted the lid. Inside lay the most exquisite necklace Sarah had ever seen. A simple emerald pendant hung from a single strand of pearls. She stared at it, too stunned for a moment to speak.

'You do not like it?'

She looked swiftly up at him. 'It is lovely—I have never seen anything so beautiful. It is only…' She bit her lip. 'It was hardly necessary…thank you. You are very kind.'

'I fear I have been rather remiss in presenting you with gifts.'

'I really do not expect you to.' She gave him a little smile. 'Merlin was quite adequate.'

A quick grin crossed his face. 'I fear that won't pass muster with my sister.'

'You must wear it, Sarah,' Jessica said. 'Dev can help you with the fastenings.'

'I…'

'Turn around, Sarah.'

She did and felt his cool fingers fumble with the clasp of the locket she wore, his fingers brushing the hair from the nape of her neck. His touch did odd things to her pulse and she stood perfectly still, hardly daring to breathe until he stepped away. By then her face was heated.

'See? It is perfect with her gown,' Jessica exclaimed. 'What do you think, Adam?'

He grinned at Sarah, clearly amused by the embarrassment on her face. 'She looks exceptionally lovely tonight. I think marriage must agree with her.'

'I think so, too,' Amelia added. She had come to stand next to Jessica. A little smile was on her lips. She looked over at Dev. 'You have not yet given us your verdict on Sarah's appearance.'

'Very nice,' he said curtly. But the flash of heat in his eyes as his gaze swept over her face belied his indifferent words.

Sarah backed away, almost tripping over Merlin. She bent down and picked up the cat, heedless of her gown, trying to hide her confusion.

'Is the cat coming as well?' Adam inquired.

'I've no doubt he would like to,' Dev said. 'He stowed away in my coach when I left for London. I discovered him when I was a mile down the road.'

'Oh, dear.' He sounded so disgruntled that Sarah couldn't help smiling. She set Merlin down. 'Thank you for bringing him back.'

An answering smile tugged at his lips and for a moment the barriers between them dissolved.

Adam's voice broke the spell. 'We'd best leave before the rain turns into a veritable downpour.'

'Yes.' Dev's smile faded. A little of the warmth left Sarah's heart as well.

As they settled into the carriage, the rain pattering down outside, she wondered if it would ever be possible to overcome the wall between them.

Dev stood at the side of the ballroom and watched Charles Kenton fawn over Sarah. She sat on a chair strategically placed near the edge of the room so that she could sit and watch the dancers when she became fatigued. All his efforts to remain indifferent had fled

and he wanted nothing more than to stalk over there
and inform Kenton he had no business even looking
at his wife.

'Really, Dev, it is not all the thing to be so obviously in love with one's wife. And I doubt very much
that Maria would appreciate a brawl in the middle of
the ballroom.'

He looked down to find Lady Violet Townsley at
his side. 'I've no intention of starting a brawl,' he
said shortly. 'And what brings you here, Vi? I
thought you and Jonathan avoided house parties like
the plague.' Since she'd remarried and had a child,
shocking the rest of the ton by her devotion to moth-
erhood, she rarely ventured into society.

She laid a hand on his arm. 'Why, to appease my
curiosity, of course. When I heard of your marriage
I could scarcely believe my ears. Particularly to
Sarah Chandler. Not only because of her brother, but
because I thought you held her in the most violent
dislike. At least it seemed so in London.' Her lips
curved in a smile. 'I can see I was quite wrong.'

'Were you?'

'Yes. And I can see you don't plan to admit a
thing.' Her blue eyes snapped with laughter. 'Come
and dance with me, then. At least I might keep you
from throttling Charles Kenton.'

The musicians had just finished the last set and the
dancers were leaving the floor. He raised a brow.
'I've no idea why you think I plan to do Kenton
bodily harm.'

'Don't you? Although it might do you some good.
Or perhaps you should just quit the ballroom and
take your wife somewhere more private.'

'Hardly a proper suggestion, my dear.'

She laughed. 'I promise I won't tease you.' She tugged on his arm. 'Come, we will dance and I will tell you all about Matthew. He is nearly two, and the most adorable creature alive.'

He allowed himself to be led to the floor. He resisted the urge to look in Sarah's direction. He feared, if he did, that he would be very much tempted to take up Violet's suggestion and drag Sarah off to a private room where he would make her forget about any man but him.

Sarah fixed Charles Kenton with a polite smile. He looked very elegant in a corbeau coat and black pantaloons and she should be grateful for his pleasant conversation. Except it was all she could do to keep her eyes from straying to her husband, who had left his place against the wall and now waltzed with Lady Violet Townsley.

Not that it should matter a whit, even if the rumours were true and the beautiful Lady Townsley had once been his mistress. In fact, she should be grateful for it. At least he was no longer glowering at her as he had all evening, reminding her all too forcibly of the month in London. This time she couldn't escape him as soon as she left the ball. No, now she was forced to go home with him.

She felt cross and tired. She'd danced with Nicholas and once with Dev, but that dance had been so filled with tension that she had said she was tired and wanted to sit out the rest of the ball. He'd stalked off, although he'd brought her a glass of lemonade before standing up with Jessica.

She realised Charles had asked her a question. She

jerked her thoughts back, feeling rather guilty. 'I am very sorry. I fear I was not properly attending.'

A wry smile touched his lips. 'I think you have other things on your mind.' He glanced at the dancers where Lady Townsley whirled gracefully in Dev's arms. 'She is very happily married with a son she adores. And her husband is just in the next room.'

'I see.' Sarah flushed a little, embarrassed that her thoughts were so transparent.

'I will leave you for now. I am obligated for the next dance.' He took her hand and bowed over it. 'And you know that if you need anything, even a sympathetic ear, I will be more than happy to be of service.'

'Thank you.' She was grateful for his kindness, but it only made her feel lonelier.

The last notes of the waltz died away. She carefully avoided looking at the dancers as they left the floor.

A man suddenly appeared at her side. She glanced up and froze when she saw his face.

Cedric Blanton smiled. 'Ah, Lady Huntington. I wanted to tell you how sorry I was to hear of your injury. An accident, I believe?'

'Yes,' she said coolly.

'How careless of your husband.'

'It was hardly his doing.'

'But he should take better care of his wife. I certainly would have not allowed anything to happen to you.'

'I really do not wish to converse with you,' Sarah said. She rose, wanting to escape him.

He moved into her path. 'No? Then stand up with me.'

'I am not dancing.'

'Then walk with me around the room.'

Did the fact that he'd purposely tried to compromise her and that she was now married cause him no shame? Apparently not, for he was regarding her in the same annoying way he had before, and was persisting in his attentions despite her every effort to rid herself of him. She took a deep breath. 'Mr Blanton, I do not wish to walk around the room with you, to stand up with you or to converse with you. Particularly after all that has passed between us, I consider your acquaintance most unwelcome.'

His eyes narrowed unpleasantly and then he smiled. 'I am sorry to hear that. However, if you do not walk with me, I will feel obliged to spread about the tale that I enjoyed a rather improper flirtation with you before your marriage.'

She stared at him in disbelief. 'But that is completely untrue!'

His gaze was bland. 'Is it? My dear, you led me on in a most shameless manner. In fact, until that last night when Huntington so disobligingly interfered, I had no doubt you meant to accept my proposal.'

Sarah glanced around, praying that no one else could overhear him. If any such tale was spread about… She looked at him and, despite the complete revulsion she felt, she said, 'Very well, I will walk with you.'

'I think perhaps I would prefer a dance.' His smile held triumph. 'There is no need to worry about your arm, I promise I will not hurt you.'

Sarah was too disgusted to answer. She allowed him to take her hand and lead her into a set, thankful he did not attempt to engage her in any sort of conversation. Not that she would have responded at any rate. She was too occupied in watching for Dev.

'Sarah, whatever are you doing?' Amelia asked in a loud whisper. She and her partner had taken their place next to Sarah and Blanton.

'Dancing,' Sarah replied distractedly.

'With him? Sarah, have you run mad? Unless you want bloodshed.'

'He forced me. Amelia, please can we discuss this later?' From her cousin's expression she feared Amelia meant to call Blanton out herself.

To Sarah's relief, the dance finally began with no sign of Dev. Perhaps he'd gone to the card room. She forced her attention back to Blanton. As their hands met, he sneezed. His eyes were rather red as if he was suddenly catching a cold. However, that didn't prevent him from fixing her with a look that was far too intimate. 'You are exceedingly lovely tonight, my dear.'

She would pretend not to hear him. She gave him a vague look. He leaned towards her and sneezed again. His eyes were starting to water. 'Are you well?' she asked.

'Quite,' he snapped. His air of bland indifference was rapidly dissipating.

The steps of the dance parted them. If only it would end. And then, as she executed a turn, her heart nearly slammed to a halt. Dev stood near the doorway. As if drawn by a magnet, his gaze fell on her. The black look on his face was impossible to miss. As was the fact he was starting towards them. Completely thrown off balance, she lost her place and stepped into Blanton.

'I beg your pardon.' She stared at him, amazed to see his right eye was swelling. 'Whatever is wrong?'

He glared at her. 'Have you a cat, Lady Huntington?'

'Yes.' Whatever did that have to do with anything?

'That explains it.' His expression held loathing. 'I must beg your pardon, my lady, but I cannot finish this dance.'

He stepped out of the set, nearly crashing into Dev. He stared at Dev, a look of pure fury on his face. But then he recovered himself. 'I fear, Huntington, that you will have to issue your challenge at a more convenient time.' He brushed past Dev, who stared after him.

By now most of the dancers had come to a halt, although the musicians continued to play.

Sarah stood frozen. Dev took Blanton's place in the set. 'I can see I arrived just in time,' he drawled. A cool smile crossed his face, but she had no doubt he was furious. He looked at the others. 'Please, continue.'

He caught Sarah's hand. 'So, you decided to dance after all. Perhaps it only took the right partner to persuade you.'

'No, that was not—' She broke off. 'I refuse to argue with you in the middle of a dance. If you wish to do so, we can do it in private. But if you must know, I am in an extremely foul mood and my arm is sore and I really wish I was at home!' To her chagrin her voice trembled.

He stared at her. 'To hell with the dance.' He pulled her out of the set and led her from the floor. He manoeuvred his way through the guests and out of the ballroom. Once in the hallway outside he looked down at her. 'We can be private in the study.'

Undoubtedly he intended to take her to task. But she was too tired to argue. Meekly, she allowed him to lead her across the circular hallway.

Dev pushed open the door, relieved to find the room empty. A single lamp burned on the desk. He stepped aside and allowed Sarah to pass him. 'Come and sit.' He indicated a wooden chair near the mantelpiece.

She obediently sat and looked at him, her expression resigned as if she expected him to ring a peal over her. Not that he blamed her, after his irrational behaviour she probably considered him the worse sort of man. 'Are you all right?' He spoke more coolly than he'd intended.

'Yes,' she replied. She suddenly looked extremely weary. 'I dare say you wish to scold me for standing up with Blanton. I pray you will proceed and then leave me in peace.'

'Sarah.' He gave a short laugh. 'Do you really consider me such a harsh taskmaster? That I would bring you here to upbraid you?'

She rose to her feet. 'I really don't know what to think!' Her eyes flashed with sudden anger. 'You stand up with me once as if it is the most painful duty and then leave—not that I wish you to dance attendance on me, for I do not! But then you must spend the entire evening glaring at me from the side of the ballroom as if everything I do displeases you! And, to make matters worse, you storm into the middle of a dance looking as if you wish to strangle me for standing up with someone I...I detest!' Her voice trembled and she looked completely and utterly defeated.

'Sarah.' He went to her side. 'Don't look like that.'

'I…I am not looking like anything.' She kept her gaze fixed on her feet.

'You are. Can I at least see your face?'

'No.' She sniffed and he knew she was fighting tears.

He stepped forward and tilted her chin gently up. 'You have tears in your eyes. I did not mean to make you cry.'

'You…you did not. I am just ra…rather tired.'

'Of course.' He brushed a strand of hair from her face. 'Come here.' He pulled her gently into his arms, careful not to hurt her injured arm. She was stiff at first and then gradually relaxed against him. He gently stroked her hair as he had Jessica's when she needed comfort.

Except she was not Jessica. Her sweet, light scent, the feel of her soft curves against him, told him that. It was all he could do to keep from crushing her mouth beneath his until she was his entirely. Which would hardly comfort her. 'Sarah,' he murmured.

She looked up at him, her lips parted slightly. She looked soft and vulnerable. He caught his breath and, with every ounce of will power he possessed, put her gently away from him.

'Are you better?' His voice was much more husky than he intended.

'Yes,' she whispered. She looked as bewildered as he felt.

He ran his hand through his hair. 'Good.' He stepped back, trying to regain control of his senses. 'I think perhaps it is time to go home.'

'Oh. Yes, if you wish to.'

'I do. You can sit here. I'll let Maria know we will be leaving.'

She sat back down. 'Thank you.'

He started towards the door, then turned to look at her as a thought hit him. 'By the way, what the devil did you say to Blanton that sent him running from the dance floor?'

She looked puzzled. 'I really do not know. He asked if I had a cat and when I said yes he suddenly left.'

A grin sprang to his lips. 'Perhaps your cat is useful for something after all.'

Chapter Seventeen

Sarah looked up, expecting to see Dev enter the study. Instead, Amelia came in. Sarah rose. 'Did Dev send you here? I am sorry to have taken you away from the ball.'

'Not at all. I was rather worried when I saw him haul you from the ballroom with that determined look on his face. But Jessica assured me you would be quite safe, so I restrained myself from going after you.'

Sarah flushed. 'Oh, dear, it was all so mixed up! I fear Lady Coleridge must be quite angry.'

'Oh, I don't think so.' Amelia smiled at her. 'You look so fatigued, no wonder you wish to leave. But I fear none of us are leaving tonight. It has been raining the entire evening and the roads are probably mudbaths.'

Amelia sounded quite cheerful, but Sarah wanted to groan. 'Are you certain?' she asked.

'Yes, which is why I am here to take you up to bed. Lady Coleridge quite agrees you should go directly to bed. She has a room ready for you and a nightdress as well.'

'That is very kind.' Sarah felt rather bewildered. 'But you and Jessica?'

'We can share a room.' She took Sarah's arm. 'Come, you look ready to fall asleep where you stand.'

The room was small and comfortable with a dressing room attached and a tent bed on one wall. Amelia glanced around. 'Very nice.' She moved to the bed and picked up a cotton nightdress already laid out on the covers. 'However, I fear this is a bit large.'

'It will do.' Sarah sank down on the bed, suddenly exhausted. And where was Dev? She wanted to ask Amelia, but she feared her cousin would tease her.

Amelia put the nightdress down. 'I shall find a maid to help you undress and then you can sleep.' She kissed Sarah lightly on the cheek. 'I will return.'

Sarah gave her a quick hug. 'Thank you.'

Amelia left, closing the door softly behind her. Sarah remained sitting for a moment, an unexpected wave of loneliness washing over her. She wondered where Dev had gone to. Perhaps he had returned to the ballroom.

She could hardly sit here brooding. Sarah rose and went to the dressing table and pulled off her gloves. She could at least remove her sling and pull the pins from her hair while she waited for a maid. Her wrist felt much better, but she still had difficulty making much use of it.

There was still no sign of a maid after she completed those tasks. She might as well remove her stockings and kid slippers. Undoubtedly, with so many unexpected guests, all the female servants were quite occupied. She had just taken off both slippers and stockings when there was a knock at her door.

She straightened up. 'Come in,' she called.

And then her heart skipped a beat when she saw Dev in the doorway. 'May I come in?' he asked.

'Yes, of course.' She stood and smiled, unexpectedly happy to see him.

He took a few steps into the room and shut the door behind him. He looked extremely uncomfortable.

'Is there something wrong?' Sarah asked, her smile fading.

'No.' He took another step towards her and stopped. 'I fear I must share your quarters with you tonight.'

'Oh.' Her mind went completely blank.

He shifted and tugged at his cravat. 'There are not enough rooms to accommodate all the guests. Maria assumed that we would not object to spending the night in the same room. A natural assumption, I suppose.'

'Well, yes,' Sarah said weakly.

'I will, of course, sleep in the dressing room.'

'If you wish.'

He cleared his throat. 'Well, are you ready to sleep?' He peered more closely at her. 'You are not in your nightdress.'

'No. Amelia said she would send a maid.'

There seemed to be nothing more to say. They looked at each other for a moment, the silence stretching between them. Dev finally spoke. 'There's no need for you to remain on the opposite side of the bed. I've no intention of ravishing you.'

Heat flooded her cheeks. 'I hardly thought you were.' She forced herself to move towards the bed.

'I suppose I can sleep in my ballgown.' It suddenly seemed infinitely safer.

'I doubt that would be comfortable. How is your wrist?'

'It aches a little, but nothing to signify.'

'Sit down.' He gestured towards the bed.

She perched on the edge of the bed, feeling more self-conscious than she ever had in her life. The room seemed to have shrunk, and she hardly knew where to look. The only consolation was that he looked just as dismayed as she felt.

And where was the maid?

He must have read her thoughts. 'I'll see if I can find an abigail.'

She nodded. He quit the room, closing the door quietly behind him. Sarah stared at it, her heart thudding. There was no reason to be so apprehensive, they would merely spend the night in the same room. She'd shared rooms many times, with Amelia, friends from school, other cousins.

But Dev was no cousin. Nor, obviously, was he female. And he was her husband.

But there was nothing intimate about their relationship. Not like Amelia and John, whose attraction for each other was apparent, who could not wait to close the door behind them, shutting out the world.

Their marriage was a sham, and the prospect of spending a night together was as disconcerting as if they had been strangers. Perhaps it would be better if she left Ravensheed. Her leaving would have the effect of announcing to society the true status of their marriage. It would be painful, but not half as painful as pretending there was a marriage where there was nothing at all.

* * *

A quarter of an hour later, Dev entered the bed-chamber and shut the door behind him. Sarah looked up, her expression apprehensive. Unfortunately, what he had to tell her would probably do nothing to ease her uneasiness.

Or his.

He kept his face expressionless. 'I fear there is no abigail available.'

'I see.'

He moved to the mantelpiece and leaned against it. 'I asked your cousin to come but she suggested I play abigail and left. I could not find Jessica either.'

'I am certain I can manage.' With her hands clasped in her lap and her wavy thick hair curling past her shoulders, she looked young and vulnerable. And incredibly desirable.

He crossed his arms. 'How? You've only one arm and women's garments are devilishly difficult when you have use of both hands.' He tried to keep his voice matter-of-fact. 'And, if you recall, you performed a similar service for me not long ago. So, it is my turn to reciprocate.'

She blushed and bit her lip. 'But this is different.'

'How?' Although he knew perfectly well it was not the same at all.

She lifted her chin. 'I can sleep in my balldress.'

His brow shot up. 'Can you? Then I compliment you. I doubt if most ladies can. At least from what Jessica tells me.' He strode to the bed and picked up the nightdress, which appeared made for a woman three times her size. 'You'll be better off in this, particularly with that arm of yours.' He glanced at her face which had that calm set look to it. 'My dear,

I am probably not the most competent of abigails but I fear you'll have to do with me.' He smiled sardonically. 'And I promise not to attempt a seduction if that is what you fear.'

She reddened to her roots. 'It is not that.'

He shifted away from the mantelpiece. 'No? Then come here.'

She rose, her face heated with colour and the look of someone who was about to face a firing squad. She stood in front of him. Which was when he noticed her feet were bare.

A shaft of desire pierced him at the sight of her delicate, pale feet. He tore his gaze away. 'Turn around,' he said curtly.

She did, holding herself stiff. He fumbled with the tiny buttons on the back of her dress, trying to think of anything but the slender curve of her neck and back. Or the way her hair hung soft and enticing about her shoulders. It was all he could do to keep from pulling her back against him, burying his face in the cloud of her hair. His fingers felt as if they were made of lead, but he finally undid the last button and then slid the garment from her shoulders.

It fell to the ground in a pool of pale green silk. His groin tightened. He strove to keep his voice calm despite his desperate urge to crush her to him. 'Now, your stays.'

She jumped away from him as if burned. 'I…I can just sleep in them.'

He glanced at her face, which was hot with colour. She looked vulnerable and confused, and humiliated to her core. It occurred to him then that not only was this probably the first time a man had seen her undressed, but had touched her in such an intimate way. How the devil could he have forgotten she was a virgin? He plucked the nightdress from the bed. 'Hold this in front of you.'

'Th…thank you.' She took the garment, a flash of gratitude in her eyes. It had the effect of making him want to take her in his arms and make love to her until all thoughts of modesty fled. 'Perhaps I can just put this on now.'

He spoke without thinking. 'These won't be the first stays I've seen.'

'Oh. I suppose not.' She blushed even more.

Now she probably thought he was a libertine. He scowled at her. 'I assure you, however, I do not make a habit of the practice.'

'I did not think so. Not…not that it is any of my concern.'

His brow shot up. 'Not your concern? What the devil do you mean by that?'

'I mean…' She closed her eyes for a brief moment. 'Please can we not finish this?'

She sounded as if she was being tortured. He felt the same way. He began to untie the laces of her stays. The intimate act was almost his undoing. The garment fell away.

'Now your petticoat.' His voice was hoarse. He loosened the ties of the remaining garment and then she stood in nothing but her shift, the neat, graceful curves of her body outlined by the thin fabric of the garment. It would be so easy to wrap his arms around her and pull her against him.

The hardness in his loins was almost unbearable. He shut his eyes for a moment, trying to regain control. The last thing he could do was make love to his wife.

He forced himself to speak and stepped around in

front of her. 'I will help you with your nightdress.'
He kept his eyes on her face. Which proved to be an
error. Her tawny brown eyes were soft and wide, her
auburn hair tumbled about her face, and her rosy,
half-parted lips invited his kiss. And when his eyes
fell to a small mole just above her right breast, he
nearly groaned.

He wanted her in the worst way possible.

She looked at him nervously, still clutching the
nightdress to her chest. 'I believe I will just sleep in
my shift.'

'As you wish.' He wasn't about to argue with her
at this point. Not when he was in such desperate need
of a cold bath. Or a bottle of brandy.

'Thank you.' Her eyes didn't quite meet his and
her face was still red.

He inclined his head. 'I will be in the dressing
room if you need me,' he said curtly.

'I will be all right.' She looked at him then. 'And
you?'

'Yes.' A strange, fierce longing shot through him
that had nothing to do with lust. 'Goodnight, then.'
He turned and stalked to the dressing room.

Nearly two hours later, Sarah finally opened her
eyes and rolled to her back. Sleep was impossible.
From the sounds coming from the room next to hers,
she doubted if Dev was doing much better.

She shifted so she could see the half-closed door
of the dressing room. In fact, it appeared he was not
even trying to sleep. A light still burned in the room.

He had left the bedchamber once while she pretended to be asleep. Nerves on edge, she had waited
until his return, scarcely daring to breath when she

heard his footsteps. It wasn't until he crossed the bedchamber and entered the dressing room without a pause that she had finally let out her breath.

Oh, she had wanted the most wanton things from him when he was helping her undress. Even now, her body felt heated at the thought of his dark head bent towards her, his hands brushing over her skin. She had wanted to press into him, feel his hand touch her in places no lady should desire.

Not that he had been anything but the perfect gentleman. In fact, he had been so impersonal she had almost thought him completely unaffected. Except for that odd, almost vulnerable look on his face just before he left her. And she knew then that he felt as alone as she did.

She heard the creak of the chair as he shifted again. She sat up, pushing the hair from her face. It was no use sleeping, not when he was awake and probably exceedingly uncomfortable. She had no idea how a man of his height could possibly expect to sleep in a chair. She could at least offer him the bed.

She swung her legs over the edge of the bed, the blood pounding in her ears. She located the nightdress and managed to drape it around her shoulders. At least she felt a little less exposed than in only her shift. She moved as quietly as possible towards the dressing room, not wanting to wake him if he should happen to be asleep.

At first she thought he might be. He sprawled in the chair, his legs stretched in front of him, his eyes half-closed. He was clad only in breeches and shirt. One arm rested on the small table next to the chair, next to an open bottle. He held half a glass of what she thought was brandy in the other hand. He looked dangerous and masculine. And very much alone.

She started to back away and his eyes shot open. She froze.

'What are you doing up?' he demanded.

'I couldn't sleep.'

A mocking smile touched his lips. He leaned back further in his chair. 'I fear I cannot help you in that regard. Unless, of course, you care to join me in a brandy.'

'I don't care for brandy.'

'I somehow didn't think so.' He set his glass on the table, this time leaning forward. He had that wild, reckless look in his eye she seen once before in the tower. 'So, Sarah, why are you here? To keep me company?' His eyes bored into hers.

She bit her lip. 'Yes. If…if you'd like.'

He laughed. 'My dear, I fear your company is far too dangerous. Go back to bed.'

Her fingers tightened on the nightdress she held around her like a shawl. 'I really cannot sleep.'

He slowly stood and came towards her, his movements slow and menacing. 'Shall I put you to bed, then? Tuck you in?' he asked softly.

He meant to scare her away, she knew that. She kept her gaze on him. 'Yes, if you please.'

He stopped. 'You have no idea what you're saying.'

'I think I do.'

He laughed again. 'I doubt it. For if you did, you would know I would be in the bed with you.'

'It would be more comfortable than this chair.'

The heat in his eyes nearly made her run. But it was too late to back away even if she had wanted to.

He took one more step towards her, his gaze hot and hard. 'Shall we find out?'

'Yes.'

He advanced on her then. She had no time to think before he swooped down on her and lifted her in his arms as if she weighed no more than a feather. The nightdress fell from her hand. He carried her to the bed and laid her on the tumbled blankets. He knelt beside her on the bed.

Whatever had she done? She could smell the brandy on his breath and realised he was probably more than half-drunk. His dark face hovered over her, his desire hot and primitive in his eyes. He appeared almost a stranger. She suddenly felt vulnerable and afraid. 'Dev…' she whispered. And then she saw the flicker of tenderness.

'I won't hurt you,' he said roughly. He stretched out beside her and pulled her to him. His mouth took hers. He tasted of brandy and maleness and passion. He left her lips, and trailed kisses down her neck. His hand cupped her breast through the thin cotton of her shift, then he circled her nipple with his thumb. She stiffened at the intimate contact, her hand tangling in his thick hair. A warm, throbbing need began to build in her lower belly.

He returned to her mouth, his tongue seeking entry. She opened to him, and shyly touched his tongue with her own. He groaned and crushed her to him. Hot pain seared through her wrist which was caught between them.

She yelped. He instantly released her and lifted his head, his eyes dark and heavy with passion. And then his vision seemed to clear. 'I did not mean to hurt you.'

'You didn't,' she whispered. His face so close to hers was making her dizzy, making her forget her wrist. She had the most insane desire to pull his head to hers.

He sat up. 'I beg your pardon. I never meant to let things progress this far.' His face was expressionless, his voice stiff.

He didn't want her. The knowledge hurt. She managed to sit. 'I quite understand. I fear brandy and late hours might compel one to do things one ordinarily would find quite repugnant.'

'That's not what I meant.' He rose and stood by the bed.

'Damn it, Sarah, it should be quite obvious by now that I want you.' He laughed shortly. 'Quite desperately, in fact. But I've no intention of making love to you when I'm this damnably drunk. Nor do I want you to come to my bed because you pity me and you think to save my soul. You had better want me as much as I want you.'

'I don't pity you,' she said, stung. But he had already turned away. She did not look up as he crossed the room and silently left the bedchamber. And then she crawled back under her covers, too numb and bewildered to even cry. And this time she fell into a restless sleep without knowing whether he ever returned.

Dev awoke the next morning with a pounding head, a dry mouth, and a body aching from a night spent on a sofa in the drawing room of Lacey Manor. He sat up with a groan and rubbed his stiff neck. Through the window facing the garden he saw the sun was shining with the particular brilliance that followed a night of heavy rain.

He closed his eyes against the pain in his head and the events of last night flooded his mind: the slender, graceful curves of her body and the feel of her silky skin under his hands as he helped her undress; Sarah standing in the door of the dressing room, her eyes soft and vulnerable as she offered to keep him company.

And, most vivid of all, the feel of her in his arms, her hair spread around her face on the pillow, her lips and arms opening to him.

He nearly groaned. What the hell had possessed him? By the time she had come to him, the drink he had consumed, combined with the torture of helping her undress, had smashed what little was left of his careful control. When she had called his bluff, he had been too far gone to resist.

He'd never intended to let it go so far. He had not been so drunk that he had not noticed the flash of compassion in her eyes as she stood there. He knew she saw his loneliness and it had scared him. And so he had advanced on her with some idea of pushing her away from him.

But she had not fled. And he realised that she would have given herself to him, if only out of her misguided sense of pity.

And he would go to hell before he would accept that from her.

Chapter Eighteen

Sarah shoved the jewellery box under a tangled pile of gloves in the drawer of her dressing table. She would have preferred to send the necklace back to her husband with a carefully worded note telling him why she could not accept such a thing from him. Except he would probably fix her with his cool stare and tell her she was being ridiculous.

She scowled and went to the window. Ever since the ball two nights ago she had been completely out of sorts. At first she had been mortified by her brazen behaviour in inviting him to her bed and then humiliated by his rejection.

Those emotions had been replaced by a growing anger. How dare he tell her he wanted her, and at the same time accuse her of feeling nothing for him but pity! As if she would throw herself at him for such a weak reason. Worse, he had not even bothered to listen to anything she had to say!

He had retreated to his usual cool shell as if nothing had happened at all. Perhaps he had been too foxed to remember, hardly a comforting thought. She would have felt completely despairing except last night at dinner she had caught him watching her with an odd longing, and she realised he wanted her more than he wanted to admit.

She sat down on her bed with a sigh. Tonight they were to dine at Harrowood, something she did not look forward to in the least. Perhaps she should plead a headache and thus avoid another evening of Dev's scowling stares and her own discomfort.

Would anything ever change between them? She had just about made up her mind to invite herself to stay with Amelia and John for a month. But then their happiness with each other would only emphasise her own empty marriage.

And the fact that Amelia enjoyed seducing her husband.

She sat up a little straighter, thinking. Amelia had offered to help her with Dev. Whether it would work or not was questionable, but nothing else had dented his barriers either. And nothing could be much worse than the night of the ball.

Her cousin sat in the library leafing through a lady's magazine. She looked up as Sarah approached. 'I have just found the most delightful gown. Although I do not know if I would like it in canary yellow. Perhaps pale blue.' She laid the periodical aside. 'But I see you have not come to discuss gowns. What is amiss, Sarah?'

Sarah clasped her hands together. Her face was already heated. She forced herself to speak. 'I thought perhaps you could…could…'

Amelia arched a brow. 'Dear Sarah, I am certain your request cannot be all that unreasonable. What is it?'

'You once offered to help me.' Sarah took a deep

breath. 'I…I want to seduce my husband.' She waited for Amelia's reaction.

Amelia smiled. 'I think it is about time.'

Sarah glanced at herself one last time in the looking glass. Amelia had loaned her a gown in a salmon silk, the colour making her ivory complexion glow. The bodice was low, exposing the soft creamy mounds of her breasts. And it moulded itself to her curves rather more tightly than she liked. Although Amelia was an inch taller and had a more generous bust, Amelia and Liza had very skilfully managed to fit the gown to Sarah's more slender body. Amelia had also insisted in adding a bit of padding to fill out the bodice.

'Very nice,' Amelia said, coming to stand behind Sarah and peering at her reflection over her shoulder. 'You look quite enticing. I will just help you with this necklace and then you will be ready.'

She slipped a gold chain with a diamond pendant around Sarah's neck. The small jewel nestled between her breasts in a most suggestive way.

'Perfect.' Amelia stepped around in front of Sarah, a mischievous smile on her face. 'It will draw the eye downward to a most interesting place.'

'I am not certain I really want that.' Sarah had no desire to have anyone leering at her bosom. Not that hers was particularly impressive by any stretch of the imagination, even with the additional padding.

'But you do. You want him to notice everything about you. Not that he doesn't now, but he needs a little encouragement to think about doing more than look.'

'Amelia!' Sarah exclaimed, shocked.

Amelia arched a delicate brow. 'Well? I thought that was what you wanted.'

'Yes, but…' Sarah coloured hotly. Not only at Amelia's words, but at the memory of his hand cupping her breast. The very thought made her body tingle with heat.

She picked up her fan. Merlin watched from his customary perch on the dressing table. She scratched his favourite spot under his chin and he rubbed against her hand. 'I certainly hope I know what I am doing,' she told him. He merely closed his eyes.

Dev's gaze flickered across the table to where his wife sat between young Lord Mobley, and Lord Bentwood, an ageing dandy. They had both spent the dinner vying for Sarah's attention, and from the worshipful expression on Mobley's freckled face, he was in the throes of calf-love.

Dev wanted to gnash his teeth together. Or throw his glass across the room. What the hell was she doing? She seemed determined to make a conquest of every man in the room, excepting Blanton, smiling and flirting with a practised ease he'd never dreamed she was capable of. She had even favoured him with several of her demure smiles and more than once on the trip to Harrowood had placed her hand on his arm or accidentally touched his leg. He'd nearly jumped at the light contact.

Worse, she wore a dress that made him want to pull her from the room and demand she change into something with a neckline up to her chin. The necklace she wore dipped between her breasts in a way that made him think of cupping them in his hands and displacing the jewel with his mouth. From the way Lord Bentwood's eyes focused on her chest, Dev strongly suspected his thoughts ran in a similar train, which filled Dev with the desire to knock the man's teeth down his throat.

She looked up and her eyes met his, her lips curving in a slow, seductive smile. Heat coursed through his loins. He yanked his gaze away and saw with great relief that Lady Filby had stood, indicating the women were to retire to the drawing room. At least for a short time, Sarah would be out of his sight, and that of the rest of the males at this damnable dinner.

Sarah sat in Lady Filby's drawing room, trying not to notice that the men had entered. She kept her eyes steadily focused on Lady Filby and Mrs Kenton who were discussing tomorrow's picnic. She was undoubtedly violating Amelia's instructions but, after tonight's dinner, Sarah was certain there was no hope of ever catching Dev's notice.

She had never been so grateful when a dinner had ended. Trying to follow Amelia's instructions to engage in light flirtation with her dinner partners all the while casting glances at Dev had proved taxing. Particularly as she had no desire to encourage Lord Bentwood at all. His ridiculous compliments had quite ruined her appetite. And Lord Mobley, a gangly youth of no more than eighteen, turned bright red whenever she made a remark and stared at her with the adoring eyes of a puppy. The last thing she had wanted was for a naïve young man to develop a *tendre* for her.

Besides, Dev had hardly seemed to notice her. He had been occupied with Lady Townsley on one side and Caroline Kenton on the other. Lady Townsley

had laughed and conversed with him with an ease
Sarah could never hope to emulate.

Now, Lady Filby leaned forward. She was a
slightly plump woman with large teeth and a knowing smile. She glanced over at one corner of the
room. 'Lady Townsley certainly seems determined to
renew her acquaintance with your husband.' She
tapped Sarah's arm with her fan. 'My dear, I don't
believe I should allow it if I were you.'

'Really, Selina! What a thing to say to Lady
Huntington! I am certain you have nothing to worry
about, Lady Huntington. Particularly since Lord
Townsley does not seem to mind.' Mrs Kenton gave
Sarah a reassuring smile.

'I am not,' Sarah said with a confidence she was
far from feeling. 'What a lovely necklace, Lady
Filby.'

'A present from my dear husband on my last birth-
day.' She looked inordinately pleased and, as Sarah
had hoped, was distracted into a discussion of jewels.

Sarah excused herself and rose, tired of the gossip.
It was impossible to miss Dev standing near the open
doors, Lady Townsley smiling up at him with a familiarity Sarah envied. He seemed not to notice
Sarah. Disheartened, she turned away and saw
Charles watching her from across the room. She
smiled at him, and then her gaze fell to Lady Coleridge who sat next to Charles. She watched Dev, a
shadow crossing her face.

Sarah looked back at Dev and Lady Townsley and
made up her mind. He could at least pretend some
affection for her, if only to spare Lady Coleridge's
feelings. And Jessica's as well. She knew that the

strain between them was a source of distress to both of them.

And it seemed his attentions to Lady Townsley were now a source of gossip.

She marched across the room, a determined smile on her face. She reached Dev's side and placed her hand on the sleeve of his coat. He looked at her hand, his expression startled. Lady Townsley stopped in mid-sentence, her eyes widening slightly. Then she smiled. 'Lady Huntington, I fear you must think me very ill mannered to occupy your husband so thoroughly. I think I shall turn him over to you and find my own husband, who undoubtedly feels rather neglected.'

It was Sarah's turn to be surprised. 'Thank you.'

'Not at all.' She looked at Dev with a little smile. 'The evening is quite nice. Perhaps a stroll in the garden. Harrowood has a most enchanting garden.' She walked off.

Dev looked down at Sarah. His expression was cool, although from the tightness about his mouth she realised he reined in his temper with a great deal of effort. 'Is something amiss?' he asked.

She dropped her hand and smiled up at him. 'Not at all. I think I would like to walk in the garden, however. It is rather warm in here.'

'Perhaps Kenton would oblige you.'

Did he really wish to pawn her off on Charles? She kept her smile steady, refusing to let him see her hurt. 'I think I would rather walk with you. I have not had a chance to talk with you at all this evening.'

'You have been rather occupied with the rest of the company.'

'As have you.' Her own temper was beginning to

rise at his surly tone. How dare he sound so cross when it was apparent he wanted little to do with her? Well, she was not about to back down. 'I would like to go to the garden, if you please.'

He inclined his head. 'I am, of course, your servant.'

'Are you? I do sometimes wonder.'

His brows snapped together, but when he spoke his voice was polite. 'Very well.' He held out his arm.

She tucked her hand in the crook of his elbow. He led her out of the doors to the small balcony which was directly outside the drawing room. They descended the steps that led to the lawn and shrubbery in silence. At the bottom, he paused and looked down at her. 'Which direction?'

'Whichever direction is the most private.'

He raised his brow in his mocking way. 'Why? Do you wish to be private with me?'

She gave him her sweetest smile. 'Yes.'

To her satisfaction he looked taken aback. He recovered rapidly. 'I will own I am quite curious as to why. Perhaps a hint?'

She resisted the urge to give him a severe setdown. 'Not until we are further away from the house.' She gave his arm a little tug. 'Come.'

He went with her, but the half-smile on his face was dangerous. 'A game, Sarah? I would not have thought it of you.'

She managed to keep her voice calm. 'Sometimes I like games.'

An arrested expression appeared in his eye. 'Do you? Then I hope you know the rules.'

'Well, if I don't, I will make up my own,' she said

with more bravado than she felt. Not that she was certain what he was talking about. Or what she was, for that matter.

'Not very wise, my dear.' They entered a walk between a row of tall yews. At the end of the narrow avenue she could see a fountain.

'Really.'

He frowned but said nothing more until they reached the fountain. He pulled her around to a bench that faced the fountain. 'Sit down.'

'Only if you will also. I dislike having you hover over me.' The dark look on his face was making her apprehensive.

He complied, his gaze on her face. She forced herself to sit and, remembering Amelia's advice, positioned herself so her leg pressed lightly against his. He flinched, hardly an encouraging sign.

'So, my dear Sarah, what is this?' His voice was dangerously soft.

'What is what?'

'You announce you wish to be private with me. So, what exactly is your game?'

'I really don't have one. It was you who suggested I did.'

He leaned back and crossed his arms. 'I stand corrected. What is it you want?'

It was all she could do to keep from announcing she wanted to return to the house. She managed a smile. 'To see you. I have scarcely seen you at all the past few days, except at dinner.' She forced herself to hold his gaze.

His eyes flickered. 'And what do you wish to see me about?'

'Nothing in particular. I merely wanted to…to see you.'

'So you invited me to a nearly dark garden with a desire to be private. My dear Sarah, that is an exceedingly dangerous proposal to make to a man.'

'Even if you are my husband?' she asked innocently.

His gaze narrowed for a moment. 'Yes. Even then.'

'Why?'

'Because it may lead to certain consequences.'

'Really? Such as what?' From his expression she feared one of them was strangling.

He leaned towards her, his hand carelessly brushing her cheek. 'You are playing a game, are you not? Not just with me, but with all the others tonight. Why? To make Kenton jealous?'

She stared at him and then shoved his hand away. She leaped up. 'How…how can you say such a despicable thing? Or think such a thing of me? He is a friend, but I…I would never….' She fought for control. 'If you will excuse me, my lord.' She whirled on her heel.

He rose in a single movement and caught her hand. 'Sarah! Wait!'

'What?' She looked up at him, angry tears in her eyes. 'Please release me! I have no desire to hear you insult me more.'

All traces of mockery were gone. 'Sarah, I am sorry.'

'I know that you have no great liking for me, but must you accuse me of unfaithfulness? Do you think I would do that to you?'

'No.' He dropped her arm and stood looking at

her. His expression slowly changed. 'No, you would not.'

She looked away. 'I think I would like to return to the house after all.'

'Let me take you. It is getting dark.'

'No, I would prefer to walk on my own.' She whirled on her heel and marched towards the house. She heard him behind her, but refused to look back.

She entered the drawing room where card tables had already been set up. Several of the guests had sat down to play. She saw Caroline in one corner, Blanton with her. Caroline looked rather desperate, a feeling Sarah knew all too well when dealing with Blanton. Sarah crossed the room, deciding, for tonight at least, she would rather face Blanton than her infuriating husband.

'Good evening Caroline, Mr Blanton,' she said.

An expression of distaste crossed his face before he bowed. He stepped away from her as if he feared she had a cat concealed on her person. 'Lady Huntington.'

Sarah smiled at Caroline. 'Perhaps you'd care to take a turn around the room with me. I've not had a chance to talk with you.'

'I…yes, I would.' Caroline gave Blanton a polite smile. 'If you will excuse me.'

'Of course. I look forward to seeing you tomorrow at the picnic, Miss Kenton.'

'Oh, yes.' She looked quite relieved to take Sarah's arm. Once they were out of earshot, she leaned towards Sarah and whispered, 'Thank you so much. I had no idea how to escape him. I really cannot quite like him, but perhaps I am unreasonable.'

'No, you are not. He is not a very proper person.' She only hoped Caroline would not ask her why she said so. She very much hoped he had not set his sights on Caroline.

She heaved a sigh, and prayed this truly horrible night would soon end.

Chapter Nineteen

The next morning dawned sunny and warm, quite perfect for an outing. The prospect of a picnic did nothing for Sarah's sour mood. She'd slept little and the last thing she wanted was to spend time near her husband.

She was relieved to see no sign of him as she seated herself in the landau across from Amelia. Amelia's gaze took in Sarah's expression and her own changed to sympathy. 'Don't look so distressed. I am certain everything will work out in time.'

'Only if I never speak to him again,' Sarah snapped. She had poured out the details of last night's disaster into Amelia's sympathetic ears. But not even Amelia's assurances that he was only showing a very promising jealousy had soothed the hurt and anger she'd felt at his words.

Amelia started to say something and then a peculiar expression crossed her face. 'I am afraid that will not happen. He is coming now.'

Sarah quelled the urge to duck. 'Really.' Instead, she stared straight ahead, intending to ignore him.

Dev stopped next to her. 'Good morning, Lady Marleigh.'

Amelia smiled. 'Good day. Are you perhaps planning to join our party?'

'Yes.' He turned, and Sarah was quite aware his eyes were on her face. 'If my wife will permit me.'

She tightened her hands and looked pointedly at a spot over Amelia's shoulder. 'You may do as you please, my lord.'

'May I? Then perhaps you will not object if I sit next to you.'

Sarah looked at him then. 'If you must know, I do object.'

'You may sit next to me, however,' Amelia said with a mischievous smile.

Sarah shot her cousin a speaking glance, which Amelia ignored. Sarah turned her head away, determined not to pay the least heed to him. To her great dismay, he sprang into the carriage directly across from her. She pointedly shifted her position so she was across from Amelia. She had no intention of having his long legs anywhere near hers.

Jessica and Adam rode up next to them. Jessica cocked a brow at her brother. 'You have decided not to ride today?'

'No, I thought I would prefer the carriage.' His gaze rested on Sarah's face and, in spite of her desire to remain unaffected, she felt colour rise to her cheeks.

Jessica grinned. 'A splendid idea.'

A loud meow distracted them. In one graceful movement, Merlin sprang up beside Sarah. He rubbed against her cheek and then settled next to her, folding his paws under him.

'Sarah's chaperon, I take it,' Adam said. 'Are you planning to bring him or does he run off?'

'I suppose we could bring him,' Sarah said. He looked quite settled as if a ride in a carriage was an everyday occurrence. 'He likes carriage rides. If he looks as if he wants to jump out, we can bring him back.'

'Or put him in a picnic basket,' Dev said.

She directed an icy frown at him, forgetting she had vowed not to look at him. He merely grinned, which made her feel even more cross.

Dev gave the coachman the signal to start and they were off, Adam and Jessica riding alongside. Sarah stared resolutely at the scenery, allowing the conversation to be carried by the others. She was undoubtedly behaving childishly, but the hurt was still too fresh. And after last night she had no idea why he was in such a good mood or why he kept staring at her in such an annoying fashion.

Her temper hardly improved by the time they reached the tower. The party from Kentwood was already there. Dev helped Amelia out and then held his hand out to Sarah.

She looked down her nose at him. 'I am perfectly capable of alighting on my own,' she said coldly.

He looked up at her, a little smile touching his mouth. 'I've no doubt of that. But I wish to help you.'

'I would prefer you did not.'

'Then I shall stand here until you change your mind.'

'We will look ridiculous.' She looked quickly over at the others who paid them little heed at the moment. Amelia had already gone over to speak to Mrs

Kenton. 'Besides, I wish to stay with Merlin so he does not run away.'

'I am sure Samuels can handle him.' He nodded towards the groom.

Samuels sprang forward. 'Most certainly, my lady.'

Very well,' she said ungraciously. She gave him her hand and stepped down, attempting to make as little contact with him as possible.

He did not release her hand and she was forced to yank it out of his grasp. 'Perhaps we should join the others, my lord.'

'Not yet.' He stepped around in front of her. 'Come and walk with me first.'

She folded her arms and glared at him. 'I don't want to.'

'Probably not. However, if you don't I will be forced to carry you off.'

She gasped. 'You wouldn't dare.'

'But I would.' His eyes held hers in a distinct challenge.

'That is hardly fair.'

'No. But I don't wish to play fair at the moment.' He held out his hand. 'There's a place by the stream where we can talk.'

She refused his hand. 'As you wish.' She stalked past him, chin raised.

He easily caught up to her and took her arm. 'You are going in the wrong direction. You'll end up in the sheep pasture.' His voice held a hint of laughter.

'I like sheep,' she said coolly. So now he was laughing at her. She quelled the very strong and most unlady-like urge to hit him.

He took her to a small grassy patch near the stream

and released her arm and turned to face her. All laughter had left his face.

Sarah forced herself to look at him. There was something in his still posture that made her defiance seem unnecessary. However, she gave him a cool stare. 'More games, my lord?'

'No,' he said quietly. He looked away for a moment and then back at her. 'I regretted the words I said to you last night more than any words I have spoken in my life. I can offer no excuse, except that I envy your friendship with Kenton.'

Sarah glanced at him. 'Why?'

He shrugged. 'I suppose because I would like the same sort of easy conversation with you, would like your same high regard.'

Astonished, she stared at him. 'But you have my regard.'

He gave a short laugh. 'There is no need to spare my feelings. I have coerced you, insulted you, ridden roughshod over you in every possible way since that night at Henslowe Hall. I nearly caused your death. And long before that, I gravely wounded your brother in a duel. I've no reason to expect you to look upon me with anything but contempt.'

'But I do not!' She was astounded he could be so mistaken about her feelings. 'I have never held you in contempt. How could I, when it was my own brother who committed such a wrongful act against you? He had no right to take another man's wife.'

He looked away. 'But he did not.'

She looked at him, not understanding. He stared out at the stream. 'Mary intended to go to her old nurse. She made it as far as an inn in Yorkshire before becoming ill with influenza. The innkeeper and his wife took her in. As she became more ill they insisted she must have someone they could send for. And she named your brother.' His voice was flat, but when he looked back at Sarah, she saw the raw pain in his eyes. 'There was something else, you see. She was pregnant with your brother's child.'

She did not dare move as much as she wanted to go to him, take his pain within herself. She waited, very still, for him to continue.

'I did not discover that until I finally traced her to the inn. She asked for an annulment the day after the wedding. I refused, of course. I had no idea what was wrong, why she should suddenly change her mind. I thought perhaps her father's death had caused some sort of collapse. She asked again, a week later. I, of course, said no. And so, desperate, she fled. I drove her to her death.'

His face was bleak, the wound to his soul still raw. Sarah moved then, and laid her hand on his sleeve. 'No, you did not. It is odd—Nicholas, Lady Coleridge, you, me—we all blame ourselves for her death.'

He looked down at her, and his mouth twisted. 'You as well? I've no idea why.'

'I invited her to stay with me. Do you remember? It was after your betrothal ball. But Mama was very ill and I could not often leave her side. So I sent Nicholas and Mary out together. I never thought anything, except it was nice my brother and my dearest friend got along so well. And now I wished I had not been so stupid, that perhaps if I had not invited her, she would be alive.'

'You are not omniscient. You could not foresee what would happen between them.'

Her hand tightened on his arm. 'No. And you are not omniscient either. You did not know that Mary carried such a secret with her. Lady Coleridge did not know either.'

'No.' He pulled his arm away and turned, looking out at the gurgling water. 'But I must have given her such a fear of me that she could not bring herself to tell me. And, in truth, I cannot fault her. My damnable temper...I swear I never laid a hand on her, but I said things that should not have been said.'

'Dev...'

'That's not the worst of it. I tried to force her into my bed.'

This time she took his hand, hardly knowing what to say. She could imagine the growing bewilderment and frustration of a husband with a new bride who did not want to be a wife, and the shame that Mary must have felt when she realised she carried another man's child. And Sarah knew that was why she had left.

Her fingers tightened around his. 'No. You did not drive her away. I think,' she said slowly, 'that Mary left because she could not bear to face you or her family. She would not have wanted you to raise another man's child as yours. She could not be your wife when she had already given herself to another man. She would have deplored the deceit above all else.' She glanced up at him. 'She never blamed you, even Nicholas admitted as much. It was her own guilt that drove her away. I think now she must have sent for Nicholas because of the baby. She would have wanted him to know.'

His head was bowed. She waited in silence. He

finally lifted his head and when he looked at her she saw the tears. 'Sarah—' he began.

'Don't.' She wrapped her arms around him and pulled him to her as tightly as she could with one bandaged hand, and buried her face in his chest. He hesitated for a moment and then he crushed her hard against him, his face in her hair.

They stayed that way for an eternity with the soft babble of the stream and the songs of the birds mixing with the strong beat of his heart under her ear. It was only when something pressed against her legs and mewed that he slowly released her.

'Your chaperon is hinting we should return to the others.' His eyes were on her face.

'Yes. Are you all right?'

'Yes…no.' He gave a shaky laugh. 'I think I will be.' His expression sobered. 'I've no idea what to do next.'

'About what?' she asked.

He made a helpless gesture. 'About you. And me.'

'Perhaps we could be friends,' she suggested tentatively.

'Friends? Is that what you wish?' For a moment, he looked almost disappointed.

'It might be a start.'

'Yes.' His mouth lifted in a ghost of a smile. 'It might be.' He held out his hand. 'Shall we return to the others? They probably think I've abducted you.'

'Yes.' She placed her hand in his and, with Merlin at her heels, they walked towards the tower.

Caroline rose to her feet. 'If I sit much longer, I will fall asleep. I need a walk. Does anyone wish to join me?'

They had finished the lavish meal and were seated under a spreading tree on a blanket. The men had wandered off to look at the stream and several of the women had gone to sit in the tower garden.

'A walk sounds splendid,' Jessica said. 'Sarah?' She stood and glanced down at Sarah.

'I think I will stay here,' Sarah said. She felt tired, not only from her poor sleep last night, but from the conversation with Dev by the stream. She had not yet thought much about it, preferring to let her thoughts and emotions rest. For the first time, she had hope that they might have a friendship, but at the moment she shied away from thinking of the possible implications.

She stroked Merlin, who sat beside her, and idly watched the others. Amazingly enough the cat had not run off, but seemed content either to follow the groom around to whom he'd taken a liking or to sit with Sarah. At least it had kept Blanton from joining the ladies on the grass after the meal. He had instead gone off with the men.

She glanced around. Amelia was engaged in conversation with Lady Townsley and Penelope Kenton. She frowned a little when she saw Blanton had returned and managed to corner Caroline again. He'd spent most of the outing trailing her around. Sarah had the uneasy feeling he had targeted Caroline as the next object of his affection. What if he decided to compromise Caroline just as he had tried to do with her?

She slowly stood, Merlin in her arms. As large as he was, she could still carry him if she avoided supporting much of his weight on her wrist. She walked purposefully to Caroline. 'Good day, Mr Blanton.'

He turned. A look of revulsion crossed his face when he spotted the cat. Sarah smiled. 'Would you like to pet him?'

He backed away. 'No, I quite detest cats.'

'I adore them,' Caroline said.

'Then would you hold Merlin for me? I...I must find Dev, and I don't want him to run off. And Jessica is looking for you.' At least she could rid Caroline of him for a few minutes.

'Certainly.' Caroline took the cat who snuggled in her arms and fixed Blanton with an unblinking yellow stare. She gave Blanton a polite smile. 'If you will excuse me, Mr Blanton.'

'Of course.' He bowed a little, his expression genial, but when he looked at Sarah, the fury in his face made her recoil.

She left Caroline and Merlin with Jessica and then wandered towards the stream. She leaned against a tree and tried to decide what she should do about Blanton.

Should she talk to Charles? But then he would want to know why she had such a dislike of Blanton. And she had no desire to seek out Charles for a private talk. Not with the very tentative truce between herself and her husband. But she could talk to Dev and he could drop a hint in Charles's ear.

'Hiding?'

She gasped. Dev stood behind her as if conjured up by her thoughts. 'Can you not announce your presence?' she demanded.

A brief grin crossed his face. 'I just did. What are you doing here alone?'

'Thinking. Although I had just made up my mind that I wanted to speak with you.'

'An amazing coincidence. I had wanted you for the same purpose. Will you walk with me?' He smiled and for the first time she had a sudden glimpse of the charming young man that had been Mary's fiancé.

She caught her breath. 'Yes, I…I would like that.'

He held out his hand. She placed hers in it and his strong fingers curled around hers. 'Shall we visit the tower or the stream again?' he asked.

'The stream, if you please.'

He said nothing until they'd reached the same place they had been earlier. 'Shall we sit?' he asked. 'There's a bench of sorts. Although it may be too rough for your dress.' He indicated a rough bench made of a felled log supported by two stumps.

'It will do nicely.' She sat, arranging her skirts. He sat next to her, the hard length of his body pressing against her on the small seat.

'What is it you wanted, Sarah?'

She glanced at his strong profile. At the moment, she suddenly thought she would like nothing more than to have him kiss her.

Flushing, she quickly looked away, and strove to keep her mind from such disturbing thoughts. 'I wanted to speak to you about Cedric Blanton.'

He stiffened. 'Has he been near you again?' he asked sharply.

'No. Not since the ball. In fact, I think he rather dislikes me,' she said quickly. 'It's about Caroline Kenton. I am afraid he may be trying to fix his interest with her. I do not think she likes him much at all, but I fear he may try to force her as he did me. But perhaps I am mistaken in my concern.'

'No, you are not.' He frowned. 'You are right to

be concerned. You were not the first woman he tried
to force into marriage.'

Sarah looked at him, horrified. 'There was another? I had no idea. I knew he was dreadful, but...
please, Dev, will you speak to Mr Kenton about it?
I have already told Caroline he is not very proper,
but I worry it is not enough.'

'I will.' He lifted her hand to his lips and pressed
a light kiss on her wrist. 'My sweet Sarah, don't
worry. Caroline will be fine.'

His touch sent a shiver through her. He dropped
her hand. 'So, what else did you wish to say to me?
Last night, that is. Now that we've decided to be
friends, I rather thought we could start where we left
off last night. What did you wish to say to me when
you desired to be private?'

His mood was odd, one she'd never seen before.
It was if all the tension had left him. She was finding
it difficult to get her bearings. 'I had nothing particular in mind.'

His brow arched. 'Nothing? You merely desired
my company?'

'If you must know, yes.' Her face heated. If she'd
had Amelia's skills, she would have been able to
come up with some witty repartee. Instead she felt
clumsy and extremely naïve.

'I see.'

She stole a glance at him. He looked bemused.
Then his mouth lifted in a self-mocking smile. 'I am
highly complimented. It is not often that a lovely
woman desires my company.'

Was he about to erect another barrier? She gave
him a little frown. 'I find that difficult to believe.'

'Why?'

'For one thing, the gossip says otherwise. And for another....' Her mind went blank.

'Yes?' His brow inched higher.

She was about to give him a set-down when her mind suddenly fastened on another tack. 'I think you highly underrate your attractions.'

He stared at her as if she'd suddenly spoken in Greek. 'What does that mean?'

She allowed her gaze to drift over him. 'Well, you are quite dashing. You are tall, very handsome and intelligent, and can be quite agreeable when you set your mind to it. They are attributes most women find quite desirable.'

A tinge of colour appeared in his cheek. He folded his arms and leaned back against the tree. 'I'd no idea you had been taking inventory of my appearance.'

'I have,' she said complacently.

He looked straight ahead. 'So, last night you wanted my company so you could...' He floundered.

'Observe your attractions.'

He scowled and stood. 'I fear, Sarah, you are playing games again.'

'Am I? Perhaps.' She smiled at him. 'But I do think you are quite handsome.'

'Are you flirting with me?' he demanded. His brows had snapped together even more.

'Yes. Well, attempting to,' she amended. 'You're making it rather difficult. Bésides, I am not very good at it.'

'You don't need to flirt. You're too dangerous as it is.'

She stood up and took a step towards him. He took a step back. 'Really? You told me once before, but

I will own, I have no idea what you are talking about.'

'You are too…' By now his back was against a tree. He scowled again. 'Too desirable as it is.'

'Oh? Is that a problem?' she asked innocently. He looked extremely flustered and the knowledge she had that much power over him was quite heady.

'It is.' He folded his arms. 'Stop playing games.'

She took another step towards him. 'Why? Are you worried I might decide to ravish you?'

'Hardly,' he snapped.

The conversation was so nearly like the ones they'd had before with their roles reversed that she nearly giggled.

She might as well bring out the full artillery. 'Actually, you should worry, because I have been trying very hard to seduce you.'

'Seduce me?' His mouth fell open and he looked as if she had threatened to murder him.

'Well, yes. Do you remember? The night of the ball at Lacey Manor you said—'

'I know what I said,' he snapped.

'What do you think?'

He paced away from her, then turned and ran a hand through his hair. 'Damn it, Sarah! This is hardly the place.'

'I hadn't really planned on it here,' she said calmly.

'God, I hope not!' He stared at her. 'Another game?'

'No.' Any embarrassment she might have felt was rapidly giving away to exasperation. 'I am not playing a game. And I do not pity you. You told me the night of the ball that I had to be certain…'

'I did. But I hardly expected—' He stopped and frowned. 'We can't discuss this here. We will discuss this at home.'

'Yes, my lord.' They might have been planning to talk about the purchase of new furniture. If it wasn't for the fact that he looked so confused, she would have been angry.

He spent most of the trip back in abstracted silence, his gaze more than once fixed on her face as if he hardly knew what to make of her. And when the carriage stopped, he helped her down, then dropped her hand as if her touch burned him.

She was beginning to wonder if all men were this difficult.

Chapter Twenty

Dev yanked his gaze from Sarah's mouth and forced himself to take a bit of the lobster set before him. He had scarcely registered the first few dishes set in front of him or the conversation flowing around him. His mind was completely on the woman next to him.

He could think of nothing but her startling words by the stream. Did she really want to seduce him? Or was it some game? Except why would she play such a dangerous one when she knew where it would lead? And there had been something in her face that told him she played no game.

The thought she might desire him as much as he desired her was driving him mad. He'd hardly been able to concentrate on anything else.

He wondered if she already regretted her words. She had scarcely glanced his way since they had arrived home. Instead, she had been as preoccupied as he, barely appearing to notice what she ate or when someone spoke.

He looked back at her again, his eyes drifting down to her bodice where her soft breasts were outlined by the silky fabric of her gown. He could almost feel their fullness in his hand, a thought that nearly made him groan. He reached for his wineglass and Amelia spoke. He started and the wine suddenly spilled across the table towards Sarah.

She gasped and jumped up, startled out of her reverie.

He leaped up. 'Damn! I beg your pardon!' He reached for the glass and set it upright, heat rising to his face. 'Did I spill any on you?' he asked swiftly.

'No.' She gave him a nervous little smile and he realised it was the first time she had looked directly at him all evening. 'I am quite undamaged.'

'Good,' he said. He stared at her, his pulse quickening. There was a slight cough from behind him and he suddenly remembered they were not alone. 'A slight accident, I fear.'

Amelia met his eyes, her own full of laughter. 'Yes, we can see that.'

'I fear my brother has not been attending at all,' Jessica said.

Adam glanced over at Sarah and grinned. 'At least not to us. I fear his mind is occupied elsewhere.'

Dev scowled. By now the footman had finished mopping up the spill. 'Perhaps we should continue with the meal,' he suggested tersely.

'I am afraid that we are nearly finished,' Sarah said apologetically.

'I see. So you are about to withdraw, then?' He felt even more the fool.

'Yes, if you do not object.' Her face was still suffused with delicate colour.

'No.'

She carefully avoided glancing his way again as

she left, followed by Jessica and Amelia. As he
watched her leave the room, the thought occurred to
him it must have taken all the courage she possessed
to tell him such a thing.

And his response had been to push her away. As
he had the night of the ball.

Perhaps it was time he went to her.

Sarah rose from the wing chair. Following the conversation between Amelia and Jessica was nearly impossible, her mind was elsewhere. She glanced at the
clock on the mantelpiece. If past nights were any
indication, the men would join them soon. 'I believe
I shall go to bed.'

Amelia looked up. 'So soon?'

Sarah managed a smile. 'I am quite tired after today's picnic.'

'Goodnight, dear Sarah,' Jessica said with a smile.

Amelia stood. 'I will return directly, Jessica. First,
I must talk to my cousin.' She walked with Sarah to
the door and then paused, her brow arched. 'Whatever has happened now? You disappear into the
bushes with Dev. When you come out, he appears
stunned, as if he's been hit over the head with a
poker and, I must say, you are hardly much better.'

Sarah knotted her hands. 'I fear I did the most
revolting thing!' She briefly closed her eyes and then
looked at Amelia. 'I...I told him I wanted to seduce
him.'

Amelia blinked. 'Well, that most certainly explains
it. What did he say after such an announcement?'

'He said we should discuss it later.' Sarah still felt
mortified even thinking about it. 'I can hardly bear

to look at him. He must think I am deranged, or quite brazen.'

Amelia laughed. 'I doubt that. Not from the way he was gazing at you all during dinner. Or the way he spilled his wine. I imagine you just took him by surprise which, come to think of it, might be for the best.' A smile touched her lips. 'Perhaps this is the time for your discussion.'

'I rather hoped it could be postponed.' For the rest of the century preferably.

'No. Most certainly not. You'd best do it now while he's thrown off balance. Men are much more compliant then.' She gave Sarah a little shove. 'So, go and have your way with him.'

Sarah nodded, having no intention of following Amelia's advice.

She walked across the hallway, fervently hoping she could escape to her bedchamber before seeing her husband. Her courage was rapidly failing. Not only with fear he might not want her, but with fear he might. It wasn't that she was completely unfamiliar with the intimacies between men and women. Before her death, Sarah's mother had gently explained the marriage bed to Sarah, uncertain whether anyone else would think to perform that duty. She had not wanted her daughter to enter marriage completely unprepared. And certainly Sarah's reaction to his embraces had made her suspect it might not be such an unpleasant duty after all.

But what if he didn't really want her? Perhaps if she waited until tomorrow she could think of a rational explanation for her behaviour.

She walked quickly towards her room, thankful Dev was nowhere in sight. Perhaps the best course of action was to retire early. If for some reason he did want to talk to her, she could feign sleep. She reached her room, shutting the door behind her, feeling as if she'd just escaped an enemy. Merlin, who had been in his basket in the dressing room, came out to rub against her ankles in greeting before disappearing again on his nightly rounds.

She rang for Liza who helped her undress and into her nightdress. Liza had just departed when there was a knock on the door. She froze, hardly daring to breathe.

'Sarah?' Dev called. 'We need to talk.'

She closed her eyes. Oh, no, why wasn't she safely in bed? Perhaps if she stayed completely still, he'd go away.

'Sarah, open the door. I know you're not asleep. Your maid said she'd just left you.' This time his voice was tinged with impatience. 'I want to talk to you.'

It was no use trying to evade him. Pretending she wasn't here would only make her feel even more foolish. She reluctantly walked to the door and opened it. He stood outside, arms folded. She was disconcerted to see he wore no coat or waistcoat, just his loose linen shirt, open at the neck, over his breeches. 'Just as I thought. You are still quite awake. May I come in?'

'If you wish. I...I am rather tired so I thought I would retire soon.' She stepped back, her heart pounding. He'd been in her room once before, but that had been different. Not only did the candlelight make the room more intimate, he had been fully dressed. As she had. With her hair around her shoulders and dressed only in her cotton nightdress she felt completely vulnerable.

'This won't take too long,' he said. He shut the door behind him and leaned against it, his eyes on her face.

Sarah retreated next to the bed, hoping her mind would work better with some distance between them. 'Is…is there something you wished to discuss?'

'There is.' He still watched her as if trying to read her mind. 'I was wondering if your offer was still open.'

'My…my offer?' Her voice was hardly more than a squeak.

'Yes. The one you made by the stream today. The one where you offered to seduce me,' he said in conversational tones.

She thought she would faint. 'Oh, that one. It…it wasn't really an offer. More of a…a statement.'

'Then perhaps I should ask if your, er…statement is still open.'

She looked at him, her mind blank. Why did he want to know? Or did he actually intend to take her up on it? Her knees began to shake at the thought.

'Well? Do you still wish to seduce me?' he asked. If it hadn't been for the sudden flicker of uncertainty in his eye, she might have thought it mattered not at all to him.

'I…I don't know,' she whispered.

He moved further into the room, a slight smile crossing his features. 'I somehow thought that might be the case. Particularly since you have seemed determined to avoid me ever since then. I thought, however, we could take some steps to help you make up your mind.'

'Steps? What sort of steps?' She backed into her bed so abruptly she sat down on it.

Suddenly he was standing in front of her. 'Well, we could start with kissing.'

'K...kissing?'

His brow shot up. 'There's no need to sound so horrified. We've tried it before and if I recall correctly, you did not seem to object too much.'

'Well, no.'

'So, if you've no objections, we can start there and progress to the next step.'

'What next step?' she asked cautiously.

He flashed her a quick grin. 'You'll know when we get there. So, should we start now?'

To her astonishment, she saw a tinge of colour in his cheek. With sudden insight, she realised that, despite his nonchalant manner, he was not at all as confident of her as he appeared. He thought that she might turn him away as Mary had.

She could not do that to him. And, unlike Mary, she wanted him in every way possible. He was waiting for her reply. 'I...I suppose we could,' she whispered.

He sat next to her. His thigh pressed into hers and a sharp jab of fire shot through her. Her eyes went to his firm mouth.

His eyes darkened. 'The preliminary step,' he said. He caught her shoulders and pulled her to him.

His mouth descended on hers. His lips moved over hers in an exploratory kiss that was completely unlike any of his earlier ones. It was gentle and completely seductive.

Her arm crept up around his neck and tangled in his thick hair. And when he lowered her to the pillow, and stretched his long, hard body next to her, she made no protest. He gently moved her injured hand and then shifted half on her, so his body rested between her legs.

Hot, throbbing heat seared through her at the unfamiliar, intimate pressure. His mouth left hers and trailed down her neck in fiery kisses that made her gasp. He pushed the sleeve of her nightdress to bare her shoulder and then his mouth slowly explored the hollow beneath her shoulder, lingering on the small mole above her breast. Her fingers dug into the hard muscles of his neck, her body arching to his.

He lifted his head. 'It is your turn,' he said. His voice was husky.

Confused, she opened her eyes to find his face hovering above hers, his eyes dark with desire. 'For what?'

'To have your way with me. To do what you'd like.' He slowly caressed the small mark where his lips had been moments before. 'For instance, I have longed to kiss you here ever since the night of the ball. Now it is your turn to choose something you have desired to do.' A slight smile touched his mouth. 'It is the next step.'

She could do what she wanted with him? The thought had never occurred to her. 'Your shirt?' It sounded safe, although with his body pressed against hers and the growing need between her legs she wasn't certain safe was possible.

'You want it off?'

'Yes.'

He rose above her. She watched as he undid the buttons down to his middle and then drew it off over his head. Fascinated, she saw his chest was muscular and strong and covered with an intriguing mat of dark hair. He lay back down beside her and cupped her face with his hand. 'Now you may touch me,' he murmured.

Shyly, she touched the hair on his chest, then ran her hand over his ribs. His skin was smooth and intriguing and he lay perfectly still as she explored the hard muscles of his stomach. Emboldened, she tentatively slipped her hand further. He groaned.

She yanked her hand away. 'What is wrong?' she asked. Had she hurt him?

'Nothing. It is just your touch. Damn it, Sarah. If you continue to touch me like that I may lose whatever control I have.' His eyes were dark with passion and he was breathing hard. And she suddenly was aware of his hardness pressing into her leg.

Amazed that she could have such power over him, she touched his cheek, tracing the planes of his face. He caught her hand and pressed it to his lips, then released it. 'You are so beautiful. Do you know how much I've longed to touch you, to feel you beneath me?'

'Is this the next step?'

A sudden grin lit his face. 'One of them. Do you object if I touch you more?'

'No.' In fact, she was beginning to feel impatient. Her body felt as if it was tingling with the need to feel his hands everywhere.

He cupped her breast through the thin cotton of her nightdress and circled the nipple with his thumb. She gasped when his mouth came down to caress her nipple with his tongue. A tiny moan escaped her at the exquisite sensations he created. And then his mouth was moving up her neck, leaving a fiery trail of desire in its wake. His lips returned to hers, his tongue moving in her mouth. His hand crept beneath her nightdress and he slowly caressed her calf. He moved his hand slowly up her leg to her thigh, and then his fingers were stroking the inside of her thigh as his knee parted her legs. His hand crept further and touched the soft hidden bud, his fingers doing things to her she'd never imagined. Her body pressed into his hand, the desire for release building in relentless circles.

And then he pulled away. She opened her eyes, confused, her body heated and heavy with desire. 'I think the next step,' he said. His voice was thick, his eyes heavy and hooded. She watched as he rose above her and then quickly averted her gaze as his hands fumbled with the fastenings of his breeches.

And then he again stretched out beside her, his arms pulled her to him, and after that, it hardly mattered which step they were on.

Cedric ran a hand down the Sèvres vase. If all went well, he'd soon be able to afford such fine porcelain. All of Kentwood was well furnished with a quiet good taste that he could not quite emulate. As Caroline Kenton herself exhibited. He turned when he heard footsteps and Charles Kenton appeared in the doorway of the drawing room.

'You have a fine collection of porcelain,' Cedric remarked. His gaze flickered over Kenton's face, trying to gauge his mood, but Cedric could not quite read him.

'My mother's,' Kenton said briefly. 'You have business with me?'

'Yes.' Cedric smiled. 'I will get directly to the

point. Over the past few weeks I have had the great pleasure of finding myself frequently in your sister's company. I have come to hold her in the highest regard. She is all that is lovely, and amiable and sweet. It perhaps seems too soon to speak, but I cannot wait. In short, I desire her to become my wife.'

Kenton stared at him. 'I must refuse your request.'

'May I inquire why?'

'There are several reasons. Sufficient to say, however, that I fear you have something of a reputation as a fortune-hunter. And even if I thought my sister returned the sentiments you claim to have, I would not consider the match.'

A slow, boiling anger began to rise in Cedric. He kept his voice even. 'And may I know the name of the person or persons who dared to sully my reputation in such a vile way?' But he had no need for an answer.

'I can't see that it matters.' Kenton shrugged, clearly dismissing him. 'I am sorry I cannot spare you more time, but I have an engagement.'

Cedric quit the house, his fury barely contained. But he'd had years of controlling his desire to leap at a man's throat or slap a woman's face for various set-downs.

He mounted his curricle and cracked his whip with more force than necessary. The horses leaped forward and he drove out of the grounds, narrowly missing the gatepost. He would have his revenge. He would destroy Huntington. And do it through the thing he loved most.

* * *

Sarah looked up as Sally entered her bedchamber. She had slept late and breakfasted in bed, and had only now finished dressing in a sprigged muslin gown.

'His lordship wishes to see you in his study,' Sally announced.

'Thank you.' Sarah's pulse fluttered. In all her imaginings, she had never expected to find such ecstasy in a man's arms. Last night seemed almost like a dream, particularly when she woke to find Dev gone from her bed. But her bedcovers carried his scent and her nightdress lay on the floor and she knew their lovemaking had been quite real.

He stood at the window behind his desk, but turned as soon as she entered. 'I trust you slept well,' he said.

'Yes, very well.' A surge of disappointment assailed her. Were they about to resume their usual formal civility? Perhaps last night had meant nothing more to him than fulfilment of his male desire. 'Did you want to see me about something?' she asked politely.

'Yes.' He stepped around the side of the desk. 'Although I would prefer that you move from the door.'

She came to his desk. He smiled. 'Much better.' And then he bent his head and kissed her thoroughly.

He lifted his head. The expression in his eyes brought a blush to her cheeks. She pulled away, her knees shaking. 'Dev, the door is not closed.'

'Isn't it?' His smile was rather rakish. 'I somehow do not think anyone would object too much if they see me kissing you. Certainly not my sister or your cousin since I suspect they have waited for this since our wedding.'

'Yes, but…'

His mouth cut off her words and she found herself nearly falling on him as he backed up against his desk. He caught her, his mouth trailing kisses down her neck. He finally put her away from him, breathing hard. 'I was going to ask you to come for a ride with me, but perhaps we should forget the ride all together and retire early.'

The idea made her dizzy. 'Now? Is that not rather improper?' And what would the others think if they found out she and Dev were closeted together at eleven in the morning?

A wicked light leaped into his eye. 'Undoubtedly, but we are married.' He stood back. 'I am only teasing, at least for now. So, do you wish to come with me?'

She smiled, suddenly happy. 'Yes, but only if you conduct yourself with the utmost propriety.'

He gave her a slow smile. 'I can't promise you that at all.'

Three-quarters of an hour later, they had just started down the road in Dev's curricle when the rug at Sarah's feet moved. A familiar grey tail hung out one end. She gasped. 'Dev! Stop!'

'What is it?' He pulled up the horse.

'I fear we have a stowaway.' She bent down and pulled the cover aside. Merlin looked up at them with his yellow gaze.

Dev swore. 'Blast it, Sarah, I thought you'd been hurt! Don't scare me like that!' He gave Merlin a speaking glance. 'I should have guessed he might try this. However, I've no intention of having him along as chaperon today.'

She picked Merlin up and cradled him against her.

'Can we take him back to the house? I don't want to leave him by the road.'

He quirked a brow. 'My dear, I hope you do not think me that callous. Besides, I strongly suspect if I were to do such a thing, we would be back at daggers drawn. Or worse.'

He manoeuvred the horses around and back towards the stables. Sarah handed the protesting cat to a groom who promised to return him to the house.

They again started off along the road that bordered the estate uninterrupted by stowaway animals. He looked down at her. 'I spoke to Kenton yesterday so you may put your mind to rest. He assured me that he had noticed Blanton's attentions and even if I'd said nothing, he would not have considered the match. Apparently he has already heard rumours of Blanton's prior affair. He has warned Caroline to stay away from him as well.'

'Thank you so much,' Sarah said with heartfelt gratitude. 'I had worried, but I won't now.'

'However, I don't want you wandering around alone. I don't trust him.'

She glanced at Dev. 'Why? Surely he cannot do me any harm now.' And then she remembered the look on his face yesterday when she had given Merlin to Caroline.

Dev hesitated. 'We still do not know for certain who pushed you.'

'You think it might have been Mr Blanton?' Putting an actual name to her assailant made her shiver. At times, she had managed to convince herself that the blow to her back had been no more than her imagination.

'Possibly.' He frowned. 'Your brother has not yet

been able to determine if he was in the area or not. Or wring a confession out of him.'

'Nick?' Sarah was bewildered. 'But he seems to be on quite good terms with Mr Blanton. I have been rather worried.'

'Your brother is here to keep an eye on Blanton. He hopes Blanton will trust him enough to let down his guard.'

'Surely there is no need for all of this.' But she felt a trickle of unease none the less.

He glanced at her. 'There is. He's dangerous. Your brother wants to make certain he leaves the area without further mischief. He is concerned for your safety. As I am,' he added softly. 'So, he is watching Blanton, and I am watching you. Which is why I've no intention of letting you go off on your own. Particularly now that you're well enough to start off on one of your rambles.' He looked at her. 'Promise me you'll not go off without one of us.'

The concern in his eyes halted any objection she might have made. 'I promise.'

They turned down a road that followed the stream. He pulled the horses to a halt near a grassy patch under some trees. 'My groom will meet us here shortly and then we can walk a bit. I know a very private spot.'

She flushed at the look in his eye and he slowly bent toward her. A loud boom jerked them apart. She glanced at Dev.

He frowned. 'Damn, I'd forgotten Filby's party was out shooting today. Perhaps we should find a quieter and less dangerous spot.'

The shot came then. It seemed to happen at once, the noise, Dev shoving her down as something whizzed over their heads and then the horses leaping forward.

She clutched at the side as Dev attempted to bring the horses under control. He succeeded and turned to face her. His face was ashen. 'My God, Sarah. Are you all right?'

'Yes.' She was shaking uncontrollably. He reached over and pulled her to him. She managed to ask, 'Are you?'

'Yes.' His arm tightened around her.

'Huntington! What the devil happened?' Sir Ralph had come through the trees, Charles Kenton in his wake. 'Saw your team bolting. Thought for a moment Lady Huntington had been thrown.'

'No. But close to it.' Dev spoke over her head, his voice grim. 'Someone shot at us. He would have hit Sarah if I hadn't pushed her down.'

'My God!' Charles exclaimed. 'Who would be so careless?'

'If it was carelessness,' Dev said coldly. 'Who else is shooting with you?'

'Are you suggesting it wasn't an accident?' Sir Ralph demanded.

'That is what I intend to determine.' Dev slowly released Sarah.

More voices came from the trees. And then Nicholas emerged. He took in the scene and ran forward, his face white. 'What happened? Sarah?'

'I am all right,' she said.

'Huntington? What happened?' Nicholas demanded.

'Someone took a shot at us, either intending to hit us or spook the horses. Where's Blanton?'

Nicholas looked grim. 'The devil of it is, I don't

know. He was with us. Then he shot a bird and he and Branley went to retrieve it. When they didn't return I went off to look for them. Haven't seen either one.'

'I am taking Sarah home and then we're both going to look for him,' Dev said.

Charles stepped forward and frowned at Dev. 'You think Blanton deliberately did this?'

'I've little doubt.'

'Then I'll join you,' he said. 'He offered for Caroline today and I turned him down. To say he was not pleased is an understatement. He would have mowed me down in the drawing room if he'd thought he could get away with it.'

'You're saying Blanton is shooting at people?' Sir Ralph demanded.

'Among other things,' Dev said coolly.

'Never liked the fellow much. Man's a bounder. Caught him with his hands on one of the housemaids. Can't have people like that staying under my roof. Will tell him he has to go elsewhere tomorrow.' Sir Ralph spoke with evident satisfaction.

'We can only hope he'll decide to leave the county,' Nicholas said.

Dev smiled, but his smile was not pleasant. 'We will make quite certain he does.'

Chapter Twenty-One

Cedric walked out of Sir Ralph's study and directly out the door of Harrowood. He started towards his coach, where the footman had already loaded his bags. He climbed inside the coach, and the rage he felt, cold and deadly, started to consume him in slow flickering flames. Oh, he would leave all right, but first he intended to have his revenge. There was a small inn nearby where he intended to stay, a not-so-respectable inn, but Crump, the proprietor, owed him more than one favour.

The problem, of course, would be getting near Lady Huntington. After yesterday, her husband undoubtedly intended to keep her under lock and key until he was gone. He leaned back against cushions and stared out at the road, lost in thought. And then his eye fastened on three woman walking alongside the road ahead of the coach. He recognised Caroline Kenton and Lady Jessica at once. The other was undoubtedly a maid.

He knew what he would do now. Huntington could be destroyed in other ways than through his wife.

As soon as he passed the women, he signalled the

coachman to stop. Blanton stepped down and smiled. 'Good day, Lady Jessica, Miss Kenton.'

Sarah glanced down at the watercolour. It was the first one she had attempted since her wrist had been hurt. It was done from a sketch she had attempted of Merlin a few days ago. She was not very pleased with it, but at least the work had kept her mind off yesterday.

Dev and Nicholas had returned to the house with the news that they had not been able to locate Blanton. Mr Branley had come home, saying he'd lost Blanton soon after they had retrieved the bird and then he himself had been lost before he made it back to Harrowood.

And last night Dev had forbidden her to so much as set foot outside Ravensheed until they determined where the man was. She sighed. She was not looking forward to another enforced stay indoors.

Amelia looked up from her book. 'I dare say it will be quite tedious for you to be locked away. I thought perhaps you could come and stay with me for a while.' She hesitated. 'I did talk to Dev, and he agreed it would be the best thing until they are certain Blanton presents no more danger.'

'That is very kind,' Sarah said automatically. The intimacies of their night together had been completely overshadowed by the other events. Dev had been preoccupied, his manner cool, as if the passion they'd shared had never happened.

'We can leave tomorrow, if you can be ready by then. Nicholas has agreed to go with us.'

'How nice,' Sarah replied, although she felt like weeping instead.

They both were startled when the library door burst open. Caroline rushed in, her bonnet askew, her eyes wild with fear. 'Oh, Sarah! It's Jessica!'

Sarah jumped up. Her heart leaped to her throat. 'Caroline? What is it?'

'He has her! 'Tis all my fault! I never thought!' Caroline's breath came in short gasps as if she'd been running.

'Who? Where's Jessica?' Sarah asked swiftly with a growing sense of dread.

'Mr…Mr Blanton, he…he abducted Jessica. 'Tis all my doing!' Her voice rose hysterically.

Sarah's mind snapped into sharp focus. She dashed over and took Caroline's arm. 'Blanton abducted Jessica? Caroline, you cannot cry now! What happened?'

Caroline nodded and gulped down a sob. 'We… we were walking along the road. He stopped and asked if we would like a ride. We said no and started to walk away, but he…he grabbed Jessica and forced her into the carriage. I…I tried to stop him but he pushed me.' Her eyes filled with shock. 'And then he was gone! Betsy screamed and would not stop and so I left her. And…and Charles is gone today so I…I came here.'

Sarah stared at Amelia. 'Oh, dear God! Dev! He and Adam are gone as well.' She tried to think. 'Nicholas! I will go to him.'

'Shall I come with you?' Amelia asked quickly. She stood, her own face pale.

'No, someone must wait for Dev and Adam to return.'

She turned and hurried towards the door, then nearly slammed into Nicholas. He caught her shoulders, steadying her. 'Sarah! My God! What has happened now?'

Sarah clutched his arm. 'Blanton has Jessica! Caroline has come to tell us. And Dev is out and I was going to fetch you! You must help!'

'Sarah.' He gave her a little shake. 'Start over.' He glanced at Amelia. 'Do you know?'

They managed to tell him the story. When they finished, his face grim, he said, 'I'm going after them. I've an idea where he might have gone.'

Sarah's hand tightened on his arm. 'You do? Oh, Nick, please, I must go also!'

He looked about to argue and then changed his mind. 'Very well. Are you ready?'

'Yes, just my bonnet and pelisse.' She looked at him. 'Nicholas, do you really know where he might be?'

'Yes, he mentioned an inn once. The Crow Inn.'

Amelia followed them out. 'I will wait for Dev and Adam. And let them know.'

They'd been on the road a scarce quarter of an hour when there was a loud meow. 'What the devil is that?' Nicholas exclaimed.

Sarah froze. 'Oh, no.' The rug shifted at her feet.

She lifted the blanket. Two lazy yellow eyes looked up at her. Her heart sank. 'It's Merlin.'

'Merlin?' He glanced down. 'Good God! There's a cat!'

'It's my cat. He likes to ride in carriages. He must have jumped in and fallen asleep.'

'We'll have to put him down,' he said shortly. 'I can't drive with a cat.'

'We can't,' Sarah said miserably. 'He'll be lost.

And he was a gift from Dev.' He would probably jump anyway, once he realised he was no longer in familiar territory. Why must this happen on top of everything else?

Nicholas looked completely incredulous. 'He gave you a cat?'

'Well, yes. Even though he dislikes them.'

Nicholas gave a short laugh. 'The man must be in love.' He glanced at Merlin, who yowled. 'My dear, I doubt he's going to stay long at any rate.'

Sarah bit her lip. 'I know,' she said unhappily. 'Perhaps if I cover him.' She put the rug back over him and he protested loudly at the indignity of such treatment.

She looked up in time to see they were advancing upon a horse cart carrying a basket of turnips. Nicholas gave a shout and the startled driver peered around and urged the horse further to the side. Nicholas deftly manoeuvred his team around the cart and then he pulled them to a halt. He handed Sarah the reins and jumped down. 'Hold them.'

'Nick? Whatever are you doing?'

But he had already stridden off. She looked around to see him talking to the driver of the cart, a youth who looked scarcely out of boyhood. Merlin meowed and struggled under the rug. She bit her lip, and prayed he would remain there a bit longer.

Nick returned. He carried a basket. 'Take this.' He held it up to her.

She grabbed it. 'Whatever are you doing?' And then comprehension dawned. 'Oh, Nick! What splendid thinking!'

'We've not much time to waste. Get him in there and put the rug on top.'

She scooped Merlin up and shoved him protesting into the basket. She covered the basket with the rug and Nick set the team in motion.

The first posting house revealed no information, but an hour and a half later they halted in the yard of the Crow Inn. The inn yard was empty except for a lone carriage and a mangy-looking dog that barely bothered to glance at them. Nicholas jumped down and Sarah followed, her heart thudding. Her apprehension only increased when Nicholas grabbed his pistol. Worried Merlin would knock over the basket and escape, Sarah grabbed the basket and carried him in.

The innkeeper came forward. He was a heavyset man with a suspicious gaze who looked as if he hadn't bothered to wash in a decade. He eyed Nicholas and then Sarah, a smirk on his lips. 'Seems to be the day for the gents and their ladies. I suppose you'll be wanting a private parlour also? Or perhaps just a bedchamber.'

His smirk vanished under Nicholas's hard gaze. 'I fear you are mistaken. We're looking for a man and a young lady.'

His eyes shifted. 'Haven't seen anyone of that description.'

'Whose carriage is that?' Nick demanded.

'What carriage?'

Nick smiled coldly. 'I would like to see your other guests.'

The man folded his arms and smiled. 'Do you now? I won't have you disturbing them.'

'Won't you?' Nick grabbed him by the shirt front and shoved him against the wall. 'Show me now.'

Sarah had noticed a closed door. She quickly

walked over to it and set the basket down on a bench near it and then heard a sound. 'Who is there?' she called.

'Help me! Please!' Jessica's voice was unmistakable.

'Quiet!'

Sarah's heart lurched as she recognized Blanton's voice. 'Nick! Come here!'

Her brother released the proprietor, who staggered a little. Nick strode to the door and shoved it open. Cedric stood there, his arm around Jessica's waist, a knife levelled at her throat. His eyes narrowed when he saw Nicholas. 'I'd thought you'd be the last person to spoil sport.'

Jessica stood very still, her eyes wide with fear, her face pale. Nicholas raised his pistol and pointed it at Blanton. 'Whatever my faults, I hardly condone abduction of an innocent. Let her go.'

Cedric laughed. 'I've no intention of doing so. Huntington has interfered enough. This time I have the upper hand. So, if you'll just step aside, Lady Jessica and I will be on our way. Unless you'd like to see her lovely throat cut. Throw your pistol here.'

'I'll see you in hell before you walk out of here with her,' Nicholas said coldly. 'Let her go.'

Blanton laughed again. 'Of course, I may send her to heaven first. I suggest you do as I ask. Give me your pistol.'

Nicholas hesitated and fianlly threw his pistol down. Blanton laughed. 'Kick it here.'

When Nicholas made no move to do so, Blanton pressed the blade further into Jessica's neck. She made a small helpless sound.

The sound tore at Sarah's heart. She pushed in front of Nicholas.

Blanton looked at her, his eyes narrowed. 'Ah, Lady Huntington. How nice to see you.'

Sarah kept her eyes fixed on Blanton's face. 'I pray you will release my sister-in-law.'

'Sarah?' Jessica gasped.

Blanton's smile was cruel and ugly, all pretence of geniality gone. 'Why? I need a wife and preferably one with a dowry.'

'It is unlikely you'll get a shilling out of my husband this way,' Sarah said coldly.

'No? Then perhaps a ransom. And revenge at the same time.'

Sarah took a deep breath. 'Perhaps you will consider another bargain. Let Jessica go and take me instead. I…I will see to it that not only will my husband pay but my…my grandfather as well. Won't he, Nicholas?'

'Sarah, no, you cannot,' Jessica cried.

'Nick?' Sarah said.

Nicholas stared at her. She looked back at him, pleading in her eyes.

'He will,' Nicholas said shortly.

Blanton's smile was ruthless. 'Very well. With the same terms. If I suspect you are coming after me, then I will not hesitate to kill Lady Huntington. First, however, shove your pistol here. With your foot.'

He waited until Nicholas reluctantly complied and then said to Sarah, 'Come here.'

Sarah picked up the basket and gave it to Nick. 'Please take care of him.'

Knees shaking, she walked to Blanton. He caught her arm and pulled her to him, then shoved Jessica away. She stumbled. At the door, she turned. 'Sarah, you cannot…Dev!'

'Don't worry. I will be fine.' But the cold steel of the blade pressed into her neck and she felt sick with fear.

Blanton's arm crushed her to him. 'So, Thayne, take Lady Jessica and leave. I should warn you, however, that I also have a pistol, so I suggest you not try anything foolish. Go, or I fear Lady Huntington's lovely neck will not be quite as untouched.' The blade dug into the soft skin. Jessica gasped and Sarah closed her eyes.

'Shut the door,' Blanton said. 'You have five minutes to depart. If the carriage is not gone…' He let the words hang ominously in the air.

Nicholas's eyes were hard. 'And if you harm my sister, I will kill you.'

'But at least I will have my revenge. I think it will quite be worth it. Shut the door.'

Still holding the basket, Nicholas slowly closed the door.

Blanton put down the knife, but still held her to him. His strong, unpleasant odour nearly made her gag. 'So, my dear Lady Huntington, we are alone. Would you like to come with me? I have often thought you would look charming gracing my table or…my bed.'

'No, I would not. I think it would be best if you release me.' Sarah tried to keep her voice calm.

'I've no intention of doing so. I suspect, my dear, that Thayne fully intends to attempt a most foolish rescue. As I also suspect your husband is not far behind. I shall quite look forward to meeting him. Sit, my dear.'

He picked up a pistol from the table and held it on her. Sarah sat in the chair he indicated, her legs trembling. She could think of no conceivable way out of the room and, with Blanton's pistol trained on her, she could not possibly attempt anything. What did he intend? To shoot her? Shoot Dev?

Then she heard voices through the open window. Her heart began to thud with a new fear. Blanton rose and went to the window. 'Very good. Your husband has arrived as well as Lady Jessica's doting fiancé.'

He grasped Sarah's hand and pulled her up.

She heard voices outside the door. Her heart sank when she recognised Dev's.

'Where the hell's my wife?' The door crashed open and Dev appeared on the threshold. His eyes went to them, his eyes hard and deadly. He trained his pistol on Blanton. 'Let her go, damn you.'

Blanton laughed and raised his pistol to Sarah's head. 'I'll kill your wife before I do that. I suggest you drop your gun.'

Dev stared at him and then slowly lowered his gun. It dropped from his hand and clattered to the floor.

'This is becoming quite tedious. Kick it here,' Blanton said.

Dev kicked the pistol. It flew across the floor and landed near Blanton's foot. He pushed it behind him. 'Now come in and shut the door.'

Dev slowly entered, his eyes on Sarah. 'Let her go.'

'Not yet.' Blanton said. 'I fear, my lord, there is going to be an accident. A struggle and, alas, you will unfortunately be shot while I tried to defend myself.'

Dev leaned against the wall and folded his arms. 'It will never work. There are too many witnesses. My wife, for one. The innkeeper, not to mention Lord Thayne and Adam Henslowe.'

Blanton laughed. 'The innkeeper has been well paid. And the accident won't take place here. There is a door behind you. It leads directly to the carriage yard. We will proceed out, you first, your lovely wife with me. And if you or any of your friends attempts a rescue, you'll have the pleasure of watching your wife die before your eyes.'

'I will kill you first,' Dev said softly.

Sarah felt sick with fear for Dev. 'If I come with you, do what you ask, will you let my husband go?'

'No.' He smiled gently. 'You are only the bait, my dear. I have looked forward to this moment, removing your husband from this earth. He has interfered too many times with my plans.' He yanked Sarah closer to him and motioned with the gun. 'In front, my lord, and no false moves.'

Dev pushed away from the wall. And then the door creaked open. Sarah heard a most familiar meow. Blanton spun around. 'What the devil is that?'

Merlin's tail waved in the air as he stalked towards Sarah and Blanton. Blanton's mouth fell open. 'A cat? I'll get rid of him.' He cocked his pistol. And then sneezed.

'No!' Sarah stamped on his foot and twisted, attempting to knock the gun from his hand just as Merlin leaped on the table. Caught off balance, Blanton staggered back, Sarah with him. Merlin stared at them, his ears pinned back and she knew he planned to jump. The next thing she knew, her arms were full of cat. She yelped, as he struggled to gain his footing, his claws digging into her flesh.

'Bloody hell!' Blanton released her so abruptly she stumbled, Merlin still clutched in her arms. Dev had his arms around Blanton and was trying to wrest the pistol from his grasp. Blanton jerked his elbow back and hit Dev in the ribs. He groaned and staggered a little, and Sarah knew she had to do something. She glanced around and spotted the two pistols under the window. But the men were in the way, engaged in what appeared to be a fight to the death.

She did the only thing she could think of. She tossed Merlin at Blanton's back. His claws connected with his neck and Blanton screamed as the cat dug into his head. Fur flew everywhere, and an indignant Merlin jumped down and dashed under the wooden bench.

Blanton stumbled backwards, rubbing at his eyes with one hand. He tripped over the chair and went down, neatly landing at Sarah's feet. The pistol flew from his hand and Sarah grabbed it. She pointed it at him, her hand shaking. 'Do not move, or I…I shall shoot you.'

Dev was at her side and pried the pistol from her trembling fingers. 'Sit down,' he told her.

The door flew open. Astonished, Sarah looked up. Nicholas stood there with what appeared to be an ancient shotgun in his hand, Adam behind him. More amazing still, her grandfather was there as well.

Lord Monteville stepped calmly into the room and walked over to look down at Blanton. He, too, held a pistol. 'You appear to have things under control. Perhaps, Nicholas, you could inquire after a piece of rope and we could render Mr Blanton somewhat more immobile. Although I do not anticipate he will be much trouble.'

Blanton had sat up, but his attempts to glare at Monteville were marred by the fact his eyes were nearly swollen shut.

Dev's arm went around Sarah and then he pulled her to him. His mouth came down on hers.

It was only when Jessica dashed into the room that they pulled apart.

Merlin crawled out from under the bench. He mewed, then jumped up on the bench and began to wash his face as if nothing had happened at all.

Chapter Twenty-Two

Dev glanced down at Merlin, who sat next to him in a wing chair in the drawing room. The cat's eyes were half-closed and he purred loudly as if he knew he was the hero of the day. Dev grimaced. 'I never expected to owe my life or Sarah's to a cat.'

Dinner was over and the entire company had retired to the drawing room together. Jessica and Adam sat together, his arm tight around her shoulders as if he never intended to let her out of his sight again. Nicholas stood with Monteville by the fireplace. Amelia sat next to Sarah on the sofa across from Dev.

'And to think I nearly made Sarah leave him by the road,' Nicholas said. He gave a short laugh. 'God, I knew Blanton detested cats, most animals actually, but had no idea why. If I had known, I would have brought out Merlin earlier.'

'He wanted to shoot him,' Sarah said indignantly.

Dev raised a brow. 'You seemed more—er—upset at that possibility than when he threatened to shoot me.'

'If you recall, I did offer to go with him to spare

your life.' She thought as long as she lived she would never forget the terrible fear that had gripped her when she thought Blanton fully intended to kill Dev.

His eyes met hers, a slow smile curving his lips. 'So you did, my dear.'

She flushed at the sudden heat in his eyes and looked away. Amelia rose and stifled a yawn. 'Well, this has been too much adventure for me. I believe I will retire and dream of home where nothing much ever happens.'

Nicholas moved forward and set his empty glass down. 'I will as well.' He had accepted their offer to spend the night at Ravensheed.

Dev rose. He approached Nicholas. 'I believe, Thayne, I did not thank you properly,' he said coolly. He held out his hand.

Nicholas hesitated for a moment, then took it. They shook briefly. Then Nicholas turned to Sarah. He bent and lightly brushed her cheek with his lips. 'I am glad you're safe. And happy.'

She rose and pressed his hand to her cheek. Tears rushed to her eyes. 'I am. Thank you.'

Jessica also stood, and embraced Sarah. 'Thank you. You were so brave. I…' Tears rushed to her eyes.

Sarah hugged her tightly. 'No more than you were. Sleep well.'

'I will try.' She pressed Sarah closer. 'I love you,' she whispered. 'I…I always wanted a sister.'

'And so have I,' Sarah whispered back. 'I can't imagine one I would ever love more.'

Jessica pulled away and squeezed Sarah's hand and then she and Adam followed the other two from the room.

Monteville moved from his position. 'I believe this is my cue as well.' He looked at them in his calm way. 'I had another purpose for coming, besides wanting to thwart any diabolical plans Blanton might entertain. I wished to ascertain whether my suspicions were correct and that you were both rather fonder of each other than either of you wished to admit.' A slight smile touched his lips. 'I am pleased to see I was not mistaken.' He touched Sarah's cheek. 'Goodnight, my child. Devin.' He moved to the door. He paused his hand on the knob. 'I quite look forward to my first great-grandchild.' The door closed softly behind him.

Sarah bent down and picked up Merlin. 'I…I believe I shall retire as well. Goodnight, Dev.' She avoided his eyes.

'Sarah, I have something I must tell you.' He moved to stand in front of her.

'Do you? Can it not wait?' Merlin wriggled and she set him down. Devin's expression was serious, making her feel slightly apprehensive.

'No, it is too important.' He held out his hand. 'Come with me, Sarah.'

'Where are we going?'

'To my bedchamber this time.' He raised his brow at her expression. 'I'd prefer this discussion to take place where interruptions are unlikely.'

She went with him down the now-familiar gallery. He pushed open the door of his chamber. She realised that it was the first time she had ever stepped into his room. A large four-poster bed dominated the room. A candle burned on the bedside table. Unlike her untidy room, his was neat as a pin.

He shut the door behind him and she turned to

face him, her stomach fluttering with nerves. His face, half in the shadows, was impossible to read.

She ran her tongue over her lip in a nervous gesture. 'What is it, Dev?'

'I wanted to say…' He paused and then stepped towards her. The next thing she knew she was crushed in his arms, his mouth on hers in a kiss that sent her senses reeling. He finally lifted his head.

'Sarah, my God.' He pushed her hair away from her face. 'You have no idea how I felt when I saw you with Blanton. If I had lost you…'

'Or if I had lost you…' she whispered. She touched his face. 'I love you.'

He looked stunned. She hastened to reassure him. 'It is all right, I promise I won't make a nuisance of myself trailing after you like some sort of…'

'Sarah, what the devil are you talking about?' he demanded.

'I fear I have embarrassed you by stating that I…I hold a fondness for you.'

He gave a shaky laugh. 'Now it is a fondness? I believe you said you loved me. Would it help if I told you that I return your sentiment, that I love you?'

'You love me?' She could scarcely believe her ears.

'Yes.' The passion he tried so hard to control returned to his face. 'That is what I wanted to tell you, but I did not know how you would respond. You, as usual, have made it easy for me.'

He cupped her face again with gentle fingers. 'I think I've loved you from the beginning,' he said roughly.

'The ball?'

'Even before then. Long before then.'

She stared at him in disbelief. 'But you always fixed me with such dark looks and tried your best to avoid me. I...I thought you quite detested me.'

'Merely an effort to avoid the truth of my attraction to you. I am sorry, Sarah, for all of that.' He hesitated. 'I never thought I would be worthy of you. It wasn't until the picnic, and I realised you did not hate me, that I thought there might be hope for us. That perhaps we could be friends. And then you announced you wanted to seduce me.'

'I dare say you thought I was the most brazen creature alive.'

'Not at all.' A smile lifted the corner of his mouth. 'Taken aback, but looking immensely forward to the prospect. And then you seem to develop cold feet so I decided to help matters along.'

'You were looking forward to it?' she asked, amazed.

'Yes.' He grinned, a rather wicked one. 'I still am, my love. If you recall, last time I seduced you. Now it is your turn.'

'I see.' She smiled at him. She remembered one of Amelia's lessons. Her arms came up to circle his neck and she pulled his head towards her. 'I believe I can remember the steps. But if I forget one or two you must help me.'

'I will be more than happy to oblige,' he whispered.

He bent his head and, as her lips met his, she knew she was home at last.

* * * * *

LIVE THE EMOTION

Modern Romance™
...seduction and
passion guaranteed

Tender Romance™
...love affairs that
last a lifetime

Medical Romance™
...medical drama
on the pulse

Historical Romance™
...rich, vivid and
passionate

Sensual Romance™
...sassy, sexy and
seductive

Blaze Romance™
...the temperature's
rising

27 new titles every month.

Live the emotion

MILLS & BOON®

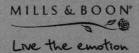

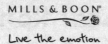

PENNINGTON

Catherine George
PENNINGTON
— After the Ball

MILLS & BOON

BOOK EIGHT

Available from 6th February 2004

*Available at most branches of WHSmith, Tesco, Martins, Borders,
Eason, Sainsbury's and most good paperback bookshops.*

PENN/RTL/8

Behind the Red Doors

Sassy, sensual...and provocatively playful!

Vicki Lewis Thompson

Stephanie Bond

Leslie Kelly

On sale 6th February 2004

Available at most branches of WHSmith, Tesco, Martins, Borders, Eason, Sainsbury's and all good paperback bookshops.